AMAZON GOLD:
COCAINE

THE ORB CHRONICLES

A. JAY COLLINS

Tellwell Talent
www.tellwell.ca

ISBN
978-0-2288-1587-7 (Hardcover)
978-0-2288-1586-0 (Paperback)
978-0-2288-1588-4 (eBook)

"*The gates of hell are open night and day; Smooth the descent, and easy is the way: But to return, and view the cheerful skies, In this the task and mighty labor lies...*"

—*The Aeneid,* Book VI, Virgil

Author's Note

This is a work of fiction. Names and characters are either the product of the author's imagination or are used fictitiously, and any resemblance to actual persons, living or dead, is entirely coincidental.

Table of Contents

Cast of Characters

ORB Operatives and Associates

Murray Stockman (Stockman)–general manager of ORB, Organization for Reorganizing Business. Ex-CSIS.

Matthew Black–senior field operative for ORB.

Lucy Stockman–wife of Murray and ex-CSIS operative.

Emma Stockman–field operative for ORB, and Murray Stockman's daughter. Also known as Emma Stone.

James Peters–ORB field coordinator based in El Pangui.

Roberto–ORB operative, highway movements, based in Loja.

Matias–ORB operative at Puerto Bolívar, Machala.

Kenny–ORB operative, mill equipment electrical rep.

Armando–ORB operative, mill equipment mechanical rep.

Nick–ORB operative responsible for open-pit equipment.

Eric–Chinese-speaking ORB operative based in the mill.

Nathan–Chinese-speaking ORB operative based in the mill.

Sean–senior field security detail for ORB.

Glenn–field security for ORB.

Mack–field security for ORB.

Deek–field security for ORB.

Others

Koski–started the cocaine manufacturing in Ecuador.

Tongyan–Chinese owners of the Zamora copper-gold property.

Ping Pei–Tongyan representative in Quito, Ecuador, for Zamora Plant.

Wang Ho Lin–Chinese embassy representative in Quito, Ecuador.

Rufus–pet tarantula.

Colonel Alberto Batista–Ecuadorian military field operative leader.

Ambassador Ramos Garcia-Lopez–Ecuadorian ambassador to the United Kingdom, based in London.

Eduardo Sánchez–assistant to Ecuadorian ambassador.

Luna–Shuar contact for ORB field operatives in Ecuador.

Rodriguez–camp manager and cook at Río Zamora.

Ecuador - Roads and Rivers

Ecuador – Topography

Prologue

"You can sell one ounce of refined but diluted cocaine hydrochloride on US streets for $2500. Or you can sell one ounce of gold for $1900. What works for you?"

Rufus loved his high, open-plan home with floor-to-ceiling windows. He could watch over his people below. They were unusual creatures who seemed to do things he couldn't comprehend. Often, one of them would take his tower down. They'd add a fresh coca leaf and some bugs for him to eat. Or they might throw in a live mouse or lizard for Rufus to inject with his mild but effective venom to kill these small animals. It kept his fangs sharp, and he could feed on them for days.

He had a reasonable relationship with humans—at least for a tarantula. For one thing, he never had to worry about where his next meal came from. But he did miss the company of female tarantulas. Oh well, he thought, that was the price he paid for wandering out that particular night when he was captured, looking for a little company in an area where humans congregated. As he had crossed a small clearing, he saw them. Frozen with fear, Rufus stood in plain sight of the giants. But one of them seemed to take a liking to him and bent to pick him up. The human seemed to think he was cute, named him Rufus, provided him with this glass home, and fed him several times a day. His new home was as good as any burrow he could imagine having. In fact, from what he had learned when he was young, he thought it was better than where most of the other one hundred or so South American tarantula species lived.

Rufus lined his home with his self-made silk thread to make it comfortable. He would have liked to stretch his eight legs more often. He even wanted to try catching his own food again, and not rely on charity. But then, that wasn't much to give up for what he was getting in return. After all, a spider's lifestyle isn't very demanding. Life was good enough the way it was. One major consolation was that he no longer had to worry about evading those pesky predators.

Rufus spent his days watching, sleeping, cleaning himself and eating. Sometimes he would climb his silk web to get closer to the air holes in the lid of his glass home, just for something to do. He wasn't much of an adventurer and was quite content to stay still for most of the time. But, just in case, he would keep at least one of his eight eyes open for any sign of movement close to him. He could also feel the minutest of vibrations that could alert him to danger. Of course, he had no idea what he would do if danger presented itself. He was, after all, trapped in a screw-top container.

Sometimes, Rufus's benefactor would tip him out onto a tabletop, and other humans would gather to stare and prod at him. They would touch his furry body and try to tickle him, or that's what he thought they were trying to do. He amused them at times by taking a run to the edge of the table, as if trying to escape. But he never made it, and he didn't want to. When the humans got bored with playing, they would coax him back into his home. They'd screw on the tin roof and slide his glass home back onto its perch.

Then, one day, chaos erupted on the ground below. His people rushed in all directions. They grabbed their things and screamed before they disappeared into the jungle. Rufus was alone to face the cause of the panic. The glass walls protected him, but at the same time, he felt trapped in his home. Although he didn't know why, he was frantic as well, stirred up by the frenzy below. He froze to the spot, looking around for his humans but seeing none, with any of his eyes. Then, all he could focus on was the thunderous, throbbing noise above. A giant machine with rotating blades descended toward him in slow motion.

Chaos erupted as bullets rained down into the encampment. Pots shattered. Tables splintered. Tanks ruptured. Chairs were destroyed. The tarpaulin covering the area was so riddled with holes, the turbulence from the helicopter blades ripped it to shreds. Rufus's sanctuary of safety fell to the ground from its place up in the frame of the shelter and shattered. He was upside down, stunned, but not hurt. Using all his legs, he rolled back upright and stood still, not knowing what to do or in which direction to run. The delicate tips of each of his sensitive hairy legs helped him make his way safely through the broken glass and out into the disquieting daylight. Bursts of intense heat came from the orange brilliance of a fire-breathing machine above him as it spat out its flame, like an angry dragon, to one side of him.

Rufus managed to crawl off toward the undergrowth. Another burst of flame shot out and turned him and everything around him to ashes. Rufus never felt a thing as he disintegrated from the savage heat. He had no time for a dying thought. But, in that briefest of moments between the whoosh of flame and the impact, he knew this was the end for him.

Chapter 1

Cocaine in the Jungle

Colonel Alberto Batista, the senior drug enforcement officer in southern Ecuador, lowered himself to the ground from the French-made Aérospatiale SA 330 Puma helicopter. Six agents followed in quick succession. They carried Steyr AUG assault rifles, the perfect jungle weapon. As they hit the ground, they sprayed the encampment with bullets. Some of the agents ran into the jungle after the farmers to chase stragglers.

Within minutes of starting, the shooting ended. The agents searched for bodies in the burnt-out ruins. They weren't looking to spare anyone, but then they didn't want to find anyone either. When it was all over, the agents had killed no one. The noise of an approaching helicopter had a habit of scaring off illegal coca farmers, but they would reappear somewhere else to do it all again.

For many Ecuadorian farmers, making crude cocaine and selling it to the local cartel was their only source of income.

Usually, eight or ten farmers worked together on one farm, and there were many of them. Seeds would be sown from December to January on the ever-expanding plots of land in the jungle. When the plants were about sixteen inches high, the farmers moved them to their final locations.

The days were long and tough, with heat, humidity and heavy rain. Farmers faced constant threats from jungle predators. But nothing deterred the farmers from gathering the fresh growth leaves from the coca bushes that ranged in age from one to forty years old. These days up to six harvests a year were possible with improved techniques and fertilizers. Regardless, the primary harvest occurred in March, after the rainy season. The second came at the end of June, and the third in October or November.

Farmers would set up their small coca processing plants under tree canopies to hide from prying eyes above. They spread the green coca leaves in thin layers on wool cloths to sun-dry them between the downpours of rain, when the hot sun would heat up the jungle. Then, they packed the dried leaves in sacks, keeping them dry, ready for the next step.

The farmers dug out and lined earthen pits with plastic or used metal drums to contain the leaves. They crushed them, added cement, water, and petrol or kerosene. Then, they mixed in caustic soda to remove residues. Afterward, they left the mixture to marinate and turn to a paste. Later, the farmers would add hydrochloric acid and potassium salts, converting the mixture to a cocaine base, a crude product that could be sold.

Each coca leaf farmer making cocaine base might make a hundred dollar profit for one week's work, after spending some one thousand dollars on ingredients and equipment. The profit depended on the volume of product they could make. There were thousands of small groups like this one in the Ecuadorian jungle making a living in this way.

Originally it was the Revolutionary Armed Forces of Colombia—or FARC as they were known to most—who connected the farmers with drug traffickers in Colombia and much of Ecuador. But, since the 2016 peace agreement with FARC, it was left to the cartels to take care of business.

Now, once the farmers had cocaine base to sell, Los Choneros would buy the solid whitish lumps to process it further. They were the primary drug cartel in Batista's territory now. Before this, their only involvement in the drug trade had been moving cocaine through Ecuador to its ports for the Colombians and Mexicans.

The cartel processed the cocaine base in-country using only pharmaceutical-grade equipment to turn it into cocaine hydrochloride, the final commercial product for exporting worldwide.

The Ecuadorians had completed their tasks once the product left their shores. But the story of street cocaine did not end there. It was the offshore drug lords who took the final step to convert the pure cocaine hydrochloride to a saleable street drug by mixing it with adulterants and cutting agents. In this way they would reduce its strength by as much as 40% before delivering it to the dealers. Good business for everyone.

Batista kicked at the burnt-out kerosene drums and canisters of hydrochloric acid and caustic soda. He also lashed out at the piles of burnt coca leaves ready for marinating. He seemed to be searching for something he couldn't find. There would be no names, no hints of identification, no personal effects. Now all there was left was a burnt-out dirt bowl in the jungle. He picked up a broken glass jar and wondered what it had held, although he didn't dwell on it. He tossed it into the still smoldering ashes. Another job well done.

But the coca farms in the province of Zamora-Chinchipe were only a small part of the drug problem Batista and his government faced.

Ecuador had become the second-highest producer of cocaine in South America. Colombia was the only country that produced more. The coca leaf grew well in the fertile soil and perfect climate of the Ecuadorian jungle. Farmers grew the bushes and made the base for very little, compared to the cost of the final product on the streets. They seemed willing to risk capture, despite the odds, when the penalty could be two years in a subhuman jail. Or they might face death at the hands of government agents if they tried to escape. But that was more a show of the government's support for anti-drug laws than anything else.

Cocaine production in Ecuador was rising and Batista knew he was fighting a losing battle, but it was one he still had to fight.

Batista managed drug enforcement in Ecuador, south of Guayaquil. His area included the Zamora-Chinchipe province, close to the eastern foothills of the Andes. It was an area of rivers, creeks, hills and valleys, covered by dense jungle and lush vegetation. The hot, humid climate was perfect for growing coca bushes in the well-drained hillside soils.

For some time, Batista felt overwhelmed by the enormity of the problem assigned to him. He was very aware that many farmers in his area sought the kind of steady income the cocaine industry offered. There were few options for them.

Batista's organized raids had almost no impact. For every manufacturing plant destroyed, two replaced it. Not only were there replacements, but the existing ones expanded. Batista resisted destroying the coca bush plantations themselves for fear of critically damaging the surrounding jungle and all it supported. He only focused on attacking the crude processing facilities when they had become large enough to see from the air.

Batista knew the business, and while he would never admit it, some of his childhood friends and extended family were part of the coca farming community. In many ways his sympathies lay with them; in another, he had to do his job. His only solace eventually came from his own government.

For years, the Ecuadorian government paid huge sums to fight the Colombian and Mexican drug cartels, who were moving their cocaine along Ecuadorian routes and using the ports for exporting their product. But there was no great financial benefit to Ecuador in what they were doing. Then, as the coca farming industry took hold in their own country, revenue began flowing in. Now, the government could make deals, gain leverage and take a more proactive role in their own drug industry.

As Ecuador continued to boost its cocaine production, Batista faced an increasing dilemma with the new written and unwritten government policies. While he had to target cocaine manufacturing and exporting to show Ecuador was complying with international laws banning the drug, he also had to be lenient with his actions. The coca farms had become vital to Ecuador's financial future and they needed protection.

Over the years, Ecuador's politics had become entwined with the cocaine industry, its largest revenue generator. The government had no intention of ruining what was working for everyone. The farmers earned an income. The cartel remained nonthreatening as long as it received the cocaine base. And the government received payments for turning a blind eye to everyone. Not to mention the secret deals many high-ranking government officials made on the side.

Then along came the Chinese.

Hiding behind their plans to build mines, the Chinese inserted themselves through cunning into the cocaine industry in Central America. An initial major endeavor was in Batista's area. It was here that the Chinese had built and now operated a large copper and gold mine, Zamora. But, while the property had a robust and bona fide mineral resource, the mill facilities included a secretly constructed and operated high-grade cocaine hydrochloride processing plant.

Local farmers started taking their cocaine base to Zamora for more money than what Los Choneros were paying. But trouble was brewing.

Zamora exported their cocaine only to China, before they sent it on to the street dealers in the West. They had not only replaced Los Choneros as the intermediaries, but they had also pushed the overseas drug dealers out of the game.

While Los Choneros were in their infancy in this part of Ecuador and couldn't resist the Chinese incursion, they were growing as their forces moved south through the country. There would come a time when they would want control once more.

That would mean, at some point, the Chinese had to go.

Chapter 2

Copper, Gold and More

In January 2020, the Zamora mine shipped 22,000 tons of copper, gold, and silver concentrate, worth over $130 million, to Shanghai, China. That excluded the $62 million street value of the cocaine hydrochloride hidden in some of the concentrate tote bags. And, according to their mine life calculations, the Zamora facility could continue to do this for the next thirty years.

The company shipped their concentrate in batches of 1,800 tons a day on fifty-six trucks. The 900, two-ton polypropylene concentrate tote bags were shipped to one of two ports. Fifty of the trucks took their loads to Guayaquil. There, the concentrate was dumped on a warehouse floor and conveyed into the holds of a bulk carrier. The other six trucks transported their tote bags to Puerto Bolívar in Machala, south of Guayaquil. Their sealed bags, containing the hidden drugs, were lifted directly into the secure holds of a waiting ship.

To the educated, it would seem strange for the gold and silver not to have been separated from the copper at the plant and cast into ingots. Or that the copper concentrate was not processed through a solvent extraction and electro-winning process to produce copper wire or copper plates right there at the site. That would have meant far less material having to be transported as waste in the concentrate halfway across the world. But no one questioned this practice of the Chinese owners. And they weren't offering any explanations. The strategy was deliberate. It was meant to ensure the cocaine had a secure place to hide until it reached Shanghai.

It was significant that the Zamora project marked the beginning of a world-class mining industry for Ecuador. This tiny country had few other major commodities to sell to the rest of the world, other than oil and bananas. It needed the mining industry, as well as the generous benefits the coca plant could bring.

A Vancouver company originally owned the property. But before investing capital to develop it, they sold Zamora to Tongyan, a Chinese government-sponsored company. Once purchased, it took fifteen years to develop the property into an operating mine.

China's strategy to boost its role in global finance, military and politics included buying key mineral assets in Central America. The Zamora acquisition was crucial. It supplied copper for domestic manufacturing and gold for inflation protection. One of the most important benefits to China's plan for Central America was the ideal growing conditions for coca plants. It meant they could expand into the production and distribution of cocaine hydrochloride at the same time as mining for minerals.

Zamora was the perfect foil for what the Chinese needed in Ecuador. Located in the eastern foothills of the Andes, on the edge of the fertile Amazon rain forest, it was tucked away in the far southeastern part of the country, with plenty of coca farmers already producing. It was also just one of a number of industrial projects in Central America the Chinese were using to hide their most valuable product for export—cocaine.

But the Chinese had not been easy to deal with for the desperate Ecuadorians. They battled the indigenous community over land rights, environmentalists over jungle preservation, and government departments concerned with their lack of planning. Also, as is often the case with developing Chinese-owned assets in foreign countries, they demanded their own Chinese construction workers, contractors and operators be brought into the country, depriving locals of work.

The China Development Bank financed Tongyan, with oversight from a cabinet minister at the Chinese central government level. The total investment expected for the Zamora mining project over its estimated thirty-year life was $2 billion. Half of that had already been spent building the facility. It was much more than it should have cost, by Canadian standards. But Tongyan had to spend a lot of money to bulldoze their way through government and local administration obstacles. It hadn't been easy for them to get to this point, but the returns were potentially enormous.

The Zamora open pit mine and processing facilities were situated in a thickly forested, undulating terrain with water courses running under and over the surface. Floods constantly eroded new and old channels through the jungle as the surface water rushed toward tributaries. All of which led to the Amazon; all of which were constantly muddied by the jungle debris and soils washed into them.

Despite being over 3,000 feet above sea level at the Zamora site, the humidity was overwhelming and relief from the heat impossible to find for most of the year.

Insects thrived in the air and on the ground, in the trees and in the water. They were so numerous in number and in species as to be impossible to estimate. They were often venomous or prickly, able to sting, or even paralyze.

The jungle teemed with wildlife and birds all chattering, clacking, clicking and screaming as though scrambling in a crowd and pushing each other out of the way. Of course, it all came with its share of danger, venom, crushing and stinging to be avoided at all costs.

The Zamora property was within sight of the border with Peru, monitored by the Peruvian military. Remnants of the Ecuadorian-Peruvian border watchtowers and barracks, remaining from when the two countries had serious territorial problems, could be seen from parts of the property. Sometimes, silhouettes of what appeared to be guards were visible as they wandered back and forth along the ramparts. It was believed that the Peruvian military still occupied some of the buildings that were a part of those old defenses.

Now it wasn't a border war that troubled them, but rather the illegal movement of cocaine coming into Peru from the Ecuadorian jungle, bringing the contraband from as far away as Colombia and Mexico.

Sometimes, coca production facilities set up near Zamora could be spotted by Peruvian guards at the border. They would keep their eyes open for local Ecuadorian farmers who would go back and forth into the jungle, carrying supplies in and—more often than not—nothing out. The information would be relayed to the Ecuadorian drug enforcement agents for action. A helicopter would swoop in. The agents on board would spray bullets on the suspect area. Fire blasts would spit out from the side doors. But the Zamora mine survived despite the war on cocaine all around them. The government ensured that they at least taxed their copper, gold and silver production.

The government permits for building Zamora allowed the Chinese to destroy acres of rainforest in the name of future prosperity for the country. The Ecuadorian Ministry of Environment had little power over the central authorities, even though the area was considered a forest protection zone, recognized by environmental agencies worldwide as being one of the most important ecosystems in the world. And yet, the Chinese were allowed to build a mine and ravage excessive amounts of jungle to do so.

The building of the mine came with more than its fair share of issues that set indigenous people against Tongyan from the very beginning. Tongyan, with help from the Ecuadorian government, dispossessed them of their land rights by mining on their land without their consent. The permitting process, implemented by the government, never considered the inhabitants and the company was allowed to forcibly evict the native people without compensation. It was rumored that local indigenous workers were badly mistreated by their Chinese employers whenever they had used them for manual tasks. Tongyan polluted the rivers with runoff during construction and was dismissive of accidents when indigenous people were injured or killed.

The Chinese owners were sued many times, especially by environmental groups and indigenous communities. But they always won with help from the federal government-run judicial system. Court filings even cited the Ministry of the Environment for failing to protect the environment. But nothing prevented the project from moving forward in the way the owners wanted.

The Zamora mine owners had many enemies. Not least of them were the Shuars, once one of the largest groups of indigenous people in Ecuador. They had tried but failed to have a say many times in the development that might match their cultural desires. But nothing worked.

The development of the project caused the loss of farmland and livelihoods for many of the indigenous groups and led to their economic dependence on the mining company. It forced those unwilling to provide menial tasks for the Chinese owners to search for other ways to support their families. Many were driven into the refuge of the jungle. They picked coca leaves and established simple but haphazard coca base manufacturing facilities, risking serious penalties if caught.

But there was a catch.

One ounce of cocaine on the streets of the US cost about $2,500. One ounce of gold cost around $1,900. Sure, selling cocaine had risks. But, with a 32% higher premium for cocaine than for gold, some might ask which business was preferred. It still remained illegal to manufacture, distribute and use cocaine hydrochloride.

Cocaine use in the US had dropped by fifty percent ten years ago. But it was popular again. Most other countries were seeing a similar increase. Cocaine was a world of opportunity, an oyster waiting to be opened. There were no international players in the game. Cartels ran it; they were very powerful. But they lacked one key element: total government support. Here, the Chinese were on their way to figuring it out. And they had an added advantage. They were using their methods to control the minds of their political and financial foes as they worked their way toward world domination.

The Zamora mine provided one of the tools used to move products—and not just copper and gold, but also cocaine. The jungle farmers eventually had little choice but to sell their coca paste to the Chinese operators. There was no other buyer now that Los Choneros had been pushed out.

The Zamora plant collected the crude cocaine in the form of what was called paste, before it could be converted to base. They processed it to commercial grade and exported it to China for distribution through their own network. That included the US, where the appetite for drugs was endless and where the Chinese were working that to their benefit.

The tide had turned from cocaine production being in the hands of Ecuadorians, to being in the hands of foreigners.

Chapter 3

The Ambassador

Murray Stockman sat in the lobby of the Ecuadorian Embassy in Knightsbridge, an upscale area of London with some of the most expensive real estate in the world.

The embassy was a modest suite of rooms, referred to as Flat 3b, occupying part of the ground floor of an unassuming five-story red-brick apartment block on the corner of Hans Crescent and Handor Place. It was only one block away from Harrods on Belmont Street, and a couple of streets away from the Cadogan Hotel, where Stockman was staying for a few nights with his wife, Lucy. They wanted to take advantage of Stockman's visit to London for this meeting to spend a few days in the city to catch up with friends and take in a show. It was as much a refreshing change from country life for them to battle with the crowds and traffic, as it was for them to be in the country away from all that. The fact was, they needed both.

As he waited to meet with the ambassador, Stockman was daydreaming, with his mind in an altogether different place.

Just a couple of days ago, he and Lucy had been relaxing in their traditional old wooden deck chairs in the front garden of their little home away from home, perched on top of the cliff in Hope Cove. It was a peaceful haven tucked away in a typically English village-by-the-sea. They had bought it several years ago on one of their visits from Montreal to London on business. The Cove was a four-hour drive from Heathrow. A short hop by North American standards.

A friend had encouraged them to see for themselves what life could be like in the country. It had taken them only one trip to this little Devonian village in the southwest of the country to realize it was just what they needed. It wasn't a retirement bug; they were still a little too young for that. It was more their need to find a place uncluttered by the mess of life around them. Somewhere that exuded peacefulness. Where there was the sea, the countryside, fresh air, little traffic, and at least one pub. It didn't seem like much to ask at the time.

They were instantly drawn to the cottage, boasting two wood-burning fireplaces and a large bay window overlooking the English Channel. It had a bright conservatory at the back, and a stunning garden with bees and butterflies, birds and rabbits, all mixed in with those darned seagulls. But their shrieks fit so well with the smell of the sea that it was hard to imagine the place without them. They drifted from air current to air current, without seeming to move a muscle, as the wind smacked into the cliffs in front and rushed upwards.

Seagulls came with the territory. But they annoyed and amused with their scavenging. They would dive-bomb visitors with no warning as they strolled through the village with a tasty morsel in hand.

As Stockman remembered, they had gone indoors just before 6 p.m., when Lucy readied a silver tray with two Plymouth Gins and Schweppes Tonic as she always did at that time whenever her husband was home with her. She put two ice cubes in each glass and a lime slice on top. Lucy took one, and Stockman the other. They sat back in their overstuffed armchairs in the bay window, took their first sip, and sighed with satisfaction.

"Just what the doctor ordered, don't you think?" She waited for a nod of affirmation from her husband, but the house phone rang in time to spoil the moment.

"Yesss?" Lucy had that way of answering the phone when she really didn't want to. It was as though to say to the calling party, "Can you call back when we aren't here?" But it didn't work that way.

"I wonder if Mr. Stockman is there with you." A serious voice on the other end of the line said.

"May I ask who's calling?" Lucy inquired in a very English sounding voice, even though she was Canadian.

"Yes, yes, of course. This is Eduardo Sánchez with the Ecuadorian embassy in London. I have something of importance to discuss with Mr. Stockman, *por favor.*"

"Oh. Just a moment, Mr. Sánchez, or should I call you *Señor*, or ...?"

"Please call me Eduardo. And you?"

"I'm Lucy, Murray's wife. Here, let me pass you to him." With that, Lucy covered the mouthpiece with her hand. "Eduardo Sánchez from the Ecuadorian Embassy," she whispered loudly. Lucy shrugged and grimaced at the same time as she held the phone out to her husband.

Stockman took the phone. His eyebrows raised in question.

"Stockman here."

Sánchez wasted no time.

"Thank you for taking my call, Mr. Stockman."

"Just call me Stockman. And your name again?"

"I am Eduardo Sánchez. Please call me Eduardo. I am calling from my home in London. I am an attaché at the Ecuadorian embassy here, but I didn't want to call you from there. Too many ears, you know."

"I'm already intrigued, Eduardo. Are those ears a problem, or is this more of a personal matter?" Stockman pressed the earpiece a little closer.

"There are matters that we—that is, the ambassador and I—are concerned with that cannot be overheard, other than by a few and we would very much like to discuss this with you. We believe you can, and may want to, help."

"Again, I'm intrigued. Is this something you can share over the phone?"

"We would prefer to discuss it with you face-to-face. Can we meet?"

"When?" This time Lucy got a little closer as Stockman put the call on speaker for her to hear as well.

"The ambassador would like to speak with you at the earliest possible time."

Stockman looked over at Lucy, who nodded.

"I can be there on Thursday. Is that soon enough?" Stockman kept his eyes on Lucy, but she had nothing to offer in return, having heard only one side of the stunted conversation.

"Yes. Yes, that would be very good. It will give me time to get some papers together for you, if you choose to help us." There was a pause when neither party seemed to know how to continue. There was really nothing else to say at this point and, in any case, they would be meeting in two days.

"I'll see you then. Let's say eleven o'clock, will we?" Stockman grimaced. It was a bit of a stretch for him to agree to a meeting without knowing the issue. But an ambassador's involvement meant it would likely be very significant and probably secret.

"Thank you, Mr. Stockman. We will see you then." The phone clicked at the other end. Stockman was left holding his phone and looked over at Lucy.

"Sounds interesting, I guess." It was Lucy who clearly didn't know what to make of this. "Let's pack and go up to the big city for a few days, shall we?"

oooo

Murray, or Stockman as everyone called him, was the managing director of the Organization for Reorganizing Business, or ORB, an international group of contracted specialists, all cleared for Class 2 security, one level down from top secret.

Stockman was in his early sixties, a smidgeon under six feet tall, powerfully built and sharply intelligent. He sported swept-back graying hair and a matching beard, trimmed in a short point below the chin. He dressed casually, had a dry sense of humor, thoroughly enjoyed sailing, and was totally devoted to his wife.

Since his military days, Stockman had worked in security for some of the most powerful people and groups in the world, including CSIS, the Canadian secret service. ORB was a natural development for Stockman. He brought his skills to this private-focused group that chose its missions. They were supported by world leaders who needed an independent organization to do work they were unable to do.

Only Stockman and Matthew Black had fixed positions at ORB. Black was Stockman's right-hand man for field operations, including sabotage. The rest of their agents were selected based on their talents for the project to be undertaken. ORB's task was to assist trusted industry leaders and government officials in managing situations that had gotten out of hand. Stockman used the advisory services of a group of twelve senior industrialists from across five countries, sprinkled with a few permanent government seniors from three countries, who opined on projects Stockman brought to the table. Sometimes he took their advice, and sometimes not. Financial support partially came from the members of the group—or rather, their employers—but principally from their client. ORB was a keystone member of a wealthy, powerful club with a global vision.

Lucy had also been a member of CSIS and had worked on the secret service side of things in Asia. These days, she played at being Stockman's confidant and would often offer her words of wisdom to him before being asked. She was a very well put-together women, as they say. Tall, elegant and charming with her own stories of action and intrigue. Beyond that, she provided them both a home and was always there by Stockman's side whenever he needed it.

Much of their time these days was spent in Hope Cove, where time seemed to stand still. The permanent population never grew. Everyone who lived there did their shopping or went to church in one of the more populated towns at least thirty minutes away by car, via the narrow country lanes bounded by high hedgerows that had been that way for centuries.

"Mr. Stockman?" A quiet, accented voice addressed him and brought him back to reality in the waiting room of the Ecuadorian embassy. He was about to discover how ORB might be of service, if they chose to be.

"Yes." Stockman stood and extended his hand in greeting. He was dressed in his usual casual but smart outfit. Shoes shined, shirt pressed, pants and jacket with no wrinkles—altogether a laid-back look with class, thanks to the quality of his clothes. He hadn't worn a tie in... ten—or was it twelve?—years.

"I am Eduardo Sánchez. We spoke two days ago." Sánchez took Stockman's hand and shook it firmly. He invited him into a good-sized office with many colorful Ecuadorian artifacts on the walls and shelves. An ornate gilded frame showed off a twenty-four-inch square photo of the president of Ecuador with who Stockman assumed to be the ambassador. Both were short with markedly dark Ecuadorian features.

A diminutive man sat behind what seemed to be an oversized desk. He stood with his hand held out toward Stockman. He couldn't have been more than five feet two inches, with a frail-looking body and a rather large head. It was his neatly trimmed black beard that seemed to give him strength and stature.

"Mr. Stockman, I am Ambassador Ramos Garcia-Lopez, but please, call me Ambassador." He smiled broadly as he rounded the desk and took Stockman's hand, shaking it firmly. "I am very pleased to meet you, and thank you so much for coming to meet me with very little context. It is very much appreciated, and I can only hope you can help us with this somewhat unusual situation in which we find ourselves." The ambassador returned to his chair. He sat down with his shoulders barely showing above the top of his desk, his head bobbing. It was an odd sight to see.

"My pleasure, Mr. Ambassador. I am intrigued by your invitation. I can only surmise you have a problem which you think my group, ORB, may be able to assist in resolving." Stockman sat in one of the two high-back green leather chairs opposite the ambassador and smiled.

"Just *Ambassador* will be fine. I understand you prefer to be called Stockman—is that correct?"

"Your intelligence is correct." They smiled at each other. The attaché sat in the chair next to Stockman. He stayed silent, attentive, and never moved throughout the meeting.

"Let me come straight to the point... Stockman." The ambassador smiled as though he had just cracked a joke. "Our country has a problem, you see, and we need to take care of it before it gets out of hand, if it hasn't already." He paused as though waiting for Stockman to make some comment, but none came. Instead, Stockman stared at him without any expression. He was waiting for the details and the reason he was here.

"You may know that we have a very consequential cocaine problem in Ecuador." The ambassador stopped again. He looked at Stockman for a sign of understanding or participation. He didn't get anything in return other than a blank look. "Cocaine, you see, has become the lifeblood of many of our traditional, and often indigenous farmers, as their land is being taken for other uses. They collect the coca leaves and manufacture enough crude cocaine to pass on up to the... let's say... bigger boys who finish the job and somehow export the finished product.

"Unfortunately, many in our government support them by looking the other way. Not all, you understand. There are still those who search out the manufacturing plants in the jungle and destroy them, but there are others who are blind to the bigger picture—those that process the raw product into commercial cocaine, those that transfer the product to the borders, and those that ship the product to other countries." The ambassador was starting to warm up.

"Don't you also have problems with the Colombians?" Stockman interrupted. "As I understand it, they use Ecuador as a gateway to other countries." Stockman knew just enough about the issue to understand some of the concerns. He also knew the governments in those countries were involved in their cocaine industry. They were only half-interested in anti-drug enforcement and never did seem to get a grip on control. It was, after all, a revenue stream they relied upon, despite the risks.

"Yes, Colombia is certainly a major concern but at least we have some understanding of the depth of that problem. The one I want to describe to you is one we cannot control." The ambassador seemed to grow taller as he looked even more earnest than he had when they started the discussion.

"I don't understand. You really don't seem to have much power over anything to do with cocaine in Ecuador," Stockman puzzled.

"That is not correct, Stockman." The ambassador wasn't annoyed at the comment. He knew only too well how the international community viewed Ecuador. Stockman's reaction was expected.

"You see, in actuality, we know a great deal about what is happening, who is responsible, and how to stop it if we need to. In fact, whether the outside world likes it or not, we are not going to stop it entirely." The ambassador seemed to shrink back into his chair. He knew he had just given something away to this stranger. Those who controlled Ecuador would not appreciate it. He could probably end up in jail himself if the wrong people knew what he was divulging.

"Oh, and is this somehow connected to what you would like ORB to do for you?" The question hung in the air for a moment. The ambassador stroked his beard as he considered his situation. "If Ecuador has no plan to stop producing and distributing cocaine, one can't expect Colombia to do so. Nor Mexico. Nor any other Central American country. In effect, it would mean open season for drug manufacturing. Enforcement would fall to the importing countries to exercise some control. Is that what you want?" Stockman paused and waited for what he knew would be a very interesting response.

"I know how it sounds to you." The ambassador seemed to have a twinkle in his eye as he said this. "But there are extenuating circumstances to consider."

"There are?" Stockman sounded and looked somewhat shocked. He was about to get a philosophical earful from a cocaine-producing country who wanted to openly defend their drug policies. He was all ears.

"Restraint, restraint, restraint. That is our motto these days." The ambassador sat forward. "There is no doubt we are not winning the war on drugs, Stockman, but we are learning to control it. And we will. Of that, there is no doubt, provided we can contain the problem to the perimeter of what we are aware of. That is, we do not want any more complications that could thwart our attempts to control our cocaine industry, for the benefit of all." The ambassador broke into a grin as he watched Stockman's reaction.

"That's one hell of a tall order." Stockman seemed stunned by what he was hearing. "Let me see if I understand what you're saying here." He paused, put a finger to his lips and looked up. "You don't eradicate cocaine production. You want to make sure the situation is contained to a business you are able to manage or control. Is that correct?"

"Yes. I think you have the gist of things, although not the entirety of the story. So perhaps I can explain a little more."

"Please do." Stockman shifted in his chair, glanced over at Eduardo Sánchez who still sat stoically in his chair without moving or changing the expression on his face, turned his attention back to the ambassador and wondered what ORB would have to do with this.

Without acknowledging the discomfort of his guest, the ambassador continued.

"While we have all been focusing on the more, let's say, traditional culprits in the world of drugs—the coca plant farmers, the manufacturers, processors and their labs, the distributors and the drug lords—there has been another element that has been eating away at their world, and ours, without anyone realizing. Can you guess what that is?" The ambassador smiled a sickly smile and placed his fingertips in a V-shape to his mouth. His elbows managed to rest on the top of his desk and he stared at Stockman, waiting for him to guess.

"I'm not very good at guessing, Ambassador, and I don't like games. So, please tell me the rest of the story, so we can move on." Stockman was not impressed by this turn of events. He didn't like the world of drugs. He knee-jerk reaction was not to get involved in it. He knew he couldn't trust anyone who had anything to do with it. But he was still interested in getting to the end of the story. "Well?"

"The Chinese, of course, Stockman." The ambassador slumped back in his chair. Stockman was caught with his mouth open and his head pushed forward. It was as though he hadn't quite heard and wanted to get closer to the speaker. He looked over at the attaché, who just nodded his head, pursed his lips and raised his eyebrows as though to say, "I'm afraid it's true."

"You see,"—the ambassador held a finger up as though to stop Stockman from asking questions too soon—"the government of China has been, let's say, encouraging some of its mining companies to become more aggressive in taking strategic positions within industry, all over the world. It has been a very tumultuous time as the Chinese pump billions of dollars into the economies of those countries it needs to invest in, to position themselves politically. But that is the way they operate. In Latin America, which includes Colombia, Peru and Ecuador, they have bought many foreign companies invested in oil and minerals. They have also advanced their projects despite local politics. All this is done in the name of China. To buy the breeding grounds of the resources they need rather than having to buy those commodities on the open market at prices governed by others." The ambassador took a brief rest as a young lady placed some tea next to him.

"It all sounds quite normal to me, Ambassador. Who wouldn't want to do what they are doing if they could afford to? The Chinese have a voracious appetite when it comes to their need for growth. Minerals are the basis for everything for them." Stockman looked up, not quite understanding where the ambassador was going with this.

"Yes, you are right, Stockman. But consider this, and I will put it as simply as I can." The ambassador took a sip of his tea, added another lump of sugar to his cup, and stirred it in slowly as he thought of how to explain things.

"These Chinese companies have now become international drug dealers using Ecuadorian resources." He let his words hang for a moment as Stockman opened his mouth to speak but thought better of it. "You see, we are sure they are the ones who are now buying crude cocaine from jungle farmers. They are somehow processing it to purity in their mineral plants, at the same time as producing the minerals they have a license for. Then they are exporting it on their own ships as a finished product, but only to China as far as we can tell. They have no middlemen, no outside sellers, no drug lords—just them. All this, and they are protected by elements within our own government. They are getting through our patrols, paying off whoever they have to, and threatening those who may threaten them." The ambassador stopped and picked up his cup.

"Are you certain of this?" Stockman wasn't quite sure what to say. He hadn't touched the cup of tea placed next to him. He was too distracted by what he was hearing.

"We know from some farmers. We know from cartel dealers. We know from our own drug agencies. Things are changing. The dynamics of this industry have become uncontrollable." The ambassador got out of his chair and strolled over to the window. He pushed back the net curtains and stared down at the street. "Oh, there is still the odd skirmish," he said. He turned and wandered back to his desk as he spoke. "A patrol finds some coca plant pickers and follows them to their little factory in the jungle." He looked over at Stockman and held his hands up. "But there are hundreds, thousands, of them out there and now we know where the farmers take their product. We are told there are collection points set up near the river where the farmers take their product. Chinese agents pay them in cash right there in US dollars, and they go back into the jungle to do it all over again."

"If you know all this, why don't you investigate and stop them?" Stockman didn't quite get it.

"Because the Chinese are protected." The ambassador was clearly emotional about the situation. "Don't you think we would if we could? Well, at least most of us would." His eyes pleaded with Stockman. "They are untouchable. More so than the drug lords we are used to dealing with. We could at least work with them. But these Chinese are beyond our ability to even negotiate with."

Stockman was recovering. He was starting to guess where things might be heading, but he still couldn't pin it down.

"What are you looking for ORB to do, Ambassador?"

The ambassador looked sad, as if he had exhausted all his energy.

"There are some of us in government who want to do something more. They have asked me to meet with you to consider how you might help us. But one thing is certain. We have to first put a stop to this encroachment of the Chinese on our mineral and oil rights. That's how sure we are they are using their industrial positions in Latin America to launder high-purity cocaine to their political and economic competitors around the world.

"They are quickly becoming the primary source for North America. They may also be supplying Australia. We have no intelligence on what they might be doing in Europe. However, we continue to work with our embassies there to investigate. If authorities find they source their cocaine from the Chinese in Ecuador, it will devastate our global market position."

"Do you have any thoughts about how we might help? If we take this on, are we going to get any help from the government or the military?" Stockman was wondering what the parameters were.

"Other than to ensure you have diplomatic immunity and safe passage for your people, there is little we can do. Whatever is done, it must appear as though our government is not involved. That means someone has to make it look as though the drug cartels are responsible. That shouldn't be hard to imagine happening. First, the Zamora mine must be neutralized, as well as their transport routes and ship-loading facilities." The ambassador stopped again and stroked his beard thoughtfully.

"Clearly you can't do any of these things yourselves." Stockman realized the predicament the Ecuadorian ambassador was in. "What about the mine? Isn't there something there you can do to stop them?"

"I am afraid not, Stockman. Any incursion into Chinese space will cause an international incident we cannot afford. That means everything they do is off-limits to us."

"I understand your situation, Ambassador." Stockman grimaced at what he was hearing, but it was a situation not uncommon for ORB to handle. Most of their cases involved situations where traditional methods of politics or policing just weren't workable.

"Let me think on this and do a little research. I'll get back to you in a few days. In the meantime, I wonder if you could round up some plans of the processing plant and the port facilities they use. We will look after the rest if we take this on."

Stockman and the ambassador spent another thirty minutes talking Ecuadorian politics. They discussed their situation with both Colombia and Peru, and how those countries handled the Chinese—they didn't, although there were a number of industrial plants that were operated by them in both countries. It was suspected they were using those facilities in the same way as the Zamora plant in Ecuador. This was new territory for all three countries. But if Ecuador successfully rid themselves of the Chinese, the others would follow.

Stockman left the ambassador to his thoughts and headed back to the Cadogan Hotel where he and Lucy had a late lunch as they talked about the situation in Ecuador. There was no doubt ORB would get involved, but first Stockman needed to meet with his board of advisors. Their advice was crucial and oftentimes added some context Stockman could miss if acting alone. They would follow the progress of whatever caper was being undertaken and provide commentary whenever they felt there could be something that Stockman might need to know. It was a group of intelligent travelers and businesspeople, including some with a military background, who were able to guide ORB through situations where governments couldn't go.

As Stockman suspected, helping to resolve the situation in Ecuador interested his advisory team immensely. Not particularly from the viewpoint of the cocaine trade, but containment of the Chinese. Their efforts to influence the minds of their adversaries—the US, Canada and Australia in particular, let alone Europe and the rest of the world—was well known.

The fact was, the Chinese considered control of cocaine distribution the responsibility of governments. If they could manipulate those governments, their job would be easier. The cocaine industry had become sprawling, rampant and controlled by the uncontrollable in a highly competitive manner by a myriad of gangs all vying for the top spot. This was where the Chinese saw their advantage. Chaos breeds chaos and it was something they were good at managing. There was no other generic global solution to the cocaine problem.

oooo

"Ambassador? Stockman here." It was several days later when Stockman called the ambassador from his hotel, the evening before he and Lucy left London to go back to Devon. He thought it best not to call him at the embassy, but rather use the private number the ambassador had given him when they had met.

"Ah, Stockman. Good to hear from you. Are you still in London?" The ambassador smiled in anticipation of getting some good news.

"Yes. My wife and I have been enjoying meeting up with old friends and, of course, thinking about your situation."

"And… what do you think? Will you help us?" The ambassador asked, hiding his excitement.

"Yes, I think we can help." Stockman seemed quite relaxed as he responded. He and Lucy had talked about their situation at some length, discussed it with board members, and decided they would move forward. It seemed like an interesting, and hopefully rewarding, project.

The ambassador was clearly relieved to hear Stockman offer to come to his country's help.

"Of course, we'll need the usual consular paperwork for our people." Stockman was now focusing on organizing details. "We'll also need a list of everyone you think we need to meet or learn about. That includes whoever it is who runs the Zamora plant." He paused for a moment. "I also assume there is some kind of a leader for the local farmers that we may have to get in touch with. Are you able to assist with those things?" Stockman was to the point and all business.

"We will get you as much information as we can." The ambassador was feeling the relief of now having someone to rely on who may be able to deal with the situation. "I will give you the names of some government contacts you can trust. There are also some well-placed military executives you can rely on, but you must ensure confidentiality. None of us knows who to trust outside of the names I will give you."

"Understood. This is something we are very used to dealing with. I would like a point of contact for any of our people if they got stuck in Ecuador and can't find their way out."

The Ambassador went quiet for a few moments. His initial eagerness seemed to have disappeared. Temporarily, Stockman hoped.

"Are you still there, Ambassador?"

"Yes, yes, of course. I am trying to think who you might best call on in any case of trouble. It isn't easy. Everyone is on edge, not knowing who to trust. Perhaps the best person would be my old friend. He is a missionary working with the indigenous groups in Ecuador and Peru. But he operates deep in the Amazon. I will make contact and establish how he may be able to assist and how you can make contact with him." The ambassador went silent again. He was unsure how he could achieve what Stockman was asking for.

"Listen, if you can get me the name, I'll have our man in the field make contact. But, unless it's an emergency, we won't call him from the middle of the Amazon. That could take days, or even weeks. So, let's leave it at that, but if you happen to come across a more, let's say, convenient person who could help, you should let me know." Stockman stopped to let the ambassador respond.

"Stockman, don't underestimate the Chinese," the ambassador warned. "I am sure they are even watching us here in the embassy, which is why we are being so careful. Our phones are scrambled, and if we generate any documents we have on this matter, they are taken off-site for storage every day. Only Eduardo and I know where that is." The ambassador paused.

"Good move. Have you spotted anyone watching you?"

"Not that I can tell." The ambassador paused, as he considered the question a little more. "Did you know there are nearly a quarter of a million homes in London owned by Chinese? Can you believe that?" He stared at Stockman, who grimaced. "In fact, a Chinese billionaire owns the most expensive piece of property in the city. It's over there, overlooking Hyde Park." The ambassador pointed toward the west from his office, as though Stockman could see. "Not that I think that means they are watching me, of course, but it's worth remembering that we are outnumbered, and it's unlikely I would recognize whether I was being watched by a Chinese person or not. There are so many that no one in particular stands out." He laughed.

Stockman smiled but didn't want to comment on the ambassador's observation.

"Well, I'd better let you go." Stockman was about to say goodbye.

"When do you think you will have your people on the ground?" the ambassador asked before Stockman had a chance to shut his phone off.

"I would think by the end of the month." Stockman's brow furrowed as he thought. "We'll have some prep work to do, paperwork to get in place, figure out a plan, and then..." Stockman let the sentence trail off as he was thinking. "Oh, by the way, I noticed the Colombian embassy is next door to you. Do you have a good relationship with the ambassador?"

"Yes, a very good relationship. We often dine together and discuss mutual issues where we may be able to exchange information that would help each other. Why?" The ambassador sounded confused.

"Well, in my research, I see that the same Chinese group purchased the Buriticá Gold Mine in Colombia. That was another one that had been owned by a Canadian company. I suppose one has to ask whether Colombia has a similar problem to your country. You know, with the Chinese processing cocaine in their plants and shipping it out." It was a good question.

"I don't know, Stockman. It may sound strange to you, but the issue with the Chinese is very sensitive. So, I have avoided sharing the details of Zamora with my friends over at the Colombian embassy."

"It may be time to reconsider. It would really benefit Ecuador if you could push the Chinese out of Central America. I don't think they would stand a chance on the international political stage if there was a concerted effort by all parties, knowing what you know. They wouldn't dare challenge you. Do you agree?" Stockman waited for the ambassador.

"You could be right, Stockman. Let me think about it. Also, other Chinese interests are well-placed in the areas where cocaine is manufactured in Latin America. Not all are mines. They are smaller, but perhaps we have to consider them all at the same time. That would be difficult." The ambassador sounded sullen. He was considering the problem and whether he wanted to contribute to the larger picture. But now was not the time to respond.

"Again, many thanks for meeting with me the other day, and of course, taking on the project."

Stockman was dubious about whether the ambassador would involve his opposite number at the Colombian consulate. Latin American countries were not known for sharing amongst themselves. They would prefer to go it alone. At least that was Stockman's experience.

Stockman smiled as the call ended. He tipped a finger to his forehead, as if he were in front of the ambassador, to say "See you again soon." It was a habit he was picking up from the locals in Hope Cove whenever they wanted to say hello or goodbye to someone.

Stockman and the ambassador had promised to stay in touch, which meant that Stockman would file reports as needed.

Chapter 4

It's So Nice to Be Home

It was one of those glorious March days that promised an early spring in Vancouver. The type of day when amateur mariners felt an urge to take to the water for their first run after winter. Cool but bright. Eight knots of wind, waves cresting, the blue sky dotted with fluffy cumulus clouds, and an almost empty bay with the only obstacles being the buoys and maritime vessels anchored as they waited for instructions to move into port.

The perfect single-handed sailing conditions for a sailor out for a joyride in his thirty-eight-foot-long Hunter, rigged to suit. The sheets, or lines, all coiled and cleated, running in parallel back to the cockpit; a furling jib and mainsail, to make things as easy as possible to manage; a cold brew sitting in the holder next to the helm and a cigar to puff on. Perfect. Destination, Gibson's Landing, and hopefully a hot toddy waiting to be savored.

Matthew Black adjusted the mainsail of *Calypso* a few degrees to take full advantage of the following wind, pushing the yacht to its nine-knot maximum speed. He watched from behind the dodger as the main sail billowed with its telltale tails horizontal, the vessel slicing through the water, leaving a curling wake behind. He reveled in the smoothness of the ride, the occasional wave breaking over the bow and spray blowing over the top of the cabin, while the boat performed with all the grace for which it was designed.

As Matthew glanced behind him to see the Lions Gate Bridge disappearing in the distance, he spotted a small powerboat weaving its way in his direction. It was the only other pleasure boat in the bay, and it was gaining on him fast at about twelve knots, bouncing over the white crests whipped up by the wind. He couldn't see who was piloting it, but he could see there was only one person dressed in a dark outfit, a baseball cap pulled down over their forehead, and a pair of oversized sunglasses hiding their face. Whoever it was, they were gripping the steering wheel as the boat settled into Matthew's wake and slowed to the same speed as the Hunter. He couldn't figure out whether this was a friend or foe, or just some joker out for fun. But whoever it was, they were annoying. Matthew pulled the mainsail into the wind and parallel to the Hunter. He tugged on the jib sheet to bring it all the way over, and then let the mainsail move to the other side as his yacht turned about to circle behind the speedboat. As he passed in the opposite direction, he spotted a smile on the face of the operator, followed by a wave with both hands, leaving the little boat temporarily to the mercy of the waves.

"Why so slow?" a high-pitched voice shouted over the water to Matthew.

"You little…" Matthew yelled back as he realized Emma was the pilot. He thought she had caught the ferry and would already be at Gibsons, but no. She was a woman who made her own decisions, and her plans were not always quite the same as Matthew's.

"See you there!" Emma shouted as she opened the throttle, moved to the starboard side of the Hunter and sped forward.

Matthew smiled. He loved that woman.

It took almost an hour for *Calypso* to reach the Atkinson Point lighthouse, a marker for boaters leaving the bay and for mariners coming into Vancouver. Rather than sailing around to the east to reach Bowen Island, before taking a left to Gibsons, Matthew adjusted his sails. He headed toward Seymour Landing on the west side before turning north to Gibsons. The other route could be a tougher passage, especially for a single-handed sailor. It crossed the busy ferry route from Horseshoe Bay to Nanaimo, two major British Columbian ferry terminals, and the rush of air outflowing from Howe Sound was known to create a crosswind that could play havoc with a recreational boat.

While Matthew had enough experience and had sailed this route a number of times, he decided to play it safe this time. It wouldn't totally avoid the outflow, but the alternative would be to face the gusts coming from the east into the Gulf and colliding with the northwesters from Alaska.

Emma stood on the dock with her hands on her hips and a big smile on her face, as *Calypso* came toward where she stood guard at a large, open berth. Matthew had already lowered the buoys over the starboard side to protect the boat from rubbing against the dock. He tossed her the bowline. She caught it and pulled the bow in against the marina, securing it around one of the cleats. Matthew maneuvered the boat a little more to get the stern in closer and tossed a line to Emma. She tied it to a cleat and reached up for a spring line, tying it off before securing the stern line more. She took the electrical cable from Matthew, fixed it into the shore power and flipped the switch. Matthew reached down and lifted up onto the deck then pulled her toward him.

"You look fabulous. Boy, I've missed you, Em," Matthew said, all smiles as he led her down the three steps to the cabin. He opened a cold bottle of Pinot Grigio, poured two glasses, handed her one and tossed his cap into the corner of the bench

"It's great to be home again." They toasted one another and headed to the forward berth. Matthew had closed the hatch from the cockpit to avoid nosy trespassers. But he opened some of the small windows to let the air in while Emma tossed her jacket to one side and pulled her sweater off. The boat had air conditioning and heating, but neither was operating. It was getting late, and the fresh sea air floated around them.

Matthew was in his early forties. He was tall, athletic and fit with a well-sculpted body, sharp features and short, thick, black, curly hair. He was intelligent, had a quick wit and was an easy conversationalist. His charm, white teeth, smile and square jaw disarmed most people. But he was not so self-centered that he couldn't stay alert to his surroundings. He was ready to react to any threat.

Interestingly, Matthew had been a welder in his early years, after he finished his mechanical engineering degree. An odd combination, but one that fit his lifestyle at that time. Those were the days he was looking for good money and excitement. Now, with ORB, money wasn't an issue and his practical talents were key to a new level of excitement. His understanding of industrial settings was essential.

After another glass of wine and more small talk, Matthew leaned over and kissed Emma on the lips, then began slowly unbuttoning her shirt. Matthew knew she was naked underneath and extremely ticklish, but that didn't stop him from playing a little here and there. Emma squirmed and giggled as he ran his fingers lightly over her skin. Then she reached out and pulled at the drawstring of Matthew's pants to loosen them, sliding them down just enough to reach her hand in.

Emma was lean, toned, and in her mid-thirties. Most often she was Emma Stockman, but sometimes Emma Stone. It depended on the job, where she was, with whom, and who she preferred to be at the time. Her everyday style preference was for short-cropped black hair, cut in a pixie style for easy management, and minimal makeup. Clothing was optional. But she preferred black jeans, a tucked-in white shirt with a stand collar, and high-cut ankle boots. Or, for even more casual moments, black Reebok Freestyle Hi's. She knew how to play up her feminine side when needed, but she was a tomboy at heart. She was a naturally sexy lady with an ever-ready urge for excitement. She suited Matthew, and she loved ORB.

The climax of the *1812 Overture* is internationally recognizable. There's a lot of noise. Lots of cannon fire. Lots of bursts of loud orchestral music. But for Matthew, it meant Stockman was calling, and one never ignored that. It was the signature tune Matthew had selected to announce that his boss was calling him.

Emma laughed and filled her wineglass. She didn't bother covering up and wandered into the cabin while Matthew answered the call. She had already taken off her jeans and stood in front of him, bare-chested and wearing the skimpiest of underwear, just enough to hide the most interesting parts.

"Hi, boss. What's happening in your part of the world?" Matthew looked at his watch and realized it was after midnight in England, if that was where Stockman was.

"I can't complain, you know. Life is good, the birds are chirping, the cows are mooing, Lucy is in great form, and I think I have a nice project for you, my boy." Stockman was content with life. But maybe that was because he had something new to tax his brain.

"Oh, do tell." Matthew wasn't sure he wanted to know at this particular moment, as he glanced over at Emma, lounging mostly naked with a wineglass at her lips, her legs tucked up under her and an arm across the back of the couch. But he knew he was going to have to listen to Stockman. That was the job, and Stockman was not only his boss but also Emma's father.

"It seems Ecuador needs our services, Matthew. Or rather, their ambassador in London and some of the less corrupt politicians in Ecuador need us."

Stockman related the story to Matthew about his meeting with the Ecuadorian ambassador. He also mentioned the potential for Colombia needing the same kind of help. At this point, Stockman had not made a plan. But he wanted the core team to get on a Zoom call soon. They needed to do a first review of the issues and develop at least the framework for a plan. As usual, timing was everything, and they scheduled a call for a week's time. Stockman was going to work on the cast of ORB characters he thought they would need.

"Let me think about that as well. We can talk again between now and next week. I certainly think Peters should be on board. I don't know if we need Plato, but we may need Colin. This could involve finance and the legal system. But let's think on it some more." Matthew had a list of good people, but Stockman's list of resources could be useful He knew a lot more people and he could even call Sloan, in London, for some help. Sloan was always a good source for the types of people ORB needed. He had contracted a number of people to ORB over the years, and this project might need some very skilled people.

"Okay, I'll send you the details for the call-in. We can do this first one over the internet, but we may need to meet face-to-face at some point. Which reminds me, how is Emma, my darling daughter?" Stockman was smiling as he said it. He already knew Emma was with Matthew—and they knew he knew, as usual.

"HELLO, DADDY," Emma called out. "LOVE YOU!" She laughed.

"Make sure you're on the call with us next week, Emma sweetheart. I have a feeling we're going to need you on this one, and I would guess you wouldn't have it any other way."

"GIVE MY LOVE TO MUMMY!" Emma shouted again, ignoring the comment from her father. He knew darned well she would want to get in on the action.

"Will do. Take care, you two. Boating can get dangerous, you know." Stockman turned his cell off, looked over at Lucy and gave one of those "What are we going to do with her?" types of looks. Lucy just smiled and went back to her reading, but she couldn't help herself.

"They seem so good together, don't you think?" She sounded almost absent-minded as she voiced her thoughts out loud and looked over at

Stockman, but he had already buried his head in his laptop again. He had his earphones on and couldn't hear what his wife had said.

"Well, I do." Lucy smiled.

Meanwhile, Matthew looked over at Emma, who had a look of mock surprise on her face at her father's assumption that she was boating, and doing other things, with Matthew.

"How does he always know?" Emma pretended to be surprised that her father always seemed to know where she was. In some ways it was a comfort. In other ways it was an annoyance. But Emma understood their concern. After all, she wasn't just a daughter, she was also a saboteur.

Matthew and Emma shrugged and smiled.

"Did it spoil the moment?" he asked as he reached for her.

"Not for me..." Emma pulled Matthew down onto the sofa. They embraced in a tight ball of love, legs stretched around each other and arms reaching around the other's neck. Their lips, their mouths, their faces and their hands intertwined in a loving embrace that only came with the intimacy of knowing. The intimacy of profound need and understanding. The understanding of what each meant to the other. Then the smoothness of contentment of flesh on flesh, flesh in flesh, and a feeling of being one, fully embraced by the other. Was there anything else to life? For that moment, at that time, they were as one, both mentally and physically. Just one. And it was exhaustingly beautiful.

Chapter 5

Team Time

"This one's a complicated one, Em." Matthew was looking at the notes he had put together, with maps and arrows pointing in a number of directions.

"Any more than the others?" Emma wondered as she looked over at him.

"Well, this one has a lot of unknown unknowns so to speak. There are some difficult logistical issues beyond sabotaging a plant, and having to deal with people very few know much about. I think just about everything I'm looking at here has to be done by an in-country team." He glanced over to meet her eyes.

"What do you mean?"

"We're on our own with this one. I don't think a Plato or a Colin or any of the legal boys are going to be involved, and no other outside help that I can see, other than Stockman, that is." He stared at her a moment longer before looking back down at the papers and scribbling a couple of notes.

There was no doubt in Matthew's mind: ORB had a complex and dangerous job on their hands with this Ecuadorian caper.

Not only were they going to have to deal with the Chinese in a jungle environment, but they would also have to convince the local indigenous farmers to redirect their crude cocaine back to the cartel. Matthew saw nothing easy about this assignment, but then none were. There were just different degrees of difficulty, and this one was near the highest.

He needed to talk things over with Emma to develop an outline for a strategy. Of course, they also had to identify what resources they needed in terms of people and supplies.

In addition to those agents ORB could make available, Matthew had some associates in South America, as well as a couple he knew with experience in Ecuador. Some spoke Spanish. Some had jungle experience. Some were even Chinese who spoke Spanish. His knowledge partly came from having worked with ORB on a project in Peru when he was dealing with Tupac Amaru. Early in his career, before ORB, he was a contract welder traveling through Chile, Peru and Colombia, working on exotic metals. He still kept in touch with many of the people he met on his travels and kept the contact with them going as they moved from job to job around the world. They were important to him. He had often dipped into this reservoir of names when he needed help on projects. This time was no different and he circled a few he thought would be useful to him now.

Emma had her own contacts in the world of heavy industry and had done her fair share of traveling from job to job. She was also a superb welder. Although she generally worked with more common materials like carbon and the more frequently used stainless steels, she also excelled at welding thin-walled—as well as extra thick-walled—small-bore pipe particularly in tight spots, where her size helped a lot as well as her level of fitness. It usually needed a lot bending and contorting to do the work she was good at, and the pay was way better. For example, she was one of the few who would wriggle into those places between the upper steam drum and lower mud drum in a boiler house to weld the inter-connecting one-inch diameter steam tubes into position.

Strangely, that's where she met Matthew—in the center portion of a steam drum where he welded the high-pressure tubes from one side and she the other. It was love at first sight, although they had to remove their welding masks first before they fully realized the other's potential.

Emma used her welding experience on ORB projects quite often, where high pressure steam drum sabotage could bring industrial plants to a complete standstill. She was a master at it and knew exactly now to scar a tube to decrease the thickness of the pipe in that location, where it couldn't be easily spotted. Or plug the ends of the small diameter pipes—or tubes, as they were called—before she welded them into place, to stop steam passing from one drum to the other. Of course, the welds never passed X-ray testing but by the time the faults were discovered, Emma had disappeared.

Mathew and Emma started laying out the scope of the project as they sat around in *Calypso*'s cabin. They could work and talk there without being interrupted and enjoy the occasional glass of cold Pinot Grigio with just a touch of friskiness in between to lighten the load.

Both searched the internet for mines in Latin America owned by Chinese companies and did some research on the companies involved. A Google search taught them how to make crude cocaine in the jungle, and what it took to make one ounce of cocaine hydrochloride, the commercial prize that made its way to the streets once it had been diluted. They researched the most likely drug export routes from Zamora out of Ecuador by road, air and sea.

From everything they read and heard, it was clear governments were losing their battle against the drug trade in Central and South America. But ORB's assignment was not to get involved in this larger picture, but in a smaller one with a focus on only the situation in Ecuador for now.

Reviewing the notes from the discussion with Stockman, they sat back to clarify their understanding of the situation as a whole.

It seemed to them, in the case of the Chinese-owned Zamora plant, there was a part of the Ecuadorian government, untainted by the attraction of illicit bribes, who needed to contain Ecuador's cocaine production to only those they had some control over—the Ecuadorian farmers and the cartel. Those whom the government had no control over had to be prevented from being any part of the country's cocaine industry, and that included the Chinese.

In their ruminations on the subject, Matthew and Emma came to understand the real problem standing in the way of the Ecuadorian government solving the drug production issue themselves was everything to do with global politics. If the government barred the Chinese from operating in-country after they had already granted mineral production licenses, it would be condemned by the international community. The Chinese would be seen as the victim. Neither could the Ecuadorian government be seen to be responsible by its own people for creating havoc with a company, Chinese-sponsored or not, which contributed so much to Ecuador's revenue and their employment.

Even the local drug agencies, sworn to uphold the enforcement laws, could not play a part in interfering with Chinese cocaine production, without disturbing the delicate balance of international politics.

The solution to the problem was a complex one, and one that could not be easily resolved unless the Chinese could be coaxed out of the country of their own free will. And that was where ORB came in.

It all made sense to Matthew and Emma as they talked about the possibilities and probabilities of Ecuador managing things themselves, and what a conundrum the situation put the government in. They wondered about any government taking such an active and controlling role in the drug industry, but logic told them it was either that or succumb to a never-ending, and very expensive, war on drugs. As the old saying went, if you can't beat them, join them.

Stockman forwarded details to Matthew, from his high-level sources, on what was known, but not publicly available, about Chinese ownership of companies in Latin America. He also sent confidential intelligence reports concerning the subversive influence the Chinese had on the governments in the region, as a consequence of their industry ownership. There were satellite photos and detailed mapping of the terrain surrounding the Zamora property. Stockman provided the names and backgrounds of indigenous groups in the Zamora area, together with the names of the most influential people in those groups. There was a brief dossier on Ecuadorian government officials believed to be accessories to the movement of cocaine through Ecuador. The list wasn't extensive, but it did include the names, contact numbers, photos and influence wielded by some powerful officials. There were also names and backgrounds of the Chinese senior operating team at Zamora, as well as in their Quito head office.

Last but not least, Stockman provided a brief on Los Choneros and Los Lobos, the two most prolific drug cartels in Ecuador. It was believed that Los Choneros were the ousted drug middlemen in the Zamora area when the Chinese plant came on stream and took over cocaine production. No one quite knew why or how a cartel would relinquish such a prize, but that was something Matthew would have to consider in the field. It was also apparent that Los Lobos were not yet a prime contender for the cocaine management in southeast Ecuador and while their reputation was well known in the north, it seemed they hadn't yet migrated south.

The details provided on the Colombian and Mexican threats to the Ecuadorian cartels were sketchy. It seemed their incursion into their neighboring country had not yet matured enough to be an imminent threat to the management of the drug industry there. They did, however, make use of both Ecuadorian cartels to move their own product south to their ports.

By the time Matthew and Emma returned from Gibsons to their homes in Vancouver, after a few days of rest and planning, as well as some well-earned physical activity with each other, Matthew had at least formed an initial strategy on how to tackle the mission. He and Emma had made a list of types of people they needed, together with matching names. They knew some might not be available, but that was where Stockman's files would be used.

It would all become clearer once they had laid out a plan of action with him.

"Hello, Matthew. Are you looking after that darling daughter of mine?" Stockman asked when Matthew called him the day after he and Emma arrived back in Vancouver.

"Of course. She's a bit of a handful, though. But then I think you know that." Matthew was smiling to himself as he thought about the time he and Emma had spent together on *Calypso* during their downtime. And that's exactly what it was.

"Ah, yes. She was always a bit of a monkey. A tomboy, really. Couldn't stop her from annoying the lads, you know." Stockman was smiling at the memories.

"She still is annoying them!" Matthew blurted out and they both laughed as Emma reached over and clipped the back of Matthew's head.

"Take care of her, won't you? Or perhaps it'll be the other way round." They both chuckled. "Lucy and I are looking forward to seeing you both. I think she's chomping at the bit to see if there's any magic between the two of you."

"I'd say there's something there." Matthew got another clip from Emma.

"I sent you a list of things I was going to send. Did you get everything?" Stockman went back to his business voice.

"I think so. Many thanks, very useful. I'm getting it all printed out now. I want to look over the aerial photos in particular."

"Sounds good. Have you thought about a strategy?" Stockman was moving on.

"I have, or should I say, we have. Emma has been with me for most of the week, and she has a good head for these things."

"Agreed. So, what have you two come up with?"

Matthew and Emma described their potential operation, and figuratively assigned each person they had come up with to a task. Stockman was asked to look for alternates in case the initial selections weren't available.

Matthew set out their thoughts, including timing, reconnaissance, contacts to be made, locations for their agents, and a general outline of some of the activities they were considering to dissuade the Chinese from continuing their operation.

"Well, it's a start but it needs a lot of flesh on the bones." Stockman was happy with the outline but knew there was still a lot of planning to do. He continued to push. "Let's set a call for the team in a week's time. By then we should have identified and confirmed our agents, and you two should have fattened up the plan a bit more. My sense is we need to move within the month. June is the next major harvesting period for picking coca leaves so I think we should be there when the activity starts."

"Sounds good, sir." Matthew was being formal. "Would you set a time and day that suits you and we'll round everyone up? Does a Zoom call make sense?"

"Yes, I think that's the way to go. Make it next Friday at ten a.m. GMT, would you?" Stockman had already settled on the timing and didn't want to waste time thinking about it more.

"Will do. Talk to you then." Matthew knew the call was finished and clearly Stockman sounded as though he was in a bit of a hurry. He didn't even have a minute to exchange greetings with Emma.

They both hung up.

"Okay, let's call around and see who we can catch." Matthew turned to Emma who had already compiled some names and numbers on two pieces of paper. She gave one to Matthew and kept the other herself.

"Do you want to call these?" Emma glanced at the paper she handed to Matthew. "And I'll call these?"

"Okay, let's get started. Anyone we can't get hold off, just send an email for now and get them to call us."

Chapter 6

Zoom Time, Stockman

Lucy wasn't much of an early riser these days, but on this particular morning she took her husband a light breakfast of tea and toast and set it down on his desk in the study.

"From my intel," Lucy started as she went over and sat in an armchair, by the window, with her own tea, "it doesn't seem as though the heavy cartels from Colombia have reached the Zamora area yet. That would mean there's time to do what you have to do before the place is crawling with too many factions fighting each other." She took a sip from her cup. "If what the ambassador says is true, the Chinese are not going to go without one hell of a fight. Not only have they filched the cocaine industry from the locals, but my read of their mineral asset is it's loaded and well worth a fight just by itself." At these times, Lucy was anything but a quietly serving wife. Her CSIS training was showing itself as she worked in the background on some of the details Stockman would need.

"I think you're right." Stockman looked thoughtful as he chewed on his toast and marmalade, wiped his mouth, and sipped his tea. "But I think Matthew is getting there. I want to make sure he isn't distracted by things he has no control over, like the Colombian cartels moving in, or the Ecuadorian government working with the Chinese. Somehow, we're going to have to manage all that."

"Don't forget the Chinese government. I'm sure they'll want to run interference if they see such a major asset of theirs disappearing." Lucy was quite nonchalant as she spoke what was on her mind. It was another important part of the puzzle that Matthew needed protection from. It would be enough for him to manage the in-country elements directly associated with Zamora without having to think about the more global picture. But then, that was what Stockman was for.

"Mmm…" Stockman lowered his reading glasses, looked over at his wife and nodded. He always appreciated her input, and as usual, she was spot-on in this case.

Stockman sat in the study of his cottage by the sea and fiddled with the papers in front of him. It was just coming up to 6:50 a.m. He was waiting for the Zoom connection with Matthew to show on his computer screen. Lucy stayed in the armchair to listen in on the discussions.

By 10:50 p.m. Pacific Standard Time, Matthew and Emma were perched together on a couch in his apartment in Vancouver. His laptop was open on the coffee table in front of them. They had spent most of the evening going over last-minute details of their plans before pressing the keyboard sequence to let them into the Zoom call.

"Hello, you two," Stockman greeted Matthew and Emma when they appeared in front of him. "Everything going well over there on the edge of the world?" Stockman chuckled. He always thought of Western Canada as being out there somewhere on the periphery of civilization. Their images were clear; their voices checked out. They had arranged the call-in ten minutes before everyone else joined so they could cover anything important but not yet discussed between them.

"I would say so, sir. It seems to be coming together fairly well, and from what I can see so far, I think we have a good team together. Any thoughts on them?" Matthew paused.

"I think it's a good package. The team looks solid. I like the idea of using our Chinese friends, Nathan and Eric, in the plant. The others seem to be well placed. I can see you're just focusing on the Zamora site in Ecuador. Any thoughts on Buriticá?" Stockman had his own thoughts on the matter of Colombia but kept them to himself for now. The fact was he hadn't approached the Colombian embassy in London yet, so that scene wasn't set. He assumed the Ecuadorian ambassador hadn't contacted them to look for possible synergies either, so there was no point in pushing that lever until he had done so.

"I know we haven't heard about Colombia, but I would prefer to just focus on Ecuador for now anyway. I think it would be seen as too coincidental for both plants to have similar problems at the same time. And if we want it to look as though it's the cartel causing the problems, it would be hard to imagine two separate cartel groups working together on something like this. No, let's just deal with one at a time," Matthew suggested.

"I agree. I'll make contact with the Ecuadorian embassy and let them know it's a go. We'll need consular clearances for our group, so that's going to take a few weeks." Stockman was happy with what Matthew had suggested—one thing at a time. And, who knew? Maybe the Colombians didn't care about the Chinese too much. After all, their share of the cocaine production would be very small compared to the whole. But it was likely the cartels would take action at some point. They weren't the type who would appreciate anyone muscling in on their territory, and they wouldn't give a damn if it was someone like the Chinese either. Everyone knew their government sponsored them, but the drug kingpins weren't scared off. They had been operating in Colombia for many years and their reign of terror and control over the drug industry was a matter of international general knowledge.

"Any thoughts on adding to the team?" Matthew wondered.

"Not really. I've been in touch with Sloan in London and put him on notice that we may need his help. He's doing a search for country and language matches. I also asked him for security agents in the event we need them. You never know—things could get nasty."

"You're right. All we know are general details about who we may be dealing with, but we haven't seen the whites of anyone's eyes yet."

"Okay, it's time." Stockman watched as the screen populated with two new faces. "I see the first couple of people waiting at the gate for us. I'll let them in."

Stockman connected Kenny first.

"God, it's good to see you, old friend." Matthew moved a little closer to the screen. He and Kenny went back a lot of years from their early construction days, when they spent their time sweating away in petrochemical plants overseas, working for American contractors.

Kenny had that same broad grin on his face Matthew remembered. He was always so positive, and so reliable. Kenny could make light of any difficult situation if that's what it took to get them through.

"You too, Matthew. It's been a while." Kenny sounded his usual self. "We need to catch up on things."

Matthew nodded, gave Kenny a thumbs-up and went back to the keyboard.

James came online next and Matthew and he exchanged memories of a couple of projects they had done together. James and his wife, Jenny, had first encountered Matthew in Iran when ORB had to disable a petrochemical plant in Sari. James was an excellent second-in-command to Matthew and they had bonded from that time. He was an extremely versatile guy with a real sense of hustle that Matthew appreciated. It was a quality that was hard to come by.

Within a few minutes, everyone had signed in and checked their audio.

"Hello, everyone." Stockman smiled as he looked at each of the faces on his screen. He knew them all. "Sorry I can't offer you coffee and pastries this time. But I'm sure you've already taken care of those things." There were smiles on the screen with a few mugs held up. A number of faces were missing, including Plato, Tony and Colin. They would get separate briefings and a video copy of the current meeting in case they were needed on this assignment at some point. Matthew wanted the in-country team to meet with him, Emma and Stockman first before involving anyone else. At this point he wasn't sure what off-site help he would need.

Stockman became serious as he looked over the top of his reading glasses at the group.

"Okay." Stockman nodded his head. "In a nutshell, this one's all about stopping the Chinese from producing refined cocaine in Ecuador and shipping it back to their homeland." He paused and looked at the bewildered looks from his audience. He was used to it. Every project he proposed had an element of absurdity about it. And that usually meant danger.

"I know." Stockman acknowledged the looks on their faces with his hands held up. "As strange as it sounds, they seem to be buggering things up for the authorities. The government is losing their grip on the country's drug industry and they want it back." Everyone raised their eyebrows in question, but Stockman pushed on.

"These Chinese are the new boys on the block in Ecuador when it comes to cocaine, and they have an interesting way of producing it." Stockman paused more for effect than anything else. "They're operating a copper and gold mine hidden in the jungle that also processes crude cocaine brought to them by the locals. It's probably not their only one, but it's the one we're focusing on for now." He had their full attention.

"Now, we're pretty sure they ship all the cocaine they produce to China for distribution to wherever. Probably to the States." Stockman studied the faces on the screen. Matthew had already explained this to each member of the team before the meeting. But it was still a surprise to hear it from the boss. Everyone was quiet as they waited for Stockman to continue.

"Before we get into the details, let me give you some in-country information you probably don't know about Ecuador to get your juices flowing, so to speak." Stockman's face went off-screen as he fiddled with something. "This is the center of our attention for this project." A slide appeared on everyone's computer, replacing their faces. "Ecuador," Stockman announced. A geographical map of the country displayed the coastline, rivers, mountain peaks, roads and towns.

"The nice thing about the place is that it uses the US dollar as its primary currency." Stockman offered a wry smile.

He pointed at the map with a pen.

"Notice Ecuador's boundaries with Peru and Colombia?" Stockman let his pen follow a line on the map representing country boundaries. "Now, while the Colombian cartels are moving product across the border into Ecuador from the north, searching for alternative transport routes to their markets, the Peruvian military are trying to stop all cocaine from crossing their border into Peru. But their issues are different from Columbia's. Peru is also a producer, so they're trying to stop their northern neighbors from flooding Peru with cocaine. So you need to be aware, the Peruvians have a military unit stationed on the border right here"— Stockman pointed to a small clearing in the jungle—"in the southeastern corner of the country, within spitting distance of Peru. That's the Zamora copper-gold plant—our target." He let his audience dwell on what he was showing them for a minute as he pointed to the various rivers, valleys and topographical undulations on the map.

"And this is the port at Machala"—he slid his pen tip west to the coastline as his voice calmed—"from where we think the Chinese are exporting their product. It's about two hundred and fifty miles from the plant." Stockman traced his pen along a road crossing the mountains from Zamora through places with names like El Pangui and Loja.

Stockman slid his pen up to the north end of the map again. "Now, just out of interest, this is the border with Colombia. Notice I've marked where we think the main area of their drug entry is. It's not relevant to this project but gives you a sense of what the drug runners go through to get some of their product out of Colombia. This is where the greatest intensity of action is and you'll see it's a long way from Zamora. And here"—the pen point moved a fraction to the west of the entry point—"between San Lorenzo and Tulcán, the drug enforcement authorities have discovered and dismantled some of the largest cocaine labs in Central America. But that's a whole different issue, and not one for us to dwell on today. It's just background so you get to understand a little more about the overall picture."

"How would you define large?" It was Emma. "I mean, are you talking about a lab in a basement, or someone's garage or...?"

Stockman returned the screen to the faces of his audience.

"Well, firstly that's where the serious business is done to convert the cocaine base to cocaine hydrochloride. Some of what are called crystallization plants can produce up to three to four tons of the final product in one week." Stockman watched the eyebrows of his audience go up as they tried to imagine what that meant at street level, where even an ounce of cocaine was a lot. "A plant of that size would have an area of about 4,500 square feet. That's, like, thirty feet by one hundred and fifty feet. It would likely be divided into a machine area and a packaging area. It would have areas for fuel and acetone storage, accommodations for, say, fifteen people, a kitchen and power generation. There would also be refining tanks, a bunch of water pumps, and an industrial kitchen where they dry the stuff with loads of microwave ovens. That sounds pretty significant, doesn't it? But there are rumors of larger ones around." Stockman eyed the team. He could tell some were doing the mathematics of value involved.

"I guess of some of you are trying to convert that to value. Let me help you. One ton of cocaine hydrochloride—that's pure cocaine—when cut becomes about one point four tons of saleable product on the streets. So, at, let's say, $2,500 an ounce on the street, it means something like $112 million in revenue. Not bad, eh?" Stockman could hear the quiet gasps on the other end of the Zoom call.

"Remember, that's for one ton. So, a three-to-four-tons-per-week capacity crystallization plant can bring in $336 million to $448 million per week in revenue by the time the streets absorb it all. Of course, that gets split up among God knows how many people along the way, and there are a lot of capital and material expenses, but you can see it's enough to get people interested in being a part of that world."

Stockman replaced his audience again with a map of Ecuador and pointed to the Zamora mine. "The mine is owned and operated by Tongyan, a Chinese company." Stockman's pen tip hovered over the area.

"This is where our problems begin," Stockman clarified. "And just so as you have an understanding of what we are dealing with, it was only a month or so ago that nine point six tons of cocaine hydrochloride, worth about $450 million, was discovered in jute bags hidden behind a false concrete wall in a Mexican water bottling company's building in Guayaquil. It was the largest cocaine shipment discovered to date by the Ecuadorian authorities. And they are sure that product came from the Zamora plant, although they haven't managed to prove it yet." Stockman paused for the relevance to sink in.

"Since then, we think the Chinese changed their tactics and avoided Guayaquil and shipped their product to Puerto Bolívar." Stockman pushed his pen tip over to the Ecuador coast on the map.

He switched back to the faces on his screen.

"Just some background now. We know that Colombia's Oliver Sinisterra dissident group, as well as the Mexican Jalisco Cartel New Generation—CJNG—and Sinaloa cartels, have a strong foothold in northern Ecuador. What we don't know is how far south they've penetrated. But we are sure Los Choneros, Ecuador's largest gang, are very active in the Zamora region, despite the fact their leader is incarcerated and their nemesis, Los Lobos, is coming on fast."

There were shuffling noises amongst the people on the call, but nobody spoke just yet. The very thought of mixing things up with drug cartels sent a shiver down the spines of most.

"So, what does all this mean for us?" Stockman looked at the faces on his screen. "Well, in part, it means that most of the nefarious drug activity occurs in the north of the country. But let's be generous and say it all happens north of the two-degree latitude that runs through Guayaquil. That means the crazies haven't got too far south yet. But you can count on them getting there soon, and before there's a bloodbath between them—the Ecuadorian cartels and the Chinese—we need to clean the place up a little." Stockman paused to take a mouthful of coffee.

"Let's take a look at the targets." Stockman posted a larger-scale terrain map of just southern Ecuador, showing the location of the Zamora site and the Pacific coastline in greater detail.

"The Tongyan group has its Ecuadorian headquarters in Quito, and a substantial Chinese workforce at its Zamora plant near El Pangui." The tip of his pen tapped on the nearest town to the mine as he continued to talk.

"As Matthew would have told you, this is an 80,000-ton-per-day copper, gold and silver mine that ships 1,800 tons of wet concentrate out every day. From what our intelligence indicates, there are approximately fifty-six trucks, each carrying thirty-two tons of concentrate in two-ton bags leaving the mine every day. Over the last couple of weeks, we tracked fifty of those trucks heading to the port in Guayaquil. There, the bags were dumped in a concentrate storage warehouse where a conveyor transports it to a waiting ship. There doesn't appear to be anything odd about this activity, although we haven't managed to get into that warehouse yet. But the transfer happens pretty fast so we think it's legit.

"The other six trucks haul their bags two hundred and sixty miles all the way to the port in Machala. That's Puerto Bolívar, a much smaller facility to the south. It's primarily used for exporting bananas.

"We think the Zamora plant is processing rough cocaine and hiding it with the copper–gold concentrate. They keep it in the concentrate tote bags and transport them on those six trucks to Puerto Bolívar in Machala. It looks as though they load the bags directly onto a ship, and once it's full, away it goes to China. We need to verify all this on the ground before we finalize our plans." Stockman flicked the screen back to the faces of the team.

"For your information, each ton of concentrate contains about thirty percent copper, so in one day the Zamora mill produces about 540 tons of copper, some 360 ounces of gold and about 3,600 ounces of silver per ton, all contained in that 1,800 tons of concentrate. You can figure out the final dollar values for yourself, but you can see it's quite a haul.

"Matthew, any thoughts?" Stockman asked.

"Not yet. But I'm guessing we should be checking out Puerto Bolívar first. From what you say, it looks like our most likely departure point. Once we confirm one way or another, we can figure out the next move."

"That's right. One thing at a time." Stockman was 90% sure his information was accurate. But there was always that 10% of uncertainty to deal with. Better to do that as soon as they could, rather than going off in too many directions at the same time.

"Okay, let's get back to the Zamora plant." Stockman's pen tip tapped at the location on the map that had replaced the faces on the screen.

"It's located on the east side of the Andes on one of the tributaries feeding the Amazon, the Río Quimi. So, it's jungle territory. You can drive from Quito to El Pangui, the nearest sizable town to the plant. There's a small domestic airport near Loja, an hour or so drive from El Pangui, and the nearest good bar is an hour's drive away." That last part raised a few groans but more for show than anything else.

"I think you all know, as with any jungle, it has all the usual stuff, like nasty snakes, spiders, and flying or crawling things. So, tents with mosquito nets are essential. It's as humid as hell, so be prepared. I'm sure Matthew will fill you in on what you need to take as well as other things you would never think you'd need.

"Most of your papers are ready. Just a little fine-tuning on some of the credentials now that we've figured out who the team is going to be. You'll all have consular papers to get you in and out of difficult situations—most of the time. But remember, the mine is hostile territory when it comes to what we need to do. For that, I'm going to pass you over to Matthew." The screen turned back to show the faces.

Matthew rubbed some crumbs from the front of his shirt, put a hand through his hair, and stared into the camera on his laptop.

"Thanks to everyone for calling in." Matthew smiled and looked at each of the faces. "You represent the field troops, so to speak." He waited a few seconds for the comments to die down. "But we may have to bring in some heavyweights for protection. And perhaps a few more to help out. The rest of the group, who aren't on this call, will be essentially non-ground personnel support. They'll be looking at things like the financing of the targets, shipping, legal, government communications and so on. Some of them are going to be involved in figuring things out for us to make life easier, like hotels, vehicles, money withdrawals, as well as running any checks we need on whoever we come across. I may ask you to contact one or more of them from time to time, but I'll leave that for now and talk to each of you later.

"Stockman has the usual site for communications. In case you don't know, I'll get you caught up." Matthew focused on Eric and Nathan, who he knew would need a refresher. They hadn't worked for ORB in quite a while, and things had been updated since then. The others had been involved more recently with ORB and knew the ropes.

"You all have a password to gain entry to the website. I want all of you to file even one-line observations on anything you think could relate to the project. As usual, Lucy will make all travel arrangements and book hotels if you need them. You may have to do that for yourselves sometimes, but make sure to keep Lucy in the loop. She's responsible for knowing where all of us are at all times. And, in case you don't know who Lucy is, I'll let you know after this meeting." There was some smiling and quiet laughter all round. Everyone knew who Lucy was, as well as some of her history working for CSIS. This was not a person to mess with.

"Now, before I get into some details of what we're up to, I'm going to let our resident dangerous animal expert, Emma, give you some snake advice. They'll be your top safety hazard down there, with drug traffickers a very close second." There were guffaws of laughter all around, but this was solemn stuff.

Emma coughed. Her notes were in front of her. She was by no means an expert in these things, as Matthew had suggested, but was the most educated of the group right now.

"A bit of background first," Emma started. "Every year in Ecuador, there are over a thousand cases of snake bites reported. So, you might imagine how many there really could be—a lot more." She could see the look of surprise on some faces. "Unreported cases likely ended in death or were treated before they became severe. If they managed to get good attention, likely in a clinic or a hospital, then they usually recovered. On the upside, there are a lot of people out there who carry anti-venom compounds of one sort or another. Not all are proven remedies, and there are a lot of old-wives' remedies—so be careful.

"We're going to give you a travel pack of antivenom. It'll contain twenty vials of Suero Antiofidico developed by the medical institute in Guayaquil and CroFab antivenom—particularly for use if you get a viper or rattlesnake bite. They aren't one hundred percent effective, but they're the best there is on the market, as far as we know. Instructions are simple. If you get bitten, inject three vials of the antivenom into your thigh. Wait for ten minutes and test your blood to see if it coagulates—there' s a test kit in the travel pack. If the blood isn't coagulated at that point, take another three vials and test again. If it's still not clotting, take seven more and wait twenty minutes. Something should have happened by then. But if not, wait another six hours. If it's still nothing significant, head to the hospital. Either antivenom will at least give you some time to get there, but at this point, don't delay." Emma paused.

"What kinds of snakes are we watching out for here?" It was Kenny. He was a native of northern British Columbia and far more conversant with the dangers of grizzly bears than venomous snakes. But then, neither frightened him. After all, who would dare mess with Kenny? Or so he hoped.

"Ah, yes." Emma smiled as she said it. Someone was bound to ask, and this was where she was a little hazy on things. "There are a lot, and they tend to come out at night and live near the riverbanks in the moisture of the jungle. That's where you'll be." She gave a fake smile and looked at each face. They didn't look happy. "The most effective bite comes from the common lancehead viper. It's highly venomous and generally has gold and brown X markings. The two-striped forest pit viper also has an effective bite. It is, again, highly venomous and a kind of pale green color. Its green is overlaid by black or red-brown pairs of spots. But remember, all vipers are venomous. And all venomous snakes have arrowhead-shaped heads, fangs and elliptical eyes. That's a really important note to remember when you come face-to-face with a snake—the shape of its head." Again, she faked a smile. "Non-venomous snakes have rounded heads, no fangs, and round eyes. But don't wait to find the culprit to take a closer look at it. Just use the antivenom if you are bitten, no matter what. You can exchange stories later." Emma looked at the faces staring back at her. People were rarely comfortable with the thought of snakes, especially venomous ones. But then, neither were they okay with poisonous spiders, or poisonous anything for that matter. She smiled to herself, knowing full well she couldn't tolerate either. "Oh, by the way, watch out for the occasional anaconda. They're not generally very interested in humans but they can— and will—squeeze the life out of you if they feel threatened." There were nervous chuckles all around.

Just as Emma was about to get into the only additional detail she had on snakes, Nathan asked about spiders. It seemed most of the group also wanted to know, judging by the noises of support for information.

"Yup. Gotta watch out for them too, I'm afraid," Emma acknowledged. "Some nasty little buggers live in the jungle. Some are venomous, some are not. Lots of tarantulas—but they aren't highly venomous, for humans anyway. We're too big and I don't think they like the taste of our clothes." This time she smiled easily and naturally, as did the faces in front of her. "Then there are poisonous centipedes, caterpillars, frogs, and, of course, mosquitoes. I can't go into all the threats here, but I would encourage you to read up on the dangers and arm yourself accordingly. If you come across anything you think we have to know, post it on the server and send me a note." Emma paused and waited for the group in case there were more questions.

"What's the closest city, Emma? I'm thinking about available support services—like a hospital?" This time it was Nick. Some of the group laughed nervously.

"Loja is fairly large," Emma responded. "About one hundred and fifty thousand people, I think. It's a hot spot for expats retiring and has a pretty good hospital. There's a small airstrip nearby with domestic flights to Quito. Also, it's cheaper than other cities in Ecuador. I think it has most things you would need."

"All clear to move on?" Matthew asked. There were no objections.

"Thanks, Emma. Okay, well, I think Stockman set things out pretty well. This time around, we'll be messing with the cocaine industry in southern Ecuador..."

"What about Colombia, Matthew?" It was Eric this time.

"I think we'll delay their problems for now," Matthew responded quickly, wanting to allay fears of having to cover off two sites at the same time. "But it's good to remember that we think the same Chinese company owns both plants, Zamora in Ecuador and Buritica in Colombia. So, we can't count them out yet. We just have to be careful with the timing. Too much of our kind of activity going on with both plants at the same time would draw some serious attention that we don't need. Nor do the governments of both countries." Matthew looked at Eric and got a nod in return.

"Let's move on." Matthew glanced at his notes. "We're pretty sure the Zamora plant is processing cocaine base supplied by the farmers from the surrounding area. We don't know how big the operation is yet, but we're pretty sure they hide the cocaine in with the copper and gold concentrate and truck it to the port and onto ships. We know China is the final destination.

"We're pretty sure the cartels will hit the area hard once they get stronger in southern Ecuador, but we think that's a while off yet—maybe a year or two. Maybe more. Whenever it is, they'll want their territory back at some point, and that could end up being a real bloodbath if the Chinese resist.

"To date, the cartels haven't pushed hard in the southeast. They seem to be mostly focused on their connections with Colombia. But farmers in that area are growing exponentially in numbers exponentially. We think there are hundreds of small cocaine base producers hidden in the jungle around the Zamora plant. If there are, it could mean Zamora is processing tons of pure cocaine every week. That's one of the things we'll need to figure out.

"Let me show you the general layout."

Matthew replaced the faces in front of him on the screen with a map of southern Ecuador. He drew a rough circle around the Zamora plant site with a black felt-tip marker and tapped the arrows pointing to it from the surrounding jungle.

"These arrows represent the flow of crude coca provided by the jungle farmers to the Chinese."

Next, Matthew highlighted the route from the plant to Loja and circled it with the marker. "All concentrate trucks come through here." He scratched a crude star shape above the name of Loja. "This is where the trucks split up." Matthew stabbed a black spot on some point that looked like a junction on the west side of Loja. Then he circled the ports of Machala to the west and Guyaquil to the northwest, and joined both to Loja using black lines roughly following the established roads. "Most head to Guyaquil along this route, while the rest head to Machala, or Puerto Bolívar, along this route." He used the marker to highlight the two diverging routes. Matthew couldn't see his audience, but there were no interruptions, so he continued.

"Eric and Nathan, I'd like you to get jobs at the plant. You'll need to go to the Tongyan office in Quito. I think that's the best place for you to apply for positions at Zamora. Try to get some operations-type jobs. It shouldn't be too difficult for you both. They only want to employ Chinese nationals, and you two come with some good pedigree.

"Now, the only opportunity we have to get Caucasians into the plant is as vendor reps. Most of the smaller plant and mine equipment is from China. So, their reps are Chinese nationals. But most of the major pieces are supplied from outside China. That's where Kenny, Armando and Nick come in. Kenny will work on the key electrical equipment, like the main transformers at the substation. Armando gets into the plant as a mill vendor. Nick gets into the mine as a shovel rep. We already have agreements with the vendors for you to represent them. You may need to brush up on your technical skills with this equipment. The vendors will coordinate with the Chinese operators to get you in once we give them the word, and Stockman will get the visa approvals for entry into Ecuador.

"James will be a point man based in El Pangui. That's a pretty small town with something like twelve thousand people quite close to the mine. He'll interface with the site people—Eric, Nathan, Kenny, Armando and Nick. He'll also be the field contact for the guys at the port and road. Matias will be at the port, and Roberto will monitor the road between the mine site and Machala.

"Now, Nick will be helping us on the mine side of things. Mitch and Tom will be our off-site technical consultants for all of you. Mitch will coordinate with Matias and Roberto if they get too busy on the transportation side of things—whether that's by road or ocean.

"Matias should stay in Machala. Roberto, I suggest you stay in El Pangui with James, or in Loja, which is a little more central. I'll leave that up to you—just let me know.

"Emma and I are roamers and we'll operate the drone if we need it. We'll scout the jungle for routes to the plant. We'll also manage the rest of you as needed. Stockman will arrange for a security team to join us and they'll get split up depending on the degree of danger I think you may be in. Good with you, boss?" Matthew aimed his question at Stockman.

"Sloan just texted me, Matthew. He has four ex–CSIS ready to go. They were part of the team we sent into Brazil a few years ago looking for those kidnapped mining executives. Do you remember Sean, their leader?"

"I sure do. Excellent guy. Thanks for setting that up. I'll let you know when I need them in the field." Matthew was very happy to get Sean on board. They had worked on a few projects together.

Matthew transferred the screen back to the group meeting.

"Any questions?"

"Timing?" It was Nick.

"Good question. We have most of the paperwork. The vendors are ready. You all need a little time to get your things together. The anti-venom serum packs are ready to send to you. I'd say we can get moving in ten days. Lucy will arrange travel for everyone. I think Eric and Nathan will be the first to go. So, look at the owner's website to see what you have to do to get in to see Tongyan in Quito." Matthew aimed his question at Nathan. "After that, it's up to the rest of us.

"James, you should get over to El Pangui as soon as you can and find yourself a place to hang your hat. Stockman has a cover story for you as one of the McArthur Foundation representatives. Matias and Roberto, you should get moving as soon as the paperwork is ready. We can line up some local people to help you get established if you need it, but the less people involved the better. Let me know if you need that kind of help." Matthew looked over at Emma, who was sitting next to him in front of the screen. "Can you think of anything else for now, Emma?"

"Take duct tape," Emma blurted out. Everyone laughed, but it was only James who asked if she was serious.

"I'm deadly serious. Before you start walking around in the jungle, make sure you tuck the bottom of your pant legs into your boots, and then tape around with duct tape so nothing can get in. Wrap it good and tight!" Emma grinned, but everyone appreciated the advice. "Oh, and ponchos," she added as an afterthought. "You'll need them. Try to get camouflaged ones, and make sure they cover most of your body, not just your shoulders. The rain there is going to be torrential at times."

"Thanks, Emma. Worth noting. We'll put together a list of essentials. Stockman will equip everyone with weapons—Rugers, I think." Matthew looked at his boss for confirmation and got a nod in return.

"Okay, everyone. I guess that's a wrap." Matthew searched the faces in front of him in case there were more questions. There weren't, at least for now. "I'll be in touch with each of you shortly to get you on your way. In the meantime, just collect what you need and wait for my call. Thanks again for helping out on this one."

There were waves, smiles and an occasional thumbs-up. The screens went blank, and everyone checked out of the Zoom session. Only Stockman, Matthew and Emma remained.

"I think that went well, Matthew. Good job. Let's get this show on the road. I'll contact the ambassador and let him know we're moving. You should get hold of Lucy and give her whatever instructions she needs about travel and things. Emma, my love, stay safe." Stockman blew a kiss, presumably to Emma, and she blew one back. He signed off, and his screen went blank.

Chapter 7

Chinese Ties

Both Nathan and Eric were unassuming, mild-mannered Chinese expats. Nathan was tall and slim. Eric was short but well-proportioned. Both had families in China but knew if they wanted to earn enough to support them in anything other than a tenement building in Guangzhou they would have to work outside the box of communism.

Separately, Nathan and Eric had found their way to Canada and worked to get some experience. Both ended up with the same employer in Vancouver who shipped them off to help manage the construction of two grassroots coal projects in China. They performed well and earned their stripes as international professionals.

After that, they realized their worth and began seeking out Chinese-run projects around the world. They offered themselves as a pair of professional operation and controls experts. That was stretching it a little far but they managed and were involved in some high-profile projects as well as a couple of small missions for ORB.

As planned with Matthew, Nathan and Eric presented themselves at the Tongyan offices in Quito. While they had emailed their resumes a week previous, nothing could be more constructive than meeting face-to-face. At first Ping Pei seemed somewhat disinterested in meeting the pair. But it was his boss who insisted he interview them. He had also received their resumes and letters. The letters showed the men to be well-educated, well-traveled, and well-experienced with large-scale mineral plants. They appeared to be just two single men working their way around the world.

As the interview progressed, Ping Pei became increasingly comfortable with these two young men who seemed to have suddenly appeared before him, almost as a gift. He knew they were a good catch and would fit in well with the other operating personnel at the plant.

Ping Pei wasted no time in signing Nathan and Eric up as his latest recruits for Zamora. He knew his manager would be very pleased with his discovery of such qualified Chinese nationals right here in Quito. They would certainly be an asset to the operations and, hopefully, help train the less-educated personnel from mainland China, who were generally neophytes in the world of mill processing. Everything they did had to be checked and sometimes re-checked.

oooo

The compound of the Chinese embassy, located in the more affluent low-rise area of Quito, sat off to one side of the embassy district. Protected from unwanted pedestrian intrusions by an eight-foot-high wall along its perimeter, the triangular property itself was hemmed in by busy roads on two sides, and a laneway on the third. The only single-entry door was on the least busy side, twenty feet from the well-guarded double metal vehicle doors. All traffic coming or going had to come through that laneway.

Wang Ho Lin, an attaché at the Chinese embassy, stepped out from the single door in the high wall and walked across the sports fields to La Cruz del Papa. It was a kind of monolithic structure erected to commemorate the 1985 visit of Pope John Paul II. It acted as a distinctive marker for those who wanted to meet discreetly, or just enjoy a little peace. It stood in a circle partially surrounded by benches, and was somewhat isolated from the incessantly noisy traffic by thick bushes.

As it happened, the head offices for Tongyan were also across the field, on the same side as the Chinese embassy, but two blocks north, on Av. Republica del Salvador, fairly close to the Olympic stadium.

And so it was that Wang Ho Lin sat on the end of a park bench close to the monolith one Tuesday afternoon. The sun was shining through the trees on this beautiful March afternoon as he waited for his associate from the Tongyan office, Ping Pei, to arrive. He lit his second Winston since he left the embassy and drew the smoke in as far as it would go, before releasing it slowly through his nose.

He and Ping Pei had been in close contact with each other in Quito for the last five years. They started when Tongyan began to commission their Zamora plant to produce gold and copper concentrate for export to China, together with their contraband. The two associates frequently wandered across the sports fields to the monolith location to smoke and exchange information. This was their favored location and it became a habit that they would meet each Tuesday at the same time in the same place. If one was not available, they would meet the following Tuesday.

Over the years, Lin and Pei had become friendly associates. They never mixed business with their personal lives. But they had come to trust each other to be honest, forthright, and free with their information. The details came primarily from Ping Pei, who was charged by his company, the operator of the Zamora plant, to keep in touch with the embassy in Quito on matters concerning their personnel and shipments.

In return, Wang Ho Lin shepherded the visas needed for the thousands of Chinese nationals coming from mainland China to work on the construction of Zamora project. Now he managed the visas for the Chinese people needed for operations. He also communicated with the powers in Beijing on concentrate shipments from Ecuador. They would arrange for safe passage for the Zamora vessels going through the Port of Shanghai customs and make the necessary arrangements to handle the special concentrate tote bags.

With over 2,000 ships arriving in the Shanghai harbor every month, it could be relatively easy to temporarily lose track of one ship in the throng, despite the sophisticated oversight. No one in the Chinese government wanted that to happen with the Zamora ships. Nor did they want them to linger, for what could be weeks, in the bay with all the other bulk carriers, waiting to deliver resources, from metal ore to grain, into the country.

In the case of the Zamora shipments, their rapid turnaround was guaranteed and essential. As soon as one of their concentrate ships entered the East China Sea and signaled for clearance, a pilot boat would be dispatched by the port authority, with the approval of a particular government official in Beijing, to guide it directly to an unloading station further up the Yangtze River.

Ping Pei was the Quito office human resources manager for Tongyan, and also managed a number of different responsibilities for the company that didn't have corporate titles. For instance, he was responsible for coordinating Zamora's cocaine processing and delivery.

Ping Pei occasionally traveled to the Zamora facility to meet with the general manager. He would visit the cocaine production and bagging areas to check that things were running as they should be. Then, he and the GM would talk about their "off-the-books" cocaine production, and finally, personnel issues.

There was zero tolerance for the slightest sub-standard performance of any kind by personnel at the Zamora mine, even if it involved casual but threatening language, or any hint of someone mentioning the word cocaine. Workers deemed unsuitable would be taken from site and sent back to China on one of the concentrate ships.

Ping Pei kept his friend updated on everyone at the plant. The Chinese were working in Ecuador using special visas. Without them, it would be impossible to work outside the country. The Chinese embassy in Quito had become Tongyan's clearing house for Zamora's workforce and shared the responsibility for their behavior.

The movements of Chinese nationals working at Zamora were restricted to the plant site, and they were not permitted to visit any other part of Ecuador without special security arrangements being made. The camp at the plant was under constant surveillance with security posts stationed around the perimeter fence. If workers had to go outside the perimeter fencing, to the tailings area or water intake facilities, or even where the garbage was burned or buried, there was always security present.

"Have you enough operators, Mr. Pei?" Wang Hi Lin asked his friend.

"So far, we have enough. But I had two Chinese nationals approach me yesterday in our office here looking for jobs at the plant. That is very unusual. All our operations people are from the mainland. But these two have traveled, have good experience, and speak Spanish. They also speak Cantonese and Mandarin." Ping Pei looked pensive. "I find it strange and almost too good to be true. I like them both. Their credentials are impeccable. In fact, I have decided to take them to Zamora myself this week to get them started." Ping Pei looked at his friend for a moment.

Wang Ho Lin saw the questioning look on Ping Pei 's face, as though he was looking for approval.

Wang Ho Lin didn't object. Relieved, Ping Pei continued.

"I will provide you with their information but I don't think we need visas. They seem to have everything they need and were just looking for some suitable work. But you should check them out to confirm their stories, yes?" Ping Pei stopped to wait for a response.

"You are right, Mr. Pei. I believe we should consider this. It is very odd, but perhaps we underestimate the young Chinese these days. They too are wanderers, much like the youth of many countries these days.

They seek adventure and other cultures. So, maybe everything is as good as it seems with these two. But we will see." Wang Ho Lin changed the subject. He too was concerned but didn't want to raise Ping Pei's anxiety any further than was necessary.

"Now, how are the relationships with the natives? Are they supplying product on a consistent basis?"

"Supply is more than we ever anticipated." Ping Pei shook himself free of his thoughts. He smiled and lit another Winston. It was his third since he left his office. "Clearly the indigenous farmers need the money and they work continuously to provide a steady supply. I think we have leveled out our processing to about five tons of crystalline product per week." Ping Pei didn't seem to be particularly impressed by the quantity, always believing they could do better. The amount was insignificant to him, compared to the amount of concentrate they produced from the mineral resource. But then, he never did appreciate the effort and resources needed to supply the Zamora plant with cocaine paste. Neither did he have any idea how many coca plants were needed to contribute to what he considered to be a small amount of product. He was quite complacent since the plant had been producing cocaine hydrochloride for three years now and seemed to have settled into a regular and constant output. Ping Pei had become accustomed to the amount and accepted it as normal. He wasn't interested beyond what he was responsible for. For that matter, neither was Wang Ho Lin. Both of them were focused on only a very narrow part of the big picture. As long as their Beijing employers were happy, they were happy.

However, neither Ping Pei nor Wang Ho Lin could ignore the value the Zamora operation was contributing to the greater good of their mother country. Once diluted and spread throughout North America, each five tons of cocaine hydrochloride a week fueled addiction. While they didn't appreciate everything about Beijing's long-term strategy, they did have some general appreciation of their contribution helping to cripple their Western foes by feeding them cocaine. The effects on a human brain had been well documented and served China's long-term plans extremely well.

Ping Pei stood and started to walk away to the east across the sports field. He and Wang Ho Lin never shook hands nor expressed any sign of their friendship. Their short get-together just ended. They would do it again in one week: same time, same place. There was no need to confirm. If something happened to either one of them or they couldn't make the meeting, they would both let another week go by before trying to meet again. There was no need for personal contact through their offices.

Wang Ho Lin got up fifteen minutes later and headed back to his own office at the embassy.

oooo

The day before Ping Pei traveled to Zamora with his two new recruits, he walked across the park on the prescribed day at the predetermined time. He went to the usual meeting place at the monolith, to sit with Wang Ho Lin. They exchanged pleasantries and smoked. They sat and stared over at the park for a few minutes, quietly watching some children kick a soccer ball around.

Then, Ping Pei asked, "Have you discovered anything about my new recruits, Mr. Lin?"

Wang Ho Lin tossed his half-smoked Winston to the ground, extinguished it with his foot, poked his tongue out and picked something off the end of it. He flicked whatever it was to the ground and turned to face his friend.

"It seems they have no background to check, Mr. Pei." Wang Ho Lin looked solemnly at his associate.

"What do you make of that, Mr. Lin?"

"I cannot make anything of that, Mr. Pei. We can find no records on either of them at this time. But we are still searching and may not have all the information yet. Next week I will put the investigation on high priority and use our resources in Washington to help us. In the meantime, we should not jump to conclusions and, for now, assume they are who they say they are. But be patient—time has a way of telling the truth. Make sure your people at Zamora keep a close eye on them." Wang Ho Lin went quiet.

Ping Pei was silent for a few moments as he thought about the situation and what he should do. He didn't like waiting. On one hand, he conjured up thoughts of being lauded by his bosses for having discovered these two ready-and-willing experienced operators. But he had some niggling self-doubt. *What if I am wrong and they aren't who they say they are?* was a thought that went through his mind. He was hesitating after the fact. He had, after all, acted quite impulsively—for a Chinese person. Generally, he didn't willingly take risks, and this could be one of the times when he did.

It would have been easy for him to have listened to his initial feelings about these two wandering apparent talents and shooed them away. But he felt excited to have discovered real potential, right here in Quito. If he brought them into the fold fast, without the usual slow red tape of two governments and company approvals, it might help to show his worth to the company.

Ho could find no reason not to fast-track the paperwork, allowing Ping Pei to take them south to work whenever he wanted.

Ping Pei didn't visit Zamora that often, but in this case, he considered it worth the special effort. He would revel in his association with these two such talented individuals, as the plant operations staff would look upon them as special. They would soon discover the extent of their experience, where they had little.

"I will take them to Zamora and put them to work." Pei was definitive and decided that Wang Ho should continue to check their credentials but not stop him from going before he could report back.

"We can meet again next week when I return and perhaps you will have more information." Ping Pei looked at his friend, expecting to see some sign of agreement.

"Hopefully I am just being cautious, but better to be that than careless." Wang Ho Lin nodded to his friend as he rose to leave.

"I will see you next week, Mr. Pei."

They walked back across the fields, fifteen minutes apart, and went back to their offices.

Chapter 8

Lima

It was early May when Matthew arranged to meet the ORB team in Lima, before dispatching each to various points in Ecuador. Nathan's news that he and Eric were on their way to the Zamora plant delighted him. They would take up roles in the operations group, as they had talked about on the Zoom call. Whatever it was, it should give them free access to the facilities within the processing plant, and that was where they needed to focus. Their jobs were to confirm where, if anywhere, the rough cocaine was being finally processed for commercial distribution and confirm how it was getting out from the plant to its export point destination. From there, Matthew would have a better understanding to help with his planning.

Matthew and Emma relaxed next to each other in business class on the five-hour afternoon flight from Vancouver to Montreal. They would have a short layover before the nine-hour overnight flight to Lima.

When the plane leveled off at 35,000 feet, Matthew took out his iPad with its Apple Pencil. He folded the cover and rested it on his lap. He wrote "STATS" in bold letters at the top of a new page. He looked over at Emma, gave her a smiling grimace, and raised his eyebrows.

"Okay, Em, let's do some work. First, we'll figure out how big an operation has to be to produce a ton of this crude cocaine in the jungle. Once we put some numbers to that, we'll have a better idea of what we're looking for." Matthew looked at her and waited for a response.

"Okay, let's get to it." Emma smiled at Matthew as she took the vodka and tonic from the flight attendant. Matthew took his, had a sip and settled the glass on the table between them.

He was always on the go during a project. Thinking, planning, calculating. That's who he was. There was no stopping him until it was all over.

"According to the drug enforcement officials in the US, it can take anywhere from three hundred and fifty to four hundred and fifty kilos of coca leaves to make one kilo of cocaine base. That means about four hundred pounds of leaves to one pound of product, if we think of it in imperial measurements. You know, that translates into one hell of a big operation for a jungle production." Emma stared at Matthew as he turned on the calculator feature on his tablet.

"Let's see." Matthew looked up as he thought. "Let's say the farmers collect the leaves in jute bags. Each bag weighs about one hundred and ten pounds, as much as they can carry on their backs. They collect four bags a day." He looked up at Emma who had a questioning look on her face.

Thank goodness she wasn't doing the carrying, she thought.

"Just saying," Matthew continued. "It looked like that in the photos I saw. It could be one hundred pounds or one-twenty, but it's as close as it has to be for what we're doing here," he commented as he watched the look on Emma's face as she was still imagining the weights he was talking about. She nodded her agreement with a grimace and raised her eyebrows.

"If that's reasonable"—he shrugged as he glanced over at Emma again—"it means one person could collect about four hundred and forty pounds of coca leaves per day. Or, putting it another way, one person could fill forty bags or four thousand four hundred pounds worth of coca leaves every ten days. If it takes four hundred pounds of leaves to make one pound of product, then they will be able to collect what's needed to make thirty-three pounds of product every month. It doesn't take a genius to figure out that with, say, six pickers for each farm, they could make as much as two hundred pounds of product in a month. Now, if I'm close to guessing there could be as many as fifty or sixty or more farms contributing, and they could be making anywhere between five to eight tons a month, give or take." Matthew blew a quiet whistle.

"We're sure there are gangs of these farmers out there?" Emma wondered, still in awe of the numbers.

"I think there have to be to make this worthwhile for the Chinese. Don't you think?" Matthew chewed his lip and punched in a few more numbers as Emma watched.

"Yes, but with that many leaves having to be picked every month to make five tons of product,'" Emma cut in, "you have to wonder whether the coca bush crop can sustain that amount."

They both had concerned looks on their faces.

"Okay." Matthew's brain was back in action again. "We know coca leaves are available at least three times a year, and there could be as many as five growing seasons. We also know that just one coca plant could provide over one ton of coca leaves each year, so clearly it is fast-growing and provides lots of leaves. That really equates to something like one ton of paste a month, if we assume one hundred bushes in each farm, and fifty farms. So, to provide, say, five tons of product, it means there have to be more bushes and—or—more farms." Matthew grinned as he looked over at Emma.

"I would say that's entirely possible given what we've heard about how extensive the farming has become. I mean, what if there are really five harvests per year instead of three, or a hundred farms instead of fifty, or an average of two hundred bushes on each farm? It wouldn't take a miracle to put out five or more tons of product every month." Emma seemed satisfied with the logistics. But there was always that element of uncertainty, and they still had to put their feet on the ground.

Once Matthew knew the amount of cocaine hydrochloride the Zamora plant was moving each day with a concentrate shipment, they would be better able to estimate the amount of coca leaves needed. From that, he could estimate the number of people required and the number of farms that would likely be in the area. They might even be able to identify some farmers who were going out to work the bushes. They could follow them to find out where the cocaine mixture was being taken for transport to the Zamora plant.

Matthew was happy with his assumptions and calculations and turned to face Emma.

"They say there could be hundreds, maybe thousands, of these coca plant farms in the jungle." Matthew's eyes widened as he realized the extent of the possibility. "Can you imagine managing the production and handling logistics required to make all this work?"

"And the area it would cover." Emma contributed her thought. "It's going to be one hell of a job for us to identify how they all get their product to the Zamora plant, if that's what they do. Where do we even start?" She looked pensive, biting her bottom lip as she thought.

Matthew looked down at his iPad, seeming to be taking everything under consideration.

"What are you thinking?" Emma asked.

"Well, perhaps we shouldn't be trying to get our heads around the whole picture, Em." The wheels in Matthew's brain were spinning. "You know, we should focus on the collection point at the plant and not where all the product comes from. We would never stop the farmers from sending their product. It doesn't matter to them who gets it, as long as they get paid. So, we may as well forget trying to map out the transport corridors. In fact, I don't think we even care how they get their product to the plant." Matthew was on a roll. "Remember, our job is to find out how the Chinese are getting the cocaine. They collect, process and move it, not the locals. Our goal is to stop their operation. Right?" Matthew looked at Emma.

"You're right. Thank God for that. I was a bit worried for a moment there." She sniggered and ordered another vodka tonic from the flight attendant.

"Me too!" Matthew smiled, and both of them slumped back in their seats. One hour to go, then a short wait for their connecting overnight flight to Lima.

oooo

Arriving at the Jorge Chávez International Airport in Lima brought with it the usual fight with frustration to get to their hotel.

First, Matthew and Emma wrestled to claim their baggage from the carousel, where everyone seemed to want to claim everyone else's suitcases. Then they fought through the customs and immigration hall where there were no defined boundaries for the mass of people trying to get through. Finally, they jostled with an unruly crowd of travelers all trying to claim a cab. But after a few minutes of strategizing, they wheeled their luggage fifty feet away to the limousine rank. There were no queues and they climbed into an Audi Q7 that took them to their hotel, the Hilton Lima Miraflores.

The hotel was an hour's drive through San Miguel and along the headland looking out over the Pacific Ocean. The route avoided the poorer parts of the city. Matthew remembered them from his last visit a number of years ago, when his cab had taken the shortest route from the airport to his hotel in Mira Flores. It was chaotic. Pedestrians dashed through and around speeding traffic. Kids played on the sidewalk and sometimes tripped into the road, with traffic narrowly missing them as though it was a game of chicken. Old ladies with baskets of flowers and fruit navigated through the traffic if they stopped at intersection lights. Dust and debris littered the side streets. He remembered it well and was quite happy not to take that route. He could only imagine how much more congested the area was after so many years since he last visited.

Not that Matthew was particularly intimidated by the unruliness of the traffic here. After all, he had driven in Montreal. Not to mention Tehran and Istanbul. Then there was Beijing and the rest of China—oh, and not to forget Kuala Lumpur. After a while one got desensitized to traffic madness despite it often taking the life of a motorist or an innocent pedestrian. As the Iranians would say, *"Inshallah"*—if God wills it.

Lima was home to approximately ten million people. Many of them lived in poverty. It showed—unless you were part of the rich minority who lived in San Isidro or Miraflores, where you could avoid the misery. But that was for the few, including the embassies, large foreign-owned corporations, private clubs, five-star hotels and restaurants.

Matthew had not stayed at the Hilton in Lima before. He usually stayed in the center of Miraflores at a smaller but very upscale hotel. This time he was looking for enough rooms to accommodate his team, as well as a hotel that could provide professional services and a reasonable-sized meeting room.

The hotel did not disappoint, with all rooms offering dramatic views of the Pacific Ocean, with only a narrow green belt between the viewer and the scenery beyond. But it was not within easy walking distance. The Hilton sat on the edge of the plateau, where most of Lima was spread out, close to a towering cliff edge that dropped almost vertically to the beach below.

A jump over the cliff's edge would mean certain death as you landed on the beach at Costa Verde, a swimming area reserved for those who could afford the opulence of the ocean-side services. One could bask in the sun or shade all day, share in the delights of the various open-air restaurants with their tables set up on the beach, or take a refreshing—if not often wild—dip in the sea.

The dramatic almost-vertical cliff provided a definitive line that separated the hotel from the beach, with a multi-switchback road across the cliff face leading to sea level. Or one could take the long way around and bypass the cliff, altogether. But that would take some time and be nowhere near as dramatic.

Matthew and Emma had separate rooms. He didn't know how much he might need his own room for face-to-face meetings with his team but he preferred that they not be distracted by sights of female clothing lying around the place. Not to worry. He knew he would share it with Emma during their downtime.

oooo

Over the next couple of days, Matthew talked to each member of his team.

While he spent time with each, the others talked in small groups, or one-on-one, as they focused on their own tasks and exchanged information. As an off-site consultant, Mitch met with Kenny, Nick and Armando, who would be working at the Zamora plant as vendor representatives. They were hoping to get a chance to talk to Nathan and Eric later, once they had established themselves at the site.

Tom met with Roberto and Matias to share their ideas on the road connecting Zamora with the port at Machala, and Puerto Bolívar itself. Tom had some experience at the port on another project. There, he worked with the customs officials on the movement of military equipment. Ecuador had been trying to trade it for updated equipment with the Pentagon.

James was to be the central clearing point for all field activities. He spent time with each of the crew, sorting out how they would communicate, as well as where and when they would meet when needed. Matthew and Emma would keep in touch with James, and only directly connect with the field agents when needed. They would look for contacts with the indigenous groups and scout for jungle pathways and flush out any weak points to disrupt at the mill. But many of their thoughts would mature once they got to the Zamora site to see things for themselves.

Stockman would be working on credentials for all the field agents. They all needed a bona fide reason to be in-country. They had to have letters of authorization, seals from government agencies authenticating their duties while in Ecuador, and work visas for those who were going to be at the mill. Except for Nathan and Eric who already had what they needed.

They discussed the possible use of a drone for what they had to do. All agreed one needed to be taken to the site, and perhaps used for any night activity. Matthew agreed and sent Stockman a note indicating what he wanted. Hopefully it would be waiting for him when he got to Quito.

Matthew liked the DJI Matrice 350 drone, equipped with a DJI Zenmuse H30T 48 megapixel, 34x zoom camera with thermal imaging capabilities for night flying. The drone weighed only six pounds, had a ceiling height of about 20,000 feet, and a flying time of just under an hour on one battery charge. It all packed neatly into a case sized to fit under a seat on a plane.

Matthew's plan for the security crew was for their leader, Sean, to watch over the Zamora plant for any signs of unusual movements. He would swap shifts with one of the others. The off-shift person would rest up at the camp where Matthew and Emma were staying. The other two security men would be assigned to the port on cross-shift, to keep an eye on Matias. Matthew had yet to decide whether James or Roberto needed any protection, but he didn't think so at this point.

"I think we're all ready," Matthew called out over the group. There were nods and shrugs of agreement. "Okay, let's move out." He shook everyone's hand, patted a few backs, gave a thumbs-up to Kenny, and then they were gone. The next time he would talk to any of the first guys into Ecuador, except perhaps James, would be when they stationed themselves at the Zamora site. Kenny, Armando and Nick would wait until they were called.

Chapter 9

Let's Go

"So far, so good." Emma squinted at Matthew's face to see from his reaction if he agreed with her.

"It was, Em. Very good. I'm happy with the team." Matthew was thinking about other things right now. "Let's call your father."

Emma's eyebrows went up, but settled down again as she responded with, "Of course." She settled into one of the two armchairs by the window with a glass of pisco sour from the jug the hotel had sent up to them. Chilean or Peruvian? Which was best? They didn't care as long as it was good, and this was.

They sat with the phone set on speaker resting on the table between them.

"We're ready here, sir." Matthew's opening to Stockman was formal and pointed. "Any updates to pass on?"

Matthew could hear some shuffling on the other end of the line. He assumed Stockman was settling into his chair in the den at his cottage.

"It sounds like at least one of the Colombian cartels is on the move to challenge the Ecuadorians, Matthew." Stockman started without small talk. It was midnight for him in the UK.

"We don't think they know anything about the Zamora facility, although I wouldn't bet on it at this point," Stockman continued. He sat by a wood fire with a small tumbler of Johnnie Walker Black. There were still a lot of drafts in the house as the wind came up over the top of the cliffs outside. He needed to attend to them come summer.

"My sources also tell me there's a shipment of concentrate headed to the coast from the Zamora plant every day. Although it seems they shut the place down now and again for maintenance, so there could be a gap of several days between trucking. You should get some eyes on that and try to figure out how they're handling the cargo, if you know what I mean." There was a pause as both dwelled on the new information. "Of course, it could be just concentrate, and we might never find out, but at least we can see what they're doing with it. Remember, we need intel on their product both at Guyaquil and Puerto Bolívar. Are there any harbour inspections, any special equipment or armed guards, and all that stuff." Stockman sounded tired but he was covering a lot of ground right now, and undoubtedly burning the midnight oil as he checked in with people around the world.

"Matias and Roberto will be there over the next couple of days." Matthew was enthusiastic about getting started. "I'll need that security team over here by the time we go in. Can you get them mobilized and have Sean select his people?"

"I'll get them on their way over the next couple of days. I already had him on standby a couple of weeks ago. I knew we'd need them, you know. Jungles and cartels and all that, eh?" Stockman played with his bottom lip and sniffed at the whiskey. He was thinking about Sean. He was likely still galivanting around in Europe somewhere with his buddies, the other three of the four-man team. But he knew they would be ready at the drop of a hat and waiting for their orders to come through.

"Great. Is there anything else?" Matthew asked.

"Any thoughts yet on a plan to get the Chinese out of there?" Stockman paused to let Matthew collect his thoughts.

"I don't think it's going to be only the Chinese we have to deal with. I think the real difficulty is going to be how we tackle the Ecuadorian cartel, Los Choneros, assuming they're the only ones and Los Lobos hasn't got to be dealt with as well. We're sure Los Choneros knows about the Chinese, because they're the ones who took their business." Matthew stopped to collect his thoughts.

There was silence on the other end of the phone. Stockman knew Matthew was thinking before he spoke next.

"We'll figure out how the crude cocaine is being supplied, first. Then, where and how it's being treated to a final product. And how they transport it to the shoreline or wherever they are exporting it from. Once it's on a boat or a plane or whatever it is, it's lost to us." Matthew stopped again, waiting for Stockman.

"Well, let's get our people into place, watch what's happening for a while, and wrap a plan around it all once we know." Stockman liked what he was hearing. "We already have a way into the Colombians through the narcos, and I can deal with that. They need to hold back until we're ready. Otherwise, all hell will break loose." Stockman sucked in a breath as he thought about what could happen if everything went down at the same time. He did not want the Colombians to know how the Chinese were involved in all this. ORB's plan had to end Chinese involvement in cocaine. It had to ensure the Ecuadorian cartels got their business back. Odd as that sounded, those were the orders from the ambassador—neutralize the unknown and normalize the known.

"Great, if you can handle the Colombians and draw them away, we can handle the rest. We may have to destroy Zamora and put some rockets up the asses of the Chinese to get them out of there, but that's what we do best. As for the Ecuadorian cartels, we'll have to see who they are first, and then try to negotiate something. Maybe we can use them to our advantage." Matthew stopped and hunched his shoulders as his neck muscles tightened.

"Okay, Matthew. Oh, by the way, a little bird told me that the Chinese were snooping around the credentials of Eric and Nathan. I have to wonder why. Maybe it's their natural distrust of easy opportunities that makes them so inquisitive." Stockman chuckled.

"I'd better let them know to keep their noses clean. I should be talking to them in a few days. Anything else?"

"All for now, Matthew. Good luck. Oh, how's that girl of mine doing?"

"Haven't seen her in a while," Matthew lied, "but she can take care of herself, as you know." Matthew got up and stood behind Emma's shoulders and massaged the tightness in the back of her neck. He knew exactly where the tight spots and knots were and spent some time kneading them into submission.

Emma's head went back as she relaxed under the pressure of Matthew's thumbs. His hands worked their way around and farther down as he gently flirted with her, almost daring her to tell her father.

"You're right there, Matthew." Stockman let a second tick by. "Bye, darling!" he shouted into the phone, and got a "Bye, Daddy" in a soft return from Emma. They all laughed, including Stockman, before the phones clicked off.

It was time for a little rest and recreation as Matthew and Emma sat back and sipped at their pisco sours. Two more and they made their way to the shower, undressed, stepped into the warmth and lathered each other up. It was luxurious. They reveled in the delight of the instant feeling of relaxation and comfort as the heat of the water washed away that uptight feeling one gets when operating under pressure. For Matthew, that feeling went to his neck and shoulders; for Emma it was everywhere, including her stomach, that tensed. But now, there was no tensing and for a moment they held each other and let the fingers of the shower gently massage their bodies. They played a little and relaxed even more as each took advantage of the other's submission. It was a bliss that unfortunately had to come to an end.

Matthew reached out of the shower and picked up two large bath towels. He wrapped one around Emma's shoulders before she stepped out, and the other around his waist. She was so beautiful, so together, so strong and independent—and yet so...

The jug of pisco sour was three quarters empty but still cold enough, and there was plenty enough for at least one more round. It was a perfect segue to bed.

Chapter 10

Welcome to Machala

"Well, my friend, I don't know how two Peruvians could be assigned to a project in Ecuador, given the problems they seem to have with each other, but here we are," Matias muttered to his new friend Roberto, as they were about to step outside the exit doors from the Mariscal Sucre International airport in Quito. It was as crowded and as confusing as the Jorge Chaval airport in Lima. They were used to this kind of seemingly disorderly mess, though.

Roberto, the quieter one, raised his eyebrows and smiled as fellow passengers pushed him on through the doors. "I think I will like it here," he said. "Smells like home."

They wandered off to look for directions to the coach station where they would get their ride to Machala.

The first thing Matias and Roberto did when they arrived in Machala, was to drive the road to Loja. Once they arrived at Loja, they decided to drive farther and get as close to the Zamora site as they dared. They didn't want anyone to see them together, so close to the plant, who might recognize them later if things went wrong.

They made notes on route whenever they came across particularly interesting areas, in case the information might prove useful to ORB at some point—like wanting to hijack a concentrate truck or delay a convoy.

The mine had finally replaced the old Río Zamora barge crossing with a new bridge, but not before it had been heavily reinforced to carry the construction equipment and all the operating machinery across the eighty-feet-wide river. It was seven miles to the Zamora plant from the bridge.

ORB had provided some basic details for potential alternative routes by air out of the area. But Matias and Roberto decided to take a look at an airstrip they spotted on one of their maps, in case ORB needed to bring in a fixed-wing plane. It was about an hour's drive north of Zamora.

The airstrip turned out to be a military one, with no private or commercial flights advertised. It had about 6,000 feet of asphalt runway in reasonable condition, and capable of landing and take-offs for a Hercules or 737-type plane. They were fairly sure the strip wasn't Instrument Flight Rules rated, but there was a windsock. It was perfect for daylight use for most private aircraft and, of course, helicopters. In fact, a few military-looking choppers were parked on the tarmac when they visited. Roberto thought they might be used for surveillance when the drug enforcement agents went looking for cocaine processing plants in the jungle. It was definitely worth reporting to James.

Matias and Roberto's mother tongue was Spanish. That's why they had fit in with the locals so well. Although they were Peruvian by birth and theoretically at odds politically with Ecuadorians, the local populations of both countries did not take any of that seriously. It was all just what it was—politics.

While they didn't spend any time together, they each enjoyed the cultures of their new surroundings. The Peruvian and Ecuadorian cultures had differences, despite what some North Americans might think. They included Spanish word pronunciation, intonations, cultural habits and teachings, as well as many other things. Each Latin American country had its own quirks. Matias and Roberto appreciated the nuances. Living in Ecuador was novel and interesting for them.

Each had accommodation local to their assigned site. Matias lived in Machala, a small port city with a population of about a quarter of a million. His apartment was just a few miles from Puerto Bolívar.

Roberto had a place in Loja, located in a high Andean valley at an elevation of 7,300 feet, with a population close to 200,000. It was almost at the halfway point between Zamora and the port.

Roberto had a particularly soft spot for Loja because it was a twin city with his hometown, Chiclayo, in Peru. He had a room in a small, cheap motel near the E-45 highway, but it didn't have the road view he wanted to actually see the Zamora concentrate trucks coming from and going to Machala. He couldn't find any accommodations that did.

The first time James called Roberto to let him know trucks were on their way, he sat in his vehicle, parked on a gravel patch near the bottom end of the last switchback they would have to negotiate, and watched as the first one came down through the mountains. Once it went past him, he followed to make sure of its routing, knowing some trucks were supposed to go to Guayaquil and some to Machala. But he need to see which ones went where.

The crossroads for highways running east–west and north–south were on the western outskirts of Loja. Traffic heading to Guayaquil would take the northern route. Traffic going to Machala would take the western route.

Roberto parked at the crossroads so he could count which trucks went to which port city.

The first fifty trucks turned north to Guayaquil. The last six went west. Roberto followed the last one until it reached a junction where it turned north. He watched as it pulled alongside the first five tucks, already parked on a gravel patch next to a motel just 200 feet from the junction, and switched off its engine.

From what he was seeing, Roberto surmised the concentrate trucks would take one day to travel from the site to Loja, and one day from Loja to Machala. He assumed they would start out again first thing the next morning. But he couldn't be certain what time so he decided to stay in his car, catch a few hours of sleep and be ready for them any time after 4 a.m.

Before he got comfortable enough to close his eyes, he watched as one of the men from the truck convoy wandered around the parking area for a while before disappearing into one of the truck cabs. *Probably going to sleep,* Roberto thought. He just hoped he had made the right decision on timing.

Chapter 11

Puerto Bolívar

Matias was bored.

For the past three days, he had been at the port, watching. Truckers had only transported containers loaded with bananas through the open barrier of Puerto Bolívar. They went to the south side of the small port to unload. There were no port cranes. Any freight coming in or out had to rely on the ship cranes. Rarely, and only if absolutely necessary, a mobile crane would be hired for special lifts.

That side of the port was dedicated to managing the export of over 6.5 million tons of bananas every year. It was a fruit that was available year-round in Ecuador, making it one of the largest global exporters of bananas.

Deliveries were made on a 24/7, year-round basis to the ever-waiting reefer vessels used to transport the refrigerated product all over the world.

The local plantation stretched for the last ten miles of the drive to the port when coming from the east. That's how big these plantations were—and that was only one. This was a crucial business for the economy of the country and the plantation owners strictly enforced the rules when it came to providing quality when the bananas reached their destination. The skins of the fruit had been treated with fungicides and parasiticides. Workers packed whole bunches as they were harvested off the trees into cardboard cartons, separating them with paper, and then transported them to the port in high-tech refrigeration containers.

Cooling and humidification systems maintained a consistent fifty-seven degrees Fahrenheit temperature and 90% humidity to put the fruit into a sort of hibernation, slowing the ripening process and maintaining hydration. Even with these precautions, every transport hour counted. The trucks never had to wait long to be unloaded; it was done as they arrived at the wharf. The reefers, also equipped with sophisticated cooling and hydration systems and deck-mounted cranes, were filled to capacity and sent on their way as soon as they were full.

Matias noted with wonder how truckloads of the crated product arrived yet were never stopped by the customs officials posted at the entry gates for inspection, or to collect any paperwork. They just waved them through, if they were there at all. Matias couldn't figure out if the customs people simply didn't care about the possibility of loading banana containers with drugs, or if there was another reason. Perhaps they were attuned to what had become a "normalized" situation between them and the exporters. But it did seem questionable. But then who could tell at this point, and Matias kept his thoughts to himself.

Unbeknownst to Matias or ORB, it had actually taken ten years for the drug cartels to reach an agreement with the plantations to keep out of each other's business. The consequence of the century-old banana industry falling victim to customs inspections, drug raids and distrust on a regular basis would mean the end of the industry.

Ecuadorians—ordinary people and drug handlers included—knew how important the banana industry was to the wealth of their country and the jobs it created. It contributed some 10% of the country's exports in terms of value and involved over 5,000 growers. Neither they nor the drug dealers wanted to compromise the security of the industry. After all, many of the cartel families and friends worked for the banana industry. It was often their only means of income. So, eventually an agreement was reached. The banana industry grudgingly paid its dues to the cartels, who left them alone; customs officials got their cut and never interfered. And all was at peace.

On the fourth day, early in the morning, Matias received a call from Roberto, stationed in Loja, to let him know that a six-truck convoy was on its way to Machala. It had overnighted outside the city limits.

By mid-afternoon, the convoy's open-deck trucks, with sideboards, thundered through the open port entrance and made their way over to one of the low, corrugated metal–roofed warehouses on the north side. One of the buildings had been specifically built for dumping bulk concentrate under cover before loading it onto a cargo ship. But the revised Zamora plan did not need that kind of a building at Puerto Bolívar anymore. They had, instead, chosen the better-equipped port at Guayaquil as the primary export terminal for bulk concentrate, and Puerto Bolívar was used only for concentrate in tote bags.

The six trucks pulled up in a line, parallel to a waiting midsize cargo ship equipped with three deck-mounted cranes, each hovering over one of three open holds.

The flat decks were laden with large, flat-bottomed, woven polypropylene tote bags. The bags were for mineral shipments and marked "2 Ton" on the side. There was a large red Chinese character stamped on the top of each bag in one corner. It had no meaning to a non-Chinese-speaking person.

As each truck came to a stop, the passenger-side door would swing open and a man would jump down onto the tarmac, release the sideboards, and take up a pre-planned position at a particular point on the perimeter of the convoy. There were six of them, one from each truck. One posted himself at the back of the convoy, one at the front, and the other four spread out on one side, away from the water and on either side of the two lagoons that separated the ship from the rest of the wharf. No one spoke, but each clearly knew what to do and where to go.

Their heads turned slowly from side to side as they scanned the port. They searched as far as they could see for any sign of anything that was out of place Each hid a hand inside their jacket, holding on to something they might need in case of trouble. There was none. Everything was as quiet as it had been for the three days when there were no concentrate trucks. No one, including the customs officials, seemed to be interested in what they were doing.

The jib of one of the cranes hovered above the first truck, then lowered its hook to the truck bed. The driver of the truck secured the hook to a bag using a remote controller. The crane winch whirred as it picked a bag, swung it over a hold and dropped the two-ton bags one at a time into the first hold. The second truck had already pulled up parallel to the second crane. Then, the third truck pulled up parallel to the last crane. The cranes lifted the loads into each of the three holds until they had unloaded all the bags, except for the first truck that still had one bag.

As the first truck pulled away, heading around one of the lagoons to the port exit road, it stopped by the warehouse. A forklift truck came out of the low building, reached up to the flat deck, lifted the last bag off, and took it into the warehouse. Each truck left the port as soon as its cargo had been offloaded, and their guards climbed back into the passenger seats. The hold covers on the ship clanged into place and one of the crew locked each of them. The ship would wait for the next convoy of trucks and the next, until it was ready to sail with a full load. Destination: Shanghai, China.

Another ship was anchored in the Puerto Bolívar waiting to take its place.

To an onlooker familiar with these kind of things, let alone customs officers who might have some knowledge of the contents of the bulk bags, it would seem very odd to see concentrate trucks guarded as they were unloaded, and then to witness it being so securely locked up on a ship. Who would want to steal a product that was still unprocessed? It still needed to be shipped offshore to add value. It wouldn't make sense.

Matias had been there at the port, working as a stevedore, thanks to ORB's influence. He was on the south side of the dock area with the banana crates and had a clear view of what was happening on the north side.

Everything that happened in the open areas of the port was visible to anyone who cared to watch. The customs office, on the second floor of the two-level building near the port entrance, had the best view. But none of the officers appeared when the concentrate trucks arrived. Neither did any appear when the bags were being lifted into the vessel. Matias couldn't make out any movement behind the shaded windows. But he was pretty sure they were watching.

Matias had spotted the bag taken into the building and made a mental note. He went back to work as the last of the trucks passed through the port gates for their return journey to the mine site and he called Roberto to alert him.

Matias wasn't sure how long he would have to wait for the next concentrate loads to come through. According to ORB's intel, he believed it was supposed to be every day. For now, he just needed to work, watch, wait, and continue to get familiar with the port facilities, particularly that building.

He would contact James later about his findings and get further instructions.

Chapter 12

El Pangui

El Pangui, known as the orchid of the Amazon, was a melting pot of Ecuadorian ethnic groups living in harmony and provided a prime example of the country's rich mix of indigenous cultures. It was also a center for biodiversity and long-term bio-commerce. Both environmentalists and businesspeople went to visit. They clamored for a chance to see the orchid fields, restored forests, and millions of new and well-tended plants. Some came to see how it was done. Some came to create or improve their overseas marketing opportunities. Some just came to see the beauty and hear the sounds of the wildlife chattering, and the exotic birds singing in this calming part of the Amazon jungle.

It was easy for James to find accommodation as a representative of the prestigious McArthur Foundation, seeking out opportunities worthy of their philanthropic support. In fact, the people in this little town considered him a special guest as they learned about his importance to their community. James carried out his fictious role splendidly as he inspected here and searched there and made copious notes on everything.

But he still had time to drive to the Río Zamora crossing. The Zamora mine trucks would cross there on their way to Machala, through El Pangui. In fact, at first James even got the help of some local boys. He paid them a couple of dollars a day to watch the highway for him, in case he was busy when the trucks came. He even gave them a walkie-talkie with a set frequency to contact him if needed. They proudly displayed it to anyone who cared to look and took up their position on a roadside bench with much enthusiasm and seriousness. James called them now and then just to give them the thrill and the experience of using the radio.

By now, James had made contact with Nathan and Eric at the plant, and it was Nathan who kept James updated on when shipments of concentrate were about to leave Zamora, including the first they would track. James passed the information on to Roberto in Loja when the boys spotted that initial convoy of concentrate trucks heading his way and radioed him.

At 7 a.m. the following morning, Roberto watched as the concentrate trucks left the parking lot on the outskirts of Loja and headed toward Machala. He called Matias to let him know they were on their way. Six hours later, Matias confirmed they had just rolled through the port gates and Roberto relayed that information to James in El Pangui.

After the first few days, the schedule for trucks leaving the plant was a no-brainer. Zamora loaded the 1,800 tons of concentrate in bags onto fifty-six trucks by mid-afternoon every day and sent them on their way, unless there was a plant shutdown.

As it happened, for the first few days Matias was at Puerto Bolívar with nothing to see, as the plant was on one of its regular three monthly maintenance shutdowns and no trucks were dispatched. He hadn't known that at the time and had wondered what was happening.

By the time trucks returned to the plant from Puerto Bolívar, the next set of concentrate tote bags would be ready to load. Even though Matias now knew when to expect them at the port, Roberto would still alert him ahead of time. Not only were messages about the trucking passed on, but there were also other things discussed, and that one short conversation each day promoted a sense of teamwork with the guys spread out as they were.

James had not visited the plant or the port yet. But he was happy with what his ORB friends were reporting to him, so far. At this point, both he and Matthew thought it best for him to stay in El Pangui for now and keep his cover. Although unlikely, visiting places where he might be recognized could get awkward. That could lead to questions being asked that he wasn't prepared to answer.

James talked to Matthew a lot. He knew when Matthew and Emma had arrived in Ecuador, and where they were staying in a camp up near the Río Zamora crossing. They discussed strategy and details for the next few days ahead. James decided to give Matthew a call now, to talk about the first shipment they had monitored.

"Hi, Matthew," James said from his self-catering apartment, as he gazed out the window at some kids playing soccer on a scrap of gravel across the road.

"Hey, James. How are things going?" Matthew was always happy to hear from James. He trusted him, especially after working with him on the Iranian and Newfoundland projects. He was dependable, bright, versatile, with a great sense of urgency—a trait that was hard to find in most people.

"Great. This environmental work is a breeze." James laughed. "No wonder there are so many young people trying to make a living out of it. Lots of the outdoors, everything is so new and interesting, and you get to study things like trees, birds and insects. And the girls! They love this stuff." There was a touch of cynicism in James's voice.

"Don't get too enthusiastic, James. Remember why we're here—and you're married with children, remember?" Matthew laughed. There was no way James would do anything to jeopardize his family.

"You're right. It's actually kind of boring. I sort of glaze over when someone starts telling me about the latest fern they discovered in the jungle." This time, they both laughed. "Okay, down to business." James sounded more serious. "You probably know the first concentrate trucks we monitored came through Puerto Bolívar yesterday. I was on the phone with Matias last night. He tells me they loaded the concentrate tote bags onto a waiting ship fast and locked down the holds. No customs—that's strange. Then the first truck out of there had one bag left which was fork-lifted into one of the port warehouses. A guard locked the building up and kept watch from his vehicle. It sounds as though there's something more important in there than only concentrate."

"Sounds like it. Can we get a look at that bag? What do you think?" Matthew was eager to investigate.

"Maybe a little early yet, Matthew. Let's see what happens on the next run. You never know, there may be more guards on the inside of that building, although Matias says he hasn't seen any others.

"I was thinking about asking Matias to take a look. But I don't want him getting into trouble, and he's not equipped for that kind of work. He'd probably freak himself out and blow the whole thing. No, we would be better off to keep him doing what he's doing for now—just watching." James paused. He knew it was the right thing to do. They didn't know enough about what was going on yet, but if the time came to take a look, it should probably involve at least two different ORB operatives.

"Agreed." Matthew was convinced to hold his patience a little longer. He needed to get a better understanding of what was going on at both the plant and the port. At least it had now been confirmed firsthand that

Puerto Bolívar was the intended port for six of the trucks leaving the plant each day. It sounded as though the ship was still at port, likely waiting for the next truck convoy.

"James, see if Matias can get some idea of how many of the cargo ship's crew are hanging around at the port. My guess is it won't be more than three or four. The rest will be in Machala taking some R&R. All they need at the port will be the crane operators and the captain." Matthew was thinking fast, wondering if they should try to get on board to take a look at the tote bags already there. "How are the others making out?" Matthew asked as he put the concentrate trucks and the port out of his mind for now. Emma was perched on a chair opposite him as she listened in on what Matthew was saying.

James described what had been set up with Roberto, Nathan and Eric. Matthew was particularly interested in what his guys were doing up at the Zamora plant.

"They're settling in at this point, Matthew. Not much to report. Eric is in the control room. Nathan is with the operations people on the floor. Perfect locations for what we need to do. First things first, they'll need to earn a little respect so they can stretch out. Nathan wants to see everything the plant offers, and Eric's been looking for anything out of place on his monitors and in the manuals." James paused, guessing what Matthew was about to ask, but allowing him to ask it anyway.

"And? Has he found anything?" Matthew seemed to tuck in closer to his phone as Emma leaned forward to try to pick up what James was saying. Matthew caught on and put his phone on speaker so Emma could hear better.

"Nothing." James smiled to himself.

"Nothing? That doesn't make sense, does it?" Matthew screwed up his eyebrows.

"Well, it does if you're hiding something. We're almost sure of what they're up to. But it's not going through the control room. So, there has to be a remote operation somewhere off-site, or we're wrong. My money is on there being a separate control station set up with no link to the mainframe. That would isolate them from any oversight." James said it, but he wasn't certain of his conclusion.

"Mmm, good assumption, James. Let's see what Nathan and Eric come up with. You may want to encourage them to move a little faster on that." This was Matthew's natural impatience showing through.

"I think they know the importance of this, Matthew. When I talked to them, they were keen on getting into all the corners as soon as they felt it was safe. But, of course, they can't talk to anyone, so they do it all on their own. And that means being really careful." James sat back in his small bedroom and waited for Matthew.

"You're right," Matthew acknowledged and glanced over at Emma. She nodded her head in agreement and gave a thumbs-up. "Emma and I are going that way over the next couple of days, so we may be able to see for ourselves. But it doesn't matter if we don't. We could always put the drone up, right?" Matthew sat back, and Emma relaxed.

"I'm sure Eric has it right. He's a pro at this. Those two have worked in a few copper and gold plants, so they know what they're looking at. I'll check again in a few days to see if they've made progress."

"Sounds good, James. Let Nathan know we're going to be in the area shortly, and I'll contact him if we need." Matthew was thinking. He wondered if there was more to cover with James. But, for now, it seemed that most things were in place. "Great work. Anything you need?" Matthew asked as he was about to sign off.

"I'm all set here. No problems, no curious people poking around, nobody asking awkward questions. So far, so good. Are you still thinking about getting Kenny and Armando into the plant?" James liked those two and he was hoping they would be around so he could spend a little time with them.

"Soon, but not until we get more familiar with what's going on over there. We're getting them and Nick processed with the plant owners now, for when they need to move in. But I'm going to hold off sending them until we can figure out what they'll need to do. If we get them in too early, they could overstay their welcome while they wait around for instructions. Remember, they'll be here as vendor representatives, so a visit shouldn't be any more than about two weeks. Let's get the plan in place first, okay?" Matthew paused to let James talk.

"Gotcha. Talk later." James hung up and continued to watch the boys play outside. It was amazing how such simple things could please these kids. They were playing on a patch of gravel, laughing and shouting at each other. Although it wasn't clear who was on what team, if there were teams, or which way they were going. Just a couple of cans for goal posts, fifteen feet apart, at one end of the patch. It looked as though it was the first to get the ball between them while everyone else tried to take the ball away. He guessed it was all about points, or was it all just for fun? It was intriguing how these little things, diametrically opposite to his own activity, helped him think, and that was what James was doing now.

Chapter 13

Operations

The drive from Quito to the Zamora property with Ping Pei felt awkward at times. It tested their ability to dodge his more personal questions concerning their background. But Eric and Nathan congratulated themselves on sounding their parts. Two wandering, educated and experienced millennials, searching the world for interesting, but not overly dangerous, adventures. At times they captivated their lonely audience with tales of their escapades, descriptions of foreign places they had visited—which was all true—and their thoughts on their hopeful future. Unbeknownst to Ping Pei, the reality was they needed money, and ORB had come to their rescue at the right time.

They arrived at the Zamora mill complex, where both the Chinese and Ecuadorian flags were displayed over the entrance to the administration building. It was surprisingly easy for Eric and Nathan to gain access as strangers. But then they were in the company of Ping Pei, the much respected and honored company representative from Quito.

The facility had been carved out of a broad valley on the eastern side of the Andes, just before it disappeared into the deep jungle of the Amazon basin. It had been a mammoth task. The Chinese had to build their way through the thick, wet clay soils, and bring in thousands of tons of gravel to provide some sort of working platform. Construction had taken over 40,000 cubic yards of concrete and thousands of tons of structural steel for the buildings and platforms. Moving the large equipment to the site was a nightmare in itself, with 100-ton pieces having to cross the Zamora River on a barge upgraded for the task.

It had taken five years for the Chinese to complete the work, but in the end, they had a self-contained facility with accommodations, their own services, and a road network worthy of any town in North America. The roads were blacktopped; the deep side ditches led to settling ponds throughout the complex, and the tailings dam stood over the plant as a symbol of their achievement to build big, regardless of what the Amazon could throw at them.

Everyone Nathan and Eric met or even passed in the company of Ping Pei bowed deeply at the waist while avoiding eye contact with such an important person. Although they did give a sideways glance of wonder at his two companions. Ping Pei introduced his newly discovered talent to the operations management team before touring them briefly through the plant and control room himself. Two operators followed at a respectful distance for Ping Pei to refer to in cases where he was unable to answer questions. He wasn't an experienced person in these sorts of surroundings. In fact, he knew little about the industry at all. But still, he managed to get by using his status for protection.

Ping Pei was not a technical person. His descriptions of what they were looking at were more of an artistic overview, with a splash of technical terms, a modicum of self-congratulation with a lot of arm waving. He was clearly uncomfortable around noisy machinery. It clanged and crashed and made him nervous. To him, it seemed threateningly close. After thirty minutes he had enough and brought his little tour to an end. He waved the two operations people forward and whispered a few words to them before leaving Nathan and Eric in their care. Ping Pei scuttled off to the end of the building and disappeared through the single door into the loadout area. They didn't see him again, and learned he left for Quito the following morning.

Nathan and Eric quickly acclimated to their new surroundings, including their more than adequate accommodations in a building designed for the plant management. The accommodations for the workers were quite different. Sparse, small rooms for two with bunkbeds, communal washing facilities and laundry, a rudimentary canteen arrangement, and an open area furnished only with mahjong and card game tables.

Following a thorough safety indoctrination on how to cope with working in this particular operating mill environment, Eric and Nathan were shown through the mill again, but this time with a senior production manager. They had a better chance to admire the open-air mill building, which had only a roof cover and partial sides from the ground up to about eight feet, typical of such buildings in warm environments. The partial enclosure was intended to protect against rain.

Each was assigned a designated station from which to operate. Eric chose a spot in the control room with a half-dozen other engineers. Their eyes glued to the screens in front of them, watching for any deviations from the programmed weights, moisture contents, densities, flows, valve openings and closings, and so on. Nathan was more of an operations person. He found a spot with the operations team and introduced himself. There was always room for another set of experienced eyes to oversee the mill from the trenches. The team checked everything ran smoothly, without overheating, leaking, or making strange noises. They also watched over scheduled and unscheduled shutdowns in the dual-line mill.

For a new facility, this one was large, even for a new copper and gold plant. It could process 80,000 tons of ore every day, seven days a week, fifty-two weeks a year, with an efficiency of around 90%, allowing for maintenance and the like. Large throughput meant low mineral grades and lots of waste. This plant was no exception. With an average copper grade of around 0.67% of the throughput, it meant that for every ton of ore, or 2,000 pounds, there would be only 13.4 pounds of copper released into solution as tiny grains. Gold was even more scarce, at around 0.22 grams per ton of ore, or under 0.008 of an ounce for each ton of ore processed (invisible to the naked eye)—and, of course, silver. Once released from the ore during the processing, the minerals would end up as a fine, damp-to-the-touch concentrate of a purity that would be diluted by the mafic, the material gluing everything together, that came with it. Miners extracted only 2% of usable ore daily, discarding the rest as waste in spoil tips. Operators then disposed of post-process waste in tailings ponds.

No gold refinery existed to create doré bars at this plant. Neither were there electro-winning facilities to process the copper into sheets or wire. In this plant, the concentrate would retain the minerals, and all refining for added value would take place offshore.

Eric wondered about that. It was odd for such a remote site not to have final processing capabilities to reduce the amount of product transported, and that would be huge for this plant. But he didn't dwell on it.

Each day, workers bagged the 1,800 tons of copper, gold, and silver concentrate that had dropped from the kiln to the floor of the loadout part of the building for shipment. Not bad for a day's work—around

$2.8 million worth of copper and over $600,000 worth of gold and silver at today's prices. And this was only the first stage of the plant's size. Inevitably, the size would double, and maybe even triple, over the years, depending on the availability of mineral-rich ore—and that required ongoing exploration. But, for now, this plant could operate for thirty years using the proven resource.

It didn't take long for Eric and Nathan to gain respect from their fellow workers once they appreciated how much experience these two newcomers had. Based on ORB's statement, they would likely handle the crude cocaine here, somewhere in the plant. All they needed to do was to locate where it was and how it was handled coming in and going out.

Nathan sidled along one of the two parallel flotation tank structures. He did this two or three times a day, while idly looking into the launders running around the top circumference of the inside of the tanks, to ensure there were no blockages and the flow was consistent. He touched the casings of each of the pumps that circulated the solution in the tanks, to feel from the vibration whether they were operating smoothly. All the while he would glance up at the door to the loadout area at the end of the building.

Nathan could see full-height sheet metal closed off the loadout area on all four sides. There was a single windowless man door from the plant with a security pad for gaining access, and an overhead door on one side to allow trucks and equipment to enter the area when the concentrate was ready for loading. There was no guard at the man door. But Nathan knew, from watching, that anyone entering the loadout area needed clearance, even if they had the security code. Somehow, he had to get access.

With the help of Eric in the control room, they devised a ploy requiring Nathan to personally check some piece of equipment in the loadout. Eric reset one of the kiln overheat alarms, and Nathan volunteered to check things out. It was likely a faulty thermocouple wire, gauge or loose connection, he told everyone. Nathan requested permission from the general foreman to carry out the check, and the GF looked at his watch, glanced over at a calendar hanging on his wall, and gave Nathan the thumbs-up. Nathan thought it odd that the time and day mattered for an approval to investigate an alarm situation. But he just shrugged, thanked him and wandered off. He made a mental note to tell Matthew about the detail.

Nathan took a mechanic and an electrician with him to provide some cover for his activities and headed down to the other end of the building. None of the three had the security code and it took three hard knocks on the door before someone came out. They glanced at their badges, then at their papers, and let them through. There were two-armed security guards standing at the head ends of the concentrate conveyors coming through from the mill. They both eyed these intruders with interest, but if they were here to fix that damned alarm noise then they were more than welcome to try.

This was the area where four conveyors from the filter presses carried the copper-gold-rich concentrate through the wall from the process side of the plant. The conveyors dropped onto two cross-conveyors, which then fed their product into rotating kilns in the loadout for drying. That was an important part of the process for shipping purposes. More than 8% moisture in the concentrate could mean it might liquefy when transported with all the shaking about. If that happened on board a ship carrying it as bulk cargo, it could slop around in the ship's hold.

The dried concentrate was discharging onto the concrete floor and would be loaded into two-ton-capacity nylon-woven tote bags for ease of transport. Usually, the bags would be emptied at the port and conveyed onto a bulk carrier ship for ocean transport. Right now, it was mid-morning and no bags were being filled, and there were no trucks waiting to be loaded. The bags were piled on one side next to a bag-loading mechanism. The overhead door to the loadout area was locked down.

The operation seemed normal to Nathan's trained eye. But he lingered a little and slowly took everything in. Then he saw it.

On the far side of the loadout space, a covered conveyor discharged something into a stainless-steel hopper. Nathan wandered over and pretended to inspect the kilns, looking for an obvious fault that could trip the alarm in the control room. But all he could see was a pile of clear plastic bags. He estimated that each could hold about ten pounds of some product. They were set close to the discharge nozzle on the bottom of the hopper, with one bag already secured in place, waiting for the next load. It wasn't obvious what the product was, but Eric made a guess. He knew he had to see what was on the other side of that wall. It was certainly not a common addition to any typical copper-gold plant he had ever seen. There was nothing it might be transferring in an ordinary mill of this kind.

Nathan went back to the local control and monitoring station at the kilns. He pretended to find the alarm fault and fixed it. He relayed his findings to the control room, who reset the gauges, and the team returned to the process plant.

Chapter 14

Zamora

"Don't move!" Emma touched Matthew's arm as they lay under a mosquito net in the early morning hours, with the sound of rain beating on the tin roof of their little room.

The dawn light filtered through the heavy clouds and open windows of the crude wooden hut they had been assigned, as Emma hugged her flimsy cover closer to her body. The air was thick with stillness and humidity. The early-morning sounds of wildlife shrieking and cawing—birds noisily competing and insects sounding as if they were chewing their way through the walls—seemed to surround them here. It was all so beautiful but at the same time so foreign. The cacophony of sounds, with the occasional howl of some unrecognizable beast, had seemed somewhat delightful in the security of their hut, provided nothing came too close. But now... Emma wasn't so sure.

Matthew slowly opened one eye, focusing on his bed mate. He tried not to move. Clearly, some kind of danger was lurking but, right now, he had no idea what it might be. There were a thousand things here in the jungle that could scare the pants off anyone unaccustomed to the creepy crawlers of the night. He had recently read about a newly identified gigantic northern green anaconda snake species in Ecuador, larger than the notorious southern anaconda, and now the largest snake known to exist. *Typical*, he had thought about the announcement coinciding with his visit to the country. Being surrounded by potential dangers would take some getting used to, and there was no guarantee that a bit of flimsy, see-through fabric would stop anything that could be lurking while one slept.

"What's up?" Matthew asked without attempting to move his head to see what was making Emma so alarmed.

"It's yellow," Emma hissed. "About four inches long. Furry, with what looks like parallel lines of inflamed red fiery suction cups gripping the net. It's curling toward your head—and the top of your head is caught up in the net."

Emma pushed her head closer to the foreign body as the shrill cry of a flock of panicking black vultures fleeing their resting tree over by the camp kitchen at the sound of pots clanging startled them both.

"Some kind of fat caterpillar, but with one hell of a ferocious look about it that seems to be focused on you." Emma pushed back, unsure of what to do. "You need to do something before it gets to you, and I don't get a feeling this mosquito net is going to help much." Emma went quiet as she backed out of the bed under the net and picked up one of her shoes.

In a millisecond, Matthew twisted out from under the net and in one fluid movement stood with a shoe in his hand. Emma stood still on her side of the double bed they had jerry-rigged together the night before from two singles, as Matthew hunted his prey with a shoe now in each hand. He slapped at the net, but the intruder clung on until Matthew flicked it to the floor and landed one of the shoes on top of it. They both heard the squelch but didn't want to look.

"Fuck me." Emma stared, mortified, at the caterpillar corpse when Matthew lifted his shoe away. It covered a sizeable area, the grossness of the squashed body a mix of pus, suckers, eyes and hair. A strange mixture of white, yellow, green and red. Matthew put his shoes on and kicked the caterpillar body over to the side of the hut.

"I think that was one of those creepy-crawly things Stockman warned us about. You remember, the good-looking one with the yellow hair and poisonous suckers." Matthew glanced over at Emma who nodded and grimaced.

"That was a close call, and it would have been closer if all that noise outside hadn't woken me." Emma shivered.

They dressed hurriedly, but didn't take their eyes off the carcass, in case the monster had a friend close by that might want to collect its dead friend—or worse, its mate—and go into hiding until it could avenge the death.

Outside, under the canvas awning supported by wooden poles, Rodriguez was preparing breakfast. Long rough wooden tables and chairs were spread around, and the smell of freshly brewed coffee had the effect of bringing Matthew and Emma back to earth. They collected tin mugs of the brew and someone waved them over to one of the tables, where two plates of food were pushed in front of them. Meat, eggs, some kind of vegetable—yellow-green in color, type unknown—and fresh-baked bread.

"Eat, my friends. I have put some food and water in the cooler for you to take today, so don't forget it." Rodriguez sidled back to his crude cooking area, where he had set up a metal plate mounted on bricks, over burning wood. The coffee pot, meat and eggs shared the space. A pan of mixed vegetables simmered in a large wok-style pot to one side.

"*Muchas gracias,* Rodriguez!" Matthew shouted over, before he and Emma tore off strips of bread and tucked into their meal. Some of the other camp residents were starting to join them at the communal table. Several introduced themselves. One or two sat in silence after an initial grunt of introduction and grabbed a tin mug of coffee. Apart from a simple *"buenos días"* to any newcomers, Matthew and Emma kept to themselves, cautious of being talkative until they knew a little more about who these people were. Likely environmentalists with smaller companies, or students and other individuals interested in studying the treasured fauna and flora of this extraordinary ecosystem known as the Amazon rainforest.

The drive from Quito to the project area had been uneventful. It had taken nine hours to travel the almost 300-mile-long winding Pan-American Highway south through the narrow Andean valley to Cuenca, where they stayed the night at the Villa Ana María hotel on the northern outskirts of the city.

Matthew and Emma had stopped at a clearing on the west side of the Río Zamora bridge, about eight miles from the Zamora plant where they had arranged to meet their local contact, Rodríguez. He had a small camp where he hosted paying visitors, mainly environmentalists interested in studying the wildlife of southeastern Ecuador.

Stockman had arranged a cover for them and James that was rock solid.

The forty-four-year-old McArthur Foundation, an internationally respected philanthropic group, had been involved in some 10,000 effective charitable organizations in 117 countries, with major commitments to socio-economic and environmental projects.

Recently they had taken an interest in studying the biodiversity of southern Ecuador, including the mid-altitude rain forests of the Andes where the Zamora plant took up a tiny section of an otherwise huge expanse of jungle. Studies in that area were scarce, even though the importance to the ecological system of Ecuador and the Amazon basin were well documented. But it had been difficult for the government to manage it and they relied on foreign investors for protection. Sometimes that came with a price, sometimes it came with a promise, and sometimes it came from benevolence and a great interest in preserving one of the world's most important natural features, by groups such as the McArthur Foundation.

The London-based Ecuadorian ambassador introduced Matthew and Emma as representatives of the Foundation with government authorization to go wherever their research was needed. Stockman's persuasion helped bring the study to the top of the Foundation's pile when they discovered that the development of a copper-gold facility in a particularly ecologically and socially sensitive area involved removing an entire mountain and threatening several of the 1,100 tributaries of the Amazon. Zamora had suddenly come under the microscope of a major international environmental group with the kind of power that could influence government.

Matthew finished his meal and pushed the plate away. He reached into his inside jacket pocket and took out an envelope, pulled out a parchment-like letter, and opened it. He slid it across the table to Emma, who edged her own plate to the side and reached for the letter. She had seen it before when Matthew first received it, but reading it again, as they sipped from their second mugs of coffee, increased her confidence in their success. She looked up and smiled at him before folding the letter, then flipped it back.

"So here we are. Eminent environmentalists, in the middle of the jungle with all the nasties, about to go into a Chinese den of drugs searching for justice." Emma smiled.

"Nicely put." Matthew reached over and stroked her hair.

The letter ensured their access to wherever they needed, although it was important that it demonstrated its relevancy to their duties. A tricky balance had to be struck between those viewing the document and Matthew and Emma, who would be presenting it. Some at the Zamora plant may question their authority, given the subject matter of their environmental interests, and what importance the plant could offer in terms of environmental compliance. Some parts of the operation were certainly relevant to their investigation, like the mine itself; it was undeniable. But the plant? Well, it would take some imagination on the part of Matthew and Emma to make a case for their inspection. Perhaps they could suggest it was more for personal interest and show a keen interest in what Tongyan were doing for the good of the country so they might be invited for a spin around inside the plant.

But who could argue with the importance of the letter they carried, and the authority it exuded? The embossed emblem displayed at the top of the letter, taking up almost one-third of the page, showed the Ecuadorian coat of arms with a condor on an oval shield. Double red-ink stamps, each with a flourish of an artistic signature representing two well-known, high-ranking government officials, was an impressive showing at the bottom of the letter. It would convince most. These two foreigners, Matthew and Emma, had the support of powerful people not to be messed with.

The wording of the letter was brief and simply introduced Matthew and Emma, under assumed names commensurate with their entry papers, as representatives of the McArthur Foundation. It provided a very concise description of their assignment—followed by a strongly worded order for the reader to assist in any way requested. It would scare anyone who might dare to question Matthew and Emma's authority. The imaginary power of the words, the stamps, the signatures and the emblem would send shivers down the spines of ordinary folk.

But it was clear they had the task of studying any environmental impacts the new mine may cause.

"Let's take a drive over to the plant and look around." Matthew smiled impishly at Emma, who nodded her agreement and grinned. He tucked the letter into its envelope and back into his pocket.

"I guess now is as good a time as any. Let's see what they think of the letter, shall we?" Emma got up and shrugged her small backpack over one shoulder before marching off to their Land Cruiser.

Once over the Río Zamora bridge, Matthew slowed the Land Cruiser down as it transitioned to the gravel road leading to the plant. There were no signs of other towns along the route. But they assumed there would be many small communities without names. They also expected to find families living off the land or cultivating coca plantations.

Matthew had always known that if he wanted to go farther into the jungle to follow the coca transfer routes, he would need the help of locals. But he would have to be cautious when trying to make contact with anyone who might be able to help, in case they were part of the problem. Right now, his plan was to familiarize himself with the lie of the land, the Zamora plant, and what isolated communities may be in the vicinity. He had no idea how big the coca territory was that fed the Zamora facility. But he guessed it was large. The network of rivers likely carried most of the product from the crude coca farms. Their cover as environmentalists would be a perfect foil for the initial investigative work.

Matthew also knew that the next major coca leaf harvest was coming up at the end of June. That would be when the jungle manufacturing plants would be at their most productive. It was imperative that he and Emma find a way to get themselves close to one or more of the communities involved and follow the process. While it had become a year-round industry, there were still only three major harvest periods: March, after the rainy season, the end of June, and finally in October or November. Between, there were more sparse periods when production diminished to a less frantic but still valuable pace. Families worked year-round for a pittance, but work was work, and money was money, and that's how their world turned. They weren't concerned with who paid them or who they worked for, so long as they could feed their families.

They slowly approached the Zamora plant limits. They could see the barbed wire fence around the perimeter and stopped to consider their plan. For now, on this initial visit, they would present their credentials and ask for a guided visit around the major areas of the site. They wouldn't need to go into the processing plant, and would prefer instead to take a look at the open pit, tailings, water, and waste collection and treatment facilities—all very environmentally threatening. It should do the trick.

At the administration building reception desk, Matthew placed his hands on the raised part and smiled at the young, good-looking Chinese lady behind her computer screen.

"Good day." He raised his eyebrows, showed his gleaming teeth and continued, "Would you call Mr. Zhao for us and let him know that his visitors from the McArthur Foundation are here to see him?"

The receptionist responded with a pleasant smile and asked, "Which Mr. Zhao would you like to see? There are five here at Zamora." Her facial expression didn't change. Her smile remained fixed, and her head cocked to one side as she waited for an answer.

Chapter 15

Ping Pei

Ping Pei considered his discovery of Eric and Nathan a success. Hopefully, in the next few weeks, he would get glowing reports of their performance. Maybe, he would be lucky to discover more wandering talent.

In the meantime, he had plans to meet his Chinese embassy friend, Wang Ho Lin, at La Cruz del Papa, their usual place across the fields.

It was time, and he crossed the Quito sports park once more and found Lin sitting on a bench facing the traffic on the west side while smoking a Winston. Oh, how he loved to smoke, and Winstons were his favorite. He couldn't believe he couldn't get them back home in China, which was why he always took a full suitcase of them back whenever he returned to Beijing—in a diplomatic pouch, that is. He had arrived early, and this was his second cigarette as he thought about what he could tell Ping Pei.

His friend sat down next to him and pulled a pack of his own Winstons from a pocket. Easing a cigarette out of its place, he slipped it between his lips and flicked the lighter. He drew a deep breath, pushed the smoke out through his mouth, and let it swirl upwards as he pursed his lips, closed his eyes, and sighed with satisfaction as though this was his last cigarette.

"How are you, my friend?" Ping Pei asked as his initial nicotine craving subsided.

"Good, my friend. It is very pleasant here, isn't it?" They eyed each other and smiled. They had both landed great jobs away from the prying eyes of their governors back in China. Wang Ho Lin worked for the government. Ping Pei worked for a private company, but one that was government controlled. Their families stayed in Beijing at their choice and for their children's benefit. Yet, Wang Ho and Ping luxuriated in the benefits of working in Quito. It lacked nothing. Their tastes were not excessive and their expense accounts covered all they desired. Despite this friendly relationship, it was all business. The two never socialized together. They feared being accused of skulduggery by their obsessively protective peers. But that's what came with the territory, and neither of them would have it any other way, given they were close to being obsessive compulsive.

"How was your trip?" Wang Ho let out a cloud of smoke and glanced over at his friend.

"Successful, I think. But I will know better over the next two weeks. And you? Did you discover anything about them that we don't already know?" It was Ping's turn to take another lungful of smoke and let it out slowly, as he enjoyed every moment of the deadly toxin. He glanced back at Wang Ho and noticed what seemed to be a moment of hesitation. Ping's brow furrowed. Wang Ho noticed that.

"Strangely, we can't find much more than their places of birth. We know where they went to study and all their usual irrelevant activities. That's where things seem to end. Oh, we did find a mention of them both in a mine operations report we found. But it was only a group photo and an article about a copper mine in Chile that completed an expansion a few years ago. After that, nothing." Wang Ho sat back, thinking. "Our people are still searching for any signs of them over the last ten years, but you can imagine there is an overabundance of information to consider, and neither of them is of such importance that they would be easy to find." He watched for a reaction from Ping.

"That's good, my friend. The fact is we don't have any reason to be suspicious, other than them arriving here at such an opportune time. But coincidences do happen." Ping smiled and seemed content.

"I am not a great believer in coincidences, Mr. Pei, although fate is quite another thing. For the sake of a few more hours of research, I think it wise to keep searching. We should even look beyond their field of expertise."

Chapter 16

A Nice Visit

The general manager of the mine, Jun Jie Khao, stepped into the Zamora administration building reception area. Unusually tall, slim, clean shaven and well-dressed in casual but smart clothes, he introduced himself with a smile and a slight bow to Matthew and Emma. They reciprocated with their fictitious names, Larry and Ann Drew. There were no handshakes.

"Please, call me Mr. Khao. I know how you foreigners can be with Asian names. So, let's make it easy for you. I don't have a Western nickname, as you might say." His English was perfect, with only a slight Chinese accent. Clearly, he had been educated in a Western environment, and his smile was stuck on his face even as he talked.

"It's good of you to accommodate us, Mr. Khao. I think you know why we are here." Matthew handed him a copy of his authentication letter, just in case their host had any doubts. He didn't appear to have any, and his face gave nothing away as he glanced at the paper and handed the letter back.

"Impressive, Mr. Drew."

"The Foundation is considering investing in the Ecuadorian social and environmental infrastructure in this area." Matthew paused as Mr. Khao nodded. Whether it was a sign of understanding, agreement or disdain was difficult to tell. "But we have to see for ourselves what risks there may be. Of course—" Matthew was interrupted by a young Chinese lady hovering in the background.

"Tea?" she asked, with that same unmoving smile the receptionist had offered them. "Refreshments?" she continued, without dropping the look, but posturing with a slight bow.

Mr. Khao offered his hand out to them, palm up, and showed them the direction he obviously wanted them to go. Matthew realized he might be getting ahead of himself. There was protocol, after all, and business was not discussed in the open with the Chinese and was usually left until after they had shared tea.

He waited until the office door was closed and they were alone together. It was a splendidly Chinese-decorated room on the second floor, overlooking most of the Zamora facilities, against a backdrop of the Amazon jungle.

While the tea was poured and passed around, Matthew remained patient until the girl left and shut the door behind her. Mr. Khao sipped his tea, looked up at Matthew, then at Emma, and smiled. He was just waiting.

"Ah, well, to continue..." Matthew forgot to take a sip of tea before he began and instead explained what they needed to see and asked for help to guide them around the property.

"Of course... Larry." Mr. Khao hesitated at calling Matthew by his fictitious first name. He was more comfortable calling people in a more official way. One could refer to a person as *Mr. this*, *Miss that*, or *Mrs.*, if they were certain the lady was married.

"Of course. I will have a driver take you wherever you wish to go. He speaks good English and is very familiar with the various parts of the plant. He may not be able to go into detail, though." There was that smile again. "He is not a plant operator. But he has been here through the construction phase and is still here. He knows his way around perfectly." Mr. Khao paused for another sip of tea. Then, he placed his cup back on its saucer with a *clink*. It was as though he wanted to prove its authenticity as bone china.

"Great. Many thanks." Emma spoke up for the first time. "I think we would like to start right away if we could." She waited for any facial expression, either positive or negative, from their host. There was none. "We're going to take a look from the thirty-thousand-foot level today and tomorrow... then, we'll be looking around in more detail." She smiled.

Mr. Khao interrupted. "Thirty thousand feet? You need a plane?" He looked perplexed.

Emma laughed. "No, it's an expression. It means we want to take in the layout—from the ground, of course—so no details right now. It's as though we were flying above, capturing the salient features that make up the entire project." She looked over at Mr. Khao, who, by the look on his face, seemed to have grasped her meaning.

"Oh, yes. I understand. A look from high above, but from the ground." He smiled, amused at the ridiculousness of the saying. How could anyone understand Westerners? he thought. Their languages were rife with slang, double meanings, and words that could mean many things but still be spelled the same.

"Yes, of course." He refrained from making any critical comment and smiled. "I will have my driver meet you at the entrance whenever you wish. Feel free to use him at your leisure." It appeared that Mr. Khao had finished. He didn't appear to be particularly interested in who or what the Foundation was, nor who they were. This was more likely a mere disturbance to his day, and it would be good to get these two out of the way.

The driver was already waiting at the entrance to the building as Matthew and Emma pushed through the doors.

"I am Kai." The driver opened the rear cab door of the GWM electric pickup. Emma climbed in and naturally took the back seat. Matthew took the front passenger seat. Neither of them had been in a Chinese-made vehicle before, but they were quite impressed by the finishes and its look. In fact, it looked very much like a Ford F-350 with a cab, come to think of it.

Kai gave them each a site map. It highlighted the main parts of the property and showed a fence around it and a dashed line with arrows to show their route. Evidently, this was a process that had been repeated before with tourists, or more likely Chinese officials from Beijing and the bank. Matthew looked back at Emma when he realized they were taking the well-worn path.

"Kai, we may need to deviate from the route you show. Our concerns could be with locations you don't identify here." Matthew sounded as concerned as he should be when speaking to Kai, hoping it might get them some leniency on the routing.

"Okay, Mr. Larry." Kai started the engine and the vehicle silently cruised away from the administration building. "But you must ask Mr. Khao first, before I can take you anywhere but to those places shown."

Matthew wasn't about to argue or make any other comments. For today, the selected route would be fine. But tomorrow, or whenever they came back, they would seek Mr. Khao's approval to go offtrack.

As they made their way around the property, Kai briefly described what they were looking at. He made no attempt to describe anything in detail and resisted answering questions. His common theme was "You will have to consult with Mr. Khao on that."

There wasn't anything Matthew had not seen before, although in different settings. But nothing they were shown seemed out of place, as they would expect.

oooo

"Sean, are you there?" A crackling sound came from the other end of the two-way radio as someone fiddled with the squelch in response to Matthew's call. It was evening back at the camp. Matthew and Emma had finished supper after a day on the property. They had stuck to the route shown on the map, but reduced their questioning to almost zero once they realized there was no point in asking any more. There was nothing that raised their temperature, so to speak, so there wasn't any need for questions. Neither did they want to ask their driver, who would probably just give the standard response. After all, this was a guided tour of a well-scrubbed facility intended to shine in the eyes of a beholder. No one would be able to see anything that shouldn't be seen.

"Yeah, boss. I'm up at the plant." It was Sean, in his spot on the hill.

"We need you to do a bit of reconnaissance over on the north side of the process plant."

"Okay, boss."

"But make sure you don't get too close. There's a conveyor belt entering the north side of the building near the far end. We need to know what's at the north end of it. It disappears into the jungle. Can you do that?" Matthew and Emma waited in anticipation. This was one of the areas they hadn't been driven to on their tour. In fact, they stayed completely away from the north and east ends of the process plant. Now that Nathan had confirmed the unmarked conveyor entry location into the plant, they needed to find out where it came from and what was at that end.

"Do you want me to take shots?" Sean had a FLIR Scion thermal monocular night vision camera. Not quite military grade, but only twenty ounces and nine inches long with an 8x zoom lens, Wi-Fi video streaming and Bluetooth. It had a run time of four-and-a-half hours, and Sean made sure it was charged up every time before he went out into the field. Glenn had the same model. He had already used it a number of times and sent the images to both James and Matthew. They showed the comings and goings around the plant, including one of Matthew and Emma going to the administration building to meet Mr. Khao.

"Absolutely. Take photos and videos of whatever you see whether it's a fixed asset, human, or anything that moves. Label them before sending, and if you don't know what you're looking at, say that. Are we good?"

"All good, boss. We'll start shooting tonight."

"Do you need Glenn?" Matthew thought it was a good idea to always have two people when there was any action that might involve risk.

"That would be good, Matthew. I'll call him right away. Is that it?"

"Thanks, Sean. Good luck." Before Sean could answer, Matthew clicked off the radio and turned back to Emma.

"We're in play. I hope Sean keeps out of trouble."

"Me too. If the Chinese get a whiff of anyone poking around other than us, I'm sure we'll hear about it." Emma didn't need to finish her thought. They both knew what was at stake if the Chinese were to find out.

"Okay, let's see where we are with things." They moved over to one of the tables, away from anyone else, and sat with a beer in hand.

"Why don't you start?" Matthew looked over at Emma as she was taking a swig of her beer. The sweat lay on her face in droplets, as well as patches of moisture under her arms and breasts. Not only was it very humid, but it was still hot, even as the sun was setting. The sound of insects chirping and birds chattering, as they all began their nightly ritual of communication, surrounded them.

"Okay, we've confirmed that the cocaine is likely packed with the concentrate. But we don't yet know how. Also, we haven't found where it comes from or who delivers the raw product. Matias has spotted the odd concentrate bag being dropped off at the port, but we don't yet know why." Emma was examining her hands as she thought and listed the knowns and unknowns. Of course, there were always the unknown unknowns, but they would hopefully become clear as time moved forward.

"We've got Nathan and Eric in position at the plant," Emma continued as she played with her fingers. "Sean and his guys are on watch. Matias and Roberto are handling the port and road, and James is in place, coordinating from El Pangui. We just got our access to the plant, met the main man, and toured the site. All in all, I suppose that's it. The framework is in place. We have to put some flesh on the bones, as Daddy would say." Emma relaxed back with her beer, crossed her outstretched legs, leaned back against the table, and looked smugly over her bottle at Matthew.

He was smiling.

"You're right, Em. We're in play." Matthew struck the same pose as Emma, and they both slurped back a few mouthfuls of beer. "Now, the next thing to do is to get some help with making contact with the indigenous community, eh?" It was Matthew's turn to look over the top of his bottle at Emma.

Chapter 17

Pieces of the Puzzle

It was a week after Nathan's visit to the loadout area before he and Eric contrived a reason for Nathan to check the water supply systems located on the side of the plant where the odd conveyer entered the building. Nathan suspected a second processing facility was attached and feeding some product into the hopper inside the loadout area. From what Eric had observed, there were no telltale signs on his control panels indicating any supplemental processing or even conveying equipment other than what was expected. Any other systems had to be self-contained and operated elsewhere.

Eric played with the control programming for the pump house they believed to be in the location they were interested in. He set some limits that would cause alarms to initialize when water levels appeared to be either too low or too high in the fire and freshwater tanks. In fact, all he had done was raise one and lower the other so the gap between the two extremes was small enough to trip an alarm.

One might have assumed it was just a water pump house constructed against the concentrator wall. But it was more than that. It was way too big. Initially, two tough-looking security guards stopped Nathan from entering the building. They backed down after one of them called their security chief who confirmed Nathan's right to enter. But they were told to watch Nathan's movements once inside and make sure his interest stayed limited to the water facilities.

Once inside the building, Nathan could see the water equipment was sealed off from the loadout bay. It was also separated from a larger walled-off space on the other side. The entry from the water facilities to that space was guarded by another security heavy and a coded lock. Nathan guessed there would be a second access point from the outside, which would also be guarded.

Nathan wandered around the water facilities. He could see nothing but the large water pumps, filters, and the usual associated equipment. He fiddled with some controls on the local panel and made an obvious inspection of the pumps, tapped some instruments, and called the control room to test the circuits.

All was back to normal. Nathan left the building, but instead of turning left to the concentrator door, he took a right. He had only gone ten yards before security, with their hands on their guns, gruffly redirected him back the other way. That short diversion was enough for him to see a covered conveyor coming from the jungle. It was heading toward the side of the building he had just come from but on the other side from the water equipment.

Nathan knew the next stage of his investigation could be difficult and dangerous. He, or preferably one of his team, had to see what was at the far end of that conveyor. He also wanted to peek inside the water building's extension. But he was sure that would be off-limits, no matter what excuse he could conjure.

Nathan decided he should contact James to seek advice on how to proceed. Perhaps, this part of the project needed someone more practiced at this kind of subversion. He was sure neither he nor Eric could push the operations people any further without raising suspicions and he certainly didn't want to be caught going outside their permitted limits.

Nathan waited until the evening, when he and Eric were back at the living compound, before he got an opportunity to call James.

"Hi, Nathan. How are you guys doing?" Although James talked to one or the other of them every couple of days, he was always pleased to hear either of their voices anytime.

"Good, James, good. I have some new information other than about the concentrate trucks." Nathan liked James. They hadn't worked together previously, but when they had met one time before, they seemed to get along well. They had similar backgrounds in industry, including mining, and had quite a few common experiences associated with work, the places they had visited and the people they encountered.

"James," Nathan started. He searched for his words. "From what we can tell, there is definitely something odd about this mill." He paused.

"Go on." James was encouraged, eager for Nathan to continue.

"I managed to get into the concentrate loadout area." Nathan knew he didn't have to explain what that was to James, given his background. "This one is a large room attached to an open-air plant, which is not that unusual, given there is copper and gold concentrate mixed in a pile on the floor. But this room is not just enclosed, it is also secured and guarded, which is more than expected. Another unusual thing is a covered conveyor coming in on the east side that dumped into a stainless-steel hopper. I don't know where the conveyor comes from, nor do I know what it was carrying, but given the subject of our project, I can hazard a guess, you know?" Nathan paused, waiting for James.

"Are you able to find out any more about where the conveyor comes from?" James asked, hoping either Nathan or Elan might be able to stretch themselves a little further.

"All I can see is that it comes in from the jungle about a hundred feet away. I'm not comfortable going there. If either of us gets caught, it might be the end of the project." Nathan clearly felt nervous about what he might be asked to do next.

"Understood. Don't worry about it, Nathan. Let me talk to Matthew and see what we can do and keep you two safe at the same time. We need you to stay in play. I'm not sure how we'll do this yet. But it's likely we'll need you two in the plant when things happen." James had changed his mind. He had hoped Nathan or Eric might try harder. But that would not be such a good move, if they were too nervous. It could only lead to some kind of spotlight on them from the Chinese. No, better to talk to Matthew.

"What about trying to get some confirmation of what's in the hopper, or what they're doing with the product?" James asked, but he wasn't expecting any help. He knew that could also be compromising to Nathan, and Eric by association. It was better to keep these two away from anything that might be risky. They were too important to any future plans.

"I have an idea, James, but I don't think we should go looking for where that conveyor comes from. That would be better left to a professional." Nathan had perked up again, having been assured he wasn't going to have put himself, or Eric, in a more dangerous position than they were in already.

"Oh, great. Do tell." James had also perked up at the news.

"Well, there are thick ten-pound-capacity plastic bags, piled up next to the hopper, which has some kind of a mounting bracket under the chute at the bottom. My guess is the plastic bags hook onto the outcoming chute and get filled with processed cocaine." Nathan stopped, pleased with himself for actually saying out loud what he thought was happening. But that wasn't all.

"Then what, Nathan?" James was impatient to hear more, but he held back his enthusiasm so as not to rattle his friend.

"I think they put the filled plastic bags into some of the concentrate tote bags, so the cocaine ends up somewhere close to the middle. Then they fill the rest of the bag with concentrate and load them on the trucks with all the other bags." Nathan was very proud of his hypothesis as an amateur detective.

"Christ. I'll be damned." James realized how simple it all was. But which bags contained the cocaine?

"How do you think you can tell which bags contain the cocaine?" James asked.

"Not sure yet, James. There must be a mark of some kind on the bag, or perhaps they leave it to the refinery in China once they open the bags." Nathan responded as best he could. But he was dubious about whether his solution made sense.

"I doubt that, Nathan. Once the concentrate tote bags get to the refinery, workers will drop the loads out pretty fast to get it into the furnace. I doubt anyone will want them messing with drugs." James was thinking, but he knew he wouldn't resolve this right now.

oooo

"Matias, can you get a photo of that bag in the warehouse?" James wanted to know why the concentrate bag was dropped off at the warehouse. But the other end of the line was quiet. "Are you still there, Matias?"

Matias was suddenly uncomfortable with where this call was going. It had started off friendly enough as he and James talked about how he was doing, where he was living and all that. Now, he was being asked to do some kind clandestine work. But he knew it came with the territory when working with ORB, and he really wanted to prove his worth at some point. Maybe this was it.

"I'm here, James." Matias sounded fragile.

"Okay." James was relieved that Matias had not automatically turned down the request and went on. "If you can get in without making a fuss, then take a picture of each of the four sides as well as the top of any bags that are there. I need to see if there are any markings that could help us figure out which bags contain the cocaine."

Again, the other end of the line was quiet. A few seconds passed before Matias answered.

"I will have to break in, James." Matias said it as though James didn't know that's what he would have to do. "And maybe there are guards inside, in addition to the one in his car outside."

"Don't do it if you aren't sure you can," James reciprocated. "Keep your eyes on the building all the time. See if there's any schedule change for the guard, and if anyone comes out from the building."

Matias was starting to gain some confidence. After all, he was pretty sure there was only one guard—and he had to sleep sometimes. Matias just needed to figure out when.

"I think the guy in the car is lazy," Matias blurted. "He stays there all day and sleeps a lot."

"What about any movements in or out of the warehouse?" James could tell that Matias was warming up to the idea.

"The only movements are when a new convoy comes and they drop off a bag. But now I see they also take some bags out as well." Matias hadn't reported that yet and was waiting to see if this was a recurring event. "Come to think of it," Matias continued, "every three days, two people arrive, go into the warehouse and stay for maybe twenty minutes, then leave."

"Wow, that's interesting. Where do they take the bags that come out from the warehouse?"

"Over to the ship." Matias didn't need to think about it.

"Wow again." James was a little flabbergasted that Matias hadn't brought this up previously.

"The doors stay locked, the guard stays in his car, and I think he lies down on the back seat during the night." Matias was sounding more confident with each passing minute.

"Okay, Matias. You need to try to get in there. Pick the right time. Make sure you take bolt cutters, unless you can pick the lock or get in another way." James was thinking quickly. Ideally, he would have liked Matias to find another way to get into the building so as to leave the lock in place. If the lock had to be removed by force, it would cause all hell to break loose. But Matias was reading his thoughts and thinking about his own safety.

"I have to find another way in, James. There is a man door at the other end of the building, and I can pick that lock. That would be a safer way." Matias felt pleased. He was relieved that he could still think clearly enough to help with the plan.

"Great. Better get it done as soon as you can." James assumed there would be between zero and three bags in the warehouse at any one time. Hopefully there would be three so Matias could get shots of all of them to compare. He wasn't sure about the visit by those guys, or what they were doing, but he guessed they might be checking that the cocaine was where it was supposed to be.

"I think those guys were protecting their interest and needed to see the product. I don't think we should bother about them right now." James sounded confident but wasn't. It was food for more thought, but right now he didn't want to make Matias any more nervous than he already was.

"Let me know what happens, Matias, and make sure you don't get caught." James winced as he said it, knowing that comment would likely put the fear of God back into Matias. But Matias laughed. He had already come to terms with getting this done, and now seemed as anxious as James to check out the bags.

James was not anxious to talk about what else was happening on the project right now. Better to restrict what each person knew, in case.

They said their goodbyes with Matias promising to call James the next day, whether he got into the warehouse or not.

Chapter 18

Hot and Humid Matias

Despite being an equatorial country, Ecuador did not suffer the intensely hot days that one might expect, especially on the coast. In May, temperatures in Machala were starting to fall. One could expect eighty-degree days but cool nights. On this particular night, there was a light rain as the wet season was trending now toward the drier part of the year.

To Matias, it was a perfect cover for what he had to do. Dark, no moonlight, rain, but with an uncomfortable mugginess in the air that made his clothes stick to his body. It would have to do.

Matias wasn't aware that his ORB security detail, Deek, was in play and watching from across the street from his apartment. Deek was short and sturdy, and wore dark clothing, with a gun in a shoulder holster. Deek followed Matias through the streets back to the port.

Matias parked his vehicle two blocks from the port entrance. He knew a way past the locked gates. He knew that the customs house would have only one or two officials on the graveyard shift at 3 a.m. They were both likely playing games, watching movies or sleeping. Shifts like these didn't usually inspire anyone to spend too much energy on patrol, especially when there were only the banana trucks coming and going. Everything else was closed up for the night.

The lone guard at the concentrate bag warehouse main entrance seemed to be in his usual slumped-over position in his car as he tried to get some sleep.

Deek had driven past Matias's car as he was parking. He stopped a little farther on and went back on foot. He managed to see Matias disappearing through a gap in the fence, to the north of the main gate, and over to north of the dock area.

Matias pulled his hoodie over the top half of his face, being careful to keep his glasses in place. He lowered his head and made his way over to the rear entrance of the warehouse. He worked the door handle in case it was open. It wasn't. He took out a small lock-picking tool kit from his back pocket. He used his phone's flashlight to light the lock as he jiggled the pick into position. He worked it from side to side for a few minutes, until the handle could be pushed down. Matias opened the door a fraction, half expecting an alarm to go off. None did. He opened it a touch more, waiting for the resistance of an internal bolt. There was none, and he opened the door only as far as it allowed him to squeeze in. Despite the rain, outside was still lighter than the inside. There were no lights on in the building or any sign of movement. Rodents were the only inhabitants showing signs of being there. They scurried around, always searching for food, and avoided the traps they had become so familiar with. But when Matias opened the door and stepped through, the rodents first froze then dashed back to their hiding places.

Deek had followed Matias through the fence gap. But he stayed as far away as he could while still keeping Matias's shadow in sight. Then Matias disappeared into the warehouse. He wondered what Matias was up to. No one had told him. But then he remembered why he was there. It was to protect Matias, if needed, no matter what his detail was doing.

Matias glanced at the illuminated face of his watch. Plenty of time. Sunrise would be just after 6 a.m. But he wanted to be out of there before twilight. And who knew when port workers would start their day. *Plenty of time,* he thought for the second time as he tried to put his anxieties behind him. He stood still for almost five minutes as his eyes became accustomed to the dark interior with the man door closed. As they adjusted, he could make out that the warehouse was empty, except for three concentrate tote bags. They sat by the main door at the far end of the building, closest to the wharf. There was also a propane forklift. It was the one Matias had watched lift bags into the building. There were no sounds, even from the rodents.

Without lighting his way, Matias made it over to the bags and placed his hands on top of the first one he came across. He took out his phone and clicked the flashlight. He looked around furtively and shone the light on the woven fabric. There was a simple "2 Ton" notice stamped on it, and he took a photo. The other sides had no markings. Matias stretched up to try to see the top of the bag. Something was there. But he couldn't quite see it clearly enough to get a shot at the angle his camera-holding hand would need. He had to get something to stand on.

Matias knew there was nothing around him to help him up other than the forklift. But he wasn't about to start it, even if the keys were in the ignition or if he could hot-wire it. The engine start-up noise could spell suicide for him. He looked around and realized he might be stuck. Then, he spotted the two propane tanks mounted on the back of the forklift. They were each secured by quick-release straps and a regulator with its hose. He only needed to release one of the tanks.

Matias carried the propane tank to the first bag. He set it down and jiggled it to check it sat flat and didn't rock. He held the first concentrate bag with both hands, one above the other. Pulling himself up onto the top of the propane tank and adjusting his grip, he balanced there and let go of the bag. Pulling out his phone, he selected the camera icon and took a shot of the top of the bag as he rested his chest against the bag. Before stepping down, he looked at the photo, and yes, there was something there. He recognized some kind of Chinese symbol stamped on one corner. He couldn't tell what it meant, but the shot was clear.

The photos of the other two bags showed similar results. Three sides of the other bags were blank, one had the "2 Ton" stamp, while the tops had the same Chinese symbol as the first stamped in one corner.

Before Matias left the building, he carefully replaced the propane tank, secured it in its place and attached the regulator. He climbed down from the back of the forklift, took one look around, then silently went back through the rear door and closed it quietly. He went over to the same spot where he had entered the port and looked at his watch. It was 4:30

a.m., still lots of time before anything happened around the port area. The humidity added to his sweat from the exertion. He was drenched. But he carefully avoided speeding back to his apartment, even though the streets were deserted.

Once indoors, Matias took out his phone again. But he kept the lights off in his apartment, in case anyone was up early and outside. They might wonder what someone else was doing up at such a time. And while they might not think of it again, it might stick in their memory in case someone came asking. He was pleased with himself for being overly cautious. Better that than making mistakes.

Suddenly a thought flashed through his head as he remembered something and sat rigid. He hadn't relocked the door to the warehouse. *Damn.*

But unbeknownst to him, things were even worse.

He hadn't known about the night vision cameras around the edge of the port. They were motion-activated. One was pointing right at the back entrance of the warehouse. The monitors were part of the customs office's communication system. One of the team members checked them every morning during the early coffee meeting. Generally, nothing had to be reported. But on this day, something would catch their attention. Someone crossed the tarmac from the fence line to the back of the northern warehouse in the early hours of the morning. Whoever it was, they didn't stay long and left with nothing they could see.

Chapter 19

Photos

"Nathan. Can you hear me?" James called Nathan at the plant the morning after Matias had sent him the photos. He knew that was when Nathan and Eric would be on their first smoke break of the day and, as usual, they would be wandering over by the camp perimeter fence, to take advantage of the privacy in case a call came through.

"Yes, I can, James," Nathan answered after a brief moment while he looked around.

"Can you talk?" James wondered, aware that it was always difficult to talk to either of them during the day, and this would be the best time to reach one of them.

"I'm sending you a photograph, Nathan. It shows the top of one of the concentrate tote bags at the port. Can you let me know what you think it means?" James pressed Send and the photo was on its way. He had forgotten to mention it was a photo of a Chinese symbol. He remembered only when Nathan confirmed getting it on his phone.

"It's a Chinese symbol, James," Nathan said somewhat surprised.

"That's what I said, didn't I?" James realized he had forgotten that detail. "Oh, maybe I didn't—but what do you think?" He wasn't about to wait to be reminded of his forgetfulness. There were important things to do.

"Well, I recognize what it says, James. 'Good Fortune,' I think. A little odd to use it as a stamp, I suppose, but perhaps it is just that." Nathan paused as he passed his phone to Eric, who looked at the picture. Eric screwed up his face a little as he stared at the photo.

"It's the kind of thing we put on flags and greeting cards during Chinese New Year, that's all. You know, 'Good fortune to everyone, and happiness for the new year' and all that." Eric stopped. There wasn't anything else to say. He kept staring at the photo but seemed a little perplexed. He didn't share his thoughts but dismissed a flash that went through his brain as nothing.

"Is it possible for you to get back into that loadout area and look at the bags before they're filled? I'd like to know if they're made with that sign already stamped on them. Or does someone at the plant put them on? I doubt you'll be able to hang around waiting until someone actually stamps them if that's what they do, but it would be good to see." James hoped either Nathan or Eric might offer to push themselves further, but he doubted it.

"I can get back in there, James, but I don't think I will be able to hang around. Those security guards around that hopper look pretty serious, and I don't want to raise any suspicions. It seems as though there is a heightened sense of alarm on site every so often and we don't know why."

"I think it may be a drill," Eric chimed in. "I was outside for some air the other day, and I watched a group of guards down by the loadout practicing some kind of military-style operation. They all had machine guns and there were half a dozen pickup trucks going back and forth around the plant as though they were searching for someone—but who knows!" Eric's voice faded.

"Okay, do what you can, guys, and let me know if anything turns up." James signed off and sat in his little room with a puzzled look on his face. "Why did he drop off one bag now and again?" he said to himself. "Very odd."

His phone rang. It was Matias.

"James. I have to tell you something." Matias paused, but James waited on the other end of the line. "I got back to my apartment early this morning and remembered I forgot to lock the warehouse door on my way out." Matias didn't sound particularly worried, but James was.

"Oh shit, Matias. Now what?" James sat up straight, focusing on the phone and already working some ideas through his head.

"No worries." Matias sounded almost happy. "I went in extra early this morning and wandered over that way. I don't think anyone discovered the door was open between me leaving and coming back. So, I locked it. Thank God for that. Boy, I was pissing myself and couldn't get to sleep. I had to wait for a couple of hours before I could go into the port with some of the early birds. But I thought I should at least tell you." Matias sounded pleased with himself despite the cock-up.

"Thank Christ for that, Matias. I almost had a heart attack."

Matias laughed with relief. "What do you think of the photo?" he wondered out loud, already forgetting James's potential heart attack.

James was still getting over the shock of Matias having fucked up.

"Good. Eh... good, Matias. Great job." It was. The photos were excellent and exactly what James wanted. Now it was a waiting game until Nathan called back.

"Thanks." Matias was smiling, then stopped short as he remembered the prime reason for his call. "The other trucks came in this afternoon and dropped off a single bag at the warehouse, the same as before. Except this time, a car pulled up as well, and two thuglike characters got out, went into the warehouse, stayed for about thirty minutes, came out, and got back into the car. Next thing I know, the forklift came out with a concentrate bag, then the other two, and took them over to the ship."

"I guess that answers one question, Matias."

"What's that?" Matias already knew but let James verbalize it.

"I think it confirms the cocaine is in the concentrate tote bags. Likely, not every one of them, but it's there, all right. Those guys must have been, let's say, the inspectors checking up on things." James wasn't looking for confirmation from Matias. He didn't need to. It seemed obvious to him, but now the question was, how much and how many bags—or did that matter? He needed to talk to Matthew.

"Thanks, Matias. Again, good job. Keep your eyes open and stay in touch." Their phone call ended. Matias crossed back to the banana warehouse to continue helping with the new load.

Chapter 20

Back in the Jungle

"Hey Boss." Sean had a distinctive, deep, guttural voice, like Sam Elliott's, that seemed to resonate with every word. Generally, he didn't need to introduce himself to anyone who had already met him. They would know in two or three words who he was.

Sean was back at the camp with Matthew and Emma. He plonked down on the bench a few feet away with his camera in one hand on the table in front of him, and a beer in the other. "Glenn's up on the hill." Sean was referring to his cross-shift, as though the others needed to know someone was covering for him.

"Hey, Sean. What have you got?" Matthew was hunched over his laptop while he ate at the same time. Emma sat opposite, doing much the same thing. Both were ensconced in finding out more about the Shuar people. As soon as Sean arrived, they both sat upright to listen to what he had to say.

Boy, Emma thought, *this is one big guy. I hope I never run into him as an enemy.*

Sean sat with muscular arms bursting out from what seemed to be an undersized T-shirt. Tattoos of creeping ivy were inked on both of them. He had legs the size of which just managed to squeeze in under the table. His neck was at least a size twenty-two. It disappeared up into his head with almost no change in width. His head was shaved to within a quarter of an inch of hair, and the sides of his chest squeezed out enough to embarrass any barrel.

"I think I've got some good shots and video on what's going on in the jungle back there." Sean looked back over his shoulder and poked a thumb in the direction of where he was referring to. "I'll send them over to you, but I wanted to let you know what I found in case it wasn't clear." Sean sounded mildly excited, unusual for someone who always seemed calm and didn't talk much.

"Send it." Matthew was eager to see what was going on, although he could guess what the overall picture would mean.

"Done." Sean pressed the camera button, and Bluetooth did the rest. The files were copied to Matthew and Emma. They waited until they came through before the talking started again.

"Okay, so what are we looking at here? It's tagged 'Plant.'" Matthew was studying the first video.

"This shows a conveyor heading over to the main plant," Sean started. "It's quite a distance. I would guess about a thousand feet or so, maybe longer. It stays close to the ground and the road goes over the top of it—right there." Sean poked a big finger at a point on the photo. "The back end comes out of a pretty skookum-looking one-story building. There's a barbed wire fence all around and a couple of dudes that look like they're on guard. You know, pretty heavily weaponized." Sean paused and stared at Matthew and Emma as they were examining the video.

"Did you manage to take a look at the other side of the building?" Matthew didn't take his eyes off his phone and looked at the tags on the other files.

"Yeah. The second file gives you some shots of what appear to be the tops of what could be a couple of silos. You can't see it properly the way the shots are, but these silos are mostly underground, with the tops exposed. You can see where one of the collection conveyors comes out from under one of them. Right there." Sean tried poking his massive index finger over Matthew's shoulder at one of the silos in the video. "See there? That's one of the tops and if you look closely, you may be able to see one that looks like it may be full of something. You may not get that detail 'cause there's a cover over it. I guess to protect against rain, or whatever." He pushed his finger against the screen of the phone as though it would help, but Sean had big hands and that one finger blotted it out. Matthew got the idea, though, while Emma followed along. She was still thinking about how big Sean was and had trouble focusing on the video.

"Did you see anyone near those silos?" It was Emma; her eyes were glued to her screen as she forced herself to concentrate.

"Yeah. I hung around for a while. I was in a pretty safe position. Then these two guys came up from the riverbank with big baskets on their backs and dumped them into what looked like this silo." Sean jabbed his finger at the photo, but Matthew guessed which silo he meant. "Just as they were leaving, another guy turned up and did the same." Sean sat back and went silent, as though that was all he had.

"Great. Good job, Sean. Let's go through the other pictures." Matthew flicked through the files. There were a couple more videos. One showed a riverboat landing area on the riverbank with a couple of aluminum boats tied up to it. There were photos of people with loaded baskets walking toward the half-buried silo. One shot captured another basket being unloaded into the hopper. Then there was a shot of a conveyor coming out from under that silo, and some shots of two doorways into a building. One man door was next to the incoming conveyor with no guard. The other door seemed to be the main entrance of the building, next to the outgoing conveyor that ended up at the loadout. It was enough for what Matthew needed.

"Thanks, Sean. Better get some rest."

"Okay. Will do." Sean got up from the table and sauntered off toward the bunkhouse.

"Christ," Emma whispered as Sean disappeared through the door to his room. "The size of that guy. Geez, did you see his arms?"

Matthew grinned. "Yeah, they're all a bit like that." He went back to staring at his screen and ignored Emma who was picturing Sean in the shower.

They put a mental picture together of what they were seeing from the photos, while talking their way through their thoughts. This would be the collection point for cocaine base, on the Río Quimi. They were pretty sure the building was the cocaine processing plant, a good distance away from the mill. The size of it fit well with what Stockman had described to them. It had armed security on the outside, protecting access to the valuables, and they guessed there would be more on the inside—and maybe even at the river, although none showed in the photos. That long, covered conveyor taking the final product toward the loadout area of the mill ended up in the annex to the water pump house.

"I think that's enough, don't you?" Matthew looked at Emma.

"Pretty organized, I would say." Emma looked from Matthew to her phone as she continued to flick back and forth between the photo files.

"So, if they process the cocaine in that plant near the river, what's in the building hanging off the side of the loadout?" Matthew wondered aloud.

"Maybe secondary processing. Perhaps some kind of dilution or stimulant plant where they add some kind of cutting agent. Who knows, but if that's what it is, this really is the final product for street distribution. Everything is done under one roof. Very clever." Emma raised her eyebrows at Matthew, and he nodded.

"I think you're right, Em." Matthew's eyebrows went up as well, and he and Emma stared at each other for a few seconds while the information sank in. "They may be doing both, bulking it up and adding some kick."

"It's no wonder the cartel wants its territory back. The Chinese have taken everything for themselves." Emma grabbed another couple of beers, wiped the sweat off her face and sat down with Matthew again.

Chapter 21

Luna

It was uncomfortable, hot and all-round tough being over 400 pounds—well, 438 to be exact—unless you were happy by nature and had been overweight from birth. Luna was, and had been.

Luna was a Shuar, one of the original Ecuadorian nomadic tribes of the Amazon. Now, here he was, forty-two years old and single. He cared for his mother, a scrawny person with no teeth, a scrappy head of gray hair, and a body lighter than one of Luna's legs. They still lived in their little hut on stilts overlooking the blue roofs of the Zamora plant camp, with their goats and chickens living underneath, as it should be.

After the Zamora mine development destroyed the other homes, Luna and his mother were among the few remaining in their small Shuar community on the banks of the Río Quimi. The rest had moved farther upriver.

The Zamora construction crews had cleared a sizeable area for the infrastructure of the mine. Why didn't they want his? Maybe his little hut was outside their zone of interest, or maybe too high up to worry about, or... Luna didn't know. He also didn't think much about it. But it was odd that he and his mother were the only ones who had not been displaced by the Chinese.

Not that he wanted to be relocated or compensated, and he certainly didn't want his home to be bulldozed as had happened to so many of his friends' homes. Thirty-two families, some 126 people, had lost their homes after the violent evictions. Zamora company officials arrived at dawn one day and ordered them to hand over their land by order of their own government. Appropriation, they said, and gave them a day to move out. No questions, no answers and little or no compensation.

But Luna and his mother stayed regardless of losing their neighbors. Their family had lived in this spot for at least four generations, if not more. This was where families had been raised, where they knew the jungle and where it knew them. They seemed to live in perfect harmony with nature, providing them with most of their basic needs as the jungle had always done for the Shuar. Even when Luna's father died two years ago, they stayed without a thought of leaving.

As Luna would tell it, his Dad had been consumed—not poisoned—by a snake of all things. He had been working his way through the jungle undergrowth one day with some of his neighbors, focused on picking camu-camu berries. As he stood up straight to stretch his back, he unwittingly came face-to-face with an enormous green anaconda, dangling there, supported from several tree branches. The others picking berries near his father said the snake looked like a small tree. The jungle's growth hid it from even the indigenous people who frequented the jungle every day, like them. In fact, one or two had even crossed its path that very day and not noticed. Perhaps they were a little too far away and didn't appear a threat, so the snake didn't move or even blink. Who knew?

Luna was not shy about telling anyone who cared to listen that while it was a rare event, it was possible for a full-grown adult anaconda—let alone a green one—to stretch its mouth wide enough, with the help of its separating lower jaw, to swallow prey much larger than itself. And this was despite it not being much more than twelve inches in diameter. In this case, Luna thought his Dad must have stunned the animal with his sudden appearance. Then the snake reacted.

From firsthand witnesses, it sounded as though Dad didn't fight much. His head disappeared before his face could show surprise. The anaconda's jaws, with independently moving parts, snapped forward instinctively and almost sucked Dad's head into its mouth. The semi-detached jaw had different pieces that formed around the foreign shape and slowly applied pressure. It would have been agonizing. Before poor Dad knew it, the anaconda's four rows of teeth began pulling in its prey. As it slid its mouth over the body, it would have crushed his dad's shoulder bones and passed him through its esophagus.

When Luna recounted the story, others noted that he appeared detached from his familial relationship to the victim at this point, and seemed to enjoy focusing on the detail of how the anaconda's slimy saliva would have been secreted to lubricate Dad's body and help it slide through the snake's digestive tract while it was being dragged through its system. Luna would shrug at this point as he was telling the story, as though to say, what could anyone do? Dad was already dead from his oxygen being squeezed out from him. Most likely, his bones would have already broken. And, if by some chance, he had not died by that point, he would have drowned in the anaconda's saliva and screamed in pain as his bones broke into even smaller pieces.

As Luna would have it, there was no going back at this point, not even with human interference. One of his friends had tried by hacking away at the snake's body with his machete, but to no avail. He had feared for his own life as the snake's tail wrapped around his legs. But with one mighty blow from his axe, he managed to escape. No one tried to help again.

Trapped inside the anaconda's stomach, Dad would have been dissolved by the powerful acids, enzymes and gastric juices doing their work. It could take a while—maybe days, but more likely weeks—for Dad's body to be completely turned to soup. No one was quite sure when Dad's last breath would have been exhausted.

The good news was that it was rare for an anaconda to eat a human—they were just too big, despite the serpent's articulated jaw.

Luna was a happy-go-lucky individual. Friendly, caring, and ready to help others whenever he could. Some referred to him as a gentle giant and never had a bad word to say about him. But the anger he hid inside himself was threatening his health, and there was no way he was going to sell his soul to the company that had ruined his life, his mother's, and that of everyone he knew. No way he was going to work for those foreign devils.

The offer of working at the Zamora plant as some kind of laborer or cleaner was repellent to him. It was not so much the work, although his weight would surely have been a hindrance to him doing anything other than a sedentary job, like sitting in front of a pile of paper. But what if, God forbid, he was cast as a security guard stationed in that cramped, hot shack at the front gate, on alert at all times in case of an emergency? Was he capable of action in the event of such as situation? No. He knew his limits.

The fact was, Luna hated that fucking plant, and he hated those fucking foreigners who came to construct and then operate it. They had brought ruin to his beloved part of the Amazon. That plant had devastating effects on the Shuar people and the other indigenous communities living in the region. It ruined everything when those damn miners came.

Instead, Luna had gathered some of his practical acquaintances—almost all of whom were good with their hands—into forming a small band of handymen who made a pitiful but adequate living from servicing a wide area of dispersed Shuar patriots and other indigenous communities. They all shared his anti-mining views. They were well-integrated. They helped each other against common causes. They all shared the need to live off the riches of their beloved Amazon. But many of them still needed income, so now they worked on coca plant farms that fed the Zamora plant. Or, God forbid, mundane, unskilled jobs in a huge room full of machinery, in an environment diametrically opposite from where they came from. From the jungle to that fucking plant.

The Shuar people had lived in their territory in the Amazon since ancient times. They adapted their life, culture, customs, and spirituality to it. Despite always being an overly large person often associated with a life of lethargy, Luna worked hard demonstrating his commitment to the Shuar culture and would tell his story to anyone showing the slightest interest.

He would search out what he thought were tourists. That would be anyone passing through—whether on vacation or business—and he would strike up a conversation. The beauty of Luna was that he could speak perfect English and a smattering of other languages, all thanks to his mother. She had scrimped and saved to send him to college in Cuenca, where he could learn languages. That was all he was interested in, and that was good enough for his *mamá*.

When Luna was twenty, he migrated to the coast in search of a new adventure. His size was enough of a qualification for him to get work on a ship traveling the Pacific seaboard. It sailed north to San Diego, Los Angeles, San Francisco and Vancouver, and it was there where Luna decided to spend some time working in the valley and perfecting his English. He picked blueberries, then became a construction laborer. Eventually, his homesickness got the better of him and he joined a freighter heading to Lima. From there, Luna caught the bus back to Guayaquil and begged rides back to Tundayme, a stone's throw from his home. By then, his English was as good as anyone's.

One day, while Luna was working with his crew on building an annex to the camp where Matthew and Emma were staying, he wandered over to share some words and a coffee with Hugo, a friend of his who helped

Rodriguez, preparing the evening meals for their guests. They knew each other well and often talked about the latest foreign guests staying at the camp. Hugo mentioned two of the guests and their association with the McArthur Foundation. Luna listened with increasing interest, and as they talked, a Toyota Land Cruiser came through the camp entrance and pulled up in front of Rod's Place, as everyone referred to the camp, named after the main cook and bottle washer.

Matthew and Emma climbed out of the vehicle and, coated with sweat, called for beers.

Hugo called out to one of his girls, "Lola, *dar unas cervezas!*" as he waved over to the two guests.

"*Gracias,* Hugo. *Muchas gracias!*" Matthew responded with enthusiasm. It was clear they needed refreshment, as Lola pushed the two bottles in front of them and smiled, displaying her pearly white teeth and beautiful round dark eyes.

Luna took hold of two more bottles for himself and slipped over to the bench on the opposite side of the table from where they were sitting.

"Mind if I sit, *señor?*" Luna smiled first at Matthew and then at Emma. He flicked off the top of one of the beer bottles with his thumbnail and took a long drink.

Matthew raised his eyebrows and looked at Emma, who did the same.

"Sure. I'm Matthew, this is Emma." He held out a hand across the table, and Luna took it and shook his hand. He did the same to Emma's hand as she offered it.

"My name is Luna," he said as he put a hand across his heart, as though the other parties wouldn't understand the term "*my name is.*"

"Great. And you speak English." Emma smiled and leaned in closer across the table. "Are you from around here, Luna?" Emma started the conversation, and right then Luna knew he had a captive audience.

"I am Shuar." He waited to see if they recognized the name. They seemed to, although they said nothing. "I live with my mother over near the Zamora plant." Luna smiled and pointed to a place over to the northeast as he waited for a response.

"We were over there today. Quite a place, eh? They must have cleared an awful lot of the jungle to develop that mill, Luna. Were you around during that time?"

Luna looked sad. His wide face seemed to sag.

"Yes. They were terrible days for us." Luna already knew who his new friends worked for, and it wasn't the mine, so he felt free to talk.

"Oh." Matthew's interest was piqued.

"They destroyed so much just for money." Luna looked from one face to the other, wondering where he should go with his story. Something about these tourists was different, but he didn't know what it was.

Luna went on, "Did you know that Zamora is the largest mine in Ecuador's history, with what will become the second-largest tailings dam in the world?" He stopped and waited for the statistic to sink in.

"Yes, we know. It's one reason we're here," Matthew responded cautiously, not sure yet who he was talking to. This large man in front of them seemed pleasant enough, spoke English well, was an indigenous person, and seemed to want to talk. Matthew wondered whether this was their man. Could he be useful? Could they use him for what they needed?

"What do you do around here, Luna?" Emma was making small talk. She could tell what Matthew was thinking and wanted to give him a few moments to put his thoughts together.

"Oh, I'm just a contractor. We do small jobs in the communities." Luna didn't want to get into the minutiae. He preferred to bang his favorite drum, so he changed the subject back to what he wanted most. "You know, its future is still uncertain."

"Whose future?" Emma wondered, and she sat back with a beer in her hand.

"The Zamora plant. There's a lot of conflict between a Chinese company and the villagers of Tundayme—including the Shuar, you know. We're focused on recovering our ancestral lands, and one day we will." Luna paused, but before either of his newfound friends could speak, he waved a hand around him and went on. "You know, this is what scientists and biologists consider one of the richest and least explored areas in Ecuador, maybe in the world," Luna exaggerated somewhat, stopped, and took his arms off the table, resting his hands at his sides on the bench. He knew he was starting to get animated and needed to calm down a little or he could frighten these tourists off.

"Yes, we know, Luna. It's an incredibly biodiverse environment. There are animal and plant species thriving here that don't exist anywhere else in the world. Did you know that they discovered a new species of snake, the largest in the world? The green anaconda!" Emma had leaned forward again and laid her arms out across the table, while Matthew sat upright and studied his beer.

Luna laughed. Matthew and Emma looked at each other and furrowed their brows, wondering what had caused Luna to break out laughing. Then he told them the story of his father as more beers were brought over with food. It was difficult for Emma to finish her meal by the time Luna got to the end of his story and described how his father had been turned into soup in the belly of a green anaconda. As Luna said, this was not a new species of snake to him.

As the late afternoon and evening wore on, Luna talked passionately about how Zamora had upended his life and the lives of everyone within a fifty-mile radius of the plant.

"And now they are going to expand the plant and raise the dam. It will become the highest in the world, and I have it on good authority it is not safe now, and even worse in the future." Luna rested a moment. Even he, as a native, was sweating from the humidity. He looked over at the table next to them. One of the group there was playing with a tarantula he had caught that day in the jungle. Luna didn't like the thought of teasing animals, but he held back from doing anything about the spider. Those tourists would likely let it go once they had enough of teasing it.

"I have to go, my friends. My mother is waiting, and I have to get the crew back to their homes." Luna struggled to raise himself from the table. There were stains from the food he had devoured on his T-shirt. He didn't seem to care as he put his hand out to his friends.

"Are you back here tomorrow, Luna?" It was Matthew.

"Yes, we have to finish that building over there." Luna pointed to the west of where they were sitting. It looked like an expansion of the camp, although it wasn't clear what it was going to be. Bunkhouses, judging by the high occupancy level of the current camp.

"Let's talk more." Matthew shook Luna's hand and waved. The big man made his way to where his crew were finishing their meals at the other end of the eating area.

Matthew and Emma looked at each other. They seemed to be thinking the same thing but didn't discuss it until they got back to their bunkhouse, showered, and climbed into bed after searching for bugs inside the net. There weren't any—at least not that they could see.

"I think I'll give Stockman a call in the morning. There's a plan formulating in my head, and you know something, Em? We may have a solution to all this." Matthew felt too alive with his new plan to play night games with Emma. He knew that would likely be the key to relax his brain, but it would have to wait. In any event, Emma was already breathing heavily when Matthew glanced over at her. She had dropped into a deep sleep as soon as her head hit the pillow. He bent over and kissed her on the forehead before lying back with his eyes open as he thought. Perhaps Luna, or someone like Luna, may be the answer they were looking for to work with the coca farmers.

Chapter 22

Cocaine in the Bag

Nathan and Eric had been at the Zamora plant now for over three weeks and had become familiar sights as they poked around. So far, so good, they told themselves. Their confidence was growing. They were looking for another way to get into the loadout area to see the concentrate tote bags. But they also knew by now that gaining entry when the bags were actually being loaded was very unlikely unless there was some kind of emergency in there.

Initially, they couldn't figure out how to return to the loadout area without attracting attention. Then, Nathan went over to the concentrate filters. He made it look like he was doing what the other operators had gotten used to him doing—checking the equipment. He made sure it was all working, not overheating, free of oil drips, and with tight connections. He lingered around the entry points in the loadout area separation wall. The concentrate was filtered and delivered next door into the kilns for drying. He realized that if he bent down a little, he could see through the rubber skirting. It provided some kind of screen over the conveyors as they poked through the metal cladding.

When he bent into a certain position, located over the filter motors, he could see into the loadout area. He waited and stared some more. He adjusted his position to make it look like he was examining some machine. Then, he saw the bags next to the loading machine. Right now, nothing was happening. The concentrate in the kiln was being heated as it moved through. But it seemed as though people were getting ready for something to happen.

When Nathan looked beyond the bag loader, he saw a collection of small ten-pound-capacity plastic bags, containing a white substance, near the cocaine hopper. The top of each bag was secured with a metal wire. A fierce-looking individual, with a small submachine gun at the ready, stood guard over the collection. Nathan suspected these bags were to be hidden into the concentrate totes.

Nathan's time was running out. Lingering too long in that one place would undoubtedly seem odd to any other operator. As he straightened up to leave, he smeared some oil from under the filter motor casing on his hands and took out his plant radio.

"Control room, this is Nathan." He knew his call would be heard all over the plant and intended it to be, so everyone knew where he was and what he was about to do.

"Go ahead, Nathan," a voice came back from the control room.

"It looks as though we have a little problem here at the filter. Some oil is leaking. Not serious, but I'll tighten the flanges for now and have maintenance change the gasket out later. I think that will work for a while, but can you shut down the number two filter pump just in case?"

"Will do," the voice from the control room answered, and immediately Nathan heard the sound of the pump motor winding down.

"Thanks, control," Nathan talked into the radio. He didn't need a response, but followed up with, "I'll contact you when I'm done."

He assumed the control room had heard his message and he took a wrench from his tool belt. He always wore one in the plant. It was in case some small fixes or adjustments were needed and were too small to bother a maintenance worker.

First, Nathan smeared oil on the concrete floor under the number two motor to make it appear as though there had been a leak. Then he bent low again, wrench in hand, and peered through the rubber curtain, being careful not to draw the thin straps back too far. That would most likely invite someone to investigate, even if they thought they could just help him in some way.

This time he took a spyglass with a powerful lens from his tool belt. It was a small black metal gadget hardly worth the attention of anyone who might glance at it, but it magnified a target ten times. He aimed the scope at the concentrate tote bags on the floor. Then, he swung it over to the cocaine bags. Two had been picked up by an operator who was moving toward the concentrate bag loader. Someone else had picked up an empty concentrate tote bag and was preparing to fit it under the concentrate loader hopper. As he did so, Nathan got a clear view of three sides, and a partial view of the top as it was unfolded and before it was flipped over one of the sides. He couldn't make out any markings but continued to focus on the loading procedure.

The concentrate started to pour into the bag as the person holding the filled cocaine bags climbed a small ladder and looked into the loader hopper. He seemed to be watching for a particular moment, and when that came, he dropped the first cocaine bag in, then the second before the flow of concentrate buried them. Once the tote bag was filled, a small column-mounted jib crane lifted it across and onto the floor of the building.

Okay, Nathan thought as he waited to see whether he would be able to see the full surface of the top of the bag.

"Need any help, Nathan?" someone asked from a few feet away. A startled Nathan swung his body around to face the filter motor. He started to sweat, not knowing who it was or what they had seen. His wrench was still in his hand as he looked up over the motor at a grinning face close to him, but not close enough to have seen what he had been doing. Nathan relaxed a little as he saw that it was one of the maintenance people who had been sent over by the control room to help check on things.

"All good here, Arturo. Thanks, I think I've got this, but you may want to check the gasket out soon." Surprisingly, Nathan's voice was calm, and he congratulated himself on having such self-control.

He watched as Arturo climbed down from the filter press mezzanine and sauntered back toward his office along the steel walkway between the flotation tanks.

Nathan allowed himself a moment to relax before he hunched down again to peer through the rubber curtain. By now, a second concentrate bag was hanging under the loader, and the first was sitting next to it on the floor. It was now in a perfect position for Nathan to see the top. He took out his phone, fixed a magnifying lens to it, and snapped a shot. *Perfect,* he thought. He didn't waste any time examining it other than to notice the same logo as the one in the photo sent to him. Selecting the photo, he emailed it to James.

As Nathan swung the spyglass back to the second tote bag under the hopper, he caught a movement near the first bag out of the corner of his eye. He quickly turned the lens back to that spot. The guy who had placed the cocaine bags was leaning over the first concentrate bag with something in his hand hovering over the logo. Even with magnification, Nathan couldn't see what it was he had done, but he took another zoom photo in case, and sent it to James. He hadn't time to tag either photo in his haste to get out of the filter location.

His time was up, and Nathan straightened, deliberately wiping his hands on a cloth he carried in his pocket, and picked up the walkie-talkie.

"All good, control. You can energize filter pump number two again."

With that, the sound of the motor winding up was a sign for him to leave the area and return to his office.

Once their shift was over, Nathan and Eric took a short stroll around the outside of the camp to compare notes.

"No one seemed concerned in the control room while you were over at the filters," Eric assured his friend.

"Good. I had to get creative to see through the rubber curtains to take some photos but I managed and then sent them immediately to James." Nathan seemed relaxed now that his part of the exercise was over. "I don't know if they will help him, but at least I was able to do what he wanted."

Now that Nathan thought about what he did, he sort of liked that rush of adrenaline and felt a little more emboldened by the escapade. Perhaps James would ask him to do something else to further the cause.

While Nathan was still feeling good about what he had done, and Eric was at his side reveling in his friend's newfound courage, they turned the corner to head back to camp for supper. As they did, they came face-to-face with four armed security guards blocking their way. Two reached out and spun Nathan and Eric around one hundred and eighty degrees to face the security building. The other two pressed rifles into their lower backs and nudged them forward.

Chapter 23

What Have I Done?

Ping Pei sat in his office, chain smoking his Winstons, and searching for some invisible solution to his problem. Well, his current problem, that was.

It seemed the Zamora plant security had seized Nathan and Eric, his two shining stars and examples of what he had been relying on to be his moment of glory. Small glory though it was, it was at least some kind of recognition that he was even on a rung above the lowest on the ladder on the Quito organization chart. But this, whatever it turned out to be—and it was likely nonsense—could cloud how the others looked at him.

Ping Pei had yet to get the full story. But it seemed that a high-resolution camera hidden in the roof of the Zamora plant had spotted Nathan near the filters, on the mill side of the loadout wall. On its face, it seemed innocent. The problem was that he had told the control room his plan was to stop a leak from a filter motor. But they had seen him on film peering through the rubber curtains into the loadout area. No one watching the security footage knew why he would be doing that if he was attending to a motor leak. Nathan was not authorized to be looking at anything in the loadout area.

It also seemed as though Nathan had been using some device. He was aiming it at something in that forbidden area. Even worse, someone could see him pointing what looked to be a cell phone through the curtain. One had to assume he was taking photos. The security service confirmed it. They searched and took everything from their bodies except their clothes and found two photos on the phone of concentrate tote bags in the loadout area. Ping Pei was unsure of their importance, but he knew he had a problem.

Apparently, Eric, Nathan's associate, was clean. But, based on the assumption that the two were so close, authorities detained him as well by default. It was assumed that if one person did wrong, they should also hold the other accountable. And so it was they were both in detention at the security office waiting for orders from Ping Pei.

It was not the day to meet his Chinese embassy friend, Wang Ho Lin, at La Cruz del Papa. But now, with this latest piece of news in hand, it was necessary to send him a signal for a meeting to take place immediately. Ping Pei had his secretary send a private cryptic message to Wang Ho Lin. It said: *The sky is gray in Beijing.* To the receiver, it meant "We need to meet today, same time, same place."

As usual, he found Lin sitting on a bench. He was facing the traffic on the west side and smoking. He didn't appear relaxed, as he usually did. His body seemed tense, and as Lin turned to see his friend coming toward him, Ping Pei could see his face was gray. That, in itself, made Ping Pei's face turn gray as well. He sat three feet away from Wang Ho Lin, took out a Winston, poked it into his mouth and lit it. This time there was no relaxing as the smoke filtered through his lips into the surrounding air.

"We have a problem, Mr. Lei." Ho Lin didn't take his eyes off the company man. He always addressed him as "Mr." whenever there was something serious to discuss. It was a disarming habit. No chitchat, no pleasantries, a simple, piercing statement of foreboding.

Ping Pei raised his eyebrows as though he was surprised.

"You already know?" Ping Pei asked.

The two looked at each other for a moment.

"Know what?" asked Wang Ho Lin. He couldn't guess what his friend had on his mind, other than what he knew himself. But the fact that he had started with "We have a problem," and that had made Ping Pei start caused Lin to assume there was something else. Something he wasn't aware of yet. It could only get worse.

Ping Pei relayed the information about Nathan and Eric, and the fact that they were both in a detention cell at the plant, awaiting their fate. He was quick to defend himself.

"How could I know? They seemed such perfect candidates—everyone at the plant respected them. They were doing such a great job. Those bastards. What have they been doing? What must I do?" Ping Pei was beside himself now as the steam he had gathered dissipated. Wang Ho Lin sat perfectly still and listened. Not even a puff of a cigarette while Pei was going through the drama.

When Ping Pei appeared to have stopped, he looked at his friend with a pathetically sorrowful look. Wang Ho Lin knew it was his turn.

"I suppose this news does not surprise me, Mr. Lei." There was that *Mr.* again. Ping Pei knew it meant trouble. He stayed quiet, his head bent. He looked like a subservient dog who knew he'd done something wrong but wasn't yet sure how bad it was.

"My news from Beijing is bad, Mr. Lei. This event at the Zamora facility supports our suspicions."

Ping Pei's eyes raised to meet Wang Ho Lin's. *Here it comes,* he thought.

"You see,"—Wang Ho Lin was drawing things out as only the Chinese can do when they have important information to pass on—"your friends…"

"Not my friends, Mr. Lin. Just acquaintances I wish I had never met. I meant no harm."

"I believe you, Mr. Pei. But we cannot change the past. I wish we had discovered these things earlier." Wang Ho Lin was drawing this out too long. It was killing Ping Pei to wait.

"It seems your… acquaintances may be working against us and spying on behalf of others. We see evidence of their previous work for companies that have suffered in the aftermath of their presence. We… Beijing and I… believe that there could be a group of, let's say, misfits amongst us working to interrupt our business quite apart from these two. That would be not only copper and gold production, but other business." Wang Ho Lin didn't have to explain what the other business meant. Nor did he intend to explain how he had found out that Nathan and Eric were spies. Or that there could be others like them at the plant. But the messaging was clear to Ping Pei. He had personally taken two intruders into their operation. Who knew what they discovered or who they contacted on the outside?

"How so?" Ping Pei was losing his sad shroud. He was realizing that there could be spies among them. The spies might be from a competitor, or a company looking to take them out and steal their mineral rights. Or worse, they could be from a company looking to take their drug business. Nothing was too subversive in this game, and the Chinese knew that game well.

"Do you think it could be the cartel?" he asked, not believing it himself. A cartel would come in guns blazing, throats slit, hanging operators from trees around the plant, all for the sake of intimidation. Spying was definitely not their style.

"No." Wang Ho Lin was abrupt in his response and slung one arm over the back of the bench as he now stared at Ping Pei. "We have been monitoring the cartels. As far as we know from what we hear, they are leaving us alone." He paused and turned his head away from Ping Pei. "We doubt they will want to mess with China, and, after all, our share of their trade in Ecuador is small compared to theirs." Wang Ho Lin was not familiar with how cartels think. Otherwise, he would have known they wanted everything for themselves. The fact that this was a Chinese operation would not matter in the least to them. Sharing, no matter what the proportions, was not their style.

They both sat staring at the traffic for half a minute, before Ping Pei offered, "Should we dispose of them? I mean Nathan and Eric."

Wang Ho Lin turned his head toward his friend, or perhaps it was now his ex-friend. "I believe that would be utterly stupid, Mr. Pei." His face was grim, and his mouth distorted to show his disgust at the thought. "Let them go," he responded to Ping Pei's obvious shock. "Let's see where they go, who they meet, what they say. Once we know more, we will dispose of them." Wang Ho Lin's face gave nothing away. But beneath that façade, there was rage, a little panic, and a lot of remorse about not finding out sooner.

"Take them back to Quito and leave them there." Wang Ho Lin slowly picked out another Winston from his pack. He tapped one end on the bench as if it had no filter. He still did it as a subconscious habit from smoking non-tipped cigarettes which needed that knock to pack the tobacco down. He bent his head a little to meet his rising hand and took the nicotine stick between his lips. Ping Pei leaned over to light it.

Ping Pei didn't ask Wang Ho Lin what would happen after Nathan and Eric were released in Quito. But he guessed that authorities would follow them, tap their phones and never let them out of sight. This would continue until they left Ecuador. Or, until the embassy's security service decided they needed to be disposed of. After that, they would be dealt with, whether they were still in the country or had left. It didn't matter. They were doomed regardless. It was just a matter of time.

Chapter 24

Chinese Signs

The photos James had received from Nathan had no taglines. Nor was there a follow-up message from him or Eric. James's thought that was very strange. But he became engrossed in studying the two pictures of the tops of concentrate tote bags, making him forget the mystery of not having heard from his guys at the plant. He pushed it to the back of his mind for now.

James wondered why Nathan had sent two shots of the same sign. He kept flicking between both on his phone. He enlarged each, a small section at a time, but by now his room was getting dark as the sun set. He wasn't quite sure, but... he could tell they were different bags from the shadows falling across them. As he stared with even more focus, and despite the fading light, he thought he saw a slight difference. Or was it some dirt, or some blemish, or the way the fabric was woven? But no. He was beginning to believe it was a part of the photo. That "speck" filled part of one quarter of one part of the sign and seemed to have a bit of a tail. *Surely,* James thought, *the stamp would be the same on all the bags.* But this one was a bit different. Not enough for a very casual eye to spot, but enough to catch the attention of someone who might be looking for it.

He wanted to compare the two signs side by side. But he couldn't do so on his phone. So, he had to flip back and forth.

James pulled a magnifying glass out of his bag. It was something he carried in the field. He thought it displayed a touch of professionalism, like a geologist with a rock pick. He was always ready to examine some sample of fauna that any one of the environmentalists thought they had discovered. They would want to share the finding with everyone, anyone. Even James.

Then it became clear. What Nathan had sent was a photo of the top of a concentrate bag with one sign. The other was of the same Good Fortune sign, but with part of it slightly changed with something like a black marker.

James's brain went into overdrive: it had to be some kind of telltale indicator. He could guess what that was likely to be. Now he needed to confirm his thoughts with Nathan, so where in hell was he?

The discovery elated him—if that's what it was. But what did it mean? That was something Matthew was going to have to figure out. He needed to contact Nathan before he made that call.

Nathan's radio was dead. There was no sound as James fiddled with the frequency just in case. He put a call into Sean's position. It could be Sean or Glenn on duty. James wasn't sure, nor did it matter. They had stationed themselves up near Luna's place. It seemed to be a dead spot for activity, but they were able to see a large part of the plant from there.

Most of the time, whoever was on duty would hold a pair of high-powered military binoculars to his eyes. If he wasn't doing that, he was surveying the place, looking for any suspicious movement. And that meant almost every movement. After all, neither had any real idea if something was suspicious or not in this environment. The comings and goings of a mine plant were completely foreign to them. But then, both knew enough to tell if something seemed out of place. If they weren't sure, they took photos and video.

"Sean. Is that you? It's James. What's new?" The radio crackled a little, and James thought Sean or Glenn might be causing it. *Whoever it is, is probably sitting in some pit with a covering of grass and shrubs,* he thought to himself. At least that was how he imagined them.

"Sean here. Nothing much, James. What's new with you?"

"Sean, I'm worried about Nathan and Eric. They sent me some photos, and then nothing. I haven't heard from them in a while. It's not like them to go missing in action. I need to talk to them. Any thoughts?"

"Well, I did see them a while ago, after their shift had finished. They were in a group of guards headed toward the security post. I couldn't tell if it was odd or not, so I took some photos. I'll send them to you. But now you've said what you said, my guess is they got themselves into some trouble. Come to think of it, I haven't seen them come out of that building yet, so it's been a while." Sean went quiet, reproaching himself for not putting two and two together earlier. Still, he wasn't posted in that spot to look out for Nathan and Eric. They should have been accepted by now as a part of operations.

"Try to get closer and see if you can make contact. Take one of your guys with you, in case." James was worried. If Nathan and Eric had really been taken by security, what if they talked more than they should? He needed to get a message to Matthew. Sean was going to have to bring his cross-shift guy in from Matthew's position.

"Will do. I'll get Glenn over here from the camp. It'll take a few hours to get organized, but we should be able to get down there when it gets dark. That would be the best time to do this, anyway."

"Good, Sean. Let me know what happens the moment you get some news. Oh, and don't go trying to bust them out if they're in some lockup. We'll need to think carefully about what we have to do to get to them if that's what's happened. Understood?"

"Got it, James. No sweat." The call was over as soon as Sean heard the crackle of James's radio signing off.

oooo

"I think we've got ourselves a problem." James put a call in to Matthew as soon as he got off the radio from Sean. He told him what he had noticed from Nathan's photos and that he assumed it indicated cocaine would be in those bags with the disfigured Chinese symbol. Matthew had agreed but both were anxious to talk to Nathan before telling the rest of the crew.

"I have to assume that someone caught Nathan snooping where he shouldn't have been." Matthew was thinking and talking at the same time.

"I've asked Sean to see if he can get close enough to Nathan to ask him what happened and see if he can confirm what we saw in the photos," James said as he adjusted himself in his chair so he could look out of the window. The boys were playing soccer again on the gravel patch.

"Okay, let's see what he comes up with." Matthew was playing with a plan in his head just in case thing went wrong with Sean trying to get close.

"I told him to make sure he doesn't spring them from there, even if he gets the chance." James hoped he had made the right decision.

"Yeah, you're probably right."

There was silence as the two of them mulled over whatever options they could muster.

"We may have to lay low and see what happens to them. I doubt there will be anything serious right now. The Chinese will want to find out what they were doing and who they're working for. At this point, we have no reason to think they know anything. Except, perhaps, that Nathan was in the wrong place at the wrong time." Matthew furrowed his brow as he thought more. He slumped onto a bench at the camp, where he had gone looking for a beer. It was the middle of the night, and no one was around. He found a quiet spot over by the small cooking area where he could keep his eyes on the landscape. Emma had fallen asleep a while ago, tucked up under her mosquito net.

"You're right. I'll call Sean in a few hours. I assume Glenn has left."

"Yeah, I heard his pickup fire up a few minutes ago. He should be with Sean shortly. I guess there'll still be time to take a look in the guardhouse before dawn if they can do it."

"I think so. They should be in and out in about thirty minutes once they meet up. They're likely in radio contact with each other about now, I would think." For some reason, James looked at his watch as though everything was on a scheduled timeline. Which, of course, it wasn't, other than they were racing against the light of the early morning in about four hours.

"Okay, James. Let me know as soon as you know anything. Oh…" Matthew just caught James before he hung up. "And tell Sean not to—"

"I already have," James interrupted, knowing what Matthew was about to say. "No heroics. No killing. No identification, and leave no traces, right?" Matthew signed off, took a swig of beer, and decided to wait it out rather than go back to his hut. It would only disturb Emma. For some reason, he felt safer from the bugs here on the bench outside than in his bunk, even though a net would cover him. It was just the way he felt. Or it was the fact his eyes were open and his ears were alert.

Chapter 25

Matias... Oh, Matias

In 2022, Ecuadorian customs, an independent organization, created a new, vital, exciting and youthful group of customs officials. They were established to battle corruption and improve integrity on the import-export front. Unfortunately, even in more pious organizations than the customs service, there were always rotten apples among humans.

Adolfo Garcia—known as Adolf to his Puerto Bolívar customs staff due to his sociopathic tendencies—contacted a Tongyan associate in Quito: Mr. Ping Pei.

Neither spoke the other's language. They might try using pidgin English if the subject was simple. But they would more likely use a Tongyan provided Spanish–Chinese translator on the speaker phone. The translator would sit next to Mr. Pei when a native Ecuadorian called and needed to talk in Spanish.

"Mr. Pei. It seems you may have a male snooper in your midst." The word *snooper* confused Ping Pei. The translator was a little slow to find the right way to translate *fisgón* to *snooper*. But eventually, not only did she translate it, but she described it better to Ping Pei.

Having gotten that out of the way, Adolfo Garcia continued.

"We saw this person, this snooper—a man we think—breaking into your warehouse here at the port. Our perimeter cameras caught his image two nights ago at two thirty a.m. It seems he's interested in what's in that building of yours. He was out of our sight for about twenty minutes and when he came out, he went back the way he came—through a gap in the fence to the east of the property. We didn't know about it until now. Then we lost track of him." Adolfo waited for a response. Ping Pei was thinking.

Of course, he knew what was in that building. There was always at least one bag of concentrate—and, of course, the other stuff—there at any one time. That's what the snooper must have been searching for. But they should be able to tell if he had rummaged in the bag. If not, then what?

"Do you know who this *snooper* is?" Ping Pei sounded hopeful that the high-resolution cameras would have done a good job. But at night? He wasn't so sure.

"We don't know... yet." Adolfo let the response drag out a little. He was pretty sure they would identify the intruder. While they hadn't done so yet, it seemed clear to him that the person knew the port's layout. That might help to narrow the search.

"Why did you wait so long before telling me, Adolfo?" Ping Pei was courteous, but annoyed that no one had informed him as soon as it happened.

"The tapes are not always reviewed immediately, Mr. Pei. They are not high priority for us. One of our people does that when things are slow and we can afford the time." Adolfo was cool and patient. Ping Pei knew that the officials at Puerto Bolívar were likely never busy and up to things not part of customs duties. But now was not the time for awkwardness.

"I see. Yes, of course, all those other duties. But perhaps you can send me a copy of the tape and we can examine it here." Mr. Pei was hopeful.

"It will be in the overnight courier bag to Quito." Adolfo was quite accommodating, since Mr. Pei was contributing to his retirement fund. "One of our people will bring it over to you when it arrives at our headquarters. In the meantime, we are still looking at the footage and trying to determine who this was." The fact that someone was coming and going into *his* port at their leisure, so to speak, aggravated him. Adolfo wanted to figure this out for himself if he could, despite the extra work neither he nor his team wanted. Apart from having to fix the gap in the fence, they also had to deal with a trespasser. But none of his team wanted to go chasing after anyone or anything. After all, wasn't this supposed to be an easy life? They laughed amongst themselves at the idea of doing anything hard. And, who knew? This could even be dangerous.

"Thank you, Adolfo. Please let me know if you identify the culprit, and I will do the same for you. Whoever it is, he is either working at the port now or *has* worked at the port, if he knows his way around like that." Ping Pei was perturbed. Two suspicious episodes now needed his attention, causing him worry. *Could this be a coincidence, or are they connected?* he wondered. Perhaps it was time to meet his embassy associate again.

After the call, Adolfo sat as far back in his chair as he could without tipping over, his hands folded behind his head as he wrestled with the problem of how to go about catching this "snooper."

One by one, Adolfo thought about the members of his small team. Who could he get to help who would take the job seriously? His thoughts landed on young Agata. Eager, energetic, fit, still keen, and willing to do anything it took to rise through the ranks. She was single, had no outside restraints on her life, and she was incredibly nosy. In fact, she was so nosy that it had become a problem, as she often poked her nose into places where a nose was unwelcome.

"Agata, would you come into my office, please?" Adolfo used the radio and waited. He saw the young customs official get up from her chair. She shook her long black hair back over her shoulders, turned and marched toward his office. *Yes,* Adolfo thought, *just the person.*

Adolfo and Agata watched the video together. They enlarged, focused and zoomed in on parts. They looked for signs, made notes, and talked through the scenario. Why, what, and who were the questions they raised between them. They spent two hours reviewing the evidence. They scratched together a profile of the offender. They deduced that he was male, slim, and not that young. They judged this from his movements and the awkwardness of his body as he bent, rose, ran and walked. He wore glasses, judging from the profile. No major facial features, such as a large nose or protruding chin. No runners, so it must be some kind of soft shoe or boot. He wore black clothes, but then what else would one expect? He had no bag or anything in his hands that they could see. He appeared nervous. He kept swiveling his head and doing other small things that didn't matter much. But, together, these things could discount many people. The short, the fat, limpers, the young, those without glasses, and so on. It wasn't great, but it was some kind of profile to focus on.

Adolfo concluded that it must be someone who currently worked at the port. The warehouse's comings and goings were somewhat new to the port. In fact, it had only been going on for a matter of a couple of years at this point. The intruder would have to know something valuable was in the warehouse. It would have to be worth the trouble to break into the port secretly in the middle of the night.

Yes, Adolfo and Agata agreed, they needed to start by focusing on the banana crew. They were the only constant workers at the port. Any one of them could watch the drivers of the concentrate cargo. It was at least a good start.

Agata was excused from her customs duties. She went to the banana warehouses and made a visual assessment of every worker as they came on duty and left. Long hours, but for a nosy person, very rewarding.

It took Agata three days to narrow down her list of suspects to only three. One of them was Matias, the newest member of the crew and an out-of-towner at that. He fit the vague description perfectly, but then so did the other two. He was a loner with no friends. He never went out except to eat. He didn't mix at work and was always glancing over at the concentrate trucks when they were at the port. He was especially obvious when an occasional concentrate bag was dropped off at the warehouse. His head would swivel between the building, the trucks and the rest of the port. It seemed like he expected to get caught doing something he shouldn't. It would take Agata another two days to set her sights firmly on Matias and report to her boss.

"Good, Agata. Very good." Adolfo was pleased with what Agata had concluded. He agreed with her conclusion, for lack of a worthy alternative. She had earned her bonus and was sent back to the drudgery of being a customs official with little to do.

Chapter 26

Mack and Deek to the Rescue

Mack and Deek were ORB's assigned security detail for Matias. They had been keeping an extra careful eye on him since he broke into the warehouse.

Mack took the midnight-to-noon watch, and Deek covered noon to midnight. It wasn't possible to see Matias at all times during the day when he was working at the port. He often disappeared into the banana warehouses, where anything untoward could happen to him. But they decided that if anything went awry, it would not likely happen when there were other people around. The more dangerous times would be when he was alone, pacing the port by himself during breaks, or when his shift was over and he went back to his rooms.

Time governed the routine Matias had set up for himself. His ritual was very reliable, on time to within fifteen minutes. Except when he was helping with the banana crates. Mack and Deek depended on Matias's consistency to watch for problems. If Matias was late, it could spell trouble. The key to avoiding trouble was not to find out about it later. They needed to anticipate Matias's moves in advance.

But all seemed quiet. Matias went about his daily routine. He worked hard to avoid suspicion after the warehouse incident. He hadn't been warned of his discovery by Adolfo, for fear he would run. Certainly, there would be questions, searches and suspicions. But Matias seemed content that he wasn't the subject of anyone's interest. The problem with Matias was that he only looked at his immediate surroundings. This was much like him not noticing the port perimeter cameras. Nor had he noticed—or even thought about—Agata, as she made the rounds of the facility. She sometimes wandered through the banana warehouses. She looked casually at the crates and chatted with the workers. Matias never gave her a second thought, even when she stopped to make small talk with him.

Matias never gave Mack and Deek a second thought either. He didn't know they were in place, although he assumed he was probably being watched over by ORB in some manner. They were somewhat out of place in his neighborhood. But he never thought they were targeting him. If he had known they were watching him, he would have been nervous. He might have done something stupid, like talk to one of them as they passed in the street. No, Matias kept his distance from everyone. But a few times a week when he was holed up in his rooms, he enjoyed chatting with James and Roberto.

Mack and Deek had taken an apartment across the road from where Matias stayed. It had a good view of his three-story building's main entrance and the windows of his second-floor apartment. But it was too far to see faces without a scope. Sometimes, the person on watch during Matias's downtime would sit at their window, behind the sheers, and stare at the apartment across the road. Sometimes, one of them would walk the street. Or they would sit in the nearby circle where locals gathered to drink and smoke. Now and again, one of them would pass Matias on the sidewalk. But they never nodded or acknowledged him. And Matias ignored them too.

When Matias was at work at the port, one of them would park their vehicle on the road outside the gates. Or they would prop themselves against the roof perimeter wall above the bar. From there, they could watch the warehouse. They were long days, most of them devoid of interest.

Mack and Deek were never without some sort of firearm within easy reach. They had two favorites, standards from ORB. One was the Ruger Mark IV.22 pistol. It had a ten-plus-one capacity, was light, slim and easy to conceal. The other was the long-range and very accurate Ruger Precision Rifle. It had a more than adequate firing range. The rifles were in the apartment. Each had a Sidewinder Hawke scope and a PARD clip-on night vision converter. Everything fit into a black lightweight backpack with thin Styrofoam protection.

oooo

"It seems we have our culprit, Mr. Pei." Adolfo felt pleased with himself for reaching a conclusion before Pei did. But what Adolfo didn't know was that Mr. Pei had already come to a more "global" conclusion about the intruder.

"Ah, Adolfo, you do not surprise me. I knew you would come through. Now, tell me what you have discovered." Ping Pei sat back in his office chair, with two of his minions listening in on the conversation over the speaker and his translator sat next to him.

"It seems this 'snooper' is none other than one of the banana crew. Matias Alvarez, a Peruvian, one of the last to join the banana crew at their port warehouse. A very nervous individual, lives alone, does not socialize, but fits our profile well." Adolfo waited for more accolades. He didn't get any, yet. "We do not know who he works for, if anyone, or why he is so interested in your warehouse. But perhaps you know better." Of course, he also knew what drew the intruder's interest. That was no secret to Adolfo. It was the reason he and Pei maintained contact and Adolfo's savings increased.

"Leave it to me, Adolfo. Of course, we will reward you for the great service you have provided us. But for now, do not interfere with this person. I don't want him to get scared and take off running." Ping Pei signed off without any pleasantries and turned to his minions. He said nothing to them, nodded before they rose and left the room. As they were about to close the door, Ping Pei whispered to them loudly enough for them to stop and turn.

"Be discreet. Leave no trace." Ping Pei rested back in his chair. The door closed behind his people. He pressed his fingertips together against his lips. *What is going on? First these two conspirators at the plant, and now this. What am I missing?* he wondered. He felt frustrated. He was trying to piece something together to make sense of it all. He knew it had something to do with the cocaine, but what? And who was behind it?

Then it came to him. *Of course!* Ping Pei said to himself. *The cartel. It has to be them. They're sniffing around. They're trying to determine how much cocaine we make and how we get it out of Ecuador. Yes, that has to be it.*

At first, Ping Pei felt pleased with himself, thinking he had solved the problem of who and why, but then his mood started to change again. What if he disposed of Matias, a cartel member? What would happen then? He fought through the scenarios and decided that disposing of Matias without a trace would leave the cartel with only a missing man. They would pull out all the stops to search for him. But they would find nothing, connect no one, and replace him with another body. By then, the port would be secured. The warehouse would be triple locked with armed guards on duty 24/7. It would be impenetrable to anyone, unless they had a tank.

Ping Pei remained in his chair. His fingers were still pressed against his lips and formed a steeple. He pursed his lips tighter and felt his resolve growing. This would not be the last time he would have to deal with the Ecuadorian cartel.

Chapter 27

Trouble in Machala

It was Sean who alerted Mack and Deek to the potential for trouble. Matthew had told him the Chinese had discovered who broke into the warehouse.

"Sounds like we have a bit of a problem, Matthew." Stockton had called one day in the early hours of Matthew's day. "My contact at the Chinese embassy in Quito tells me they have a name for the intruder. It seems Matias is in their sights. I haven't heard what they intend to do about it, but it would be best to keep a closer eye on him. We need to stop whoever may come after him, otherwise the game may be up. I think the embassy thinks it's the cartel, but I can't be certain of that."

"Will do. Wonder what gave him away? Matias sounded pretty pumped up and happy about the work." Matthew was scratching his head, trying to figure out who might be watching any of them.

"I don't think we need to worry yet." Stockman sounded grave but optimistic. "It sounds as though they had cameras in places Matias wouldn't know about. We should have given the place a more thorough going-over before we sent him in there."

"We couldn't see anything on the plans, sir. I thought we had everything covered."

"My guess is that they put in extra monitors once the concentrate started to roll in with its special cargo." There was a pause as both were thinking. "Can't help it now. Just have the guys keep their eyes open."

They finished their call with a brief update. Matthew promised to call again in a few days with his plan.

Matthew had no doubt that Stockman was right. He put a call in to Sean and then James to let them know what was needed.

At 2 a.m., a few days after Sean's call, Deek watched as two shrouded figures skulked by Matias's apartment building. He had a couple of small rooms on the second floor. This time it was too suspicious to ignore. They had passed this same way on the last three nights, but earlier. At those times, they looked up at Matias's window and watched as his light went out at 10 p.m. Then they moved on and didn't return. But now, they were back.

No one bothered to lock the main entrance to the apartment building, day or night. The early hours of the morning were a dead zone: the streets were quiet, and hardly a soul would pass. Despite being a dock area, people considered it safe mainly because of the presence of dock workers. Who would mess with them? If there were pedestrians at that time of night, they had a purpose. They focused on their destination. Or a vehicle would speed by.

Deek took no chances and called Mack to take up a position near the main entrance.

It was just after 2:15 a.m. when both figures pushed through the front door, stepped inside and stopped. The dim lights in the main-floor hallway barely lit the area. They slowly made their way to the bottom of the stairway and stopped again, obviously listening for any sound that might signal their presence. That's as much as Deek could see through the night-vision scope on his rifle.

No lights were on in any of the apartments. Matias's had been turned off shortly after he got into bed, as his ritual called for.

Deek called Matias.

"Get out through the back entrance, Matias. Now!" he whispered loud enough to startle Matias awake. The warning broke through his sleep. Deek watched Matias's shadow from across the street. Matias moved across his room and into his bathroom. The bathroom had a door to the back stairs. Deek felt Matias had understood the message enough to get out of there using that exit.

Deek adjusted his body to hold his Ruger Precision Rifle for firing. He pushed it through his open window, aiming at Matias's bedroom window, 500 feet away. It was already fitted with the night scope assembly. A shadow appeared and a head jutted into the night light from the window. It was looking in all directions for the kill, when a bullet from Deek's rifle slammed into its forehead. The rifle made a muted *thunk* as it fired. The body the bullet hit slumped over the sill, and the window pane slid down onto the back of the dead man's neck. Deek didn't stop to look again. He rushed down the stairs of his apartment building, as quietly as he could, and out the front door into the shadow of the adjacent building.

By now, the second figure had seen his accomplice slumped half out of the window and took flight, stumbling down the stairs and through the main entrance. He looked in all directions with panic on his face and his arms a tangle of uncertainty. It was as though he was trying to decide which route to escape the killer he couldn't see. He decided, without logic, his best option was to aim straight across the street to the building opposite. As he stumbled off the sidewalk, a strong hand sprang out of the darkness from behind and clamped over his mouth. He was jerked backwards, and a serrated, eight-inch-long army knife sliced across his trachea. It cut deep enough to almost separate his head from his body, as it sawed its way between two hyaline cartilage rings.

Mack stripped off his T-shirt and wound it around the bloody mess, trying not to let the head separate completely. Then, he dragged the body into the alley beside the apartment building and dropped it down. The signs of blood on the sidewalk and road were inevitable, but the less the better.

Meanwhile, Deek had made his way to the rear of the apartment building and intercepted Matias as he fought to open the gate from the rear courtyard. He said nothing as he put a hand to Matias's mouth and signaled for him to wait where he was. Deek stepped through the back door and came out fifteen minutes later with the body he had shot, wrapped in a rug slung over his shoulder.

Mack and Deek crammed both bodies into the back of their truck, and headed out of town.

"Matias, we're with you." It was Mack. "Take it easy. You're safe but we gotta get out of town."

Matias looked scared, but he was settling down as he realized these two were there to help him. But he knew something must have gone incredibly wrong for things to have come to this. Two bodies were unceremoniously dumped behind where he was sitting, and the two hefty individuals up front were not giving anything away. He dared not talk until they did.

On the north side of the port, the seashore was a mass of rocks jutting into the ocean. It was not a place for swimmers or boats, or for any casual strollers. In fact, it was unlikely that anyone ever ventured there, but it was a perfect place where two bodies, weighed down by rocks, could rest in peace for a very long time, even under shallow water.

"You need to leave, Matias," Deek started as soon as they had disposed of the two bodies and begun their drive north. "This is no place for you. Your job is done, and now you've been compromised." Deek looked over at Mack, who nodded his agreement, then put a call in to James.

"Better collect his things from the apartment right away before it gets light and take him to the airport in Quito. Avoid Guayaquil in case anyone comes looking for him. That's where they would go first. He needs to get a flight to Lima and hunker down for a while. Let him know I'll call him when I can." James didn't show his surprise at the turn of events after the call he had from Matthew, but the discovery that someone from his team had actually been found, shook him. Then he remembered Nathan and Eric. Things were getting complicated, he thought. Better get Matthew involved.

Mack and Deek headed back into town. They picked up all of Matias's things they could fit in one bag. Then, they drove him out of Machala and north to the airport in Quito, before dawn revealed what had happened.

Chapter 28

Get Out of Town

James called Matthew to get him up to speed on the events in Machala.

"How's Matias? Is he hurt?" Matthew voiced his concern. But his brain was working hard on what had happened and how they would deal with this. 'Two men dead. Two Chinese men—but sent from where, from Zamora? Is that likely?" Matthew's brain was working overtime. He hadn't suspected the Chinese embassy. So, he never suspected their government of planning such a thing. It was all too quick for them to react like this. But it was possible, he conjectured.

"He's rattled but okay. He'll be sitting in the Quito airport in the next few hours, waiting for a flight to Lima, I guess." James sounded a little uncertain. "Well, he might be going to Trujillo, his hometown, but that's okay. He has family there."

"Okay. What's happening to Sean's guys?"

"They're going to be on hold in Quito, waiting for orders."

"Okay. Any idea who found out about Matias?"

"No idea. All I know is about your call with Stockman. But how the Chinese found out is anyone's guess. Probably the customs guys at the port. A few days ago, two Chinese guys turned up. They walked up and down outside his apartment. Then... well, you know what happened. Matias didn't seem to know anything either. Big surprise to him." James was still shaken by the events. He blamed himself for not having done a thorough recce of the port and discovered the perimeter lights. Oddly, Matthew had the same thoughts of recrimination. But that was history now.

"Have Sean's guys take a break and I'll be in touch." Matthew paused, thinking. "What about Roberto? Any word from him? Do you know if he's okay?"

"He seems to be. Lying low, I assume. I can't see how anyone could get suspicious of him. All he's doing is watching the road for concentrate trucks." James wasn't worried about Roberto.

"Okay. Have him look for a truck-mounted crane. Also, a place to stockpile some of those concentrate tote bags. It has to be in the same area as the drivers take their overnight break." Matthew started pacing and talking at the same time. "We're going to take some of those bags while the drivers are all tucked up in bed. But it has to be done so they don't know when they wake up and carry on to Machala. Understood?"

"Okay, but what happens when they get to the other end and find they're missing some loads?"

"I don't think they're going to miss them at the port. They're just the drivers. I doubt they even know what they're carrying or how many bags they have. Make sure Roberto knows to rearrange the remaining bags on the truck to create the appearance that nothing was taken." There was a pause as Matthew was thinking, and James knew enough to let him have that moment. "They're only going to miss those bags once the cargo gets to China, and that's what we need." Matthew was still thinking through things as his thoughts spilled out.

"But listen. Make sure Roberto only lifts two of the marked ones from each of three trailers. No more than that, or the gaps on the trailer will really show. Drop the bags onto the truck and take them to a place out of sight. You may need to get down there to help Roberto out."

"Maybe we should also send one of Sean's guys, or both."

"Good, James. Sounds like a plan."

There were details for Roberto to work out for his job. But with James on call and a couple of ORB security team to help them, the plan seemed promising.

"Okay, Matthew. I'm on it. We'll go after the concentrate haul in two days. Provided we can get things organized by then." James knew this was pretty optimistic, given Roberto had to get hold of a lift truck, but it was at least a target date.

"Only if Roberto can get that truck crane organized in time. If not, it'll have to be the next one. But contact your men in Quito and have one get over to Roberto as soon as he can." Matthew was happy that things were coming together on another piece of the plan.

The next call Matthew made was to Stockman. He briefed him on what had happened with Matias, and how Mack and Deek had handled the guys who had come after him.

"Not surprised really, Matthew," Stockman didn't sound shocked or even bothered. "Couldn't let them get away with what they were bound to do to Matias. I don't know yet how deep this will go with the Zamora people or with the Chinese in Quito. But you can be sure there won't be a lot of noise. The fact is, they were caught with their pants down, and if exposed, someone from their side is going to have to pay." While the violence was not something Stockman took any joy in, he knew when it had to be meted out.

Chapter 29

What Photos?

"What do you think they'll do to us, Nathan?" Eric looked and sounded worried, as he should.

Nathan put on a brave face for his friend, who hadn't done anything in all this. At least not on this particular occasion. After all, they only happened to know each other, Nathan convinced himself. Maybe that would at least get Eric freed. So, he thought, there was really nothing for him to tell. Well, other than about the pump shutdown and, oh yes, the problem in the loadout with the control room alarm. But how would the Zamora bosses ever discover that they were the ones behind the false flags?

"They'll let us go in the morning when they realize they've made a mistake, I think. There is nothing they can prove. We're just two innocents—so make sure you sound pathetic if they talk to you." Nathan searched his friend's face for his understanding and got a slight nod in return.

"No problem with that." Eric looked glum and lay down on the hard bench. Then he stood up, took off his coveralls, wound them into a ball, lay down again, and pushed the ball under his head. "In that case, I'm going to sleep."

The Zamora security office was larger than one might expect for a mine. Normally, there would only be a small trailer off to the side near the entry gate. But at Zamora, it was much more substantial given the problems they had in the past with indigenous protectors. But it wasn't a common occurrence to have to detain anyone at a project site. If it was a serious issue, a guard would escort the suspect to their room in the accommodation center. The guard would lock the door and sit in the corridor to ensure his ward was secure. Of course, there was always the window for a potential escapee. But they were generally so small that not even a 120-pound twig of a person could get through. And if they did, where would they go? The next day, security would escort the perpetrator off-site in one of the concentrate trucks to Machala, to be put on the next available concentrate ship. And that would be it.

The Zamora security facilities were not lacking in ways to securely detain unwanted intruders. In fact, the facilities seemed overly designed to Nathan and Eric as they wallowed in one of the concrete-block rooms—or a cell by any other name. The door was locked. There were no windows. There was only a wooden bench on each of the four walls to sit or sleep on. A bucket was in one corner and a tin pot with water was in another. This was clearly the end of their relationship with the Zamora operations people.

They didn't know what their captors knew. But, as they had given up their phones and the scope, the captors must now know something about what the two, or at least Nathan, had been up to. It was doubtful they had any kind of a full story, and while neither was about to tell them, there was always the possible threat of torture to look forward to. They never claimed to have been trained for this type of thing. In fact, if push came to shove, they would admit to being cowards the moment someone raised a hand to strike either one of them.

Nathan would make up a lame explanation like "I was just being nosy" or "I thought I heard a noise" when asked why he was looking through the rubber curtain. He knew his excuse wouldn't go a long way but who knew? Maybe, *maybe,* their stupidity would be recognized for what it was.

As Nathan lay there on the concrete bench, he pondered his potential fate, unless ORB sent someone in to help them escape. He couldn't imagine why no one from security had said anything to them yet, nor why they weren't being held in more bleak conditions. But perhaps that was just his imagination kicking into high gear. He managed to convince himself that those kinds of lolled-up things, like torture, didn't happen in real life, although the other side of his brain told him they did. What if they sent them back to China? What then? Well, he knew that would be game over.

Like Eric, he had wrapped his coveralls into a ball and tucked them under his head. Eventually, though his mind was still going through the possibilities awaiting them, his mental exhaustion overcame him and his eyes flickered to a close.

Chapter 30

Get Them Out of Here

His eyes snapped open, and without breathing, Nathan tried to make sense of the scraping noise he heard coming from the other side of the door to his cell. It opened slowly. He could see the black shape of a body. It loomed larger as it came toward him. He sat up and cowered at one end of the concrete bench in the corner of his cell, not daring to make a noise. Before he could gather himself enough to make a sound or attempt escape, he felt his arm being held tightly by a strong hand. The hand was far stronger than his.

"Easy, Nathan. Easy. I'm with James," Sean hissed right next to Nathan's head and still held him tightly as he pressed a finger lightly against his mouth. Not that he thought Nathan would cry out. Who would care? He took his finger away.

"I. Okay. Who are you and how d–did you get h–here?" Nathan's voice trembled a little, but he was more surprised than afraid. In the back of his mind, he wondered if James would send someone to get him out rather than risk losing the project.

"Listen, the guard is going to be back in a couple of minutes, so no time for explanations. You guys okay?"

"So far, no one has told us why they're holding us. Are you going to get us out of here?" Nathan sounded hopeful, but it didn't last long.

"No, you gotta stay until we find out what the Chinese are up to and what they know. What did you find out?" The hand around Nathan's arm relaxed. The shape was still black and featureless. There was no way Nathan would ever be able to recognize this person again.

By this time, Eric had woken up and lay on the slab, scrunching his fists into his eyes, urging them to see better. But he had caught the drift of what was being said and lay there quiet and motionless.

For a moment, Nathan was confused before he grasped the question being asked.

"Tell James the marked-up sign on the bag is the one with the drugs." Nathan had relaxed some.

That was all Sean needed.

He locked their door, crept back out the way he had come, and stopped when he reached the reception area where the guards would collect their orders each morning. He picked up a small hessian sack he had brought with him and left by the desk before he searched out Nathan and Eric, untied it and dumped four pit vipers on the concrete floor.

The snakes stayed absolutely still for a moment with their arrow-shaped heads erect, Their eyes took in their new space before they slowly slithered off in different directions to seek shelter. One slithered under the reception desk and up onto a narrow ledge in the gap with the back of a drawer. Another disappeared into a washroom and slithered under a countertop into the far unlit corner where dirt had escaped any attempt to brush it away. The third found comfort behind a tall filing cabinet and managed to squeeze through a gap between the bottom drawer and the frame. The last viper slid under a sofa chair and up into the soft inner padding, in an anteroom. They could stay in their positions for days, if necessary, until they knew it was time to either strike, or attempt an escape.

Meanwhile, Nathan and Eric were left in their cell to wonder what the hell had just happened.

Eric was going to say something but thought better of it. He wasn't sure what was meant by the message Nathan had given to the stranger, but he knew it was the reason they were where they were now.

oooo

Nathan and Eric woke up. They didn't know the time, nor could they see whether it was daylight. They lay talking and wondering what was going to happen. Hopefully, it wasn't going to be violent. Neither was up to that. If their captors knew how easy it would be to get the information, they would likely just raise a hand as a threat, and out it would all pour.

The door to their cell burst open, and two guards pushed them out into the common area where another couple of guards were waiting. No one said a thing. Fifteen minutes went by before two tough-looking civilians came into the office and signaled the guards to take Nathan and Eric outside. It was daylight and Nathan guessed it must have been about 7 a.m. judging by the noises they could hear around them. Still no one spoke, even as they were hustled into the back of a van with no side or rear windows. Just a couple of seats, a water jug and another bowl. *Just in case?* Nathan thought with a worried look on his face. One of the civilians slammed and locked the door. The front doors slammed shut and the engine started up. The van moved forward and picked up speed once they heard the front gate open and close.

Nathan and Eric guessed they were being driven away from the property. Then, it felt like they were on the highway with other traffic going by them in the opposite direction. There was no talking, no torture, nothing. Just removing them from the Zamora property and away from where they could cause more trouble. Why? They had no idea.

The van stopped twice. Once for gas and food, and then for a toilet break and a change of drivers. By nightfall, they arrived at the Mariscal Sucre International Airport in Quito. There, Nathan and Eric were dumped unceremoniously at the passenger drop-off area to find their own way. Zamora security personnel had bagged their things from their bunkhouse and now tossed them out the van's front. They drove off without a word, glance, or a wave goodbye.

Nathan and Eric looked at each other. They shrugged and quickly checked their bags to make sure their passports and wallets were there. Clearly, neither of them now had a phone. The scope was missing, as were a few other personal items that mattered only to them. Perhaps their captors were being overly suspicious, Nathan thought, and not taking any chances. But he doubted this was the end of their worries. Maybe the Chinese deliberately took their seemingly harmless personal items, such as photos of their families and contact addresses of friends, to instill fear in them and stop them from talking about their adventure.

Nathan and Eric wandered off into the airport in search of a public phone. They needed to contact James. Neither of them noticed the two shadowy characters following them, one on each side about twenty feet or so away. When Nathan crammed into one of the open phone booths, one of the characters crammed into the one next to him. At this point, neither of the friends was watching for any suspicious activity, including the attention they were getting.

As Nathan dialed the number for James, Eric stood fifteen feet away, gazing at the crowd in the opposite direction, and oblivious to the character in the booth next to his friend. The character was standing back from his receiver, focusing through the glass on the dial pad in front of Nathan, and listening intently.

"It's me, Nathan. We're out." James had answered on the first ring.

"Wow. That's great." James felt shocked but happy they were both safe. "What happened? The last thing I heard was that you were in lockdown at the site. But I got the message, thanks." James was somewhat lost for words as he acclimatized to this new situation. It was certainly a strange turn of events and somewhat suspicious. "Where are you?"

"They drove us to the airport in Quito. That's where I'm calling you from." Nathan sounded pretty steady and didn't appear to be under any undue pressure. "Some civilians picked us up from the plant this morning and drove us straight to the airport. Don't ask me what anyone said. No one spoke to us from when they marched us out of the plant to when they dumped us here. We have no idea what they know or what they're planning, if anything. Maybe they don't think anything and just wanted us out of the way." He waited for James.

"Wow, again. You guys had better get on a plane and head anywhere but North America for now. Go somewhere you can keep an eye open on anyone who might be following you, like the desert." James wasn't joking. He was cautious about letting them go so easily. Maybe the Chinese believed that Nathan and Eric would lead them to whoever they were working for.

"Okay. I've been thinking about that. We'll catch the first flight out to Antofagasta and drive up to Escondida. Can't be any more out of the way than the Atacama Desert! We have friends in operations there. They can help us get into the visitors' section of the camp while things settle down. If anyone is following, they will have a hard time keeping up. That road up into the mountains is wide open and we'll see whoever comes behind us. Plus, they wouldn't be able to get through the security gate, and if they did, they wouldn't be able to get any rooms at camp." Nathan seemed pleased with himself. It sounded like a good idea. Eric was taking in the crowds and not paying attention to his friend on the phone. The person in the other booth was still listening to Nathan's conversation. He was trying not to miss any part of what Nathan was saying. He heard the words "Antofagasta," "Escondida," "Desert," and "camp."

When the call finished, Nathan went to Eric and talked to him for a few minutes. Then, Nathan took out a credit card and they went searching for the LATAM airline ticket counter. They were in luck. The next flight was the 8 p.m. to Lima and onto Antofagasta, getting in around 4:30 a.m. the next morning. They would pick up a worker's bus from there to the mine site and arrive around noon.

Two hours later, Nathan and Eric were in their airplane seats. They were happy to see the end of the runway as the plane took off to the south, far from their Zamora problems.

"Wonder why they took our other stuff?" Eric said. He looked worried about what the Zamora security people had taken from their rooms. It included information about their families. Their families were still in China. Their phones also held their lists of friends around the world.

Nathan shook his head. He also worried and considered what motives the Chinese could have that would be anything less than troublesome. He knew this wasn't going to be the last they heard of Zamora.

Chapter 31

The Plan

While talking to Matthew, Stockman sat in his favorite chair in the bay window of his cottage in southwest England. Lucy was off somewhere in the kitchen.

"From what we now know, despite the display of harmony Tongyan and the Ecuadorian government try to show, most of the concerns of the local population are still ignored." Stockman paused and took a sip of tea. As he talked, he took in the time on the pendulum clock sitting on the mantelpiece. It was coming up to 12:30 p.m., making it 7:30 a.m. for Matthew.

He carried on.

"Lawsuits against the Zamora operation have shown that, if not diffused, the plant will just carry on operating the way it has been without the community's involvement or consent. That can only cause a social disaster in the long term, as well as be a constant irritant to the Chinese. But I don't think it's going to be enough to get them out of the country, after what they've already been through to get this far." Stockman took a bite from the sandwich Lucy had placed next to him on the side table. Smoked meat and sauerkraut. His favorite.

"It's not just that, you know." Matthew took advantage of the pause to chime in. He had found a quiet spot in the camp and huddled around the phone with Emma.

"Even top scientists aren't sure what makes that area so biodiverse. They're totally against disturbing it at all, until they've at least figured things out." Matthew took a breath and glanced over at Emma for some sign of support. She nodded and gave him one of those solemn looks. It implied she agreed.

"Doesn't every environmentalist oppose change, Matthew? Is this another of *those* things?" Stockman was being cynical. "These protests by environmentalists generally don't help much. They're always trying to prove something's wrong but they never offer solutions. And still they all drive gas-guzzling cars and use tons of paper and all the rest of it. They dispose of their plastics as litter rather than recycling, just the same as regular people, don't they?" He paused as though in thought, but not expecting an answer. While Stockman was committed to the cause, he was not an extremist.

"They're not environmental scientists," Matthew pressed on. "They're social-cultural anthropologists." He paused, expecting a sarcastic comment from Stockman. He didn't get one and carried on. "This area of the Amazon basin requires explanation. Apparently, they think it's all due to the limestone soil beneath the area. It has millions of tiny seashells, very unusual in the Andes. Can you imagine? The Amazon was underwater at some point in its history." Matthew paused, knowing Stockman would have something to say.

"I guess the McArthur Foundation is having quite an effect on you, my boy." It was an odd sign of affection for Stockman when he used the term "my boy." The message conveyed was one of paternal interest. It showed understanding of the other party's passion.

"To some extent, and although that's interesting, my interest goes a lot further than that." This time, Matthew didn't wait for some comment from Stockman and instead pressed on. He realized he had gone off track a bit.

"I'm still gathering and collating information," Matthew said quietly.

He came back to earth when he realized Stockman hadn't heard his comment. Emma gave Matthew a sign to move on, by rolling her hands one over the other.

"Let me explain a little more, sir." Matthew rarely called Stockman "sir." But he used it sometimes to get back on topic, as he was now. "The area we're talking about here is important to more than only environmentalists. It's also vital to others with even more basic interests such as where life in the Amazon came from. This could actually help us with our mission." Matthew had got back on track. He heard Stockman put his cup back in its saucer, making a clinking sound. Yes, Stockman was a saucer man. Or at least his wife was, so he was too.

"Go on, Matthew. I sense you're getting to the point of your call." Stockman smiled to himself. He sat farther back in his chair, staring out the window. He watched the bushes in the garden sway in the breeze. He saw a lone sailboat, with jib and mainsail set, rise and fall across a crested sea. But he returned from his meandering thoughts. Now, he focused on Matthew. He felt this was the point in a project when things would snap together. This was the part he loved most.

"Okay. As far as I now know," Matthew continued, "there's still a lot of tension and mistrust between the government, the company and the indigenous people over the Zamora plant getting permits to build in the first place. In fact, I'm told they started work before they had any permits at all.

"The local communities were decimated. They didn't have time to gather themselves to fight, but then neither were they keen on starting a civil war. There were at least seven towns affected by the project, as well as five Shuar settlements.

"So, they took the project to court," Matthew continued, "but it didn't go well. One of the most respected Zamora opponents was found brutally murdered. Signs of torture were on his body. This is just one example of the intimidation they faced.

"The first and highest-profile legal action argued that environmental rights had been violated. The state countered that the Shuar community had no collective land deed demarcating the presence of an ethnic people who had to be consulted. The judge ordered an expert anthropological evaluation. But the report was inconclusive, and a Quito judge sided with the government and dismissed the case. The fight has never stopped, but they built the plant and put it into operation. Now they're planning on raising the dam against some fierce opposition."

Matthew stopped to take a break. He waited in case Stockman wanted to add anything.

"Go on, Matthew. This is all very intriguing, but I sense a punchline coming." It sounded more like a question, and Matthew was ready.

"There are all kinds of criminal complaints against the Chinese company. Most are associated with environmental damage to water sources. But the biggest one coming down the pipeline is one associated with their tailings dam."

"Oh!" Stockman startled at the word *dam*. Their failures were at the top of the list when it came to international disasters resulting from man-made structures. As far as he could remember, the last major dam to fail was Brumadinho in southwestern Brazil not that long ago. It killed more than 270 people. Over 13 million cubic yards of liquefied tailings mud flooded the site. It took out the neighboring settlements and a railway bridge. There had been worse ones, but that was the one stuck in Stockman's mind. Despite decommissioning the dam several years earlier, it was an unmitigated disaster.

"The Zamora dam will eclipse all the others and will be the largest earthen dam in the world when it's finished. They plan to raise it another four hundred to eight hundred and fifty feet high. Can you imagine?" Matthew waited for Stockman.

"I'm very suspicious when it comes to dams, Matthew. We've had a lot of failures over the years as a consequence of things like design flaws, unknown ground conditions, bad construction, or poor management. It really annoys me when I hear it called a man–made disaster. This is the age of scientific knowledge and scrupulous safety regulations. It shouldn't be happening. Jesus, they apparently even know how to design for catastrophic events like earthquakes, so what gives?" Clearly Matthew had hit a nerve with Stockton. He didn't know he had such a strong sentiment about dams, but then the subject had never come up before.

"Well, in the case of the Zamora dam, it's a lack of everything, and the indigenous people know it, as do the technical people who have come out and opposed what is happening. No permits, no approvals, the dam slopes are too steep, and the construction is sloppy. But what can anyone do when nothing has happened—yet? The government certainly isn't going to make a move. They have a partnership with the Chinese company. It gives them access to one of the world's largest copper deposits." Again, Matthew paused.

"Wow. Now that's a disaster waiting to happen." Stockman was shocked.

"Local leaders and engineers say the existing structure is a serious threat to life of all kinds, let alone the expansion." Matthew was unusually passionate about the subject. "It would cause a huge landslide of tailings and would exterminate the surrounding communities and destroy many of the Amazon's tributaries. Damage like that would take years to repair itself, if it ever did." Matthew listened for any sound from Stockman on the other end of the line. There was some shuffling and rustling of papers.

"You know,"—Stockman had come up for air—"I was reading something about this yesterday. Let me see." There was more rustling and the sound of chair movement. "Ah, here it is. Let me read it out to you: *'Indigenous Shuar communities and local mayors in southern Ecuador have demanded immediate help in light of the imminent potential collapse of a massive dam holding mining waste, set in the high rainforest of the Cordillera del Cóndor, a key watershed of rivers in the western Amazon.'* That's it, isn't it?"

Stockman kept staring at the article as he waited for Matthew. But then he didn't give Matthew time to interject and read on. *"'Another study showed that builders constructed the Quimi dam at Zamora with a forty-five-degree angle. They used a slope of one foot up for every one foot across. This deviated from the Environmental Impact Study's specification of one foot up for every two feet across. Institutions such as the U.S. Army Corps of Engineers and the European Commission recommend slopes of one to five.'* That's what they say, Matthew. This is terrible news. What are you thinking?" Stockman was truly rattled. He had operatives in a region where a potential mammoth disaster could happen at any moment. And there would be collateral damage and loss of the surroundings.

"Well, with all that background..." Matthew had absorbed what Stockman had read out; it confirmed what he was telling him. "Emma and I have been meeting with a Shuar person who lives in the Zamora area. The events at Zamora disenfranchised him and his people. They're really upset by all that has happened to their communities and their traditional Amazon land." He paused, gathering his thoughts. "Now this increase in the height of the dam is risking worse catastrophes. He doesn't think his people will survive." Matthew paused again to allow Stockman to interject if he chose. He didn't.

"So, we're developing a plan we think will get the Chinese out of there as well as prevent a disaster from happening. We need to shut the place down completely, and we can use environmental good practice to help us do it." Matthew sat back, happy to finally be able to get to the point. "And you're going to have to help with that, sir."

"Oh, yes. Yes, of course. Just let me know when the time comes, and I'll do what I have to do." Stockman paused to consider the help he was expected to provide. But he certainly liked the way Matthew was thinking.

"Now, I assume you don't mean to breach the tailings dam, Matthew." Stockman recovered from his moment of thought. "It may not be at its maximum height yet, but it has to be up to somewhere around four hundred feet high. That's still a lot of tailings behind such a steep structure." Stockman sat back in his chair as Lucy came by to pick up his plate and put another cup of tea in its place. He waved a "thank you" and blew a kiss.

"Nothing that extreme. But using the environment against them will be our best play." Mathew looked over at Emma who sat listening, nodding, smiling and giving him the thumbs–up sign now and again.

"Well, I like the thinking, Matthew. But do you think that will be enough? I mean, will the government shut them down for anything but a catastrophic failure? I think not." Stockman was skeptical but encouraged. His feeling was that they were on the right path, but it needed more substance on the bones.

"I thought the same," Matthew said honestly. What Stockman had done was to push him into doing more. He was right. The Chinese were supported by their government. They would do everything to get the plant running again as quickly as possible after any accident.

"Good. Good. Well, it's getting better, but—now, thinking out loud here, Matthew. What if we had a pit wall failure on top of all this, and even take out the main transformers? Yes, they could replace the transformers. Perhaps, with a line of smaller ones. They would be off-the-shelf in China, but it would be another stumbling block to slow them down. But the pit wall? That's altogether a different matter." Stockman had got to the core of his thinking. Yes, these things should be in the plan.

Stockman rolled on. "Environmental agencies would be crawling all over the place. Mining inspectors would be everywhere. Safety inspectors, government agencies, the global critics all coming down heavily on Tongyan. Critical parts of the plant would be out of service.

"It would take the Chinese millions of dollars and years to get back on track. Meanwhile the coca farmers would be looking for an alternative buyer for their cocaine base." Stockman stopped as he envisaged the chaos all this would cause.

Matthew had no immediate reaction to the pit wall failure addition to his plan, but he liked it. Stockman let him think, and they both took a bit of a break from talking while they mulled things over.

"It means getting Nick into the mine as soon as possible," Matthew started again, "and Kenny has to be at the plant for the transformers. But I think we can do it. Nick's a dab hand with explosives, but I don't know yet whether he will be able to get the things he needs from the site stores." Matthew left it for Stockman to respond.

"Let him work on that, Matthew. He's a pretty resourceful fellow as you know from your previous experience with him. I also need to get entry permits and company credentials for the guys." Stockman was writing some notes.

"What about the cocaine? Any thoughts?" Stockman loved immersing himself in planning and plotting.

"Yes, I do, sir." There it was again. But this time he used the term "sir" as though he were about to add the icing to the cake.

"Okay, I'm all ears." So far Stockman found the plan they were developing fascinating. This one sounded difficult but doable. Maybe even with less risk than other ORB projects. Or perhaps not. It depended on what Matthew was thinking about the cocaine, and he was about to hear what that was.

"As we talked about last time, we have confirmed that ships transport the cocaine. They take it to Puerto Bolívar in Machala, on the southwest coast of Ecuador. We also know the transfer schedule for concentrate tote bags from the plant to the port. And, of course, we know the route they take. We're pretty sure the cocaine is in ten-pound bags they bury in the concentrate as they fill the tote bags at the plant.

"Now we know all the concentrate bags on the six trucks that head to Machala contain the cocaine, I'm thinking we should skim a few bags so they're short when they reach China. At that point, there's going to be hell to pay, and everyone's going to be blaming everyone else. Before you know it, it'll be a free-for-all. Two governments involved, and each one finds it's missing its share of the take." It was a simple plan. Perhaps difficult to execute, with the detail still to be worked out. "What do you think?" Matthew waited for Stockman.

"Well, it's a simple enough plan, but perhaps a little skimpy." Matthew couldn't see the expression on Stockman's face as he said it, but it was all scrunched up in thought. "I don't know how long it will take for the Chinese at the other end to figure things out. It could be a slow fuse." Stockman wasn't totally convinced yet. He liked the idea of skimming the cocaine. But he wondered if there was something they could do to speed things up with Beijing. Ideally, all these things should come together at around the same time. The environmental mishap, the pit wall failure, the transformer outages, and someone siphoning off the cocaine. Plus, whatever they could do to disable the equipment. That was a lot to orchestrate at the same time. Timing them to coincide was imperative.

"Let me think on things a little more. Overall, I think we have it," Matthew enthused, "but I agree we need to shorten the fuse for Beijing to get involved. They might pull the plug before they get into more trouble. On the other hand, if they smell a rat, it might piss them off enough to make them come in guns blazing." Matthew smiled to himself. There was no certainty the things he would orchestrate would scare the Chinese out of Ecuador, but perhaps there was one thing: drug cartels. It was a thought he preferred to keep to himself right now and let the words permeate instead.

"Well, I doubt the Chinese will come in with guns blazing, Matthew. They're more likely to keep trying to smooth things over and handle everything under the table. We know they have the hierarchy of some of the Ecuadorian government in their pockets to do their dirty work, so…" Stockman trailed off, ready to end the call. But Matthew wasn't quite ready.

"Okay, let's be in touch in a few days on that." Matthew went on to tell Stockman about the photos of the concentrate tote bags and what had happened to Nathan and Eric. He seemed confident they were safe at the Escondida mine in the Atacama Desert. But he had a nagging feeling they weren't totally free of the Zamora folks quite yet.

"Nathan seems pretty concerned." There was a pause as Matthew let his words sink in. "It sounds like the Chinese took some of their things when they packed their bags at Zamora, including information about family and friends. We're going to have to watch that situation. I'm going to send one of the security crew over there to look after them." Matthew had already decided to call Sean about sending his man, Mack, from Quito to Escondida.

"Good idea. From what I hear, the Chinese may have dug up something on them. I don't know what it is yet, but a contact tells me they were for the chop even before they got those photos." This turn of events had perturbed even Stockman. He wasn't sure if ORB could face the consequences, but he knew he had to do something to solve the issue. He would think about it before sharing his thoughts further with Matthew.

"Okay. Let's think about it and see what comes up," Stockman suggested. "Meanwhile, perhaps you can get Nick and Kenny organized to come over. We may also need Mitch on standby over here to help Nick with the pit blasting."

"Sounds good. Let's both think about shortening that fuse we talked about. I have an idea I want to work on." Matthew was finished and ready to sign off.

"Great. Sounds good, Matthew. Oh, how is Emma doing? Is she helping or hindering?"

"I heard that, Daddy." Emma couldn't help herself, but she knew her father would know she would be tagging along. "GIVE MY LOVE TO MUMMY!" she shouted over Matthew's shoulder and into the phone.

"I will, sweetheart. Take care. Let's talk in a few days' time, Matthew." Stockman put his phone down and turned to Lucy. "Did you hear all that?" he asked her.

"I did, my dear," Lucy replied and continued sipping her tea. She would undoubtedly have some observations for her husband. But, for now, tea was her priority.

Immediately after the call with Stockman, Matthew put one more call in.

"Sean, are you there?" Matthew used the radio. Some spluttering occurred on the other end as they squelched the frequency to reduce the hiss.

"Here, boss. What's up?" The line was clear, and Sean was back in position halfway up the hill overlooking the Zamora plant. He was covered in leafy twigs, grasses and other jungle things poking out from his clothes, bandana and hat. Not even the local wildlife would be able to spot him he was so well camouflaged. But it was better than having to dig a depression in the sodden soil and lie in it for eleven hours a day. His only problem was the possibility of disturbing a snake, particularly a viper.

It wasn't often a viper, or any snake, would attack just for the sake of it, unless it was searching for food, like a rodent or a frog or some other tasty morsel. But Sean was vigilant and surrounded his area with a mix of compounds used to prevent most kinds of small animals at bay. The nights were the worst. That's when a lot of jungle creatures came out to feed, and neither he nor Glenn wanted to be a snake's last meal.

The Andean pit vipers were the worst of the ambush predators most active at night. During the day they spent most of their time coiled and camouflaged on vegetation anywhere from ground level up to twenty feet high.

Pit vipers didn't see very well but had heat-sensing pits, or organs, between the eyes and nostrils. They could sense heat coming from the body of their prey, and once sensed, could attack their prey even in the dark. So yes, Sean was very cautious, and both he and Glenn always carried their anti-venom kit and a military grade spray can of eugenol.

The eugenol, derived from cinnamon and clove plants, wasn't a hundred percent guarantee as a general snake repellent but it seemed to work on pit vipers, who kept their distance whenever they came close to those scents.

"Better get your man in Quito to put eyes on Nathan and Eric, Sean. They're up at the Escondida plant site, a few hours' drive east of Antofagasta. It sounds like they may have some unwanted folks in tow. I think they're safe in the camp for now, but I can't tell for sure. We'll arrange a room for him at the camp as close to the boys as we can. How soon do you think you can get him mobilized?" Matthew stopped pacing and waited for Sean.

"I estimate it will take two days for him to arrange a flight and get up to the mine. Can't make it any faster unless you charter. I'll send Mack. He's good in the desert."

"Good, see if you can charter a flight for him right into the site and have a vehicle for him on standby when he gets there. They have a small airstrip there for private planes. I'll get the approvals. That would help your man take in what he needs without having to go through customs."

Matthew knew that dealing with customs officials for private flights was always easier than going through the usual process at commercial airports. He was eager to get some protection for Nathan and Eric as soon as he could.

"Sounds like a plan." Sean was a man of few words, but very sharp.

"I'll send you a contact name for entry to the site and camp. I may not let Nathan know that Mack will be there. I don't think Mack should be seen with them, or he'll be a target as well."

"On it, boss. Anything else?" Sean would put a call into Mack in Quito and have him arrange what was needed.

The two signed off, and Matthew took Emma by the arm and gently led her over to their Land Cruiser.

"Time to head out. Let's find Luna."

Chapter 32

Jungle Farmers

Matthew and Emma found Luna holding the bottom end of a very old twenty-foot wooden ladder. It was propped against a sadly built single-story hut—or maybe it was going to be a house. It was hard to determine whether someone or something was inhabiting, constructing, or tearing it down, whatever "it" was. Two of his crew poked their heads over the roof's perimeter as Matthew's Land Cruiser pulled up. Luna turned his head, gave a broad smile at his newfound friends and let go of the ladder to walk over to greet them.

"Ah, my friends." Luna's face lit up at the idea of sitting and talking rather than working. Even thinking about work or holding a ladder counted as work.

"Don't let us take you away from your work, Luna." Emma smiled at him and waved him back to the ladder with a flutter of both hands. But he insisted they shake hands. "Please, just go ahead and finish up, and then perhaps we can talk some more." She raised her eyebrows as a sign of positive expectation, while keeping a smile on her face.

"Yes. Yes, of course." Being reminded that there was still work to do clearly disappointed Luna. But he acquiesced. "Excuse me while I inspect their work before they come down from the roof. Have to keep my eyes on them, you know." He gave a knowing look to Emma, then to Matthew, tapped the side of his nose with a finger, and waddled back to the ladder, knowing he was being watched. He took hold of the ladder's sides, put his right foot on the lowest rung, looked back and gave Matthew and Emma a wry smile with a toothy grin that could be mistaken for a grimace. Then, he put his left foot on the second rung and stood still for a moment, as if wondering what to do next. He looked back again. His smile sank into a full-faced grimace as he placed his right foot next to his left. He was clearly uncomfortable with the prospect of going higher. But he did.

They had to applaud Luna's courage. He made it to the rim of the roof, about ten feet above the ground. He grabbed the edge of the roof to hoist himself up further before gravity took over and his 438-pound body pushed through the old wooden rungs. He fell all the way back down to the ground as the two ladder posts fell to the sides. Luna rolled onto his back and lay there, staring up at the sky, not daring to move in case he had been injured. He never did like the sight of blood.

Matthew and Emma hurried over to Luna's body, sprawled in the dried mud, and attempted to lift him. It was impossible, until his two crew members somehow appeared at the doorway of the hut, without the help of the ladder, and ran to help, all the while gabbling and wailing. It took all four of them to raise Luna to a sitting position. Even then, one of them had to get behind him, back-to-back, to keep him upright. It took some colossal strength and complex positioning to heave Luna up to his feet.

"Looks good, guys." Luna waved a hand casually at the roof of the hut as he walked, or rather limped, away. "You can go home," he said to his two crew members over his shoulder. They were still trying to brush the muck off their boss. "But be sure you're back here first thing in the morning. We've got work to do." His men hurried off. Luna blushed a little. But he never spoke of his accident. He also never mentioned that he didn't get to peek over the roof's edge to inspect the work. Neither did he bother to clean the rest of the mud off his clothes. "I knew that ladder was broken" was all he said.

"Beer?" He looked from Matthew to Emma as a broad grin split his face in two when he realized there was no blood, and apparently no bruises or broken bones.

Rodriguez set up some beers for his guests when they got back to the camp. It included one for Luna, who always seemed to be freeloading. They sat around talking about their visit to the Zamora site and discussed what they had seen, what they would have liked to have seen, and an agenda for their next visit to the plant property.

Luna was tucking into a plate of barbecued chicken Rodriguez had pushed in front of him. The bones were piling up. Luna listened to his new friends as the sauce from the chicken splattered his T-shirt. If one examined that T-shirt, one might see what Luna had eaten over the last few days. The stains gave it away.

They had spent some thirty minutes listening to Luna talk about life in the jungle. The indigenous people faced many problems after their benefactor, Koski, had left them. The Chinese forced some to work as laborers at Zamora so they could provide food for their families. Slowly, as the Chinese gained more of a foothold and the Zamora project rose from the ground, the culture of the indigenous communities in the area began to erode now that living by clocks and money was governing their lives.

"Koski? Who was that? It doesn't sound like an Ecuadorian name." As the name was raised, Emma and Matthew looked at each other, perplexed.

"Oh, he wasn't from Ecuador," Luna said, as though they should know. "I think he was Canadian originally, but he lived in Peru for a long time, helping the Piqueneros mine for gold." Luna stopped and looked at Emma, as though that was all the explanation needed.

"Piqueneros?" Another quizzical look passed between Emma and Matthew. This conversation was losing them.

"They call them gold bandits. Somehow, they're able to almost smell high-grade gold from the surface and dig holes down to intersect the rich pockets. Koski turned up out of nowhere and helped them make their processing more efficient. He spent years with them learning Spanish. Then, the owners and police drove him away. The government is more tolerant of the locals doing those kinds of things—it's a part of their culture—but not foreigners." Luna stopped to pick at more chicken legs and thighs that Rodriguez had conjured up.

"What happened to him to get involved here?" This undocumented information intrigued Matthew.

Luna wiped his hands on a nearby cloth, dipped his fingers into a bowl of water and drew his hands across his T-shirt.

"He crossed the border not far from here." Luna pointed at some point southeast behind him. "I think he was looking to do the same thing here as he did in Peru, but we don't have the same kind of terrain. Ours is jungle. Theirs is all dry and stony, so you could easily travel between the digs and see their line of holes ahead of you. I don't think we have the same kind of geology either. There's not as much gold, or something like that. I'm not really sure." Luna looked up at the sky and squinted as he thought, a chicken leg dangling from his hand. "No, he seemed to join the cocaine farmers for some reason. I guess his background in working with chemicals made it easy for him to switch products." Luna was lost in thought. He slid a beer toward him and cracked the top off with a nearby spoon.

"What made him leave?" Emma was curious.

"The cartel. They were onto him. It seems he was getting too good at the processing. The cartels like their cocaine delivered as a paste so they could play with it their own way. But Koski had other ideas. He started to get the farmers to process the cocaine past the paste stage to a base. The cartel didn't like that. It meant they had to pay the farmers more for that upgrade. But Koski just kept going, and the farmers were getting richer.

"He was here for quite a few years. The manufacturing was getting better all the time, and the cartels were getting super mad. They sent their people in a few times, but the farmers were protecting Koski and kept moving him. Strange old stick." Luna took a second to chomp on the chicken leg.

"Eventually," he started again, after dropping the bone and licking his fingers, "I guess it got too much for him when he had no new places left to hide, so he just vanished. No one knows where he went, but we haven't seen him here for a few years now, maybe more. As far as I know, the cartel is still chasing him. They don't forget, you know, and I think they figure he did them out of millions of dollars." It sounded as though Luna had finished. He was staring down at his hands.

"Hey, Rodriguez. Any more of that chicken?" he shouted over to his friend.

"So, what happened then?" It was Emma. Both she and Matthew found this story of a Canadian, Koski, intriguing. But Matthew doubted it would change their plans. The man was gone.

"Well, that's when the Chinese came in and built that plant of theirs," Luna continued. "They rounded up the farmers and pressed them into sending only the cocaine paste over to them and cut out the cartel. Well, that didn't go down well with either the farmers or the cartel. But Los Choneros were never that strong down here in those days. Plus, they had their own problems with the Colombian drug gangs up north. Always fighting. And now we have the Chinese in the mix. If the other cartels get here at the same time as the local ones return, there's going to be a war." Luna looked dejected. There was no more chicken, he was tired, and showed signs of hurting from the fall. But he still didn't say anything about it.

"Do you think things would be better without the Chinese?" Matthew was cautious, but this was the crux of the matter with Luna. If he were on their side, it would make things a lot easier.

Luna perked up. His eyes widened as he placed the palms of his hands on the table and seemingly forgot his pain. He had no idea where this was going, but he liked the trend.

"I think we would all like the Chinese to disappear." Luna's face lit up. "Sure, they take at least the cocaine paste and pay. But they're destroying our land and culture. They cause real problems for the cartel, and in the end that means trouble for us. The cartel is supposed to be here." He looked at Matthew and Emma. They just stared at him with wide eyes. Luna realized that sounded odd.

"Well, I mean, the cartel is always going to be around"—they still stared at him—"in one form or another." He hunched his shoulders as if asking if they understood. "If it isn't cocaine, it'll be something else." He continued, "They're a conduit for us to sell anything we can make to the outside world. That's what makes everything go 'round here, as it's supposed to. The farmers do their thing, the cartel does its thing, the government shows up now and then, and everyone wins. With the Chinese here, no one wins. But what can we do? You know all about the efforts we've made to stop them. And we know we won't be able to." Luna's eyes almost pleaded for their understanding. Strangely, they wanted it too, given the circumstances.

"Maybe you can help us, Luna." Matthew felt elated about the discussion and the alignment of things with their mission's target.

"A couple of environmentalists with big money behind them? I doubt it." Luna smiled broadly. He had suddenly become somewhat suspicious of these two. He wondered for a moment what was coming next.

"Let me tell you something, Luna. I think we have mutual needs. Strangely, we want to get rid of the Chinese for the same reasons as you." Matthew and Emma watched Luna's face as he considered this. "But first, we need to know if the farmers agree. Let's face it, they're being paid, and they sure won't want that to stop. So… maybe, if we find a way to convince them the money will still flow, then perhaps we can, let's say, convince the Chinese to get the hell out. What d'you think, my friend?" Matthew could see Luna was mulling things over.

"How could you do that? I mean, get the Chinese out of here?" Luna needed some convincing before he put his neck on the line.

"Leave that to us. We can't discuss the details, but believe me when I say they will want to leave once we're finished with them." Emma was quick to take up the discussion. "And... there's a large group of powerful people who want the same thing. All of us will be pushing in the same direction at the same time." She was getting a little carried away here, but Luna was listening.

"What about the cartel?" Luna looked worried.

"Don't you think they will want the same thing?" Matthew asked.

"I guess they will. Wow, what a turn-up for the books! Who would have guessed that a couple of environmentalists would come to our help like this? I thought you might help save some frogs and trees and things, but this! Will there be any police, courts, and judges involved, or military?" Now Luna was warming up to the idea, but he had questions as he ran through the things that concerned him most.

"None of that. And besides, most of them will be on our side." Matthew looked smug as he turned to Emma. It was like the pièce de résistance.

Luna caved, smacked his palms on the table, and let out a *Wowwww*. "Let's do it. I hope this is for real."

They talked on for another hour before calling it quits for the night. Everyone felt tired. But Matthew wanted to make notes from their talk with Luna. He would read them later, but he knew he needed to record them because they were important.

As they said their goodnights, Luna turned to them with a huge smile on his face.

"This could be our time." He turned back and walked to his broken-down old pickup. It had no radio, no passenger seat, seat belts, gearshift knob, or mirrors. He had sold them all for food.

Chapter 33

For A Few Bags Less

The old red Ford picker truck seemed lost tucked away at the back of the contractor's yard. It was partly hidden by other sad-looking construction equipment in various states of disassembly. But, if it worked, and the knuckle boom still operated, it could be just the right vehicle Roberto needed. He wasn't an expert in these things, but he knew enough to check it out and even operate the boom if needed. The job wasn't hard. All it had to do was lift some two-ton bags off parked trailers and move them to a hiding place he had yet to find.

The owner was more than happy to fire up the old beast and let Roberto play around with it, although it couldn't go off the premises without a permit. Roberto had some experience with these kinds of truck-mounted cranes, but not an '88 model. On the other hand, older was generally simpler to operate with fewer, if any, electronics to learn. He wasn't looking for a long-term relationship with the truck and would probably be finished with it in a few weeks. After that, well, he would park it somewhere and let others worry about disposal.

Everything seemed to work, although there was a fair amount of black smoke pushed out of the exhaust when the truck moved from first to second gear. Good old Ford engines. They seemed to go on forever, despite making the kind of noises that, in other machines, might indicate it was about to fail. But the owner assured Roberto that the old beast had been a faithful donkey over the years and served him well, helping around building sites. The five-ton capacity crane was more than enough for the majority of ground-level lifts he needed. The knuckle boom's advantage was its articulation. It could work in tight spaces and needed less vertical room to load and unload. Roberto wasn't sure if this was important for the work he intended, but versatility could be useful. The crane would have more than enough capacity and they wouldn't have to extend the stabilizers to pick up the bags. That meant a nimbler operation.

Oddly, but fortunately for Roberto, the contractor wasn't particularly interested in selling his picker truck. He preferred to lease and maintain ownership for use on his next project. The deal was struck, and Roberto drove the old Ford off as it belched its way through the gears, struggling when it saw any kind of incline ahead.

By this time, Deek had joined Roberto from Quito, and Glenn had driven over from the El Pangui camp. Neither of them showed themselves during the transaction with the owner of the picker truck. There was no point in identifying themselves to strangers as associates of Roberto. They stayed in different hotels, communicated by radio and didn't eat together, but it was clear what they had to do.

The six Zamora truckers needed over twelve hours to drive from the project site to Puerto Bolívar in Machala, up and over two mountain ranges, along narrow roads through busy towns, and twisting almost all the way as they dealt with constant highway gradient changes and hairpin bends along the route. Then, they had to turn around and go back to Zamora. Wisely, the company arranged for the drivers to stop at a midway point on their way to the port near Loja, as well as on the way back. The round trip would take them three days: Zamora to Loja; Loja to Machala, and back to Loja; and finally Loja to Zamora. Arrangements were made by Tongyan for rooms permanently on hold at Motel Tabbú, off the E-35 highway, on the west side of Loja. It had a large, rough, graveled surface on the north side, able to accommodate the six tractors with their trailers, as well as the six returning vehicles from the port. There would always be twelve drivers and their guards at the motel on any night. Unless there was a plant shutdown for any reason.

At noon on the third day after getting the truck crane, Roberto was ready to go. Then, he got confirmation from James that the next concentrate trucks were coming his way. It would take the trucks roughly six hours from that moment to reach Loja and arrive as sunset was about to happen at around 6:15 p.m. The trucks returning from the port should arrive at around 9 p.m.

Roberto had already examined the area around the motel. He watched for two nights as the convoys came and went, and noted a spotter was posted all night in one of the trucks with the concentrate tote bags on both occasions. As it happened, the trucks heading to the port with their concentrate loads had parked parallel to one another, facing the highway, with the last truck closest to the motel on the downside of the slope. The spotter had taken up position in that last one. The returning trucks arrived at 9:25 p.m. and parked parallel but opposite the others, and didn't need to post a spotter.

On that first night of operations, Roberto drove the picker truck around the north side of Loja at around 5 p.m., taking the northern E-35 route as far as the traffic circle, where he took the third exit onto Av. Lateral de Paso Angel F. Rojas heading south down the hill to the bend immediately north of the motel. He had already spotted a good location for parking out of sight of the motel and had rented space in a secure metal shed nearby for the stolen bags to be stored. Deek and Glenn followed in their Land Cruiser and parked on the gravel pad next to Roberto.

It would be a while until nightfall when the action would start. Meanwhile, they seized the opportunity to reconnoiter the area together, discuss what needed to be done, and assign tasks before driving in the Land Cruiser to a small café, Piedra's Grill, north of the roundabout and well away from prying eyes. The welcoming sign included a skinned pig hanging on a hook at the entrance, ready to cut and wrap. It was hard to miss.

Roberto had left the truck crane up the hill from the motel. Shortly before 10:00 p.m., they glided by the motel in the Land Cruiser. Roberto saw all twelve trucks parked in the same pattern for the night as he had seen on the previous two nights.

Deek could make out an outline of a head in the cab of the truck Roberto had mentioned. Deek's job was to ensure the spotter wasn't doing too thorough a job while Roberto and Glenn had to work with the picker truck.

By 2 a.m. there was zero traffic on the side road as Roberto put the truck crane into neutral and glided, with no lights, down the hill. He steered with some difficulty onto the gravel parking area farthest from the truck where the spotter sat or slept.

The parallel parking in combination with the two sets of trucks facing away from each other meant there was a gap between the backs of the trucks. It could have accommodated the old Ford, but Roberto was hesitant. He preferred to stay as far away as he could from the occupied truck and decided to operate from the front side of the trucks returning to Zamora. The knuckle boom's reach and capacity were perfect. They could reach up enough to clear the cabs' height and extend across to the concentrate tote bags on the trailers. He only needed to reach three of those trailers to do what they needed: six bags in total from each convoy, two from each truck.

Deek stayed on target, staring at the silhouette of the spotter's head in the first truck. Glenn stepped down from the Ford and scooted over to the trailer farthest away from where Deek was focused. He climbed on top of one of the rear tires and pushed himself up and over the sideboard, rather than dropping the tailgate and risk making a noise if it slipped and thudded down.

Roberto watched as Deek positioned himself with a narrow beam flashlight over the bags. He stopped, turned, and gave Roberto a thumbs-up as he confirmed the defaced Chinese marking on the top of the first tote bag. The old Ford came to life with a little roar and a lot of smoke. Roberto kept his foot off the accelerator to minimize noise. All three froze as the engine came to life with a modest rumble, but the head in the first truck didn't move.

After counting to twenty, with no sign of the spotter having noticed anything, Roberto raided the boom and swung it over the trailer farthest from him then aimed the head end toward where Glenn crouched. He lowered the hook enough for Glenn to grab on and feed it through the loops of a bag. There was a muted whining as the boom's sheave hoisted the bag over the sideboard. The boom retracted and swung the bag onto the Ford's trailer bed. Glenn returned to release the hook. First lift complete, five to go.

It took less than forty minutes to lift the six bags off three trucks and shift the loads around to hide the gaps that had been left.

Glenn climbed back into the truck cab with Deek following. Again, Roberto counted to twenty to ensure the spotter had not been disturbed. The old Ford made its way up the hill to the storage building. The horizontal boom lifted the six stolen bags into place, with space remaining for more bags to be stored.

They locked the storage and changed vehicles back to the Land Cruiser. Then they headed back down the hill to check the motel for signs of activity. There were none, and once they reached the highway, Deek pressed his foot on the accelerator. They would repeat the procedure the next two nights. Then, Roberto would ask James for more instructions.

Chapter 34

Let's Do More

"You know, James, we should take the cocaine out of those bags Roberto and the boys took. Then, put them back on the trailers to replace the next ones they take." Matthew felt encouraged by the smoothness of Roberto's operation in Loja. He saw no reason not to take things a step further.

"You mean carry on lifting six bags at a time from the trailers and replacing them with cocaine-free bags?" James laughed. "That would really piss off the Chinese."

"I know. That's what we want, though. Talk to Roberto and see what he thinks. He's going to have to dig those cocaine bags out in short order if he has to put them back on the trailers, and he needs to think about the timing."

"I like it, Matthew. By the way, is there any news on Matias?" James was still smiling at the thought of what they were hatching.

"He's still at home in Trujillo. I don't expect him to show his face anytime soon. Let's give him a couple of months, then move him on before anyone tracks him down."

"Okay. What about Nathan and Eric?" James stopped smiling and felt concerned.

"One of Sean's guys should be there now to keep his eyes on them. So far, so good, but I'm not getting a warm and fuzzy feeling. We may need to airlift them out."

Matthew had heard from Sean that Mack was at Escondida and scouting for signs of anyone following his charges. But so far, it was clear.

oooo

Roberto guffawed when he heard James and Matthew's suggestion. But he liked it and put in a call to Glenn and Deek. They were in the area, waiting to move on the next convoy. They all laughed at the idea and decided there was no time like the present to put the plan into action.

Back at their adopted unofficial office, Piedra's Grill, they worked out some of the details. Getting it done would mean digging out the cocaine bags immediately after they had unloaded the stolen concentrate tote bags and storing them in the rented shed. They could finish by dawn, rest, and be back for the evening's work. Roberto decided to leave the old Ford at the storage shed and shuttle back and forth to his digs with Glenn and Deek. That would avoid driving the truck to and from town every day and risk someone taking notice.

Using military-style folding shovels, the three of them broke into the six concentrate tote bags at the storage shed and dug around for the cocaine bags. They weren't hard to locate, about one foot from the top. It had taken only thirty minutes to retrieve the twelve bags, two from each concentrate tote. The next time they would fill the holes left, after taking out the cocaine bags, with concentrate from the next set of bags, re-tie the cords and place the refilled bags on the next convoy in place of the new ones they would take. And so on. A work of genius.

The concentrate tote bags without cocaine were lifted onto the picker truck, ready to be taken down the hill to the incoming trailers later that day. The next six bags were brought back to the shed. The three men retrieved the cocaine bags and set them in one corner. They laughed at the thought of the Chinese discovering the lack of their lucrative product and wondering how it could be. Were they shortchanged at the Zamora? Was it mismanagement? Or were the truck drivers involved? How could this happen?

Of course, they had no idea about the sample of concentrate tote bags sent to the blue warehouse at the port. Had they known it was a check by the Chinese on the security of the cocaine before the concentrate tote bags were finally shipped out, they may have taken things more seriously. In fact, they wouldn't have done it at all.

The first looting had gone unnoticed at the port because, of course, they had chosen a bag with the cocaine still hidden in it to be taken to the warehouse for checking. And no one at the port realized they were actually short by six bags. They weren't counting. Nor was anything suspected with the second convoy. After the third convoy unloaded at the port, and the single bag removed to the warehouse, it was time for an inspection.

There was no guarantee that any of the bags in the warehouse would be free of cocaine, as other bags on the trailers could have been selected and would have passed the inspection.

As it happened there was only one cocaine-free tote bag in the warehouse bearing the mutated Chinese symbol, but it was enough to sound the alarm. The two inspectors thought it was perhaps an error on the part of the Zamora plant, marking it incorrectly.

The inspector boarded the ship to examine some of the other sign-bearing tote bags. Most marked concentrate tote bags contained cocaine bags but a few didn't. The alarm was raised. At this point it was rated as orange, which was second only to red, the highest alarm level.

The frantic call from the inspector at the port to Jun Jie Khao's office at the Zamora plant was put through to the general manager immediately. His immediate reaction was to lock down everything—no one coming in and no one leaving. The workers in the loadout area on day shift were rounded up and detained by security.

Two separate pairs of security eyes scrutinized the concentrate due for departure that day as they filled the tote bags. They watched as the cocaine bags were dropped into place in the six selected totes. Another two-member security team had already examined the final cocaine product coming into the loadout hopper and all was as it should be. The full armed security team was on high alert. The ones not in the loadout were near the perimeter gates and all plant doors.

General Manager Khao called Ping Pei on his private scrambled phone. Both were unable to understand what had happened, but they agreed that the plant and the port needed additional security.

"We know that we processed the product," General Manager Khao started. "Our cameras confirm that it was bagged in the usual way and placed in the concentrate tote bags." He paused to take stock of his line of thinking and whether there was any room at any step for anything to go wrong. He could think of nothing, but his thoughts did wander to Nathan and he wondered whether there could be a link. He didn't mention it right away.

"The six carrier trucks were loaded. Again, we know this from the cameras." He paused again, thinking his way through, picturing the bags being loaded onto the trailers, the drivers and their guards getting into cabs, and the trucks disappearing through the front entrance of the property.

"They left for Machala," he continued, "then, after the fifty-truck convoy turned off at Loja for Guayaquil as usual, the other six trucks arrived at the motel outside Loja, also as usual. There were no stops in between. The six trucks departed the following morning at seven a.m. and arrived at Puerto Bolívar at the usual time. The bags were immediately unloaded onto the waiting ship, leaving just one in the warehouse. All as planned." He sounded tired and out of ideas.

"General Manager Khao," Ping Pei started, "if everything you say is correct, and there is no reason to think you are wrong, something must have happened between the Zamora plant and the port." He waited for some sign of agreement or alternative thought from the general manager.

"It must be the drivers, Mr. Pei. How else could it have happened? Only the drivers have access to those bags once they leave the plant and before they arrive at the port."

Ping Pei was nodding. His hand reached for his pack of Winstons, picked out a cigarette and twirled it in his hands. He was thinking. He was thinking hard. He was thinking about Matias, the fellow at the port who had gotten into the warehouse. *What was he doing there?* Ping Pei never did find out. Nothing was missing, nothing was out of place, but he was there without permission, and the only thing of interest would have been the cocaine. Yet the bags didn't appear to have been undone. Regardless, this was all too much of a string of coincidences with that fellow Nathan, then the person at the port and now the missing cocaine bags. It was extremely concerning and he knew he would have to contact his people in Beijing. He may even talk to his embassy friend, Wang Ho Lin, in the event he had heard anything of interest, or could help him piece these things together. After all, they were both tied to this business by assignment through their masters.

Chapter 35

They Know

"Better pull the plug on your Loja operation, Matthew. It sounds like the Chinese are onto something." Stockman sounded serious.

Stockman had called Matthew as soon as he got word from his contact at the Chinese embassy in Quito.

"Oh? What's happening?" The sudden warning took Matthew aback. Roberto's team in Loja had only pulled a few bait and exchanges now and they seemed to have gone without a hitch.

"I guess no one realized the Chinese were checking those concentrate tote bags dropped off at the port warehouse." Stockman wasn't happy.

"Oh, shit." Matthew couldn't help but be surprised and disappointed at the same time. Why didn't he realize that was going to happen? He should have guessed that was the reason for dumping those bags off. Someone was checking before the boat sailed.

"Do you know if they're aware it's an operation out of Loja?" This was grim news. He needed to get his guys out of there, or at the very least get them to go to ground.

"They haven't put it together yet. As far as I can tell, they think it's an inside job. They've rounded up the guys in the loadout at the plant but haven't gotten as far as the drivers yet." Stockman went quiet as he thought.

"I'd better stand our guys down." Matthew was disappointed their ruse was up so quickly. "I guess this is one way to get the word back to Beijing faster." Matthew almost wished he hadn't said that, but Stockman laughed.

"A blessing in disguise, Matthew." He laughed again and suddenly became serious. "Listen, my boy. This could be the trigger we needed to get moving. They'll be focused on whoever took their gold. If they can't pin it on insiders, then all hell will break loose. My guess is they'll start looking at Los Choneros or other cartels, and that will put a match to the fire."

"You're right." Matthew perked up a little. "This might be just what we need. If they start looking at the cartels, we'll have a perfect cover." Now Matthew was getting excited. Most pieces of his jigsaw were in place. He needed to get the troops together to go over everything as soon as he could. But first things first. Get Roberto, Deek and Glenn out of Loja.

"I'll let you know what I hear, Matthew. In the meantime, it's better to get moving and chase those buggers out of there." Stockman didn't spend time on small talk. He was too preoccupied with this latest turn of events and needed to go back to his embassy contact for an update.

Matthew put a call in to James.

"James, have Roberto get rid of the picker truck and get the guys out of Loja—fast." Matthew relayed the information he had received from Stockman to a surprised James. "Better do it right away. I have no idea how far the Chinese have got with their coverage, but my guess is they're all over the place by now."

"Will do. I'll send the guys over your way to help with things," James responded with an urgency in his voice that matched Matthew's.

"Good idea. I'll make sure there's room in camp here for a few more environmental experts." They both relaxed a little and chuckled.

James had already called Roberto earlier to let him know another convoy had passed him and was on route to Loja. Now he had to call him again before he headed up to the Grill with Glenn and Deek and got ready for another raid on the concentrate trucks. They had no idea what had happened earlier that day at the port. Had they turned up at the motel looking for those trucks, it could have been a disaster if the Chinese had doubled security with more than one spotter at the truck stop.

Despite the warning from James, Roberto and the others drove up the hill past the motel to see if anything was happening. But they agreed it could seem suspicious to anyone watching if they went by the motel too slowly with all three heads gawking out the window. They kept a steady fifty miles per hour in the Land Cruiser as Glenn pressed a camera against the rear passenger window, ready to take photos. As it happened, there were no trucks or trailers in the gravel parking area, despite it being two hours past their usual arrival time.

"Looks like they could have driven straight through," Deek commented. He kept staring at the empty lot, which was disappearing fast behind them. "Probably headed to the port with no stops."

"I think you're right," Roberto answered and called James to give him the news.

"I guess that answers something for us." James was not surprised by the turn of events. "Better get rid of the truck and get out of there."

"First thing in the morning, before we leave for El Pangui. We should see you around noon." Roberto was nervous about the turn of events, but he stayed calm in the calmness of his company. This was their style of operation, while he was normally a peaceful, boring person.

Chapter 36

The Case for Luna

Matthew and Emma relaxed by the heated pool on the grounds of the small boutique-style Hostería Quinta Esperanza, in a small town forty-five minutes south of Loja. They needed to spend some time away from the field to think about how to deal with the indigenous cocaine farmers, many of them Shuar. Undoubtedly, Luna was their key, and while they weren't sure to what extent his influence reached over his native Shuar people and the other communities living within the same area, they intuitively felt he could be trusted to convince them of their plan to distance themselves from the Chinese and the Zamora plant. He had certainly got fired up during their discussions, so perhaps he really was dedicated to the concept.

Emma sat cross-legged on a sunbed with a computer tablet in her lap and papers strewn around her. She wore a locally made large-brimmed woven hat which protected most of her body from the sun. Next to her was a small table with a tall iced drink, some local fruit, and a spray suntan lotion bottle. Her skimpy black bikini was tied with the bare minimum of strapping that had fallen from her shoulders, showing off her lean, well-toned body. Matthew sat in a chair opposite. He was already partly tanned from his sailing trips back home. His hat, much smaller than Emma's, was perched on the front of his head and tipped forward to shade his eyes. His swimsuit matched hers in that it was also small and black. In the privacy of the hotel grounds, they could get away with wearing nothing if preferred. There were no other guests and only a couple of staff on duty here in the middle of an afternoon on a weekday.

Stockman had the hotel especially selected. He wanted somewhere to accommodate the whole ORB field team for a few days while they put together the final details of their mission. Time was moving fast now. The Chinese were beginning to look further than their own people as they thought more about the incident with Nathan and Eric, then Matias at the port, and finally finding out about the missing cocaine. They knew there was a story to piece together from these things. But, as far as Stockman knew, they hadn't figured it out yet, although he had heard they were focusing their attention on the cartels. He wasn't sure which one yet but assumed it would be the local Los Choneros chapter.

Matthew and Emma had driven to the hotel early that morning, checked into a room, and looked around the premises and considered it suitable for the team to meet. They ate a small lunch by the pool, then with their laptops and papers in hand began to piece together what they had learned so far about the Shuar and what part they would play in the mission. It became very clear that all their communications with them would have to go through Luna. There just wasn't time to do it any other way.

Emma flipped through her information and looked up at Matthew. She placed her oversized sunglasses over the brim of her oversized hat.

"You know, these poor people—" she started.

"Who?" Matthew looked up with a puzzled face at Emma.

"The Shuar, of course." She had thought Matthew was on the same page as she was and started again. "Those poor people. It's a sad story." Emma's emotions somewhat distracted her as she stared at the report in front of her. "Battling through their entire history for the right to stay on their own land. Land they had always lived on and that provided everything they needed to survive." She put her partly closed hand to her lips as though to cover her expression. She was imagining Luna and his mother fighting for survival, and putting faces to a catastrophe was always emotionally devastating.

"First, they had to fight other indigenous groups looking to spread out. Then, the Spanish colonizers and those pesky missionaries tried to wipe out their culture. And now, their own government with all that foreign industrial pressure." Emma kept staring down as she read from her laptop, as if she was engrossed in what she was reading.

"This is interesting, Em. From what this says," Matthew took up the conversation without looking up from his point of reference, "they were the first formally organized indigenous people in Latin America, and yet they kept losing ground to everyone else." He picked at his chin, deep in thought about what he was reading. "I can't tell from what I see here whether they were outnumbered or too simple. Maybe a lack of leadership, or plain disorganized, but they ended up ceding their land to settlers or leaving the area out of frustration with what was becoming overpopulation. Whatever it was, those who stayed seemed to have been driven to restricted areas to eke out a pretty bare living—as Luna has done. It reminds me of the North American Indians and what they endured."

"You're right," Emma agreed. She could see the parallel, except it had happened to the Shuar people over hundreds of years, like a slow and agonizing loss that one only realizes after the fact. Emma went back to reading.

"From what I can tell after talking more to Luna and reading what I can find on the subject, it seems they hitched their wagon to this guy, Koski. He was a complete stranger, found by a small hunting group of Shuar, coming out from the Peruvian side of the jungle." Matthew paused as he went on flipping through the notes in front of him and then stopped at a page.

"Luna seemed to have a lot of respect for this Canadian." Matthew was trying to make sense of the notes he had rapidly made after he talked to Luna. He had embellished in some places to make his notes flow. "This Koski guy was a mild-mannered, kind and thoughtful person with a twinkle in his blue eyes, which the Shuar took to be an omen of good fortune for their future." Matthew looked up at Emma and made a face. "Perhaps they needed someone special to believe in after all the other foreigners seemed to just prey on them. Or were missionaries interested only in twisting their religious beliefs for their own purposes. Whatever it was, Koski seemed to embrace the Shuar's cause as one worth working for."

Matthew went back to his notes.

"It seems, for years Koski worked with the Shuar people, helping them orchestrate their defenses against foreigners looking for mineral or oil rights on their land. He showed them how to deal with lawyers and court systems, and while they lost most of their struggles, they learned to move forward and send many of their people to colleges in Guayaquil and Cuenca and even Quito to learn about the law and other useful courses to help the indigenous communities. That's where Luna learned languages, and a lot more he isn't telling us." Matthew looked over at Emma who nodded her agreement with his observation.

"I think you're right. There is lots he isn't telling us, but then, does that matter? I don't think it would change the story." Emma got a facial look of acceptance of her point from Matthew.

He continued, "They needed a lot more money than they could make to finance their agendas and send their people to get educated. They had always relied on the jungle to provide almost everything they needed to live. But, as he said, those times had changed... and according to Luna, Koski provided a ray of hope. He first taught them to search for their own minerals, as the Peruvian Piqueneros had taught him." Matthew paused again. "It's a little difficult deciphering what Luna was saying or trying to say. I don't know if he was ever involved directly with Koski. So much of this may be hearsay or second hand, and Luna is passing information on, but let's keep going.'"

Matthew looked at Emma, who nodded as she picked up the glass of what was a cold drink. Matthew continued.

"But, according to Luna, there were slim pickings. The minerals were disseminated through the ore as microparticles, not given to underground mining." Matthew paused. "That's what I think he meant. Rich veins of ore with nuggets that could be extracted weren't there, unlike in Peru. Open-pit mining is the only way to recover the minerals in southeast Ecuador." Again, Matthew paused and looked over at Emma. "He's bang-on there. He may not know a lot about mining, but he does know the difference between nuggets and no nuggets." They both laughed, in part to break the tone of what they were learning. This was a downtrodden group who couldn't seem to get a leg up on life.

Matthew carried on.

"Koski kept thinking of other ways he could help and as he watched a small group of farmers picking coca leaves, he realized they were harvesting several times a year. Then, they prepared a product they claimed they could sell to local gangs. They weren't sure what that was, but they did know that if they were to chew the leaves, they felt happier. Koski took the process further, realizing his friends were producing the paste they could sell for what would become refined cocaine, a prized drug to the outside world."

"Quite a revelation, I would say." It was Emma.

"It sounds like the beginning of a successful industry, Em, and the one that brought us here."

Matthew continued interpreting his notes.

"It seems this Koski person improved the process and encouraged other farmers to form a cooperative. He began negotiating with what he realized was a branch of the Los Choneros cartel to buy the crude product. They didn't like each other at all. Luna told me that if it wasn't for Koski being needed on both the business and manufacturing ends, Los Choneros would have happily done away with him and dealt directly with the farmers, who they knew could be manipulated.

"Luna goes on. Koski's notoriety became well known, not only with the hierarchy of Los Choneros, but also with Los Lobos, who were gradually replacing them as the predominant criminal organization, after the leader of Los Choneros was imprisoned.

"Soon, word reached farther into Colombia and Mexico, where the cartels were preparing to push south into Ecuador's new cocaine territory. It seems that while Koski worked with the Shuar in the south, he only had to hide from Los Choneros, but he knew that the other cartels would follow—he didn't know how long it would be, though. The Shuar knew Koski was being hunted and kept moving him from one community to another. Eventually, he had to leave once the cartel began torturing and killing innocent villagers to find where he was hiding. No one knows where he went, or whether he is still alive. But his legacy lives on. Except now, with only a small and ineffectual group of cartel members to deal with, the Shuar and their burgeoning industry have been manipulated by the Chinese. Once again, they are at the mercy of foreigners." That was the end of Luna's notes.

"Boy, it's one hell of a story. If we put that together with everything else Luna told us, it's no wonder they want the Chinese out. My guess is he won't have any problem convincing the others not to keep going the Chinese way, even if they have to deal with the cartels. At least they're from the same country—well, Los Choneros is, at least. This is as much a cultural thing as it is a financial one, I think."

As chance would have it, Matthew and Emma had struck gold when they met Luna that day in camp. Despite his size, that look of simplicity and a sort of happy-go-lucky attitude, they had come across a key to one of their problems. He was desperate for his people to regain solidarity and independence from foreigners.

"Okay, so what do you think we have to do to help him along?" Emma stared at Matthew, who had put his papers to one side and flopped onto a sunbed next to her. His hat was over his eyes as he thought.

"I don't know, as we have to do a lot, Em. That is if we trust Luna to round everyone up. We need to get with him again and go through the framework of our plan so he understands the timing. My guess is he's going to have more trouble keeping to that than we are. It's a hell of a lot of ground for him to cover. If there are a crazy number of farms out there, he has to get to every one of them, convince them to stop what they're doing on a particular day and trust that they'll do it."

"Well, that's where we can help." Emma had a mischievous look in her eyes.

"Oh, do tell." Matthew smiled and waited.

"I doubt Luna has to go to every one of those communities himself. If I know him even a little, my guess is he'll have others do it for him." She paused for any response from Matthew. He tipped his hat back off his eyes and looked over at her.

"You're right, Em. Go on."

"We need money to float these groups for, say, a month while we wait for the cartel to pick up the slack. And you know that won't be long."

"Okay. We can arrange that. And?" Matthew knew she hadn't finished.

"To make sure, we shut down the Zamora cocaine processing plant and conveyor from the river as well as their staging area." Emma sat back. Her eyebrows went up as she smiled.

"What about the annex at the plant and the incoming conveyor?"

"Leave it. It's all useless without the feed cocaine." Emma leaned on one elbow and reached for her drink.

Matthew sat up and mulled over her ideas, searching for weaknesses. He couldn't think of any right now.

"Let's do it, Em." Matthew reached over and pulled her toward him. They kissed, laughed, got up from the loungers and dove into the pool together. It was going to be a beautiful evening, but over the next few days, they needed to get hold of Luna to go through the plan and timing.

Chapter 37

Almost There

Nick, Kenny, and Armando arrived at the Zamora site a few days apart from each other. Stockman had made the necessary arrangements. His Ecuadorian ambassador friend in London helped get visas and other necessary documentation. The papers identified each of his ORB agents as a guest of the country. The companies they represented vouched in writing for them to do their specialist duties.

In essence, they were presented as experts in their field, performing tasks that could not be undertaken by an Ecuadorian. This was typical of the requirements for those seeking to work in-country. Even as temporary vendors, which is what they were claiming to be. The companies involved were the original equipment manufacturers for some of the major pieces of equipment being used on the Zamora property. China was not known for the types of equipment these particular manufacturers were world-renowned for, particularly in terms of performance, size and capacity. Some outsourcing to other countries was inevitable.

Nick rumbled up to the Zamora property security gate in his old open-top jeep. He sported an overgrown ginger beard, short ginger hair, arms covered in more ginger hair, and a T-shirt and shorts that seemed to be several sizes too small. He was six feet two inches tall with a big-boned frame which, when combined with his other features, intimidated the hell out of the two security guards who met him at the gate. Nick flipped open his papers, looking as though he was ready for a fight if anyone stood in his way, but the guard just waved him through unceremoniously. He chuckled to himself as he threw his things on the undersized bed in his room and wiped the sweat away from his eyes for the hundredth time that day.

"Fuck, what a place," Nick whispered loudly under his breath as he stomped off down the hall in search of a cold beer. He wasn't going to find one, but it didn't stop him from looking and eventually giving up for an iced soda instead.

Nick carried credentials as a representative of Komatsu. The Zamora's mining fleet included their WE2350 loader, the world's largest. They also had their 4800 XPC electric rope shovel. Both were matched for working with 400-ton haul trucks. They also had two ZT44 blasthole drills. They were gigantic. The bucket of the shovel could grab 135 tons of blasted rock at a time and fill a 400-ton capacity truck in three swings. Nick knew enough to get by in each, but he was no expert. He did, however, have a geotechnical and mining background and was very good with explosives.

Two days later Kenny arrived in his filthy, somewhat battered black Range Rover that had seen better days. He was the antithesis of Nick. All smiles, lots of teeth, short, stocky, and with the general look of a small, difficult-to-stop football player. He had a smattering of Spanish; he looked like a Spaniard and had been living on the Mediterranean coast near Gibraltar for about five years, indulging in a life of mild debauchery. But for all that, ever the womanizer, Kenny came with a cuddly smoothness and smile no one could dislike.

Kenny entertained the security guards at the gate, promising them all kinds of trinkets he had brought with him and handed his papers over for examination. They patted each other's back as Kenny jumped into his SUV and drove on through to the camp. His bed was perfectly sized, and while he also used up a lot of napkins to soak the sweat from his brow, he took it all in stride and made his way over to the plant, where he would introduce himself as the ABB representative, here to check out the three main transformers.

Armando arrived in a cloud of men's perfumed fragrance, making the guards keep their distance as they rubbed their noses to work the release of antihistamines out. Slicked-back black hair, a face that seemed very recently shaved, and an outfit that could fit into the casual side of a city, Armando, an Ecuadorian himself, passed his credentials over and instructed the guards to let him through—he had business to attend to. The guards reacted with deference to the apparent importance of this individual, one of their countrymen, saluted and let him pass.

Armando strode through the camp, chest out, and stood upright to his full height of five feet four inches. He found his room, dumped his two bags on the bed and headed to the canteen for refreshments. Along the way, he greeted the Chinese occupants with a surly *"hola"* and strode on past with seeming purpose. They just looked at him, screwed up their faces as the waft of perfume hit them, and wondered how another Caucasian had been allowed into their domain.

Armando was an educated man and had traveled extensively from project to project in various capacities, from mechanical engineering to project management. Now, he spent fifty percent of his time working on ORB special assignments in either advisory or field roles. He had become an expert in sabotage techniques associated with mechanical equipment. He also managed small jobs for them requiring his technical expertise to temporarily disrupt an operation while others worked on the bigger picture. Or he helped someone like Matthew, who might need guidance on how to best handle a particular assignment with a mechanical component that was beyond his knowledge. But one had to pay the price. Armando came with a degree of cockiness heightened whenever he felt his knowledge surpassed others', and at those times, he seemed to bathe himself even more extensively in the colognes and perfumes that were a signature of his presence. It was one of those oddities of his life that couldn't be explained.

The three new men intentionally didn't mix and avoided each other whenever two or all three of them happened to be in the same place at the same time, especially in the dining hall. But they managed, and while none of them had even a smattering of Mandarin, most often spoken by the predominant Chinese mainland workers, each of them tried their best to integrate with the workers in attempts not to stand apart from the crowd should the need arise.

For the next week, Nick familiarized himself with the open pit operations at the mine, motioning to the operators what he was doing and getting a lot of nodding in return. As the day and night crews became more familiar with his presence, including jumping up into the seat of each piece of equipment he was "checking out," he only went so far as to start engines, listen to the revs for a few minutes as though searching for foreign sounds, then turn the engines off with a nod and look of satisfaction that everything was performing as it should. Any more than that, and he would get the operators to show him on the pretext of testing their abilities and invited their comments on equipment performance. Fortunately, two of the more senior operators spoke reasonably good English, although neither was confident enough to actually have a free-flowing conversation with him.

As soon as Nick felt comfortable that everyone up at the mine knew who he was and why he was at Zamora, he drove over to the ANFO plant, where the ammonium nitrate, kerosene used for fuel oil, and caps were stored. Concrete block walls separated the individual components stored in the same building located nearly a mile from the nearest inhabited facility—as it should be. It was also nearly a thousand feet from the nearest pit wall, and Nick was very happy he had his own vehicle to hide and transport what he needed.

There were two busy times for the explosives plant over a twenty-four-hour period on most days. The first was preparing for a mid-afternoon blast, and then for a second blast at 3:00 a.m on most days. The rest of the time at the mine was spent drilling the blast holes, packing the explosives, and hauling the blasted rock out to either the mill or to the waste piles.

Once the blast components were taken up to the mine to charge the blast holes, the plant would go quiet. Only one person was left to clean the equipment before the next preparations.

Nick watched as Eduardo, one of the Ecuadorian men with the explosives contractor, finished his work. He locked the double sliding doors to the plant and stepped into his trailer twenty feet away. He would be there for the next four hours until his shift ended and someone took his place to prepare for the next morning's load.

Once Eduardo's head disappeared below the window of his trailer as he settled himself down to rest, Nick pulled up to the side door of the plant. He picked the lock and stepped in. Over the next week, Nick poured kerosene out from the bulk storage tank into his own containers, carried out bags of ammonium nitrate, and enough boxes of caps for what he needed.

Nick's duties at the pit were light, to say the least. Everyone appeared happy with the equipment, and whenever questions came up, Nick would send appropriate messages to Komatsu dealers in the US for responses. That way, he kept well ahead of any suspicion as to his expertise. But he needed to use the ZT44 blasthole drill to complete one more task in preparation for what was expected of him.

Meanwhile, Kenny was checking out the transformers as well as the interfaces with the substation and control room. To him, it was all routine, with very little prep for what he had to do when the time came. The three transformer beasts had taken over fourteen months to be delivered. They had arrived in one full piece each, requiring special transport permits, a slew of pilot vehicles to guide each along its route from the port, high-capacity cranes, and high-voltage electricians to make the final connections at the plant to the incoming power lines from the new hydro station up-country on the Río Zamora. Everything took a lot of time, coordination, and specialized skill sets. Everything was expensive. And nothing could be replaced at the drop of a hat. Kenny was just the person to totally annihilate it all, and it made him smile.

As he wandered around the substation in the fenced-off enclosure, where the transformers were mounted on their concrete foundations, Kenny checked the sizes of wrenches he would need to loosen the bolts on the oil fins. He checked the location of the pressure gauges and where the communication lines ran. He crawled under the fins to see if there were additional drain plugs or wiring added that other similar installations didn't have. He could almost do what he went to Zamora for with his eyes closed. But he also knew that in bad weather or with security guards around, he might appreciate extra preparation. He was ready now.

Armando swaggered through the mill, in his custom gold-colored safety hat, with a look of superiority that made the operators stand back to let him pass. He rarely stopped to talk to anyone. But, within a day, everyone knew who he was and why he was there—the guru of mills, the oracle of all things mechanical, the perfumed prince. If he needed anything, jump. Make sure he gets it, and fast.

Armando familiarized himself with the location of all his targets, including the control room, noting entry points, stairways, alarms, and whatever cameras looked over the area in which he was interested. Fortunately, most of his work would be in the basement under the mills, where there was only one camera mounted under each side of the operating floor and facing down into the sumps, where problems would most likely occur, if at all. The basement was where the lube oil packages and large slurry pumps were located. Any work he was going to do there could easily be done out of sight of the cameras. He was happy and ready, except he still needed to locate some wedges for the mill trunnions.

Each end of a mill was mounted in trunnions that supported it and allowed it to rotate smoothly. Bearings were made to allow frictionless rotation of the equipment during operation. Keeping them well lubricated was vital. They also had to be aligned perfectly to keep the mills from running off center and destroying themselves with vibration.

When the mill motors weren't operating and the mills were not rotating, dedicated inching drives could be used to slowly turn the mills for maintenance and liner replacements. They were simple pieces of equipment but extremely sturdy and exact. As the inching drive turned, it would engage the mill gear and slowly, very slowly, rotate the mill at the liberty of the operator. Should Armando be able to install very thin wedges—and they had to be made of steel—between the inching drive and the mill gear, the mill could be slowly turned using emergency power until the gear became misaligned with the pinions. Easy? Maybe. Armando had never tried it, and there was a possibility that the inching drive would not be able to overcome the resistance of the wedge, or the weight of the mill simply destroyed the wedge—but he was going to try.

Chapter 38

Beijing

Wang Ho Lin sat a bench in their usual meeting place in the shadow of La Cruz del Papa, to meet his friend Ping Pei in private.

As he waited, he considered the situation. From his perspective, it would seem that the drug situation, as he preferred to call it, had been discovered. As yet, he had no idea who was behind what had happened, who these people they had identified were, or who they worked for. He hoped Ping Pei had more information to pass back to Beijing.

As he lit another Winston, he spotted Ping Pei coming toward him. His friend looked dejected and deep in thought as he sat down at the other end of the bench. He didn't look up, nor did he say anything in greeting. Instead, he took a Winston out of his pack, lit it and sucked the smoke in deeply. It was only then—as though the cigarette gave him courage—that he looked over at his friend, nodded and spoke.

"It is a worrisome time, my friend. We have uncovered a conspiracy— we have some perpetrators in our sights, some of our... value has been taken, yet still we don't know who or why." Ping Pei stopped, inhaled another lungful of smoke, and slowly let it swirl through his mouth into the air. "Do you know anything that might help us discover who these dogs are?"

"Mr. Pei," Wang Ho Lin started as Ping Pei angled his head toward him, wondering why the formality of his friend's voice. He must have something new to disclose. *But they will recall me to Beijing to answer for these problems... perhaps.*

Ping Pei's thoughts were interrupted.

"Our sources tell us Los Choneros cartel is closing in. Could it be the cartel who are causing your trouble? Perhaps they are looking for their share. Or they are looking to get rid of us. Who can tell?" He stopped and waited for a response.

Ping Pei thought it a little far-fetched that the cartel would use non-Ecuadorians to do their work. He mused that they would like to get involved or take charge of the whole show if they could. After all, they were the ones who had been replaced when Tongyan came along.

"Thank you, Mr. Lin." Ping Pei was formal in his return. "Perhaps you are correct, but our feeling is there is something else going on."

"Oh?" Wang Ho Lin wasn't given to sounds of wonderment, or any kind of emotion. "If this is not the doing of the cartel, then who?"

"I don't know if you are aware, but before we arrived at Zamora, there was a foreigner of high regard among the natives. Someone called Koski, who we understand taught them almost everything they know about this special industry of ours." Ping Pei looked up at his friend to make sure he understood what he meant. "While he seemed to have disappeared a number of years ago, he may have returned to help them once again." It was Ping Pei's turn to pause.

Wang Ho Lin shrugged. "A man. Just a man. A foreigner. I am not aware of this person. Are you sure of what you're saying?"

"I am sure of the man. I am sure of his name. But I am not sure where he is or whether he is the root of our problems."

"I will see what we can do." Wang Ho Lin was deep in thought. "Do you know his country of origin?"

"Canada, but I don't know where. But I can tell you that these indigenous people treat him as a god. He can do no wrong, and that includes all the product suppliers in the jungle. They talk about him freely and respectfully, but all refuse to say where he is." Ping Pei didn't know any more and neither was he going to assume anything. But he desperately needed to identify who was behind all their problems. Otherwise, he would be recalled for things he had no knowledge of.

"Leave it with me." Wang Ho Lin picked another cigarette from his pack and lit it.

Chapter 39

Time for Action

"We're going to have to mess things up a bit." Matthew looked around at his crew, sitting in the meeting room overlooking the pool. They had collected at the small hotel he and Emma were staying at, the Hostería Quinta Esperanza, to get a little R & R and discuss their plans going forward.

Stockman reserved all twelve suites in the hotel for a few days, so there were no other guests. He had also arranged the room to conference in, and a large TV was set up in the room for him to join them. There was an easel set to one side, with a large map leaning on it of the Zamora area showing the pertinent parts Matthew would be referencing.

"We'll likely kill a lot of plants and some animals that won't be able to escape," Matthew continued. Stockman looked on. "But it's much better than a tailings dam breach." Matthew glanced up at Stockman on the screen. He nodded in agreement but didn't say anything.

"Sean, you and Glenn need to blow out the bolted joints on the tailings discharge pipelines from the plant over to the tailings pond. Emma will show you where that is." Matthew glanced over at Emma, who nodded her understanding and made a note on her laptop before getting up and crossing over to the map. She pointed out the location of the tailings pipe and pond to the southeast of the plant.

"The joints are about five hundred feet apart, and each blast will destroy the flange and ruin the two ends of the pipe at each location." She paused and looked at her audience. "There are eight of them."

Emma nodded as she sat down and looked at her notes.

"Thousands of gallons of copper processing waste will have been released into the undergrowth by the time the Chinese figure out what's happening. No big flood, no wave of tailings, no huge force, but more of a big leak." Matthew grinned as he said the word *leak*. He knew it would be more than that, but still it wouldn't be anything like what a breach of the dam would create. That would have meant millions of gallons of waste plus the dam materials hurtling into the Río Quimi and wiping out everything in its path.

"We're not going to avoid polluting a lot of tributaries," he said. "But the waste should wash through the waterways within a few days of the power going out." Matthew looked over at Kenny. "That's where you come in." There were some raised eyebrows as the extent of his proposal started to sank in. But there were no comments at this point.

"What do you need me to do, boss?" This wasn't the first job Kenny had done with ORB, or Matthew. They got on well, had worked on similar projects in their pre-sabotage days and possessed an almost innate understanding of what the other needed before they even said it.

The whole gang was there, listening to every word. Emma sat at a front corner of the table, with James opposite her on the other side. Her laptop was open to the notes she and Matthew had made before the meeting. She would offer prompts to him if needed and take extra notes.

Roberto, Nick, Kenny, Armando, and what remained of the security team—Sean, Glenn, and Deek—filled the rest of the table. The only ones missing were Mack, Matias, Nathan and Eric.

At this stage in a project, everyone was a field operative in the execution plan. Each person would be assigned a specific detail based on their expertise or assisting another team member with their own.

Matthew continued, "I'll get to that, Kenny. Let me just finish up with Sean and Glenn." He poured a fresh mug of coffee, took a sip, and began again.

"Once you're done with the pipelines, head over to the pond and set some explosives on the reclaim water barge's flotation tanks so it sinks and takes the supply line with it." Matthew pointed to the barge on the map, at the opposite end of the pond from where the tailings waste entered. It floated in the freshwater part of the pond, where the solids had settled out and pumped the now clear water back to the plant. "When that's done, we'll be able to report to the agencies and get them to shut the place down." As Matthew said it, his optimism about the success of the overall strategy, which had yet to be completely outlined, was growing. An environmentally enforced closure would be a certainty. But it would only be temporary, maybe a matter of months or a year at the very most, before Zamora would be up and running again. It wouldn't be enough to put them completely out of commission.

The fact was it was possible to rectify. The Chinese could think big and fast when pushed. They could gather all the needed materials quickly, even if that meant shorting someone else. They could even send in additional labor crews at the drop of a hat, albeit they may have to press them into service.

The pipelines were made of thick-walled high-density polyethylene. Easy to transport, and quickly fit up in the field, especially if their ends were already beveled. They would be fuse-welded using special heating equipment that wasn't complicated and didn't need computer software or specialized talent to operate. They could import all the fusion machines they needed and use laborers to handle the pipe and even do the welds. It was just a matter of lifting two ends of the pipe onto the machine. Then, pushing the ends together and lowering the heat source that wrapped around the joint. Once that was done and the joint cooled, the pipe would be dragged forward and the next two ends fitted up for fusing. New bolted flange connectors would be needed every 500 feet to allow the lines to be turned every so often to balance the internal wear, but they would also be easy to acquire for the Chinese.

"And just to make matters worse for them, do the same with the water reclaim lines." Matthew was thinking fast. He pointed to a pair of dashed lines on the map with a pump station located close to the center. The two 36-inch diameter carbon steel pipelines, laid on the surface, brought the fresh water back to the plant.

"These are fully welded lines, so it's better just to blow them out at the pump station and at the two ends. Demolishing the pipe at those few places will have devastating consequences for the plant.

"It's fresh water. So, it won't harm the environment. It'll seep into the ground and leave no residue. That piping is steel and more difficult to handle, though. It will take months and months to get replaced, even for the Chinese. It's all thick-walled, large diameter, so it's not just lying around in the yard, even in China."

In his mind, Matthew was still not convinced the Chinese would be permanently affected.

"Do you think that will be enough to shut the place down, Matthew?" It was Nick. He was echoing the same thoughts Matthew was having. And Matthew knew Stockman would be thinking the same. They had already talked about it.

"I don't think so, Nick. They could probably get one line running in a couple of months to put the plant into at least half-service. Then they could likely replace the second line in, say, a month or two, if they ordered all the pipe at the same time. As for the barge, well, they could probably replace that in a few months as well. We're going to have to do more, and I'm going to come back to you in a moment. Their biggest issue is getting the environmental agencies on side again. But who knows who they're paying off there. "

Matthew looked over at Kenny again.

"Okay, my friend." They had become firm friends a number of years ago after they helped each other sabotage a small power station in Eastern Europe, during the early hours of one bleak morning typical of that part of the world. That silent communication skill they seemed to have developed might have been what saved them when they were discovered after the station blew up.

"You need to take out those primary transformers." He watched as Kenny's eyes lit up. This was the kind of thing that excited him about working with ORB. Always doing something thrilling.

"Tell me more, or do you want me to use my imagination?" Kenny was all smiles as he rubbed his hands together. The others in the room laughed at his enthusiasm.

"Go after the cooling oil." Matthew's suggestion was about as simple as it could be, and Kenny liked that. "But it's all in the timing, my friend. Last thing we want is to take power out at the wrong time."

The plant had to reduce the incoming high-voltage electricity provided from a new generating station further north of the Zamora site through the transformers to 220 volts before distributing it to the rest of the facility. For a plant of Zamora's size, it meant having three 90 megawatt transformers with two operating and one on standby—enough to power well over 100,000 homes. The units were oil-filled to prevent overheating of the coils and core. Pressure drops and heat alarms in the control room signaled oil leaks in the oil bath or sensory lines. If not detected, the loss of oil would first cause short-circuiting. If it continued to exhaustion, it would overheat the transformers, greatly reducing power as the heat built up, and eventually they would burn out.

It was imperative for Kenny to first disconnect the communication wiring to the control room, which would set off the alarms once Kenny started to disable the transformers. Then he would cut the oil-feed lines to the pressure gauges to help drain the oil from the top of the tank. Finally, he would need to remove the bolts under the cooling fins. This would allow the oil to drain into the concrete containment bund, where the transformers were. Without early detection, the transformers couldn't be saved. They would keep operating until overcome by heat.

But Kenny knew all this. There was no need to explain the details. He just nodded. "I guess it's all in the timing." He looked up at Matthew and over to Emma. They both nodded, knowing that Kenny knew what he had to do. This was a one-man night job, and Kenny was just the man they could rely on.

"We'll have to get our schedules synchronized, so let's work on that for the whole team after this meeting. We need to blow out the pipelines first with the barge. Then, the power and everything else. But I need to go through it more precisely. So, you all need to give me your task timelines." Matthew knew that this was going to have to be a set of events timed perfectly. There was going to be no margin for error if they wanted to catch the Chinese off guard with having to cover so many emergencies at the same time.

Okay, so Matthew had added more detail, but it still didn't mean the Chinese were out of Ecuador. Maybe they would keep processing and shipping the cocaine, with or without the copper to hide it. The cocaine processing plant had to be destroyed.

"Roberto, while Kenny is over at the transformers, you and Emma need to get over to the cocaine processing plant on the riverbank and deal with it. Make sure the power is out first, then take out the conveyor supports, cut the belt and blow the building. It all sounds a bit crude, but I don't see any other way to handle it. It has to be totally destroyed. Okay?" Matthew looked from Roberto to Emma. They both nodded. Roberto had the explosives experience and Emma had the moves to make it all work. Again, they would be operating in the dark but for them there was an additional disadvantage: it would be in the jungle and at night.

"Now, while we're on the subject of cocaine, Emma and I will deal with the jungle farmers. They're suddenly going to be without a landing stage for their product, and we need to be ready to deal with them." No one asked Matthew to explain any further. That was well outside their scope of thinking, but Matthew already had a plan in mind that he needed to talk over with Luna.

"Are we going to have to run interference with the cartel?" It was Nick again.

"We're not sure yet, Nick." Matthew looked to Emma for support.

"We're hoping our friends with the Shuar are going to help with them," she offered. "They need the cartel to take over from the Chinese, so it's in their best interests to cover them off. We don't know what their reaction will be, but we should know over the next couple of days."

"Armando." Matthew turned to his Ecuadorian friend. They had worked together before on some mechanical sabotage at a steel plant in Chile. "I know you've done this before, and this is a repeat performance, but this time you'll be doing it inside the mill in the semi-darkness with no power other than emergency. So again, wait for the power outage and get to work. James will be with you to share the load. There will be auxiliary power, so keep hidden. My guess is that if the security people aren't already tied up with the tailings lines, they'll be all over the transformer area. But there are going to be operators fumbling around the mill making their way out of the building. Give them time to do that, then watch for anyone else who may be around before you make your moves." Matthew looked at Armando, who seemed to want to say something. But then, he always did. He was keen but a little undisciplined. However, he was very capable. He knew mill processing equipment like the back of his hand. James would be a great partner for him. Together, they should be able to disable the most important part of the plant—the mills themselves.

"The emergency power will be enough to turn the mills with the inching drive," Armando eagerly chimed in. "It has to be." He hunched his shoulders, as if to say, *You all know that, right?* "Otherwise, if the power goes down and they can't turn the mill, the slurry inside settles out. It's a real pain to get the mill going again. So, they use the inching drive to move it around very slowly and keep the slurry live." Armando was eager to explain his thinking. "So, once we set the wedges in the mill gear, we'll turn the inching drive. James will have to stay at the mills and make sure the wedges hold. A couple of turns on the inching drive and those mills should go off-center and be useless." Armando stopped and looked at Matthew. "If we can't do that, we'll have to blow up the trunnion bearings.

I don't like that but"—Armando could see the concern on their faces—"at this point, I don't know if we can turn the mills past the wedges. So, what else can one do in such a short time?" Armando shrugged and held his hands out, palms up and cupped. It was as if he was looking for something to put in them.

"James, take some C4 in case. But if you have to blow it, make sure it blasts the gears and the trunnions." Matthew didn't like the idea of blasting inside the plant. He was afraid innocents would get hurt. But he couldn't think of an alternative. Maybe contaminating or draining the lube oil system would stop the mills, but he wasn't sure of the timing. He didn't know how long it would take for the mills to seize up without lubrication.

Armando was happy and looked over at Kenny.

"My friend, can you tell me the best way to knock out those mill motors? I know how to screw up the slurry pumps, but not so much the main motors."

"Of course. Let's talk after this." Kenny was smiling. He was in his element.

"Before you leave the plant, Armando, if you have time, put sand in the mill lube oil tanks. You can get pick up some bags from the fire stations. I can't imagine it, but if they do manage to get the mills started up again, they'll all get shut down soon enough with only sand in the system and not oil." It was Matthew's turn to smile as he thought about the havoc that would create.

The lube oil system for a mill was a complex network of pressurized lubricating oil distributed to all moving parts of the mills. There would be one system skid for each mill, located underneath, on the basement floor, and all it would take to disable a mill was to contaminate the oil in the feed and collection tanks. Normally, the oil would be distributed from the feed tank to all the points of the mill needing lubrication. It would return through a filtering system to remove any deleterious particles collected on route before being circulated again. The purity of the oil was crucial for the equipment and the sand would clog everything going in and coming out.

Armando signaled his understanding with a thumbs-up sign and looked over at James, who just nodded. This was probably the simplest set of tasks of all the work needed, provided they weren't disturbed.

Matthew looked over at Nick.

"Now, perhaps this is going to be the thing that really puts a stop to everything. How do you feel about creating a pit wall failure, Nick? And how would you go about it?" Matthew asked as he settled back into his chair and gave his mouth a rest from talking. He glanced up at Stockman on the screen, who winked and smiled back.

"Wow. Yeah, that would do it, Matthew. Nothing like a pit wall collapse to finish operations off. Not that it has ever stopped an open pit. But I guess with environmentalists being mad about the tailings spill, the transformers going down, the cocaine plant being blown up and the mills being put out of action, the Chinese could find that enough to give up." Nick laughed, and everyone joined in.

"My sentiments exactly," Matthew said. "I don't know if we will stop them for the long term, even then..." He paused as the team stared at him, waiting for the other shoe to drop. "But let's try our darndest."

"Well, I can get the pit wall to collapse without too much trouble." Nick was charged up. "But what more are we going to have to do to get them out of there?"

"Gentlemen." It was Stockman for the first time during the meeting. "We may not be able to stop them from operating in the long term, despite how hard we try. But I can tell you this..." He paused for effect and watched the faces in the room with their eyes glued to the screen. "If we can create some breathing room, the coca farmers and the cartel will have a chance to get things back to normal. Then, we will have succeeded in our mission and I doubt very much if the Chinese could get that business back, even if they get the mill up and operating." Stockman watched as heads cocked and smiles broke out on the faces as everyone realized the game plan.

Nick raised his hand.

"Go ahead." Stockman focused on Nick.

"Then what would be the point in my blowing out the pit wall?" Nick asked.

"To add to the mayhem, Nick. The more there is, the longer it will take the Chinese to recover, and by the time they do, they will have missed the cocaine train altogether, so to speak. We don't care about the copper and gold—we need them to get out of the cocaine business." Stockman paused and waited in case there were more questions. There weren't.

"Okay, everyone. Take a break for the rest of the day." Matthew took over the meeting again. "All of you come back here after supper to go over timing. Nick, let's talk this evening about the pit wall." He waited for acknowledgments. "We still have tomorrow to go over anything else, so meet here for breakfast at seven a.m. before we break up. All clear?" Matthew looked around and glanced up at Stockman.

"Are you going to join us later, sir?" Mathew asked.

"Wouldn't miss it for the world. I'll call in at seven. Does that sound about right?"

Matthew gave the thumbs-up and Stockman's screen went blank.

"What do you need me to do, Matthew?" It was Deek. He hadn't got an assignment yet.

"I haven't forgotten you, my friend." Matthew smiled, walked over, and put his hands on the big man's shoulders. "You're the best marksman we have, Deek. Your job is to protect all of us in the field. Meet us for the schedule discussion. You're going to be a busy guy, covering everyone off."

"I like that." Deek smiled and shrugged.

Once the job in the field was completed, Matthew would need to cover off any agreements Stockman had been able to arrange with the cartels, and how they would affect the Shuar and the farmers.

Things were coming to a head quickly.

Chapter 40

Trouble at Escondida

In an otherwise barren landscape, the largest copper mine in the world, Escondida, was carved out of Chile's Atacama Desert, 10,000 feet above sea level. The area was completely devoid of inhabited communities, except for the one the mine created for itself.

It was hard to imagine the size and scale of this project. The massive 150,000 tons of copper ore mined and processed every day of the year, comprising multiple open pits and concentrators, churned out copper pulp. The plant pumped it over one hundred miles to the coast for processing, while pumping desalinated fresh water from the Pacific Ocean back to the plant.

With almost 20,000 bodies to be housed on any day of the week, not to mention the temporary stopovers such as vendor representatives, dignitaries, government inspectors, and, of course, head office interlopers, the expanse, complexity and logistics of housing so many were mind-boggling. An encampment the size of a town with its own make-do churches, shops for essentials, vehicle repair garages, junior schooling for some and kindergartens for others, and a substantial security detail constantly watchful for troublemakers, lawbreakers, drunks and all the other riffraff that came with a hodgepodge collection of humanity, where men outnumbered the women three to one, required special attention. Not all workers stayed on-site, but the commute to the nearest serviced city, Antofagasta, meant a 100-mile ride through the desert each way. Very few did that on a daily basis.

The sprawling camp started in 1990 as a uniform and relatively modest collection of trailers. As the operation grew, the camp became an intertwined network of mobile and container homes, construction trailers, fenced compounds, roads, pipe corridors, passageways and playing fields, with its own utility services and catering. Some areas were for management. Some were for women or visiting dignitaries and executives. Others were for contractors with their own camps. By far the largest area was dedicated to the hourly-paid workers who came and went every week or two on rotation and were driven to and from the travel hub of Antofagasta in company buses. Most traveled to points beyond, depending on the terms of their rotation agreement. No one traveled through the Escondida site on their way to anywhere. It was the end of the line.

After the fiasco at Zamora, Nathan and Eric felt safe. They were in one of the double-wide converted containers on the edge of the self-contained management area, passing their time in the recreation facility. They weren't sure what they were waiting for. They assumed someone from ORB would give them directions if they needed to move. If they had to move, it would be in response to a sign of danger. That's when they needed to worry.

Unbeknownst to either Nathan or Eric, Mack had taken up residence in a single converted container within watching distance of where they stayed. They all ate at the same 1,000-person capacity cafeteria, relaxed in the same recreational area with multiple TV and cinema rooms, but they never came face-to-face. Some of the accommodation units were assigned to married persons if they had rank, and some were even for families with young children. The fact was, even the manager's area was too big to see or know everyone in residence unless you lived there for years, as some did.

As the days started to drag on, Mack began to wonder if what he was doing was futile. While keeping an eye on his wards as well as he could by himself, he was gradually succumbing to the thought that it was a waste of time. He couldn't imagine how anyone could enter this place without credible authorization, especially if they were of Chinese descent, which he assumed the enemy in this instance would most likely be. Everyone needed a work pass, or a visitor's pass, signed by site security after approval by whoever was the invitee. Mack could feel himself losing his edge as time went by. He wasn't used to such a lack of action. Yes, he may be holed up on missions for a few days at a time sometimes, waiting for his opportunity to pounce, but this...

It was three weeks after his arrival when Mack decided to put a call in to Sean to let him know how quiet things were. He would suggest leaving

Nathan and Eric at Escondida. To him, the Chinese probably thought the pair were no longer important. They were just tiny fish to be forgotten in a huge pond. Maybe they could even get jobs, Mack fantasized. They could get lost in operations while he went back to Ecuador to join the others. That's what he wanted to do.

Eric walked out of his container home with a coffee mug in hand, placed his sunglasses over his eyes, and looked out over the myriad of camp roofs stretching to the horizon on yet another bright, wonderfully fresh, early morning that was so typical of the desert. Two white plastic chairs sat opposite each other on the small wooden deck outside their front door. The backs of the chairs were set against a three-foot-high privacy fence on both sides.

He placed his mug on the flat surface of a chair armrest, plopped down into the seat facing the sunrise, and searched for the latest world news on his laptop. This had become his habit each day, in time to catch the sunrise before the heat of the sun soaked into everything. On this day, Eric was a little late. The sun had already peeked over the horizon, splashing light into his eyes. It blinded him for a few seconds, despite the tint of his glasses.

As his eyes were still adjusting, he never saw the thin wire loop drop over his head from behind, without touching him. But he did feel something against his throat as it nestled into place. Before he could grasp what had happened, his attacker rose from behind the fence, stood in close to him, and holding the handles of the wire, deftly pulled them in opposite directions. The wire fit the contours of Eric's neck much more snuggly as the intruder quickly jerked the wire to set it. He then kept pulling his hands apart, sinking the wire deeper into Eric's throat. As his airway was cut off, Eric couldn't make a sound. His hands instinctively shot upwards to feel for anything he could get hold of that might help him fight off his assailant. But he was clutching at air as his eyes rolled up into his head.

Eric was helpless to resist by using his hands. His feet automatically struggled to find a hold on the deck to give his legs the leverage they needed. But they just slipped as his body was pulled backward against the chair. Moments after the garrote sank into his windpipe, blood flowed from the gash around his neck. Bloody bubbles gurgled out of his partially open lips with his final breath and his eyes stood out almost an inch from their sockets.

Eric's laptop dropped to the ground, with coffee spilling over the keyboard and screen, and the broken mug rolled away. He slumped in his chair, pushed farther back and at an angle so it forced the fence to bend outwards. It stayed that way for thirty minutes before a driver spotted Eric's hunched, lifeless figure in a blood-soaked T-shirt. Mack was nowhere to be seen. He couldn't be everywhere all the time and hadn't picked up on Eric's morning ritual.

Nathan was woken by a loud banging on the front door of the container home by one of the two men who had stopped their truck and jumped out to check on Eric. They were on their way to start a shift in the plant. Nathan flung the front door open to see who was knocking so urgently. But he stopped short when he saw Eric's partly covered lifeless body still sitting in his chair. Blood was everywhere, and Nathan realized in that split second that this was no accident.

An emergency ambulance siren wailed louder as it came closer. People were coming out of their homes to see what all the noise was about, and passing vehicles stopped for their occupants to crane their necks for a view.

The company security team arrived within minutes. They hung yellow "NO CRUZAR–NO CRUZAR" tape around the home and pushed people away from the carnage. Mack looked on, helpless to reach out to Nathan, and too late to help Eric. Clearly, this was not the time to contact Sean to suggest a withdrawal of his services. Somehow, someone had managed to infiltrate the camp complex, identify where Nathan and Eric lived, and do what they needed to do. The question now was whether he, she, or they would make an attempt on Nathan's life. Mack had to assume they would.

Nathan shuddered with shock. Someone held him by the shoulders and led him back inside, wrapped a blanket around him, prepared some coffee, and sat opposite him just to watch. It seemed like an eternity before everyone left to give Mack an opportunity to take Nathan to one side.

"Listen. I'm really sorry about your friend, Nathan, but we have to leave, now." Mack stared into Nathan's red, swollen eyes.

Nathan looked stunned by this new turn of events. It had been a surprise when that stranger, Sean, had appeared in the Zamora cells three weeks ago. But here was another stranger telling him what to do. He couldn't find the words and started to shake again. This time it was with fear.

"I'm with ORB." Mack looked into his eyes as he said it, and suddenly Nathan seemed to understand what needed to be done. He made a dash through the rooms, threw things into a bag, grabbed his wallet, phone and passport, and almost hurled himself through the front door.

Within minutes Mack's truck rolled through the gates of the compound and out onto the road toward Antofagasta. Neither of them talked for nearly thirty minutes as Mack continually checked his side and rear mirrors in case they were being followed.

As they began to relax, they found their voices. Nathan needed answers. Mack provided none other than his relationship with ORB and what he had been assigned to do. He admitted his failure and apologized profusely. How could he have known after three weeks of peace with not a sign of anyone following or showing one iota of interest in the two of them? No one passed by their way at night. No one hung around them in the dining or recreation facilities. No one seemed out of place.

A few hundred yards ahead, they would pass under a pipe bridge. It supported the desalinated water pipelines coming from the treatment plant on the ocean's edge, as well as the copper-rich pulp pipelines going to the solvent extraction plant on tidewater. The crossing required traffic to stop before moving slowly forward under the trusses to avoid the possibility of any mishaps occurring in that particular location. It was really overkill, and most times traffic just slowed down unless security was watching.

Mack played it by the book and came to a stop twenty feet in front of the first column holding the structure. A single shot rang out, and a bullet smashed through the front side passenger window and struck Nathan in his neck. Blood spurted out over the dashboard and windows. A second shot rang out and struck the front passenger door panel with a loud smack. The third shot passed through the broken passenger window and out the other side, but by then Mack had lunged downward and over to push Nathan as much as he could into the footwell. He couldn't tell if Nathan was alive or not, but it looked to be a fatal wound, and there was a huge amount of blood squirting in all directions. In his crouched position, Mack collected himself and slowly opened the driver's side door and rolled out onto the ground, his Ruger pistol already in his hand.

From under his truck, Mack could see the legs of two attackers. They were coming slowly toward his vehicle. He lay tucked into a small ball behind the driver's-side front tire for protection. As their full bodies came into view, he could see neither of them was Chinese. Mack silently chastised himself for inventing what trouble would look like. One of the assailants bent to look quickly under the truck, but Mack's body was in tight against the oversize wheel, enough to avoid detection from just a quick glance. He guessed they thought both he and Nathan were dead in the vehicle, or at least severely wounded, since they were heading over to his position so soon after the shooting.

Mack heard whispering as they got closer. This time, Mack moved away from the tire's safety and shot the kneecap out of the one with the rifle. The body fell to the ground with a scream of pain. As he hit the dirt, Mack put a bullet into the top of his head.

The first shot had made the other assailant stop short as his companion went down. The second shot made him move. With a knife in hand, he stopped and ran to the passenger side of the vehicle. There, he found Nathan's lifeless body slumped in the footwell. He realized he had acted too quickly by coming forward so soon. Then, he had not checked under the vehicle, where the shots must have come from. He stood and twisted to go toward the front end for cover. But too late. Mack had fired that second shot and immediately rolled under his truck, where he came face-to-face with the lower legs and twisting frame of the second assailant just as he was about to move forward.

Mack's knife sliced first one and then the other Achilles tendon at the back of the assailant's ankles. The killer collapsed straight down as his disconnected leg muscles had no feet attached. Mack crawled out to watch his prey holding the knife he had probably used to kill Eric. This time, Mack leveled his pistol at the man's face and pulled the trigger.

Leaving the two bodies stretched out in the desert, Mack got back into his truck and headed to the coast. It wouldn't be long before security discovered the bodies, made their calls and spread out to find whoever committed these heinous crimes.

"Sean." Mack called his boss as soon as he could get a reasonable signal as he raced along the dusty highway at over one hundred miles per hour.

"Mack. What's going on?" Sean was preparing himself for his sabotage assignment.

"They got to us. We lost both Nathan and Eric before I could do anything. I'm heading out with Nathan's body now."

"Jeez." Sean felt shocked and was at a loss for words. "What happened to whoever came after you all?"

"Left them for dead out here in the desert. They ain't going anywhere."

"Okay, okay." Sean was thinking fast.

"What d'ya want me to do, boss?"

"Get rid of Nathan's body and get back here." Sean was recovering enough to realize there was nothing they could do now for Nathan and Eric, but he needed his man. "We've got work to do. Let's talk this through with James and Matthew when you get here." Sean ended the call.

Every five miles along the copper-rich solution pipelines, workers built large ponds lined with plastic. They collected any spilled solution should a pipe fail. Mack chose one of the ponds. He settled on a way to dispose of Nathan's body and buy time to get back to Ecuador before someone found it. That was unlikely to happen very soon since the pond areas were deserted, but Mack had no idea whether inspection teams came through, diligently checking for potential pipe ruptures or even sabotage, and might get out of their vehicles to look around.

Mack drove to the far end of one of the more distant ponds.

He parked and looked for any signs of movement of anything as far as he could see. There were none.

Mack dragged Nathan's body from the passenger floor and rolled it down the slope into the dry pond containment. He had seen, and been involved in, these kinds of personal situations before. But he had always found the mettle to overcome the emotions that could overcome him if he couldn't control himself.

Mack whispered some heartfelt words as he took the time to watch Nathan's body roll down the slope and stop when it reached the flat bottom of the dry pond. From the road, at a distance, it would be difficult for anyone to see the dark spot of Nathan's lifeless body against the black of the plastic lining covering the bottom and the sides of the depression.

There was no time for lingering remorse. Mack's job was done. His instinct was to get out as fast as he could.

They needed him at Zamora.

Chapter 41

A Little Planning Goes a Long Way

With the map of the Zamora plant spread out on the table, everyone sat, stood, or leaned against something. Stockman was back on the screen and the group was ready to talk about timing.

They had already talked strategy before getting to the map and agreed that the plan was realistic and possible. It fit the block of time they allowed themselves: one night, from 10:00 p.m. to 5:00 a.m., before sunrise.

It was vital that everything happen quickly, otherwise the Chinese would get a chance to double and maybe triple security on finding their plant was being sabotaged. Should that happen, ORB may never get the opportunity to complete its work.

Sean had already reported extra security measures around the plant had been put in place by Tongyan after the incident with Nathan and Eric. But he had also recently noticed that they had started to relax some of their more frequent inspections inside and outside the plant. Now they had settled into a routine, and posted two-man guard teams at all entrances and sent another team into the plant at regular intervals. Sean knew their schedules and had clocked the comings and goings for over a week now.

"Let's talk." Matthew was keen to get into the details.

Emma nodded. "Perhaps we should break this all down and figure out the best time to take down the transformers. That's the central pin here. Power has to stay on for some things and be out for others."

"You're right, Em. As I see it," Matthew said, pointing at the tailings waste pipelines, "these need to go first, then the reclaim lines, then the barge." He moved his finger from one to the other. "We do it all with the power still on so we flood the area. But the question is, how long will that take?" He looked over at Sean, and then at Emma.

"Well, we need to remember that the pipelines are going to be full and flowing if the power isn't off. So, when those explosives go off, the contents are going to spray like shit all over the place before things settle down." It was Emma again. She had done this same kind of thing before and knew how it worked.

"We don't want the power off before that, though." It was Matthew. He was looking at the map as he talked. "Let the flow go for about thirty minutes before putting the transformer out of service. That should be enough to soak the countryside sufficiently to make it look as bad as it needs to be for us to call in the agencies."

"Give us three hours to take out the pipelines and the barge, including the half hour." Sean looked around as everyone nodded. "Let's say, we start at ten thirty, we should complete by, say, one thirty a.m. I'll give the word when we're done, and Kenny can shut the power down." Sean had been looking at his watch as he estimated, as though it helped him.

"Well, that's provided everyone else is ready as well." It was Emma, still making notes, cross-checking with what the others were estimating, and cautioning against overoptimism too early. "Mind you,"—she looked up—"Sean and Deek are the only ones who need the power to be available, so I guess when they're finished, Kenny can move."

Again, everyone nodded.

"Kenny." Matthew looked over at his friend. "How long?"

"I should start cutting the wires and draining the oil before the blasts. It'll take a little while to drop the levels enough to start the overheating. Then the transformers will take about an hour to build up enough heat to knock them out." Kenny was smiling in his usual self-confident manner. "So, assuming I start at midnight, we should have built up enough heat by around two a.m." He looked around for any sign of doubt.

"That should do it, Kenny. What do you think, James?" Matthew asked.

"Assuming the blasts will be enough to have security scurrying around looking for the source, and then alerting control to turn off the power to those pumps, that timing for the transformer should be okay." James continued, "If control acts fast, as they should because they'll see the pressure drop, they can disable the lines in thirty minutes at the most. So, *voilà,* it fits. By then, security will be all over the tailings area and they won't be over at the transformers. That should let Kenny do his thing in peace." James was happy with his take on things and turned back to Matthew.

"Armando, you'll be pretty well free to do what you need to do when you want, once the power is off."

"I'm thinking I could start around two a.m., so it sounds as though their timing fits." Armando enjoyed being the focus of everyone's attention; that was his nature. "That's when things are quiet. The operator's shift is halfway through, and they're all back at the canteen for lunch. Roberto and I can slip in, pick up some sand on the way, disable the lube systems first, then get on with the big items."

"Any issues with the power being on or off?" Emma asked.

"Only when we need to use the inching drives. Those mills need to have lost power by then. Otherwise, there's not much we can do. Same with the big pumps."

"So, Kenny's timing is good?" Emma asked.

"Perfect. We'll wait, and once the emergency power comes on, we can get moving."

"How long?"

"An hour or so, but we should be out of there by three thirty a.m." Armando appeared very confident as he smiled over at Roberto.

"Okay. Good. Let's move over to Nick." Matthew made a few notes and looked across the table for Nick to input.

"Nick, I assume you'll have to set your explosives a couple of days ahead of time." It was Emma.

Nick was nodding and thinking about what he was going to say to the team.

"I'll need some help there." Nick looked over at Matthew.

"Sean, take Deek with you when Nick goes up to the pit to set those charges and help him out, would you?" Matthew looked over at Sean.

"Got it." Sean nodded. "Can't forget there's a night shift happening," he noted.

"I can't imagine anyone from the mine's night shift will take any notice of Nick over on the other side of the pit, even if they could see him at night. That's a long way for anyone to recognize a shadow."

"You're right." It was James.

"Nick, if I'm guessing correctly about the best location for you to do the blast," Matthew continued, as he hunched over the map and pointed at one side of the pit, "this is far enough away from anyone who would be up that way." He jabbed his fingertip against the spot he had selected. He kept it there as he stood and looked at Nick.

"We've all agreed that I need a couple of days ahead of time to set the charges." Nick looked over at Sean and Deek, who would be there helping and watching his back. They nodded their understanding of what they needed to do.

"That's fair. Do you have everything you need?" It was Emma.

"Let's say Zamora provided everything, thank you very much." Nick smiled and looked around as the others joined him although they weren't sure why.

"What about drill equipment?"

"We're all set. When I first arrived on site, I had the mine drill out a blast pattern to my specifications. It was where you pointed to on the map, Matthew. On the far side from where the mine is right now, and at varying depths and diameters. I told them I needed to understand their methods. I said I wanted to try a few things, so I needed a practice area. They agreed, so that's done." He smiled again.

"Well done, Nick. Great job. So, you only need to set the ANFO and charges?" Matthew really liked where this was going. He paced back and forth between the bed and the couch as he thought. But Nick hadn't finished yet.

"The holes range from five to eight inches wide and down to a minimum of forty-five feet. Some are much longer, but I'll explain why later." Nick paused in case there were questions, but there weren't. "I've been accumulating the ammonium nitrate for a while now, and I have a stockpile of kerosene in cans all ready to go. Sean and Deek can help with getting it all up to the mine and sending it down the holes. We'll leave them covered until we're ready to blow. The night we decide to move, we can set the blast caps and trail the cables over to the remote controllers. When I get the signal, I press a few switches, and there we go, but I'll need some help that night. I know Sean and Deek will be onto other things, but..." Nick shrugged his shoulders.

"I'll be there." It was Matthew. They were one man short, so he was going to have to step in as well as play center forward for the rest of the team.

"Okay." Nick held his hands up in front of him as though to say, "Easy." It wasn't that easy. There was a lot of grunt work to do in the dark. It could even be pouring rain.

"How do you know this will cause such a catastrophic failure, and the pit wall will actually collapse, and not just create another bench?" Matthew wondered.

"If you look at the Geotech work,"—this is where Nick excelled, and he put his finger on the map—"you'll see there's a fissure going through that area, right where my holes have been drilled, running north-south." He stabbed his finger a couple of times at the area he was referring to on the map. "It runs very deep. Under normal conditions, operations would have to do some fancy blasting to get around it without disturbing the whole countryside. But they haven't got to that part of the plan yet. They're still messing with the easy stuff.

"Now if you really want everything to go, we blast the shit out of the rock on both sides and let the fissure help you collapse it all. The holes I had drilled are at angles that cross the upper part of that fault line, so when the explosives are set off, the shock waves fire off in all directions—up, down, and side to side. That's how we get the biggest bang for our buck, so to speak. But there's something else. In answer to your question earlier, Matthew, I mentioned that I drilled the holes deeper than forty-five feet. They're down a long way, that's for sure. So, when the blast happens, it happens at a few different depths at the same time. I could never have done all this without that drill rig they have. It's the best, and very powerful. Boy, what a beast." Nick's whole face pushed upwards. He seemed to be imagining the power of the equipment.

"Wow." Matthew and the others were in awe. This guy knew his stuff, and God help anyone who might be near that pit wall when it goes. They hoped that he was being cautious enough to avoid anyone on the other side of the pit, except maybe by sound. But thousands of tons of rock were going to bury the mine equipment at the bottom of the pit, and it would definitely not survive.

James was bending over the map, tracing the outline of the pit with his eyes and noting where the current pit work was occurring. It was quite a distance between the two spots, probably a thousand feet or so. The mine had finished its initial work where Matthew had pointed. It had slowly worked its way around the other side, shaping the pit and benching down forty-five feet each time.

"You're going to have to be in place to detonate at the same time as the rest of the team does its work." It was Emma, thinking out loud. It was a rhetorical statement, but she was wondering about logistics and timing. "You need to get up there before any of us start our work over at the plant, to set your caps, check connections and so on. I would say you need to be at the pit around ten." She looked over at Nick and the Matthew. They looked at each other and nodded back to Emma.

"That's about right, Em," they said to her at the same time.

"So,"—Matthew wanted to wrap things up—"if I understand, when the transformers have to go down, Nick doesn't need electricity for his work. Sean needs it until about two a.m. And Armando can only start once the power is off?" Matthew raised his eyebrows in question as he looked around. They all agreed. "Okay, there you have it, Kenny. Can you disable the transformers by two a.m. at the earliest?"

"As I said, they should be in a critical overheating mode by then. I can't guarantee the exact time, but it'll be close if I look at the heat-time curves. I'll have to keep an eye on the heat buildup as the oil level drops. I may even have to put an extra few holes in the fins to speed up the leak." Kenny was still smiling with confidence, although with him, it often hid issues he didn't want to share. But he had a backup plan. If all else failed, he would trip the entire circuit on the high voltage wires to allow the other guys do their work while the transformers still leaked.

Everyone was nodding, but there were no other questions at this point. They all needed time to absorb everything and would have an opportunity the following morning to follow up if they needed.

"I think that covers it." Emma clapped her hands together, with her eyes wide open as she was still looking at Nick as though she were seeing him in a new and more powerful light. "Once you all have finished with Zamora, it should be a shell of its former self. Does everyone agree?"

"Ah. What about you, Emma? You're going over to the cocaine processing plant, remember?" Her father was watching her from the screen and smiling. The others had bemused looks on their faces.

"Yes. Yes, of course." Emma had almost forgotten herself. "Thanks for reminding me, sir." She looked up at the screen and winked at her father. "Well, I don't think we'll be doing our thing until the power is down—so around two a.m., I guess." Emma looked over at Roberto for a sign of agreement. He nodded.

"Once we hear from Kenny, we'll move in. The only way we can do this is to use explosives. There are going to be guards to deal with, though. Roberto looked at Emma. This was probably the only location outside of the mill where there would be security guards posted permanently.

"Do you need help?" It was Matthew.

"It would be useful if we had a spotter or two who could take the guards out if necessary. We'll be able to attract their attention if they're inside the building, to get them into the open. But I can't be sure how many there will be or how well armed they're going to be." Emma was more than capable of defending herself, but in this case, she was right to be cautious.

"From what I've seen,"—it was Sean—"there could be anywhere from two to four guards at any one time. Sometimes one stays inside the building, with three walking around outside. At other times, two are inside and two are outside. So, I guess that means there's always at least one guard inside all the time. And there always seem to be four guards in total. "

"Okay. Sean, once you and Deek finish at the tailings, go to the cocaine processing plant and find a spot to cover Emma and Roberto. And Emma, don't start until you hear Sean or Deek radio when they're finished their assignment. That means you don't get started until about three thirty a.m." Matthew looked around. "Everyone good?" He looked at Stockman as well as the others in the room. There were no objections. "Okay, get a good night's sleep everyone and we'll meet here for breakfast at seven."

"Good work, you two." Stockman looked at Matthew and Emma after everyone else had left. "There's a lot of moving parts with this one, but it sounds like you have a great team. My advice is to get it done asap before the Chinese catch on." They waved to each other and Stockman was gone.

The following morning, the team got together for breakfast and ironed out some details. Nothing of consequence came up although Sean wanted clarification on the type of force he should use in the event of problems with the security guards. The answer from Matthew was short.

"Do what you have to do if they're armed. If you come across operations people, try not to kill them."

By the time they got back to the camp, Mack had returned from Chile. He was clearly deflated by what had happened in the last thirty-six hours. But he faced his debriefing as a professional. No detail was left out of his story, and while everyone felt saddened by what had happened to Nathan and Eric, they knew there was nothing they could do to reverse the situation. They were sure Mack had put everything he had into the mission.

Matthew outlined to Mack the plans they had been working on in his absence. He would be taking Matthew's role to support Nick on the night the caps were to be set at the pit.

Chapter 42

Luna and the Cartel

If there was anyone who knew everyone else's business in the Shuar and other indigenous communities in the area, it was Luna.

He had spent much of his adult life wandering from person to person and from family to family gossiping, telling stories, reminiscing and laughing. He went from gathering to gathering and from church to church. He stopped here to just say hi and paused there to chat and hopefully be fed along the way.

Everyone liked Luna, shared their food with him, and gathered around whenever he visited. He never refused a meal, was always ready to laugh, share a story, grieve when needed, and give his humble opinion whenever invited. That was his way. While he lumbered through life as a friendly, smart and well-spoken giant, he brought with him a wisdom and deep pride in the Amazonian culture he was committed to keeping alive. The native people loved that about him, and made time to listen to his stories, meanderings, and dreams. Because of this, he and some of his community members were able to spread the message quickly—it was time for the Chinese to leave. Then they would explain how it would happen.

No one had to be convinced of getting the Chinese out but, to a man, they needed assurances that they would not be left with nothing once they were gone. Of course, Luna knew this would be the prime obstacle and had discussed it at length with Matthew and Emma. They assured him there would be money available to support the farmers until they regained their relationship with Los Choneros. The parties also agreed to pay a sign-on bonus immediately upon reaching an agreement with the various native factions. After that, each farm group would receive payment on a weekly basis based on the amount of cocaine base they brought. Luna was the prime mover of this initiative. He wanted the farmers to go back to making base. That way they would be able to sell for more than just paste, and they were good at it.

Luna also knew the members of the local chapter of Los Choneros cartel. Right now, they were a small band of criminally inclined individuals, shrunk in size from when Koski had originally introduced them to buy cocaine paste. Paste manufacture was as far as the farmers could go with their knowledge. At the time, Koski knew they had the resources in the north to convert the paste to base and process it to a cocaine hydrochloride grade for export. But shortly after making those arrangements, Koski taught the coca farmers to make their own base and took that part of the process away from Los Choneros.

The news spread quickly all over Ecuador, and all the farmers did the same. While it was a small part of the overall process, the volumes involved caused the cartels, both Los Choneros and Los Lobos, to lose millions now that they had to pay the farmers more for the cocaine paste upgrade to base. As Luna had described, this was what made the cartels eventually drive Koski out of Ecuador, but he had at least left behind more educated coca farmers.

After Koski had gone, the Chinese arrived to develop Zamora, with their monstrous equipment, thousands of workers and plans for taking control of cocaine processing and distribution, cutting out Los Choneros who were too few and unorganized to resist.

Although Los Choneros were ruthlessly active in the north of Ecuador, their full migration into Luna's beloved Zamora-Chinchipe in the southeast came to a grinding halt when authorities captured and imprisoned their leader, Adolfo Macías, also known as Fito. He was now a "guest" in Guayaquil maximum security prison. While his influence was still felt countrywide, it was diminishing. As a consequence, Los Lobos, their main competitor in the world of drugs, as well as the Colombians and Mexicans, were moving in on Ecuador's cocaine market.

It seemed the cartels were so busy fighting each other in the north, they overlooked Luna's area for now. It flew under their radar of immediate interest. Despite this, it was still home to a small band of leaderless Los Choneros who weren't interested in pushing the agenda of their northern brothers if it meant harming their own people. In any event, there were too few of them these days. But they were useful messengers for Luna and he used them to convey the plans to get the Chinese out of the drug industry to Fito in Guayaquil.

ORB believed that once Fito heard, he would instruct his people to get back in the game.

If it all worked out as Luna described, he would be a hero to everyone, including Los Choneros, for leading such a coup against the Chinese. No one would stop to wonder how he did it. No one would even care, so long as the cocaine flowed as it should.

oooo

Yerush Tigre was a Shuar coca jungle farmer and a family man. His wife, Yanúa, spent most of her days preparing food, washing clothes, sweeping the dusty floor of their hut, and tending three goats, six chickens, two cows, and four children all under the age of ten. Their little home, perched on a hill overlooking the Río Quimi, was five miles north of Luna's home and the Zamora plant. They had always lived there, and their parents and grandparents before them.

Yerush was one of eight other Shuar farmers in his area, tending several acres of coca plants, thriving on the slopes on both sides of the river. The jungle had been cleared just enough to still conceal the bushes, hiding them from the prying eyes in helicopters 10,000 feet above the ground. When they weren't collecting the coca leaves and converting them to solid, whitish cocaine lumps, they would be clearing new areas, planting seedlings and weeding.

The farmers were preparing for the new harvest by bringing in more help from farther afield. They needed leaf baggers, carriers and laborers to help with excavating new pits and cleaning out the old ones. Most farmers near Yerush would take their product in beat-up aluminum boats, with small outboard motors, southward on the Río Quimi to the collection point close to the Zamora plant. There would be other boats coming down the much larger Río Zamora and its tributaries to the confluence with the Río Quimi, bringing their contributions. Many of those boats couldn't motor northeastward up the short stretch of the Río Quimi against the flow, to the collection point. They would have to unload onto waiting pickups at the confluence and the trucks would take their loads up to be unloaded and weighed. The product would then be emptied into hoppers and transferred to the processing plant.

Before the season began, both parties agreed on the payment for one pound of rough cocaine product, or cocaine paste, provided by the farmers. The scale punched out a ticket when they weighed their boatload. It showed the unique number for each farm, plus the date, time and weight. Some farms delivered several batches a day. At the end of each fourteen-hour day, one farmer would collect the tickets for his farm and share the total weight recorded that day with his people. One of the station staff would toss a copy ticket into a bucket and collect them at the end of each week and use them to quantify payment for each farm.

At the end of a seven-day week, each farm's representative would travel to the transfer station to meet with a Zamora representative. They would compare the tickets and weights before payment was made. A mistake was rare with such a simple system.

The location of the collection point was the common location where all suppliers visited. It was near here that Luna and his close friends greeted the farmers as they came by after unloading their produce. This was where they could discuss the future plans and ensure everyone involved heard the story and asked questions.

Yerush and his friends had listened to Luna one evening as they finished their deliveries, before they returned to their homes. They sat together and shared the food and the refreshing *chicha* their wives had made for them that day. It was like any other communal event: conversation flowed freely and everyone laughed. For a short while, they forgot about their work and thoughts about how it consumed their days. But at the same time, the message was getting through. There was an alternative to the Chinese, and it was about to happen.

Luna smiled, listened, told stories from his visits along the way, and described what the plans were for ousting the Chinese. Initially, concerned looks, grimaces and confusion greeted him. Things had been going well for so long—why change? Luna explained that a gang war would soon grip them. The factions would fight over control of the drugs in their part of the world, as they did elsewhere. It was better to keep the Chinese out, he told them. If they were involved, the fighting would be far worse. They would find themselves in the middle with no place to sell their product. And who needed the Chinese anyway? There were nods all around as worried looks turned to smiles on the faces of his friends.

Over the final three days of meeting and greeting, there was unanimity amongst the farmers that they would be better off without the Chinese.

But without them, they knew they still needed money and the expertise of others who could convert their product to a better one. They needed the cartel to take their cocaine, in base form, so they could return to the Koski system. They all agreed it was better to keep things amongst Ecuadorians, than allowing foreigners to take control. They had not yet considered that other foreigners were already there—the Mexicans and Colombians, muscling in on their territory. But that was a problem for another day.

Yerush was happy; Yanúa, not so much. Culture and the environment were one thing, but feeding a family was quite another, and if it came to a choice, she knew which way she should go. But she also knew that time was against her. From what she could understand, things were about to change rapidly. In the end, she agreed with her husband mainly because she envisioned being overrun by gangs known for their ruthless ways.

Yes, Yanúa thought. Perhaps it would be better, much better when she thought about it, if her family had some Los Choneros protection. Then, the other gangs might leave them alone. Little did she know it was wishful thinking, with the other cartels chasing new business. But for now, getting the Chinese out was something even Yanúa looked forward to.

Chapter 43

One Last Meeting

Wang Ho Lin walked beside his friend, Ping Pei, as they crossed the park together on their way to their favored bench in the peaceful La Cruz del Papa plaza. They didn't speak until they sat down, picked a Winston cigarette out from their own packets, lit each other's and took a long, deep pull.

Once they had exhausted their smoke into the fresh air, Wang Ho Lin started without looking at Ping Pei. Neither of them wasted time on personal informalities. Each of them found it too difficult to think of anything else during these strained and difficult times. Their jobs were on the line. Their Beijing bosses were not at all happy about the threat to the operation.

"This Koski person is a waste of our time," Wang Ho Lin stated without emotion. "He is gone. Nobody knows where."

"So, you don't think he is behind our troubles?" Ping Pei was more worried than he had been before. If it was Koski they would be better able to contain him. If it wasn't, the only alternative was the cartel. But which one? He didn't know much about drug cartels in Ecuador, not even their names if there were more than one. Even though he knew a lot more about the Mexicans and the Colombians, his knowledge was still limited. But what he did know was they were born killers. They protected each other and their trade with a ferocity beyond anything he could imagine.

"No, he is gone." Wang Ho Lin clearly didn't want to talk about Koski anymore. To Ping Pei it sounded as though his people in Beijing were likely unhappy that he had even brought them the name. They had wasted so much time on him. They knew he had left Ecuador shortly before Zamora went into production. They also appeared to know at least one of the drug cartels was searching for him, and that would mean Koski had no chance of being their culprit if he was in hiding.

"It is Los Choneros." Wang Ho Lin wasn't going to waste words. He was annoyed, although Ping Pei wasn't sure if it was with him or someone else.

"Why do you say that, my friend?" Ping Pei needed to get Wang Ho Lin to talk a little more. At this point, his curt responses weren't helping to solve anything.

"Our man in Guayaquil tells us that Fito has instructed his people to take control once more." Wang Ho Lin wouldn't provide any additional explanation unless prompted. Ping Pei wasn't sure why.

"Who is this *Fito?*" Ping Pei had no clue who this person was, what he was, or who his people were.

Wang Ho Lin turned his head slowly and looked at Ping Pei for a moment.

"Mr. Pei. If you don't know who Fito is, then you don't know who Los Choneros cartel are."

Wang Ho Lin's stare was riveting enough to make Ping Pei very uncomfortable, and he squirmed on the bench.

"*Fito* is Adolfo Macías, the leader of Los Choneros, the cartel Zamora had replaced."

Ho Lin sat back and looked straight ahead, as though ignoring his friend.

Ping Wei's face had distorted into a mask of fear. Now he understood. The cartel was making their move to regain control. He asked himself, *Could Zamora fight the cartel without Beijing's help?*

"How long do you think we have, Mr. Lin?" It was Ping Pei's turn to be more formal. This was a very serious situation. His mind was turning over the possibilities of what might happen.

"We need to get our friends in the Ecuadorian government to help. We need their military. We need their police. You cannot protect the plant with the security personnel you currently have. It was quite different when you were building and had so many people. It would have been extremely intimidating to the cartel. They were just a small group in those days, but from what I hear they are growing stronger, and with Fito pushing them…" Wang Ho Lin paused and searched his friend's face for some sort of understanding of the seriousness of what was happening.

"Can you help us, Mr. Lin?" Ping Pei sounded dejected, not knowing whether his friend would help.

"Of course. Of course, but remember, Beijing cannot get involved. They will not involve themselves *directly* in the matters of any country. And to think they would become physically involved in fending off a drug cartel in a foreign country would be ludicrous." Wang Ho Lin paused to take in another lungful of nicotine. "We will, of course, be working at the highest levels possible in Ecuador to protect our interests—and theirs." He looked away as though focusing on something in the distance. "But, we can only hope they will want to protect them. There have been so many difficulties with our presence here, we cannot say for sure where their sentiments lie. I suppose we shall see."

"As you may know, we have dispensed with two of their operatives." Ping Pei changed the subject. "The ones who took photos of the plant." He was still trying to piece things together. Somehow, he wasn't as convinced as his friend that the cartel was involved.

Wang Ho Lin looked at Ping Pei as though to say, *"They are no longer our problem, so what does that matter now?"* He didn't say it, but instead responded with a polite "I know."

"The tragedy," Ping Pei continued, "is that both men we sent to dispose of them were themselves killed." He paused and looked at Ho Li's face for some sign of his understanding what the significance of that statement was to him.

"Oh." Wang Ho Lin turned to face Ping Pei. "I was not aware."

"Yes, and by what appears to be a professional assassin." Ping Pei raised his eyebrows as though to accentuate his words.

Wang Ho Lin was completely taken aback, and for once, seemed lost for words.

He waited for Ping Pei to continue.

"As I am sure you can imagine, it seems there may be others at play. But perhaps I am being overly suspicious and it's the cartel seeking to eliminate any resistance we may put up. We send two assassins to kill two people who may be theirs, and an assassin kills ours. That does not make sense. There has to be another party involved." Ping Pei lowered his head as though deep in thought. He was really waiting for his friend to offer some comment. Perhaps it would support his own theory.

"Ah, so. I see where you're going with this. But the cartel must have caused all the problems you've had. It is simple. They want their business back, and they want you out." Wang Ho Lin appeared adamant, or perhaps he simply didn't want to make the issues any more complicated than they already were. In any event, having the cartel as the antagonist was an easy sell to Beijing. It was something they could not ignore as an issue they might not be able to resolve easily.

Ping Pei wasn't satisfied. If Wang Ho Lin was right, Beijing would want to distance itself from the problems. Maybe they wouldn't even look to the Ecuadorian government for help. But then what? Would Beijing really give up control of Zamora? It would mean losing its two-billion-dollar investment, as well as the revenue from a very profitable venture, not to mention its global strategy. Not likely. But, for now, Ping Pei had to be satisfied with what he was hearing.

"What will you do, Mr. Pei?" Wang Ho Lin asked his friend.

"I will bring in more security. Maybe a hundred, or two hundred, if I have to. But we are not going to give in to those mobsters after all we have done. And besides, how would they be able to operate the equipment we have at the mill? It would take them years to learn. No, we won't surrender." Ping Pei rose to leave.

"Mr. Pei, I will call the Ecuadoran ministers to see what help we can get from them. But we must not let Beijing know they are involved, unless it becomes impossible for us to contain this situation. If it gets to that point, we will tell Beijing we have been overwhelmed. Until then, all they need to know is that we have some problems with the locals which we are attempting to resolve. Do we understand each other?" Wang Ho Lin also rose from the bench.

"I understand." Ping Pei held his hand out to his friend. "And I agree. Whoever the perpetrators are, we will remain vigilant and determined to resist them at all costs."

The two old friends walked across the park together. They went their separate ways once they got to the east perimeter of the park and walked slowly back to their offices.

Chapter 44

No More

It was time.

Yerush Tigre did not go to his farm that morning. Instead, he and some other representatives of nearby farming groups traveled by boat down the Río Quimi to the confluence with the Río Zamora. They turned south. Eight miles farther on, toward El Pangui, they steered their boat into a muddy backwater and pushed up onto a low bank. A few low-level buildings were set back from the river. A sign hung loosely from one of the doors to guide them. This was where they mingled with representatives of other farming groups waiting to be paid their sign-up bonus now that they had stopped taking their product to the Chinese.

It had been left with James to coordinate with Luna. They had to plan how to pay the farmers once they no longer took their crude cocaine to the Zamora plant. They settled on a one-time payment to each farmer of $200, with up to $140 per seven-day week depending on the amount of product they had produced. To avoid crowds, only one representative from each group was invited to collect the money for the rest. Luna and James did not know how many farms would be there to collect the money that day. But they guessed it could be sixty to eighty, or maybe more. There could even be more coming when others who didn't make this first trip heard the arrangement was for real.

James had brought almost $200,000 on his first day to ensure a sign-up payment was available for everyone. Part of Luna's job was to verify the representatives. He would go over the terms and have each one write down the names of their farm's members and sign for their money. He emphasized to each person the importance of continuing to produce cocaine base, but then weighing and storing it while they made arrangements to have Los Choneros take it off their hands.

Over the course of that first day, representatives of eighty-four groups arrived by various forms of transportation. Some came by boat. Others ride-shared in old pickups. One or two arrived on motorcycles. One came on a trusty moped. Luna personally knew the more local leaders, whom he greeted as old friends. With others, who traveled from more remote parts of the Amazon he rarely visited, he was at least acquainted enough to inquire about their health and share some common interest stories.

Not all were Shuar. But they all had a common goal: survival in the jungle. They had enough understanding of current jungle affairs to know who best to follow into the near future. They knew trouble was brewing for control of their product. But this time they understood they needed to be proactive and take control, rather than waiting until it was too late.

James had arranged for enough US funds to be available every seven days to make the weekly payments. But ORB and their clients knew those costs were well worth the price of removing one major hurdle standing in the way of their success. It was almost worth that price to James just to see the fixed smile on Luna's round face, whose thoughts were wrapping around the impending success of his long campaign to oust the Chinese from Shuar territory.

Over the following two days, James and Luna waited for stragglers. A few more came, got paid in the same way, and with huge grins announced they would return on the eighth day for their next payment. Luna reminded them they needed to keep working and store their product. They laughed, waved and made signs indicating their understanding of what was expected of them as they drifted back to their homes.

James and Matthew had anticipated this first step of supplementing the farmers for what they thought would be about four weeks, before Los Choneros could take control. Stockman would send more money to Banco Pichincha in Guayaquil for James to collect on a regular basis. Luna went back to mingle with the farmers and share in their celebrations of what was to come.

The call from James at the end of the three days was music to Matthew's ears. He and Emma had thought their most difficult problem, and one they had little control over, was going to be convincing the farmers of their plan. It turned out to be the least of their worries. But then, they had Luna's talents on their side, and he knew his people.

Matthew needed to signal his team to put the rest of the plan into action. It had been raining for three days nonstop. The sky was full of dense gray clouds. Sheets of water came down, surrounding the Zamora area and stretching to the horizon.

"Perfect." Matthew turned to Emma as they lay in bed under the netting and listened to the rain smack against the tin roof. How they slept through it was a difficult question to answer, but Emma would just say, "Aw, you get used to it."

The heavy rain was a bonus that Matthew appreciated. It would camouflage their activities both from a visual and noise perspective. While it would make things more difficult for the team, he knew the pros outweighed the cons for what they had to do.

"Let's give the word to move, Em. Tonight's the night. Ready?" Matthew put his arm around Emma. They lay listening to the rain pounding on the roof.

"Where are you going to be while all this is going on?" Emma whispered into his ear.

"With the drone, over where we're going to park the vehicles. It's close enough to the action there to get out and help if I need. I want to keep over top of everyone to watch for any threats. Apparently, this baby is supposed to operate perfectly in these conditions, but I haven't tested it yet. If it does what it's supposed to do, I should get good sightings. But I won't be using the radio, unless there's a problem of some kind." He didn't want anyone using the radios any more than they really needed to. But a threat would be an emergency he would not hesitate to react to immediately, although he would speak in a code only his people would understand.

"Christ, that reminds me." Matthew lifted the mosquito net and fell out of bed. It was the best way to get out of there.

Emma didn't bother lifting her head to see what he was up to. She just glanced over with one eye at what he was doing.

Matthew opened the 350 drone case and checked both batteries for power. They were at a hundred percent and ready to go. He opened his phone, pressed the flashlight and ran his fingers over the contents making sure everything was where it was supposed to be. He had brought six spare rotors just in case the drone crashed. The most likely thing to break would be one or more of them.

Happy everything was as it should be, Matthew closed the case, pushed it under his clothes out of sight, and climbed back into bed. Before turning to face an already sleeping Emma, he made sure to push the mosquito net firmly all around him.

Chapter 45

Get Moving

Deek squatted in the same location as Sean had been, overlooking the majority of the Zamora site, surrounded by the camouflage of the jungle with some of it attached to his clothes.

He had become accustomed to watching for pit vipers that might be hanging from the trees, ready to strike if confronted. He used the butt of his rifle to make a path through the jungle, and occasionally managed to poke one or two snakes from their hiding places and watch them tumble to the ground and wriggle off into the undergrowth.

He couldn't see the pit, the tailings line, or the waste pond. But he could see the security building. He wondered if he should go down and block the entrance. He resisted the urge after judging the potential risk of being discovered and setting off a security alert for the entire complex.

The day Matthew gave the word to move, the temperature was in the mid-nineties. It was still raining, and with it came the intensity of humidity as the oversized drops splashed onto the ground and partially evaporated immediately, forming an eerie blanket of mist over the landscape. There were advantages to this weather, though. It tended to lower the risk of discovery by the security guards, who would be distracted by the discomfort of being pounded by the rain enough to lower their sharpness for detecting unusual movements. It would also slow them down considerably should there be any kind of chase, if one of the ORB agents attracted their attention.

The downside for ORB was the difficulty they would have in maintaining traction over the slippery jungle undergrowth. They had to avoid the ponds and mud flows and the many fast-running streams the rain created. It lowered their wariness of animal predators, including snakes, in the trees and on the ground, although many would seek drier refuge away from the barrage of beating rain.

Deek had pulled the hood of his plastic poncho further over his head, as the interminable dripping of rain bounced off its rim and ran into a pool created by his cover, straddling his arms. He would shake the water loose now and again, or let it overflow, if he felt any restriction on his movement as the pond of water grew in size. His Ruger Precision Rifle was also covered. It was mounted on a fixed stand and aimed at the door of the Zamora security building, five hundred feet away. It was his safeguard, in the event of an alarm being triggered through the plant, should one of his team members get themselves noticed, and the guards scrambled through that door in their haste to pursue.

Deek's orders were to slow down the guards at all costs if any of them were seen investigating. It went without saying what that meant. Ideally, and if he had to, he was to keep them from leaving the building should they try, by shooting at the entrance. There was no other entry, and the window at the front overlooking the plant was the only one on the perimeter wall. From the recce Sean had done when he visited Nathan, he knew that window didn't open.

The building was like a small fortress. It was almost impenetrable, but also very hard to escape from. He knew this wasn't a war and human casualties should be kept to a minimum, but should the situation become untenable, he would have to go a step further and wound some or worse.

Regardless of the rain, the PARD clip-on night vision converter Deek had fixed to his scope performed more than adequately. It had an extended hood over the far end to protect against rain. It let him see his target as clearly as if the weather were clear, despite the downpour.

In the vehicle parking area, Matthew unclipped the drone case inside his Land Cruiser and began setting up the equipment. The DJI Matrice 350 drone simply lifted out, the rotor arms unfolded, the blades snapped on and the Zenmuse zoom camera clicked into the gimble slot underneath. The whole unit sat on skis that lifted it such that it could sit flat with the camera dangling below. Matthew activated the control unit, calibrated it with the drone, checked the camera was transmitting to the control base, tested the rotors and took the unit out into the rain. Within a few minutes the drone was airborne and heading up to around three hundred feet directly above Matthew before he set it off to the east. At that height it couldn't be heard.

He tested it at two hundred and then one hundred feet for noise. Again, he couldn't hear the whine of the motor in the rain.

Despite the torrential downpour, the video feed back to the control unit was perfect, with heat sources showing up as unrecognizable green shapes when using the thermal imaging setting on the camera. With the camera set on night mode, the visuals were remarkably distinct especially when zooming in.

It was just before eleven when Deek spotted the recognizable shape of Kenny. He was half-crouching, making his way over to the transformer substation on the far side of the plant following the route they had talked about during the planning session. There was no one else in that area. The only other movement he could see was near the plant. Two guards were milling around by the loadout area next to the overhead doorway. But nothing was happening there. His eyes caught the sudden movement of two more guards coming out from one of the main plant doors. They stopped there in the rain, and covered their hands as they lit cigarettes under the canopy light. They would likely stay there for another hour or so before their shift was over and two others would take their place. Deek wasn't sure whether there were any other guards lurking in the shadows, out of the rain, but keeping their eyes open for trouble. He could only monitor movement.

Deek swung his scope over to the fenced area around the substation. Kenny had made it through the gate and over to the first of the three transformers. He would soon cut the pressure lines. Deek wondered when the control room would notice the red warning light on their panel showing up the broken gauge before Kenny cut the communications lines. The chances were that no one would be dispatched to the substation in this rain even when they did see the gauge wasn't working. They would probably think the weather caused a short and wouldn't investigate until the morning.

"Go, One." A quiet voice came over the radio on a preestablished, generally unused, frequency. To anyone who might be listening, it was such a short and unclear message as to be easily ignored. But the ORB agents had a coded message system. Tonight's calls on that channel meant something to them but to no one else. In this case, "Go, One" identified Sean and Glenn as Team One. The "Go" meant they were initiating their part of the project. "Out, One" would mean they had accomplished their mission and were moving on. "Stay, One" would mean things were taking longer than expected, while "Down, One" would mean they were in trouble. Emma and Roberto were Team Two; Armando and James, Team Three; Nick and Mack, Team Four; Kenny was Team Five. Deek was Team Six. He had some of his own codes, including "Trouble, Six," which meant what it implied—he was firing shots. After that, it may not matter so much, and he would be free to warn the others of impending problems. Matthew used "Lead" as his moniker.

Deek shifted his sights to where he could just make out Sean and Glenn right on time as they poked their heads through the cover of the jungle in the pre-planned location, watching for any signs of being followed. It was just after 10:30 p.m. They would be heading to the first flange on the tailings pipeline. That would mean a blast would follow soon. Deek twisted his scope back to the security door to watch for any guards. Luckily, the rain on their tin roof would muffle the noises. Deek relaxed with his arm on the Ruger. His finger was on the trigger, the safety off, and his other hand held the rifle steady.

Sean and Glenn moved into position at the first flange on the two tailings pipelines. The lines sat on the ground, held by concrete anchors to prevent them from over-buckling in the heat of the day. Left unrestrained, polyethylene pipe expanded by almost thirty percent of its length as the sun beat down and caused it to bend in all directions. It would shrink back as it cooled, but it would leave a misshapen line in its place. Anchors were needed to confine distortion, not so much to keep the pipe straight. But the pipes still moved from heat and created short, misshapen alignments between them. It was going to happen, but it needed to do so in a semi-controlled manner.

The drone hovered overhead in the dark. Matthew could see the guys working below him. There was no one in their vicinity so he aimed the unit over toward the plant site.

The pipeline anchors were placed apart at 100-foot intervals. But there were also anchors on both sides of the flanges at the 500-foot mark. It made the job easier for Sean and Glenn when they came to bind their explosive packs to the pipe. The anchors lifted the pipes enough for them to work their hands underneath and around with tape.

Both Sean and Glenn preferred a modified Semtex 1H high-performance plastic explosive. In this version, PETN was replaced by BCHMX, and RDX was replaced by HMX. They used a plain number-eight electric detonator. Sean carried the pre-cut blocks of explosive.

Glenn carried a box of detonators and two 12-volt batteries. He also had pre-cut copper wires ready for attaching to the detonator and the battery. They both wore headlamps with a narrow beam to only focus on what they were doing. They divided the components between them as a safety precaution. They had learned to do so by working together in the Middle East.

The detonators were one and a half inches long and a quarter inch in diameter. They had a base of high explosive and a primary charge of an initiating explosive. The charges were pressed into an aluminum tube. Leg wires were soldered to a fuse head inside the detonator. A pyrotechnic delay element provided a predetermined time delay and Sean had selected 120-second delay detonators, each with twenty feet of extension wires. Placing the explosives in the correct position on the pipes was important. They needed the rupture to face away from them and angle downwards.

Sean unwrapped the first block of Semtex and placed it on the side of a pipe near the flange. It was set about thirty degrees below horizontal. He wrapped the block to the pipe with duct tape. Then, he moved to the other pipe flange. There, he fitted another block of Semtex. While he did this, Glenn had pulled out two detonators. He attached one end of two extension cords to the leg wires of each detonator and placed them on the anchor block. He rolled the rest of the line out to its full extent away from the pipes. Sean took the detonators and poked them into the Semtex blocks, then checked the wiring. Together they attached the wires to the battery switch. They were ready for the first blast.

They looked at each other. Sean flipped the switch and counted to one hundred and twenty. This gave them more than enough time to look around for unwanted visitors or other problems. Then, he looked back to watch the blasts.

The flanges disintegrated in the explosions. All four ends of the two thirty-six-inch, three-inch-thick plastic pipes bent outwards in the direction of the blasts. The pulverized mineral waste rock combined with the pressurized copper processing wastewater sprayed high into the trees and over fifty feet into the jungle, taking pieces of flange with it.

Sean and Glenn wasted no time moving on to the next set of flanges. There were seven more sets. At their current rate, Sean estimated they would finish the rest in just under two hours. They were going slower than he had planned. The rain had played a part in delaying them. It made it harder to work, run between targets, and to set the explosives and wires.

After blasting the flanges, they would still have to demolish the barge and reclaim the line. As they worked on the second set of flanges, Sean had a plan to finish in time for the others to do their work.

Sean was reasoning that there was no need to wait thirty minutes to let the unrestrained tailings slurry work its way into the jungle. That would happen from the first blast. If the control room quickly stopped the flow, it would still take time to actually stop. From his talks with James, he also knew the plant was not likely to shut down too fast while the mills were turning. That's because it would have to push waste through the processing end of the plant, where it would have nowhere to go afterwards. Instead, it would flood the mill. No, he reasoned, the operators were going to have to resort to other measures and would not likely come up with anything solid until they met with senior management. By that point, the other blasts would have occurred, and the Zamora management would know for certain they had an environmental disaster on their hands. The mill would have to be shut down.

Satisfied with his logic, he and Glenn continued on until they reached the waste pond. The dam was just over a mile long. At the farthest end from where the tailings waste was discharged, the tailings reclaim water barge floated in a pond of clear water. There, the fine waste particles from the tailings had settled out, and the water was fresh enough to return to the mill. But it meant they had to hike half a mile before they reached the walkway onto the barge.

Once they arrived at the barge landing, they reached into their bags for explosive supplies. Sean didn't want to spend time searching for the best place to attach the Semtex to the barge's tanks. Instead, he taped Semtex to each side of the upper casings of the four huge submersible pumps. Then, he pushed in the detonators.

They quickly retraced their steps to the dam's crest at the other end of the walkway. With enough extension wire to ensure they were on solid ground, Sean flicked the power toggle, and they ran to the first of the reclaim pipe anchors. Behind them, the sound of two powerful blasts and the uprush of air and water almost threw them off balance. The front end of the barge tilted down into the water. The angle was so steep that the weight of the equipment broke the knuckle joints on the reclaim lines. It pulled the walkway out from the dam and into the pond. It sank, with just one-third of itself held above water by a thread of what remained of the piping and electrical cables stretching from the shoreline.

The reclaim pipelines were buried but came to the surface at the anchor blocks set only where there was a change in direction. There were only three. By the time the first explosives were set, Sean and Glenn could hear the wailing of the plant alarm, but it didn't stop them for a second. If anyone was coming, it would take them a while to reach where they were in the saturated undergrowth. They would first stop to examine the damage to the initial set of destroyed flanges on the tailings line. Once they saw that one had disintegrated, they might think there would be more, although no additional alarms would have been activated, because there weren't any. In fact, it would be really freaky for them to think there may be more joints in the same condition.

But eventually some guards would go further along the pipe. Once they saw the second set of flanges had been destroyed, they would suspect the damage was more extensive, and race forward. They wouldn't stop at the third set but would keep moving toward the dam. By the time they got as far as the barge, the reclaim line would have blown, and water would be firing high into the air. Had it been daylight, they would have been able to see the streams above the tree line. As it was, the rupture of the reclaim water line closest to the plant was spewing its discharge over the security guard building and beyond, with a pressure well over that of a fire hose.

At the sound of the plant-wide alarm, Deek sighted his Ruger at the security door and fired three bursts just as it was about to be opened. He pulled his radio speaker from his shoulder holster, pressed the send button and announced, "Trouble, Six."

Matthew was taking video from the drone of the activity below. He couldn't make out exactly where Deek was hiding, but he could see an occasional flash from the muzzle of his rifle now and again. He switched to thermal imaging and picked up the lone green shape of Deek hiding in the jungle growth. There were no other heat sources in his immediate area. Matthew smiled to himself as he thought of Deek having a little fun taking pot shots at the security guards trapped in their building. The drone hovered for another ten minutes before moving toward the substation.

When the eight guards, who had been spending their time playing Mahjong, reading or sleeping inside the building, heard the plant-wide alarm activated from the control room, they went into a panic. Guards were stubbing out cigarettes, buttoning up tunics, pulling on boots, strapping on guns, covering themselves with ponchos, and grabbing their rifles. But the first one to attempt to open the door was met by the resistance of three sharp smacks of bullets, which pushed it back against him. He didn't fully comprehend at first, but when he realized they were bullets keeping him from opening the door, he pulled the last inch back into place, to close it tight.

A few seconds later, the door partially opened again, and Deek put two rounds into the metal frame, deflecting them into the room. This time, the door closed and didn't open for a while longer.

Inside the room, the guards scrambled to try to make sense of what was happening. Some guards were ex-military, and were not so shocked as those who weren't. They were the ones who more quickly backed away and searched the building for an alternative means of escape. They wouldn't find any. Instead, pit vipers found them.

Disturbed by the chaos around them, the four vipers slowly came alive and slithered from their hiding places to search out the reason for their disturbance. Their usual camouflage as a primary defense mechanism didn't work here. This wasn't the jungle. But their venom was as dangerous. It contained a cocktail of chemicals that included a lethal hemotoxin, and they would readily bite if attacked or harassed. In humans, its venom caused intense pain, bleeding, swelling and death.

A couple of the vipers in the security building were over three feet long. A lot less than the seven feet in length they could grow to as mature snakes. But they were still lethal.

The pit viper hiding behind the trash can struck first and sunk its teeth into the lower leg of one security guard who was otherwise distracted by the sound of bullets smacking into the front entrance. He let loose a scream of death and pulled his leg out only to find the snake clinging on to it with its teeth and fangs buried in his flesh. While he frantically shook his leg from side to side, a second pit viper struck a guard who had ventured into the washroom looking for peace from the chaos, as he sank down on the toilet seat to consider the situation.

His viper was taking no hostages as it sunk its fangs into his foot and curled its body around his lower leg.

What followed was more chaos as shots pinged against the outer door, and the last two found their marks on more guards. The scene was a frantic mess of bodies running in all directions, some writhing on the floor, and vipers hanging on to their prey.

Meanwhile, the military-inclined guards tried opening the front door once more while constantly looking behind them in case of viper attacks.

But this time, they used the two dusty, unused riot shields brought out from storage in a back room. They had never used them, nor did they know if they were bulletproof. They just came with the original security supplies, when plant construction began. At that time, it was expected there could be problems with the tribes in the area. As a precaution, a small amount of riot gear had been sent to the property.

Two guards, protected with shields covering eighty percent of their bodies, pushed out against the door with their companions behind screaming at them to get out of the building.

The first shot from Deek's Ruger caught one of the two brave guards in the ankle. Despite the thunder of pouring rain, Deek could hear the scream of pain. The guard dropped his shield to hold his foot. One of his comrades yanked him back into the safety of the building. The other brave soul crouched lower behind his shield to protect against a similar fate and edged backward after his friend had been removed. As the door pulled shut, Deek smacked two more shots into it. The guards cautiously retreated to the back wall of the room to consider their next option and bind the leg of their comrade. They needed the doctor, but none of them were willing to make themselves a target for whatever madman was out there taking shots at them. The bullet had punctured the poor man's foot right in the lateral malleolus, the bony protrusion felt on the outside of the ankle at the lower end of the fibula. It would hurt for a very long time.

In the meantime, two of the guards who had escaped the viper attacks hacked away at the snakes stubbornly hanging on to human flesh even as their heads were separated from their bodies. More panic set in as the uninjured ones searched frantically for anti-venom. There was none.

The only guards available to head over to the tailings pipeline to investigate were those in the plant and those on duty at the security gate. All ten left their posts and assembled close to where the tailings lines came out for the mill, and waited as site management considered when it was time to investigate the sudden loss of pressure in the pipelines. Work had already started on closing down the main crusher and having the mine trucks reroute their loads to the stockpiles in that area to avoid continuing to feed waste through the system. Once the feedstock from the crusher stopped and their product had gone through the mills and been discharged into the start of the process system, the mills could be shut down. As soon as the milled ore had gone through the cyclones, the process speed would be increased to push all the mineral-rich slurry through the tanks, bypassing the filters. Then all of it would be dumped into the tailings lines, including whatever copper and gold it contained. That way, the lines would be emptied despite all the waste having been discharged into the jungle. All this would take some time, but for Armando it was enough to have the mills stopped. He didn't care about the rest of the plant.

Chapter 46

Kenny

Kenny heard the blasts and saw the fiery explosions from the tailings area. Now he waited for the signal. He had been draining the oil from all three transformers for the last couple of hours after cutting the feeds to pressure gauges and communication lines as planned. So far, there were no interruptions, and he guessed no one would be crossing the yard in the torrential downpour to investigate. As long as the power was still on, no one would worry. By now, the control room would be totally distracted by the loss of the tailings and reclaim pressures in the pipelines. They wouldn't investigate something as minor as faulty gauges.

"Out, One," came as a harsh whisper over the radio, and Kenny checked the operating temperature of the first transformer.

"Go, Five," he whispered into his radio as he watched the temperature gauge in front of him move a fraction into the red zone. The oil from the transformers was spilling over the containment area curb and flowing out into the jungle. It was only meant to contain 110% of the oil from one transformer, based on the assumption that only one would rupture at any one time. The additional allowance in the containment was for the possibility of rain, and there was plenty that night.

The drone hovered over the substation and Matthew watched as Kenny drained the transformers. Then he flew it over to the plant to watch for Armando and James.

Armando knew with Kenny's experience he would be able to time the power outage to within thirty minutes. He and James were already in position to go into the mill by 2:15 a.m. As it happened, it was about the time the plant guards reacted to the alarm. They rushed from their posts to the collection point to wait for further orders. All, that is, except the guards who were stuck in the security building.

James put a restraining hand on Armando's arm as he was about to move forward. Armando looked at him with a questioning look. The rain dripped from his eyebrows and the end of his nose. James pointed to the security building as the door opened a crack, then quickly closed. They had heard Deek's "Trouble, Six" message and realized that this was where it was happening. James made the decision to go the longer way around to the plant, to put them farther away from Deek's angle of vision. Hopefully, he would know they were taking another route out into the mill, but still, it was better to be safe.

With the plant guards waiting for orders and the others pinned down in the security building, the site was open to ORB's team to do what they needed. Unless some operators decided to take matters into their own hands. It was possible, but each one of the ORB agents was armed and ready to make use of their pistols and knives if they had to. James decided to put one more message out just to be safe in case Deek mistakenly thought they were guards as they ran across the yard to the plant.

"Go, Three. Eleven o'clock to six." Hopefully it would be enough of a signal for Deek.

Armando and James made their way over to the plant with the drone hovering two hundred feet above. At the same time, the yard lighting went out, the primary crusher started to wind down to a stop, and the white noise of heavy machinery began to shut down slowly.

Before they reached the door to the plant, Armando and James heard another set of shots to their right and saw the door to the security building slam shut. It seemed as though Deek had whoever was left of the Zamora security team well contained.

By now, Kenny had finished his work, sent his "Out, Five" message over the radio, and started to head back to camp. Matthew could have flown the drone over to where Kenny should be leaving the substation, but he wanted to make sure Armando and James were safely inside the plant.

Kenny decided to take another route back to where the vehicles were parked. He had an uneasy feeling about returning the same way as he had come in. It meant he would have to cross behind the main administration building, knowing the area would be deserted at this time of night. All the admin staff clocked off at the end of a normal day, and even the cleaning crew would have finished up by now. As he made his way nonchalantly through the rain, and without the cover of the jungle, he reflected on how good a job he had done with such perfect timing. Even the horrendous weather hadn't dampened his spirits. He was smiling when suddenly a shot rang out and a pool of mud in front of Kenny's feet blasted up as he fell backwards, stunned by the attack.

Deek had been looking at the door of the security building. But suddenly, from the corner of his right eye, he saw movement coming around the back of the administration building. He thought all the guards had either gone to the tailings area or been trapped in their building. But he wasn't taking any chances, even though for a millisecond he thought it was most likely an operator, and he took a shot to block his path. He could see the fellow fall backwards and scramble to get back behind the building for safety. But Deek's adrenaline was running on high. He swung back to point his Ruger at the security building door again. He fired off two shots into it as a warning. He wasted no time and turned his rifle ten degrees east and shot a bullet into the left leg of the still scrambling body.

Kenny lay there a moment before he blacked out, bleeding profusely from his wound. It was only the beating rain on his face that brought him back to consciousness. He lay there in excruciating pain. But he still had the wherewithal to rip his bandana from his neck and strap it as tightly as he could around his upper leg to stem the flow of blood. Drenched with sweat and rain, he pulled out his radio, pressed the send button, but blacked out in the mud before he could speak.

Deek thought no more about it. The door to the security building had remained shut, but he knew the occupants would be hatching some plan, and he needed to be sharp and focused.

Jun Jie Khao, the general manager, was furious at being woken up at such a time. He was told there was an emergency with the tailings system, the power was down, and it seemed the control room could not understand the problems.

Khao did not cope well with being disturbed from his sleep by an uninvited guest. At 2:30 a.m., it was far worse. But in this case, he had little choice but to react.

He could see that the main power was out because the light in his room and through his quarters was coming from the emergency generators. He dressed hurriedly, threw a coat over his shoulders, pulled some galoshes over his bare feet, and opened the door to his luxurious quarters. His driver was already waiting, although judging by his attire, he hadn't had the luxury of time to dress and stood in his yellow oilskin over his pajamas. He was wearing an oversized pair of dark green rubber boots. He held a large company umbrella over the general manager's head, and cursed quietly each time a drop of rain missed the umbrella and hit his boss's shoulder.

They drove to the mill in semidarkness. The plant lights were now running off generators and gave off a dull yellow light where they shone. The eeriness of the silence was the first thing Jun Jie Khao noticed when he stepped through the door into the mill. For a second, he just stood there in shock. His driver stood behind him with the umbrella raised to keep off any stray raindrops that might hit Mr. Khao's head. With the mill door still open, the driver half in and half out, the rain beating down on him, he dared to gently nudge his boss a few inches forward. Khao swung around to face the person who had dared to push him.

"You!" he screamed at his driver. "You shall pay for this!" It was as though suddenly the rage within the general manager had been released—but at whom? Jun Jie Khao was not a happy man. And neither was his driver. But Khao did know one thing. Whoever caused this night would pay heavily. If only he knew who it was. The reality was that he had no real power. That came from Ping Pei in Quito, and that was who he needed to make contact with immediately.

Meanwhile, Matthew had recalled the drone for a battery replacement. He could recharge it from the vehicle battery through the computer connection. It took only a few minutes to land the unit, remove the first battery, replace it with the fully charged one, and send it up on its way again.

Chapter 47

And Now, the Rest

"Go, Two" the radio whispered, and Deek looked to his left without taking his focus away from the door. He could just see the profile of two figures. They were hunched and moving toward the edge of the jungle. That's where the conveyor from the loadout area disappeared into the cocaine processing plant. He knew there could be problems if any guards were still at that post. "Go, One to Two," whispered the radio. Deek knew it meant Sean and Glenn were in position. They were there to cover Emma and Roberto when they needed access to the processing plant.

The drone hovered overhead as Armando and James made it through the door to the mill. They each picked up a bag of sand from the first fire station and stood still, waiting to see if there was movement on the operating floor above them. They had entered the basement, where their first targets, the lubrication oil systems, sat under each of the four mills. Generally, basements would be free of operating personnel, except at times when they were needed to contain emergency slurry dumps from the mills. In this case, the area was dry. Armando selected the first two mill train oil systems, unlatched the oil tank filler cap of the first and dumped a half-bag of sand into it. He did the same for the second system, while James copied him over on the two right-hand train systems. Even as the mills were slowing down to a stop, the sandy oil would be fatally circulating through their systems.

Armando and James held their breath as boots sounded on the steel grating of the operating floor above them. With the main power going down, the emergency power had activated automatically within minutes, and an eerie glow threw shadows in all directions as the light caught equipment from different positions. It was often hard to tell if something was moving in the dim light. But Armando and James only needed to work on the inching drives from under the mills. They had enough light to do what was needed.

Over the past three days, Armando had been hiding thin stainless-steel shims, just millimeters thick, under the huge motors of the slurry pumps. They would be perfect for packing between the inching drives and mill gears. He planned to place them slowly, one by one, as they turned the mills, instead of trying to push multiple shims in at one time. It could be too thick, presenting too much of an obstacle for an inching drive to overcome.

The sound of boots on metal grating and checker plate intensified above them, accompanied by shouting that made it sound as though everyone was in a panic. But because it was the Chinese way, Armando and James had no idea if the screams were due to panic, or just the employees having casual conversation, or someone giving orders. More footsteps sounded as the night shift operators arrived to ensure that the mills were shutting down as they should be. There was little else they could do without main power.

Matthew flew the drone over to the riverbank location where Emma and Roberto would be arriving to deal with the cocaine plant.

Meanwhile, Sean and Glenn positioned themselves south of the cocaine processing plant, hidden by the tall vegetation. They wore their high leather boots, with their pants taped over the bottom of each leg, thin leather gloves, and anything else they could think of to protect against insect predators.

Snakes were different. As they lay in position, Glenn could feel one moving along his outstretched leg toward his groin. He had no idea if it was poisonous or just an irritant. But he kept still and let the creature pass. It paused every few seconds, as if smelling the air. Then it slowly slithered a little farther, but off to one side of his thigh. While clothing could act as some kind of protection, it wouldn't help if it was a viper that wanted to sink its teeth into the flesh below. But Glenn didn't know what kind of snake it was and waited, motionless, for it to move off his body.

Emma and Roberto inched closer through the jungle toward their target. The rain beat down on them in torrents, pouring from the peaks of their caps poking out from their ponchos.

"Lead to Two. Hostiles at one o'clock," Matthew whispered into the radio. It was enough.

Emma spotted the four guards as she and Roberto came to the edge of the clearing for the building. They were standing outside, riveted to the spot as a group, looking over toward the tailings area where they had heard the blasts. Their orders were to not leave their station unless explicitly ordered and, as yet, they had received no such order.

The guards appeared unaware of the potential risk to themselves as they stood there and seemed to have forgotten what they were supposed to be protecting.

Emma was the first to move. Roberto maintained some distance so as not to expose both of them if things came to it. Their pistols were drawn and the safeties released.

Despite the incessant downpour, the flames from the tailings line blasts showed above the tree line. As the other guards rushed into the jungle, the four guards at the cocaine processing plant stood still, mesmerized by the chaos in the distance.

Emma slipped into the building behind the guards and stayed out of their line of vision should they turn toward her. Roberto made the same move and ducked inside just as one of the guards turned to check the door inadvertently left opened. He walked over and closed it before rejoining his group to carry on straining to see anything more over by the tailings pipelines. There wasn't really anything for them to see. They were too far away and separated by jungle. The rain was driving at them. It was pitch black. The eerie backup yard lights barely lit the area. Only one out of three lights was working.

Emma took advantage of the guards all being outside to lock the door. They didn't notice.

From what she and Roberto could see, there were only three operators in the plant. Each was focused on what he was doing on the catwalks over the tanks. It seemed as though they were processing the last of the crude cocaine as it came up from the hopper at the river. While they didn't know it at that point, the feedstock would soon dry up, and they would wonder what had happened. But for now, processing was ongoing.

Emma and Roberto crept over to the nearest set of pumps, under what looked like the last tank in the circuit before the product was fed to a kiln for drying. From there, it would fall onto the conveyor belt to the plant loadout area. Every tank and pipe was labeled for easy identification by the operators. They followed the circuit back to the incoming conveyor.

From what Emma could tell, there were two process circuits in series.

Emma could identify everything from the diagrams she and Matthew had studied. It outlined what happened after the farmers had done the donkey work of creating the coca paste—a chunky, off-white, putty-like substance by the time they had dried it—then converted it to a cocaine base they would sell to the cartel.

Except, in the Zamora case it seemed the farmers were providing only cocaine paste to the Chinese. That meant the farmers would be paid less than if they provided a base.

The first circuit at Zamora converted the coca paste into base. The second converted the base to commercial-grade cocaine hydrochloride. After that, she presumed it was left to the street distributors to cut it with filler products in any fashion they wanted. That was unless the Chinese did it themselves in that annex to the water pumphouse. But now was not the time to think about those things.

In this plant, the coca paste, produced by the farmers, was fed into the first tank, labeled "Hydrochloric Acid." Here it was mixed with water to dissolve it. This was where Roberto strapped the first block of Semtex to one of the feed pumps with one hundred feet of extension wire. The detonator had a delay of 180 seconds, and Emma rolled the wire to the door at the back of the building next to the incoming conveyor. She placed the battery and switchboard next to it by the door and went to help Roberto with the second block.

The next tank, actually a series of tanks, was where the potassium permanganate was added. It rid any deleterious material in the coca paste and was labeled "PotPerm." The cocaine mixture worked its way through the cascade of tanks over a six-hour period on its way to the filter press. This was where Roberto taped a second block of Semtex. He pushed in the detonator, attached the extension wires and gave the roll to Emma, who walked it back to the door.

Once the precipitate was removed and the solution mixed with ammonia water in another tank, the liquid was drained and the remaining precipitate was dried to a cocaine base powder. Roberto taped the third block to the bottom of the drain tank, and he and Emma repeated their procedure with the detonator and extension wire.

oooo

Back in the mill building, Armando and James had managed to place the thin steel shim plates between the gears of all four mills and their inching drives. Before they fired up the first inching drive motor, they checked on the whereabouts of the operating crew who had been previously scurrying around up on the operating floor, looking for problems with the equipment as it came to a stop.

By the time Armando was ready to start the inching drive, the operators were done with their investigation. They had found nothing more to do and had gone back into the plant offices. Armando activated the first drive, and millimeter by millimeter, it moved clockwise and took the first mill gear with it. James watched carefully as the gear started to cross the shim and he pushed another one in its path, then another and another. It was working. Within fifteen minutes, the mill gear was very slightly off-center, pulling the horizontal alignment of the entire mill with it. That was all it needed, just a few millimeters, less than one sixteenth of an inch.

Armando performed a complete rotation of the inching drive to remove the shims and hide them back under the slurry pumps. They were dramatically deformed and showed the impressions left by the mill gear teeth pressing into them as the mill moved. It took another forty-five minutes for the other three mills to be misaligned in the same way. They were finished by 3:30 a.m. and decided to leave the slurry pumps and motors. The damage they had done was more than enough to put the mills out of operation.

"Out, Three," James whispered into the radio as he and Armando slid through the door into the yard area. It was still pouring rain, like a sheet of water, and there was no turn-off valve in nature. They heard two shots and looked over at the security building. There was a body lying outside. It was likely some brave soul who had hoped to be fast enough to run for cover. He never made it, and no one had tried to get him inside.

The drone flew overhead as the camera focused on where James was calling from. Matthew spotted both bodies with the thermal imaging feature. He also picked up Deek's location and he switched to the night camera. Deek was focused on the security building and hadn't attempted to aim over to where James was.

James held the radio again. "Out, Three," he repeated, but added, "eleven o'clock to Six." Deek heard and understood the message. He continued to focus on the security facility and fired a shot into the door just because.

"Good." Matthew breathed a sigh of relief, knowing that if Deek hadn't understood the message from James, there would be a serious fuck-up.

Armando headed to the west, with James close behind. They would get to the jungle and follow the tree line to the perimeter of the property where the vehicles were parked. It was time to head back to camp.

As they got into their vehicle, James noted Kenny's jeep was still parked.

"Didn't Kenny finish up around two thirty a.m.?" James looked over at Armando as they pulled away.

Armando thought for a few seconds. "He should have left by now." They were worried but kept driving.

"Trouble, Five," James whispered into the radio. His phone rang.

"James, it's Matthew. What's happening?"

"Kenny's truck is still parked," James whispered.

"What? Anyone seen any sign of him?" Matthew sounded worried.

"Don't know. But can't say if anything happened—it's just his vehicle is still parked, and he should have been out of here an hour ago." James was thinking about what could have happened. He didn't know. He couldn't even guess at this point.

"I'll call around, James. You guys get back to camp." Matthew was worried. Everything had sounded like it went well with Kenny, so what had happened?

Matthew aimed the drone over to the substation with the thermal imaging activated. There were no signs of heat anywhere around the transformers. He searched farther afield in the cleared perimeter. Nothing. The drone retraced the steps Kenny had taken to get to the substation, but still nothing. Matthew was at a loss and flew the drone around the plant site looking for any sign of life, even just anything still warm.

oooo

Back in the cocaine processing plant, Emma and Roberto were moving into the second stage of the plant. So far, so good, but maybe too good. It was hard to hear very well with the rain pounding on the metal roof, but Emma was sure she heard the main door open. She signaled to Roberto to keep going and motioned to him that she was going up front to check things out.

Roberto crawled between the pumps, under more tanks. This was where the cocaine was turned into cocaine hydrochloride. It was where the real money was made. If the Chinese could cook it all here up to commercial grade, it would be worth a fortune at street level.

He placed another block of Semtex on the bottom of the acetone tank, where the cocaine base was dissolved before being filtered to remove any more unwanted material. The acetone purified it to an even greater extent than before. One last Semtex block was taped to the underside of the next tank, where hydrochloric acid was added to crystallize the cocaine out before feeding it into a kiln for drying. The explosion would take out the kiln at the same time. Smaller labs would probably use microwave ovens for this stage, but here at Zamora, the thinking was much bigger. Roberto pushed the detonators into place on the last two blocks before unwinding the wire back to the rear door.

Emma had spotted one of the guards back inside the building. Somehow, he had gotten past the lock and was now on the upper platform, talking to one of the operators. He was oblivious to what Emma and Roberto were doing beneath them.

As Emma turned to go back to meet Roberto, her pistol hit a steel column. The sound reverberated through the building. It was enough for the guard to look over the railing and search for whatever made the noise. He couldn't see anything. Emma stayed still in the shadow of one of the tanks as the guard came down the steel staircase, gun at the ready.

As the guard looked around, he spotted a set of wires leading from the base of a tank, back toward the rear of the building. He stiffened and readied his pistol. He shouted up to the operators to take cover. When one noticed the gun in the guard's hand, they all squeezed between the tanks and the building's side wall. They held their notepads in front of their faces as though they would protect them from bullets.

As the guard advanced along the length of the building, still following the wires, his head bobbed up to look ahead and down to keep an eye on the direction of the wires. He wasn't looking from side to side. As he passed her hiding place, Emma stepped out from the shadows. She smacked him hard on the side of his head with her pistol. The guard wobbled but didn't fall. He managed to gather enough strength to focus and aim his pistol at her lower body. He fired. The safety had not been released, and as he struggled to hold the gun up for his other hand to pull the safety back, Emma fired her shot. It drilled into the side of his head just as he was regaining some control. He slumped forward against one of the steel columns and slowly sank to the ground with that shocked look of death on his face as his gun fell to the concrete floor.

The operations people couldn't see what was happening, but they could hear the shots over the noise of the rain. They made their way cautiously down the two flights of stairs to the ground floor and over to the front door with their hands above their heads.

The other three guards outside heard the fatal shot. They were already inside the building when the operators ran into them. As they flailed around, Emma disappeared through the back door. She pushed it shut and almost tripped over Roberto, bending over the twelve-volt battery. He was connecting the last of the extension wires to the switch as the rain dripped off his forehead and chin.

Outside the building, Emma and Roberto could hear the guards shouting and firing bullets at imaginary threats. They didn't know how many intruders there were, where they were, what they were doing, or why they were doing it. But they knew they would have to fight to survive once they saw their comrade's body. His eyes were wide open, staring at nothing in particular, with a look of anguish on his face.

Emma gave Roberto the thumbs-up, and he flipped the switch. They started counting to 180. The seconds ticked by slowly. Emma wished she had set the delay to thirty seconds. The sound of the guards inside the building arrived at the rear door. It slowly opened, and a head poked out, only to be met with a bullet from Emma's .22-calibre Ruger Mark IV pistol. The body jammed the door from opening further or closing. But a brave pair of hands pulled it back into the building by the feet.

Emma and Roberto knew it would be only minutes before the remaining two guards would go back out through the main door and come around both sides. By then, it would be too late. Emma and Roberto would have fled the scene.

They threw themselves on the bank of the Río Quimi seconds before the blasts leveled the cocaine plant. The explosions took the incoming and outgoing conveyors with it.

"Out, Two," Roberto whispered into his radio as they lay there watching the glow of fire through the trees.

No one was chasing them as they made their way back to their vehicle, parked just outside the perimeter of the property. Emma looked over at Kenny's vehicle. "Where the hell is he? He should have been here by now," she murmured and looked around as though she would see Kenny leaning against a tree with that smile on his face.

A terrible thought went through her mind, but she had no time to think about it more as Sean and Glenn joined them and climbed into their own vehicle.

"Glenn. Better take Kenny's vehicle back to camp. I don't think he's coming," Emma managed to say.

Matthew was circling the drone to all the places he could think where Kenny might be. There was no sign of him, and with the security guards over at the tailings or cocaine processing plant, or stuck in the security building, it left only his own people and the operations night shift. He was pretty sure the operations people would stay where they were as long as it was being reported there was gunfire outside in the yard area.

So, where the hell was Kenny?

Chapter 48

The Pit

Nick and Mack had been at the open pit since 1:00 a.m. Now they were waiting and watching in the rain. Miners on the other side were getting ready to blast at 3:00 a.m. They had moved their equipment far from the blast zone, with the shovel and loader waiting at the bottom of the pit to restart work. The prewarning blast horn sounded five minutes to the hour. It cut through the sound of heavy rain smacking against the ground and throwing up small stones and mud.

It had taken Nick and Mack nearly two hours to set the blasting caps in all the drill holes and connect the wiring. Then, they rolled all the wires separately uphill to the power source, far from the effects of the explosion. ANFO didn't respond to detonators used for Semtex. Nick used number-eight caps with a mixture of mercury fulminate and potassium chlorate, stuffed into a quarter-inch-diameter metal tube, one and a half inches long. The stamp on the casing indicated the value of the delay. The caps had varying delays built in and Nick had been careful to select caps with delays as close together as he could. The less the delay, the greater the blast.

The extension wires were connected to a switch box, which was connected to the twelve-volt power source. It took time to run the wires back to the box. Instead of handling the wires one at a time, Mack was tasked with grouping wires from several caps together and running them back. He had to be careful not to mix one wire from a pair of wires with another. Each pair needed to terminate in a negative and positive connection.

By 2:45 a.m., they were ready. Nick whispered, "Go, Four," into his radio. They settled down to look out over the glow from the blasts at the tailings area. The glow was reflected back through the rain from the low clouds. Pulling their poncho hoods over their eyes, they took a moment to rest.

As the last few minutes ticked by, Nick looked at his watch, his finger hovering over the switch. He knew the miners were always on time with their blasts. They were working on their next pit bench, where forty-five feet of rock would be blasted out of the wall at a predetermined length, width, and depth. It would take the shovel and loader three days to remove the broken rock, then feed it to the 400-ton-capacity mine trucks to haul down to the crusher. The mine didn't know the crusher was out of service yet. But they did know their pit lighting had gone out around 2:30 a.m. and the emergency generators had turned on. The pit boss assumed it to be a local fault, likely at the pit panel, and they would check it out in daylight.

Within seconds of the miners triggering the delayed blasts on their side of the pit, Nick activated his.

The first of Nick's blasts were in the deepest holes. The explosions kicked the pit wall outward at the bottom of that bench. Then, the upper blasts did the same at various levels, working their way to the shallowest holes. With the toe of the pit wall demolished, the upper blasts caused the rock to surge downwards and into the weak fissure. They threw it outwards so far it landed on the opposite side of the pit and cascaded downwards onto the already blasted-out lower wall.

The rock fragments, some the size of a small building, landed with a thunderous roar over the equipment left at the bottom of the pit, including the shovel and its substation. Nick and Mack watched the commotion over on the miners' side. There was pandemonium as miners stood at the edge of the pit and strained their eyes through the rain to get a glimpse of what had just happened. They would be in shock. But they would see nothing to explain the pit wall collapse. It was on the opposite side from where they had blasted. They just could not have caved in the whole side of the pit from their own side.

"Out, Four." Nick and Mack made their way back to camp.

oooo

Jun Jie Khao was mortified at what was being reported to him. He stood in the control room with his driver still at his side. Two assistants had joined them, but stood silently to one side, awaiting orders from their leader.

The general manager watched the screens over the shoulder of one of the process control operators. The subset screens for the tailings and substation were blank. No signals were coming through from those locations. Suddenly, as Khao studied the diagrams on the screens in front of him, the signals from the cocaine processing plant went blank. His eyes widened even further as he stood motionless, trying to make sense of what was happening. *What now?* he wondered as his brain worked overtime. *Here? The plant?* His whole body went into panic mode as he turned and fled down the steel stairway and out through the side entrance of the mill building. His driver could barely keep up. He wrestled with the umbrella, ready to do his duty. But his boss was already in the back of his vehicle, waiting impatiently to be driven back to his quarters.

"Wake up. Wake up," Khao whispered hoarsely into his phone. It was almost 4:00 a.m. when he called Ping Pei in Quito. A very sleepy voice answered.

"What is it?" Ping Pei answered, annoyed by the disturbance.

"We have a big problem here." Khao's voice was shrill.

Sleep had managed to provide Ping Pei with a short respite from the problems at the Zamora site. But now they came flooding back to him as he looked at the time and heard the panic in the voice of his general manager.

"What is it, Khao?" There was no time for formalities.

"We are under attack!"

Ping Pei realized that moment that he had been too slow to get extra security mobilized. He was still waiting for word from the Ecuadorian minister to assure him he had their full support and troops were on their way to Zamora. It hadn't happened yet, and Ping Pei realized it may never.

Chapter 49

Time to Reflect

James greeted the teams as they returned to camp. But he felt mortified when he realized that Kenny hadn't made it. It was almost 4:00 a.m., and it was still raining and dark. He knew Matthew was still over at the parking area with the drone scouting the plant, searching for Kenny.

"Anyone got any thoughts on what may have happened to Kenny?" James looked around at the tired faces as everyone sat around the table. Some were drinking beer, some coffee, but no one had an answer that made any sense.

"Well, we know he gave the call. He was all done, so something must have happened after that." It was Emma, searching for some morsel of sense. "He had to come back your way, Deek, if he was heading over to the parking area. Did you spot him at all?" Everyone turned to face Deek.

"I don't think so. I had a clear view of him when he went over to the substation, but he never came back that way. I heard his call, but I didn't see him come out. Maybe something happened to him before he had a chance to make it. He could be lying there, injured." Deek was thinking but hadn't linked the operator he had disabled with Kenny. It didn't enter his mind.

"I don't know why he didn't make the distress call if he was injured, unless he was knocked out or worse." It was James. "I have to go back and look for him."

"Wow, hold on there, cowboy." Emma was now not only concerned for Kenny but also for James. "Let's just think about this a little more before anyone takes risks we can't afford right now. As far as the Chinese will ever know, this was all the work of the cartel. If we take a chance and expose ourselves on the ground, the tiger will strike back. I mean, Beijing, and

God knows who else. Matthew has this handled. He's using the drone and if he needs help, he'll call."

"If we're going to do something, it has to be now." James was impatient to do something to help Kenny, if it wasn't already too late. And if it was, he needed to be extracted. "It'll be getting light in another hour. If Matthew hasn't been able to spot him yet, it may mean Kenny's lying injured in a mud hole and no thermal camera is going to catch that. We need to get in there and hunt around. I'm going in with Sean." James looked around. Emma didn't object any more. She could tell when James had made up his mind. Sean nodded and picked up his rifle. He was ready to move.

"Okay, Glenn, you drive us over and get as close to the back side of the substation as you can. Drop us off and wait there with your rifle aimed toward us. The power line from the dam crosses where we park, so you can follow the cleared path as far as the substation. That's a dead zone over there, so I wouldn't expect any trouble unless someone has Kenny and they're waiting for us. But they would have to be pretty sharp to think that's the way we would choose to get in.

"If we can't find him at the substation, we'll take the route out we think he would have taken. If that doesn't work, we're going to have to wait until things cool down a bit, identify where he is and go in and get him. Clear?" James looked at each person on his team. They were all nodding their agreement. There was no other way, and no one was going to leave Kenny there without trying.

"I'm coming with you." It was Emma. "You and Sean can head in, and I'll trail and keep you covered."

"Good idea, Em. Thanks. Let's go." James and the others got into the vehicle that made the least noise. Glenn fired it up and sped off toward the parking area.

Meanwhile, Kenny was coming to. It took him a minute to figure out what was happening. He wiped a hand across his face to clear the water from his eyes and looked down at his leg. The bandana was soaked in blood and rain. But he was aware enough to use both hands to search for his radio. He couldn't find it and slumped back into the mud. A crackle over the radio startled him. "Come in, Five. Come in, Five." Kenny recognized Matthew's voice. It gave him a better fix on his unit. It was somewhere down around his left knee. He stretched his arm until he felt the radio, and with an extra push, managed to knock it toward his chest. "Come in, Five. Come in, Five," Matthew repeated.

Kenny clutched the radio. He pressed the send button. "Trouble, Five. Trouble, Five," he managed to whisper.

Matthew broke with protocol and whispered, "Thank God. Hang tight."

Kenny smiled and fell back. He was sure one of his comrades would pinpoint his coordinates from the radio message, and somehow, he managed to relax a little.

Glenn negotiated the rough ride through the clearing, despite some serious obstacles. There were creeks running at their maximum height in the rain. Mud holes of unknown depth and debris floating around in the downpour. Frightened animals ran in all directions, away from their machine. Boulders showed themselves above the surface for Glenn to navigate over or around. His skill at driving in these conditions was magnificent, a testament to his jungle training. He stuck close to the side of the power line right-of-way. The jungle on the sides kept a lot of the debris from his path and stopped mud holes from forming. They made it to within fifty feet of the substation without serious damage to themselves or the vehicle.

While they were driving, and despite horrendous jolts, James had zeroed in on Kenny's coordinates: somewhere at the rear of the administration building. He took a chance and opened the radio channel.

"Three to Lead. Rear of admin." He switched the radio off.

Matthew flew the drone to the administration building. He dropped it to twenty feet and guided it around two corners to the rear. The drone slowed as it searched the outside perimeter with the thermal imaging. It picked up a green shape and Matthew switched to the night vision camera.

There was Kenny, bundled up against the siding of the building and very still. The drone got close enough for Kenny to hear the quiet buzzing of the rotors and his eyes snapped open. He knew then that the boys had come to get him. He gave the camera a grizzly smile as the drone went straight up to about thirty feet and stayed hovering above him.

"We're going to have to head over to the admin building, over there to the left." James pointed as he, Emma and Sean stood next to the mud-covered jeep. Glenn stayed in the driver's seat, wiping his pistol.

"Let's go." James moved forward with Sean on his right side. Both had their pistols drawn. Emma followed twenty feet behind with her Ruger rifle loaded and ready to fire. Rain bounced off their camouflaged ponchos as they walked to the substation through sodden undergrowth. Once there, they went to the left, as Kenny would have done. They moved faster over the gravel yard. Twenty feet from their destination, shots rang out, and they ran the rest of the way, while Emma lingered behind. She hadn't left the substation yet. But she could see a small group of Zamora guards moving toward James and Sean. Emma raised her rifle and looked through the night scope. The green bodies showed up through the rain. There were three stopped over by the corner of the main building.

"Trouble to your right," she whispered into her radio, but it was too late to do anything about the shots fired in their direction. Emma realized she wasn't the target and had likely not been seen. She moved slowly backwards along the substation fence and worked her way over to where she had a good vantage point of the three guards. They fired again. This time a half-dozen rounds hit the corner of the admin building where James and Sean had taken cover. Emma moved in closer to her targets, knelt, steadied her rifle against her shoulder and aimed. She would need three accurate shots to make their mark. She waited a few more seconds until the small group was close enough her shots would count.

Matthew watched James and Sean turn the corner of the building and activated the drone spotlight over Kenny. James ran over to him, while Sean walked backwards, his pistol raised and ready to cover them, in case Emma couldn't. They all heard three shots fired a second apart. Sean unpacked a folded stretcher from his back, set it on the ground, and helped James move Kenny onto it. Once they saw it was Kenny's leg that had been shot and it was already tightly bandaged, they didn't stop to tend to the wound. There was little more they could do for him in the field.

"Live bird in hand," Sean whispered into his radio, referring to Kenny.

"Three down. Coming in," Emma whispered into her radio.

"Stay and cover," James responded and knew Emma would do what he asked. There was no point in her coming any farther from the substation and having to cross open ground to the admin building. She had done her job.

They had no idea whether there were more guards in the area. Regardless, with Emma covering them, James and Sean raced back to the substation with Kenny on the stretcher between them.

Matthew had switched off the spotlight and turned the drone to follow the stretcher. He flew up to fifty feet to get a wider look around at the yard, but he didn't see any more hostiles.

When Glenn heard the three quick shots, then the "live bird" call, he moved the jeep closer to the substation. He knew Kenny would be coming out on a stretcher. Suddenly, James and Sean burst out from the bushes with Kenny between them. They had taken a safer route along the edge of the jungle from the administration building. They pushed the stretcher along the back seat. Kenny was lucid and smiling, but clearly in a great deal of pain. Emma joined them. She lifted one end of the stretcher, squeezed onto the back seat and lay Kenny's stretcher across her lap, her legs tucked snugly behind the front passenger seat. The three guys squashed together in the front with James in the middle and the gear shift between his legs, while Glenn struggled to navigate their retreat.

Back at camp, the others were still awake and waiting. Matthew had arrived and they sat around talking about the rescue.

"Christ, I think it was me." It was Deek who had suddenly put it together and realized the "operator" over by the admin building was Kenny.

Chapter 50

The Day After

Matthew and his team left camp only three hours after they had returned from their mission. None had slept for the last twenty-four hours and were unlikely to rest for at least another twelve.

They were traveling in a convoy to El Pangui to drop off James. He would be staying for a while to make the payments to the farmers. Once Luna had helped them make peace with Los Choneros, he would return home. Roberto had offered to stay with him and James immediately accepted. The two of them would make a good team to close out business. It could take a month or longer, but that's the way it was. Stockman would continue to wire funds to the Guayaquil bank. James would continue to collect for as long as it took.

The convey had pulled over to the side of the road when they reached the outskirts of El Pangui and everyone gathered around to say their goodbyes in the pouring rain.

Matthew hugged his friend.

"Until the next one, James," he said.

"Call me when you need me, boss. Oh, and thanks for the ride. Interesting as usual."

James and Roberto stood by the roadside and waved for as long as anyone from the little ORB convoy waved back.

Once the rest of them arrived at Loja, Matthew, Emma and Kenny would drive to Quito to get medical help. Sean, Glenn, Mack and Deek would head to Guayaquil in two separate vehicles and then fly back home. Armando would go home to northern Peru by road. Nick planned to head north, but east of Quito, to Colombia. He had friends in Medellín.

The group stood soaked from the night's continuing storm. They were saying their goodbyes when a convoy of rugged, dark green pickup trucks sped by. They were heading in the direction of Zamora. Sullen-looking men, drenched and poncho-covered, grasped support bars attached to the pickup boxes. Emma read "Active Security" on the doors. The large Guayaquil security company was sending reinforcements to the Chinese.

"Wow, glad we got out of there fast, guys. There must be at least fifty of them." Emma sounded very relieved. "Now, let's get out of here."

"You bet," Matthew agreed. "I doubt that'll be all. My guess is they'll have reinforcements coming in from Quito as well. Who knows what the government will send to support them, but you can be sure they won't all come by road. Those guys will use helicopters, and they'll be looking for whoever beat up the place. So, let's get moving, everyone. We're not out of the woods yet."

Matthew and Emma transferred Kenny to the back of their vehicle. "We have no idea who the Chinese think was behind all this, but I'm hoping they keep thinking it was the cartel." Matthew looked over to Emma, who pursed her lips and nodded.

"Sure hope so, or they'll be looking for us everywhere." Emma pulled herself into the passenger seat. "You good, Kenny?" She turned her head to look at him.

Kenny's pain had plateaued some with the help of some serious painkillers. But he was still uncomfortable. He sat up with his injured leg stretched as far as it would go across the backseat.

"I'm good." Kenny smiled. This time it was real. He thought about what might have happened if his friends had left him at the Zamora site. He would either die or someone would kill him.

As they waved, shouted, and even blew kisses, the crew drove off in different directions. Who knew when they would meet again.

Chapter 51

Time to Die

"I build mines!" Koski would respond to anyone who naively asked what he did for a living.

He left out any reference to his cocaine production expertise.

It was a bold response from such a frail-looking, shy man in his late sixties. But he still had a twinkle in his eyes and a wry smile on his thin lips. That was all he would say. He wasn't much for small talk.

Most of the time, his response confused anyone who asked. They had probably hoped for a clear and simple answer to a simple question. They had hoped to avoid follow-up questions. It was a simple response. But it immediately raised the need for more explanation if one wanted to pursue the subject. Mostly, Koski faced shrugs and turned backs. His audience wanted simpler challenges.

Koski would wait for the next question. He'd have the same wry smile on his face and one hand on his sleeve of beer. Meanwhile, the remaining audience considered if they should ask more. They would ponder over whether it was worth the trouble of a follow-up. They knew it could make that three-word response much more complex. It could be more than anyone wanted to deal with. They might have to embark on a lengthy challenging conversation, seeking common ground with this enigmatic stranger. No, better to just turn away with a simple "oh" and leave it at that, like the rest of them had done.

Koski didn't seem to care if they wanted to continue or not. He sipped his beer and looked over his glass as the strangers started to engage with others at the bar. His gray bushy eyebrows raised in question at the lackluster response. But it became normal for him. He shrugged it off again and kept drinking, lighting up another Chesterfield.

This time, in this saloon, in this town, Koski was left alone once more. He sat at the bar until closing time. It took him five hours to make his way slowly through his beers. Occasionally, he would have a whiskey chaser thrown in, to fire things up a little.

Despite his small size, he didn't appear drunk at the end of the night as he put his cash on the bar, tipped his black felt cowboy hat to the barman, and made his way out the door into the darkness of yet another unfamiliar town. But he was used to this life now and had always made sure, before visiting a bar, to make arrangements for when he had finished. After all, everyone needed somewhere to sleep.

Koski stumbled along the two blocks to his motel.

Perfect. He needed the fresh air—but not too much lest he black out before getting to his room. With just enough night light to feel his way forward, his keys on a chain secured to his belt loop held loosely in his right hand, he slipped into his room without turning on the lights.

Koski was a civilized man, even when drunk. He took off his well-worn black leather boots and stood them side by side with heels against the door, as though they could possibly stop an unwanted intruder. Then, he removed his clothes. Folded and placed them on a chair within easy reach of the bed, in case he needed to make a quick getaway. He pulled on some shorts and flopped onto the bed. There was no point in drawing the curtains. He liked the dawn light poking its nose into his room in the early morning to remind him that another day had arrived, and he was still alive. His snores could be heard down the hallway in less than a minute, but no one complained. They were all doing it.

Koski had been back from South America for a year. Eventually, there was no place in Ecuador for Koski to hide. No village was safe. Already on the run from the authorities in Chile and Peru for illegal gold mining, Ecuador had been his final challenge. It was time to return to Canada, although he knew that any idea of returning to his home in Wawa would never provide refuge from the cartel. They would never give up.

No. Koski knew his days were numbered, but he had no intention of making Wawa his grave. So, once home, he kept moving from town to town, from bar to bar, with the familiar surroundings of his youth always within reach should he need it.

Koski often thought about the past and what circumstances helped create this circle of fate.

The 1980s were good to gold prospectors, but, as usual, the red tape for development was cumbersome at best, and expensive. It took time. Years more than most could tolerate before their ambitions were achieved. Many moved on to other prospects, hoping the path would be shorter. It rarely was. But there were other, simpler, ways to get rich off gold for personal reasons, so to speak, if only one knew how.

In his youth, Koski had messed around panning streams near Wawa. Patience was the key, and knowing where to go was the secret. He got lucky every now and then, and stored the gold flakes away until he could figure out the rough cost of his future. It came as a surprise one day when he joined a small mining group visiting Peru in search of a worthwhile deposit. Peru was one of the friendliest jurisdictions for mining at that time, along with its neighbor Chile. Both were making great strides in mine development and reaping the tax rewards and paying the graft that came with permitting. They saw it as the industry of the future, continually discovering resources that would last for thirty, forty, or more years.

Koski happened to be in the right place at the right time. He was rekindling a childhood friendship with the son of a senior mining executive who also lived in the gold-rich area around Wawa. The place was a hotbed of gold mining fanatics in those days, some of whom carved a substantial and influential career out of the industry. His friend's family took a liking to Koski. They knew about his interest in panning for gold, as well as his occasional forays into the mining industry in the neighborhood. He had already worked at some process plants. He had also done stints at the mines, both underground and open pit. By the time he was thirty, he had become a bit of a jack-of-all-trades.

The trip to the western side of the Peruvian Andes proved fruitful for all. The Canariaco property hosted an abundance of copper and gold. The Wawa executive struck a deal by purchasing a forty-nine percent interest in the mine and the rights to develop and operate it for additional revenue. The Peruvian owners were reluctant to concede any more than that to foreigners.

While there, in the dry western foothills of the Andes, Koski had a chance to drive up to the highest point. At the top, he looked west. He could see over the town, past the foothills, and almost to the ocean. Essentially, this was desert. But that was not what caught his interest. As he gazed out over the property, he noticed holes, like perforations, but at unequal distances from each other as they reached out toward the horizon. This was his first experience with the Piquiñeros—or gold bandits of Peru. Somehow, they seemed to be able to smell the high-grade gold pockets below the surface, and manually hacked their way down until they hit small mother lodes. While being illegal, the law never bothered them. Their hauls were minimal compared to the vast amount that was down there, underground. Somehow these people had managed to carve a living out of the earth—or rock—over the past years, when others had left their properties to remain undeveloped.

Once the miner reached the gold-laden rock, it would be hammered off piece by piece. The pieces would be placed into a woven basket and hauled to the surface by a rope. The rope passed through a crude A-frame over the hole and was attached to a motorized hoist bolted to the front of a dilapidated F-150. There were other equally run-down trucks spread along a line of holes that stretched into the distance. Each also being filled from the baskets coming to the surface with their hauls.

Koski followed one of the trucks filled with ore to a crude open-air mill, a trapiche, set outside the property limits. There, the ore would feed into a round, rough stone trough; water was added, and the mixture ground down with a heavy flat wheel of rock attached to a sturdy pole. It was slowly pulled around in the trough by a dusty, tired-looking burro, creating a gritty slurry. The slurry would be directed into a chute and carried to the next part of the process.

Other trucks would dump their ore into similar troughs. They worked in parallel, each with a burro applying the needed crushing power before the mixture was pushed forward. At some point, the troughs would combine. They would sluice the total volume through a simple cyanide circuit, freeing and collecting the gold.

At the end of the crude processing line, a basic refinery made gold buttons that were stored in a crude old safe. Two heavily armed men guarded the safe, which was anchored in a concrete block for extra protection.

This was the first time Koski had witnessed the workings of a cooperative, and an illegal one at that. As basic as it was, it seemed to work. Trucks came from other properties where Piquiñeros worked. They brought their hauls here for processing and payment.

No one stopped Koski from roaming around, although the guards at the safe were clearly on high alert. He wandered from one end of this little miracle in the desert to the other, smiling all the time and shaking his head from side to side.

Koski spoke little Spanish. Enough to get by, but not enough to converse fluently. But he would come to it. This was where he wanted to be. One step above panhandling.

Over time, Koski became fluent in Spanish and even picked up nuances from neighboring countries. After living among them for several years, he joined the band of Piquiñeros as the first gringo, sharing his stories of gold panning and mining and demonstrating his passion for their accomplishments.

He never returned to Wawa until now, forty years later. But all things must come to an end.

Koski's legacy included teaching the Ecuadorian jungle farmers to add value to the coca paste they had been selling, and contracting with Los Choneros for them to buy their coca base at a higher price.

Now he was back, close to this little-known town in eastern Canada, situated west of nowhere in particular, in an old mining area of Ontario. There was no family for him there anymore; his few old friends had died, and the one bar that would once have been relied on for community had changed hands long ago and become a sports bar. The spirit of the area had left when he had, forty years previously. There was nothing but old memories remaining, although he still had property outside of town. But it was now just wasteland, and even farming had moved on.

Koski was destined to wander since his return. His lengthy straight gray hair was swept back from his forehead, and his gray mustache threatened to become handlebars. His sun-browned face, with deep wrinkles, showed his experiences. He had a constant twinkle in his corn-blue eyes, matched only by a sly twist up at the right corner of his mouth, as though he were about to smile, but never did. He wore a short-waisted, black, supple leather waistcoat unless he was in bed, the bath, or the shower. It was Koski's trademark. He was never seen in public without it, no matter the occasion.

Tonight was Koski's last. He would die without wearing that trademark, without his boots on, and without the comfort of knowing who had killed him. As he settled into the deep sleep of a drunk, he never felt the sharp edge of a blade slice deeply across his throat, almost to the spine. He never made a sound, never struggled and never woke, even for a split second, as the blood gurgled from his twisted lips.

It was a fast and humane way for a killer to rid themselves of what had become more than just an irritant to them. The assassin, a Los Choneros cartel member, had spent months tracking his quarry. Going from town to town and missing Koski by a day or two. This was the Koski who bilked them out of millions of dollars by educating the coca farmers in Ecuador to make cocaine base out of paste. It meant the cartel had to pay more for the product when they could have converted the paste themselves.

The cartels never forget. Koski may have escaped Ecuador but Los Choneros would always follow.

oooo

No one claimed Koski's body. No one knew he had returned to his homeland. The local newspaper dedicated only three lines to the news of his death, identifying him as an unknown wanderer who had been found dead, not murdered, in a local motel. It was far too much for the community or the local cops to have to deal with a murder. Better to leave it alone and not ask questions. Vagrants wandered through their town on a regular basis. Most passed through. Some stayed, and some just disappeared.

Chapter 52

Last Call?

Matthew had called Stockman while they were on route from Loja. He knew it would be difficult to take Kenny, with a bullet wound, into any hospital when they reached Quito. There would be all kinds of awkward questions, and if it was anything like home, the hospital would have to report it to the police and then who knew what would happen to them all? Certainly, they would have detained and questioned Matthew, even though he felt confident that Stockman could help get them released. It would still have been a situation he would rather avoid.

Stockman didn't want Matthew to take Kenny all the way to Quito in his condition. "From what Emma says, Kenny's running quite a fever and going in and out of consciousness. No, he needs attention as soon as you can get it." Stockman was adamant, and Matthew could hear him flipping through some papers on his desk.

"Guayaquil is the closest city with the kind of facilities he needs, but I don't have any contacts there." Matthew waited for Stockman.

"Okay." Stockman had finished fiddling with his papers. "I'm going to call an old friend of ORB's, Dr. Fabrizio Delgado. He works at the Neuroscientists Institute on Av Pedro Menendez Gilbert in Guayaquil. But he has a small private clinic on the south side of the city, where he treats the poorer people at the weekends. I want to you to stay on this line while I use the other line and call him and get you two introduced." Stockman didn't wait for a response from Matthew. He put his cell phone down on his desk, speaker up, picked up his land line and dialed a long number. Matthew could hear Stockman speaking to someone but couldn't quite make out the words. It was a short conversation and he heard Stockton's phone drop back into its cradle.

"Okay, you're good to go. I'll send you a message with the address and his phone number. He'll be waiting, but when you get there, park in the lane behind the place and knock on the door. Fabrizio will come out and get you." Stockman felt relieved to get some good help for Kenny. Fabrizio was a neuroscientist, but he also had more training as a general surgeon than most. He would do a great job.

"Many thanks. We're about two hours away. Once I get Kenny settled, we can go over how we finished at Zamora." Matthew and Emma were very relieved. It wouldn't be long now. Emma sat in the back with Kenny, feeding him sips of water and keeping his head cool.

Matthew glanced down at the message that had arrived from Stockman and handed his phone to Emma.

"Here's the address, Em. Can you plan us a course and look for a hotel close by where you can book us a couple of rooms?"

Emma took the phone and copied the address to her Google Maps.

oooo

"Well, I think it's over, sir." Matthew was relaxing in their room at the River Garden Hotel, across from the Malecón and overlooking the River Guayas in the south part of Guayaquil. Emma sat on the sofa, staring out the window at the boats and barges moving north and south, with a vodka-tonic in hand.

"And Kenny? Did he get taken care of?" Stockman wanted to make sure his agent was all right before they went into any detail about the project.

"All good. Thanks for that. It worked out really well. Kenny's all wrapped up and over in his room down the hall from us. He's going to be in pain for a while. But you know Kenny. As long as he's smiling, he'll be fine."

"So, everyone did what they had to do and made it out okay?" Stockman assumed they had, otherwise he would have heard about it a while ago.

"Yes, and we left the place in one hell of mess. I don't know what Tongyan are going to do but whatever it is, there's no way they're going to be processing anything very soon. Did you call the agencies?" Matthew tipped back the last of his vodka-tonic, put his glass on the desk in front of him and leaned back in his chair.

"They're probably there as we speak. The first thing I did was call the McArthur Foundation folks."

"Good move! They would be crawling all over this." Matthew laughed and looked over at Emma. But the speaker wasn't on so she didn't know what they were talking about. Her hands went up with a silent *"What?"* appearing on her questioning face. She motioned to Matthew to put the speaker on.

"Thought you'd like that." Stockman was smiling as he heard the line click.

"Hello, Daddy. It's me. Your favorite daughter, remember?"

"Hello, darling. Are you okay? Did you do what you like to do, and survive?" Stockman loved Emma. She was so much like him when he was younger. Afraid of nothing. Always ready to get in with the men.

"I survived. Didn't I, Matthew?"

"She did, sir. Survived and more, I'd say." Matthew smiled at Emma as she fell back on the sofa with her legs in the air.

"They were the ones I needed so we could get the environmental agencies involved fast. And I know they'll put the word out to all the others. Before you know it, the place will be closed off tighter than a… well, you know what. Place will be crawling with so many government agencies and mine inspectors it'll be a nightmare for a few days before things settle down. And then we'll see where things stand. But for now, mission accomplished, I think." Stockman was clearly pleased that Matthew and his team had managed to do almost everything they had planned and kept ORB out of the limelight completely, using Los Choneros as the perfect foil.

"We'll hang around here for a few days to keep Kenny company. Then when he's okay he can head back. I'm looking forward to reading the headlines. Are you keeping in touch with the Chinese embassy?" Matthew asked. Emma had got up from the sofa and was heading his way. She could tell the end of the call was coming up and was coming in to claim her prize.

"I'll call them in the morning, and the Ecuadorian ambassador in London will have a few things to say as well. I'll keep you in the loop. Are you coming this way on your trip home?" Stockton inquired, hoping he and Lucy could spend a little time with Emma.

"Not sure, yet—" Matthew was cut off by Emma.

"See you in a week or so, Daddy."

"I guess that's the answer then."

They hung up. Stockton went back to reading, with Lucy doing the same in the wing chair next to him.

Matthew went back to holding on to Emma, relishing being with her after all they had been through. They really needed to be close to one another on a more permanent basis and he was determined it would happen. She made him lighter, kept him grounded, more relaxed and focused on what was important. Emma crawled her way onto his lap, and felt the soothing comfort of his arms around her as they held each other tight in the knowledge of what they had just survived.

Chapter 53

Bye, Wang Ho Lin! Bye, Ping Pei!

Wang Ho Lin put his phone down and buried his head in his hands. He stayed in that position for fifteen minutes before sending a message to Ping Pei over at the Tongyan office. This one wasn't cryptic.

Meet me in thirty minutes, usual place.

It had been a call he had never thought he would get from his masters in Beijing. It would resonate with him for many years to come. He was being recalled. That was never good unless it was at the end of a specifically arranged time for a commission. In this case, it wasn't. What would happen to him upon his return would not involve accolades. Quite the contrary. It would likely involve imprisonment, or worse. After all, Wang Ho Lin had been charged with only one major task by his embassy during his tenure in Quito and that was to coordinate with Tongyan to ensure the success of Zamora. And now... well, it was obvious. There was no Zamora to coordinate anymore. At least not for him.

Ho Lin sat on the bench in the usual place and waited for his friend. This was his third Winston since he had left the embassy gates. He had lost his normal upright posture, even when sitting. He slouched forward with an arched back. His arms rested on his thighs and his hands hung lazily between his open legs. He flicked the ash from his cigarette with his thumb tip in an altogether too-casual way, which did not befit his usual style. His hat sat slightly off-center on his head, allowing the light rain to slowly drench him.

Ping Pei could see his friend from a distance and knew his news would be as bad as his. He too had a call from his masters in Beijing. He too was being recalled, and he too faced serious consequences that could range anywhere between horrendous and horrific.

They sat and smoked together for ten minutes before Ho Lin spoke.

"What happened? What the hell happened?" he asked himself over and over again. There were no other questions at this point. Everything had collapsed so quickly neither of them had a chance to resist with any more than that small contingent of poorly armed security personnel. Even the ones that came in from Guayaquil—after the fact, as it happened—were of no use. Despite scouring the immediate area and gradually working their way outwards, they came up with nothing. Not even a trace of who or what it was that had completely decimated the mills, the transformers, the tailings, the pit, and the prized cocaine processing plant. All in less than four hours. Less time than it took to play a good game of Mahjong.

Ping Pei had no simple words to describe what had happened. The fact was, he didn't know. His last conversation with Jun Jie Khao, his GM at Zamora, was beyond confusing—it made no sense at all. It was as if Khao had suddenly gone mad. He was firing his pistol at shadows, at noises, and particularly at his driver. Fortunately, by the time he got to that point, he had run out of bullets. But the last thing Ping Pei had heard on the phone was Khao shouting at some kind of a devil.

"I cannot say, my friend. I don't know. I don't think anyone at the plant knows. What I do know is that my general manager has gone mad." Ping Pei looked away.

"But was this the doing of the cartel?" Ho Lin was desperate to know. It might be the only reason Beijing could go easier on him.

"I think it was, my friend." Ping Pei looked back at Ho Lin and could see the look of desperation in his eyes, and he knew that he too needed that small lifeline.

"I think so, too. So be it." Ho Lin almost whispered as he said it. He stood and walked over to his friend who had also stood. They shook hands, put their arms around each other's shoulders, and walked back across the field together.

Chapter 54

Goodbye

As Matthew and Emma were about to leave Quito on route to London through Miami, Stockman's *1812 Overture* sounded his call.

"Hello, sir. We're waiting for departure from Quito. Should see you in a couple days' time—I hope." Matthew was relaxed and happy to be leaving. Emma sat by his side in the business lounge.

"Have you read the news?" Stockman didn't bother with small talk. There was too much else going on that was far more important. "Bring up the BBC on your phone or iPad or whatever you have. You'll like it. See you soon. Safe travels. Take care of my girl." Then he was gone.

"He's not usually a man of so few words." Matthew was almost speaking to himself.

"You can't mean Daddy!" Emma looked mildly shocked and fluttered her eyelashes.

"Hey, look at this." Matthew didn't seem to hear Emma. He was too busy fumbling with his phone and opening the BBC News app. By then, Emma was looking over his shoulder.

The headline appeared just below the report of another concerning the US political scene, but this one monopolized their attention:

Ecuador's Constitutional Court Rescinds Zamora Operating Permit

Matthew opened the story, but decided the writing was too small for both of them to share. He pulled out his laptop and opened to the same story. Emma moved closer to him and they sat side by side as they read it.

Ecuador's Constitutional Court has rescinded the operating permit for the Tongyan-owned Zamora Mine, in the southeastern province of Zamora-Chinchipe. This decision follows a series of disastrous events caused by a combination of weather and bad operating practices.

The $2 billion project copper and gold project has been operating for three years but came under intense scrutiny last week after a rupture of their tailings waste system flooded the surrounding jungle with toxic waste. The accidental discharge resulted in the death of thousands of creatures reliant on the area for food and shelter. Environmentalists report there is extensive damage to the flora and fauna for miles to the east of the mine.

In addition, the mine open pit wall experienced a massive failure, believed to be caused as a consequence of a lack of understanding by Tongyan of the geology in the area. The collapse caused irreparable damage to millions of dollars' worth of mine equipment. The pit has been left unworkable, with scientists demanding more thorough research before it can be cleared for work to begin again. They say it will take years to return to stabilization.

The plant has been left without power to allow clean-up of the area, and Tongyan is now the subject of a number of lawsuits from various government agencies over their lack of permits and approvals.

The billion-ton copper and gold asset, initially advanced by a Canada-based company, was purchased by Tongyan, a Chinese company reporting to the government in Beijing, who built and operated the facility.

The Ecuadorian paper, El Universo, reports that the earlier decision by Zamora-Chinchipe province's supreme court to suspend Tongyan's environmental license for Zamora stands.

As part of the ruling, Tongyan will have to prepare a new environmental impact study and environmental management plan for the project.

Ecuador is rich in minerals and metals, but its mining industry is relatively new and lags behind that of neighboring countries like Chile and Peru. This is partly due to court decisions and opposition from indigenous communities to mining projects.

The administration of the president is seeking to promote greater mining activity as a means of economic development, despite the legal and community-based challenges that have hindered progress in the sector over the past decade. In the case of the Zamora project, the administration has been forced to reconsider the way in which approvals have been granted and will be reviewed in the future.

When asked for comment, a representative from Tongyan, Mr. Ping Pei, said,

"No comment."

We have not heard anything more from Tongyan, but we have noted that most of their operations people have returned to mainland China, along with staff from both the Zamora property and their office in Quito.

We will bring you more as it happens.

"Wow, that about sums it up." Emma glanced over at Matthew as each read the article again. There was no mention of sabotage, cartels or gunfights. Just accidents and mismanagement.

"If that's not a cover-up, I don't know what is." Matthew took his eyes off his laptop and called Stockman.

"I guess that's it" was all he said when Stockman answered.

"There is a little more to this, Matthew. It's just not being reported. From what I hear, Los Choneros are back in the game, so that's one issue resolved for us. My contact at the Chinese embassy tells me Tongyan are pulling out of Ecuador for a while. I guess they'll regroup to lick their wounds and consider whether to go back in. They have another couple of big mineral properties north of Zamora they wanted to open up. We may see them back in a few years, but it isn't likely they will venture into the cocaine business again."

"Sounds good, sir. Can we consider this a success?" Matthew was smiling as he put an arm around Emma's shoulder and pulled her into him.

"If the ambassador does, then so do I."

"And does he?" Matthew played the little game.

"He does. In fact, he's delighted."

"What now?" Matthew was hoping for a break between jobs.

"I guess it could be Colombia, or it could be Mexico." Stockman chuckled. "Let's talk about it when you get here."

"See you soon, Daddy." Emma signed off for them both.

"Which one would you prefer, Em. Colombia or Mexico?"

"I have a nice little bikini for either. Oh, and a gun." Emma laughed, put her arms around Matthew's neck, and dragged him toward her.